THE SWEETNESS AT THE BOTTOM OF THE PIE

WINNER OF THE AGATHA, ANTHONY, ARTHUR ELLIS, DILYS WINN, AND CWA DEBUT DAGGER AWARDS FOR BEST FIRST MYSTERY

Selected as a notable book of the year by *The New York Times*, Amazon.com, the *South Florida Sun-Sentinel*, Murder by the Blog, and January Magazine

Shortlisted by the American Library Association for
2010 Best Mystery Reading List

"**Sure to be one of the most loved mysteries of the
year** . . . introduces a delightful, intrepid, acid-tongued
new heroine to the genre . . . **wonderfully entertaining.**"
—*Chicago Sun-Times*

"**Sophisticated, series-launching** . . . It's a rare pleasure
to follow Flavia as she investigates her limited but
boundless-feeling world."
—*Entertainment Weekly* (A−)

"**Brilliant, irresistible and incorrigible,** Flavia has a
long future ahead of her. Bradley's mystery debut is a
standout."
—*Kirkus Reviews* (starred review)

"If ever there was a sleuth who's bold, brilliant, and, yes,
adorable, it's Flavia de Luce."
—*USA Today*

"Alan Bradley's marvelous book *The Sweetness at the
Bottom of the Pie* is a fantastic read, a winner. Flavia
walks right off the page and follows me through my day.
I can hardly wait for the next book. Bravo!"
—Louise Penny, bestselling author of *The Brutal Telling*

"Utterly charming! Eleven-year-old Flavia de Luce proves to be one of the most precocious, resourceful, and well, just plain dangerous heroines around. Evildoers—and big sisters—beware!"

—LISA GARDNER, bestselling author of *Live to Tell*

ALSO BY ALAN BRADLEY

The Sweetness at the Bottom of the Pie

Tennis shoes Vic

Lots of hard candies

BANTAM BOOKS
NEW YORK

The
WEED
That STRINGS the
HANGMAN'S
BAG

A Flavia de Luce Mystery

ALAN BRADLEY

•••

The Weed That Strings the Hangman's Bag is a work of fiction. Names, characters, places, and incidents either are the product of the author's imagination or are used fictitiously. Any resemblance to actual persons, living or dead, events, or locales is entirely coincidental.

2010 Bantam Books International Mass Market Edition

Copyright © 2010 by Alan Bradley

Published in the United States by Bantam Books, an imprint of The Random House Publishing Group, a division of Random House, Inc., New York.

Bantam Books and the rooster colophon are registered trademarks of Random House, Inc.

Originally published in hardcover in the United States by Delacorte Press, an imprint of The Random House Publishing Group, a division of Random House, Inc., in 2010.

ISBN 978-0-553-84089-6

Cover design: Joe Montgomery

Printed in the United States of America

www.bantamdell.com

2 4 6 8 9 7 5 3

Book design by Diane Hobbing

Again, for Shirley

secure wallet for
Vic

Granola Bars!!

Camera strap

Sir Walter Raleigh to His Son

Three things there be that prosper up apace,
    And flourish while they grow asunder far;
But on a day, they meet all in a place,
    And when they meet, they one another mar.

And they be these; the Wood, the Weed, the Wag:
    The Wood is that that makes the gallows tree;
The Weed is that that strings the hangman's bag;
    The Wag, my pretty knave, betokens thee.

Now mark, dear boy—while these assemble not,
    Green springs the tree, hemp grows, the wag is wild;
But when they meet, it makes the timber rot,
    It frets the halter, and it chokes the child.

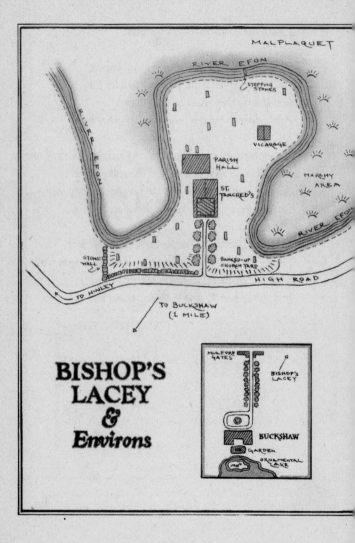

FARM

RIVER EFON

OLD TOWPATH

GATE STREET

THIRTEEN DRAKES

SHOE STREET

PIT SHED

LIBRARY

COW LANE

HIGH STREET

TO DODD INKSLEY AND REDING END

BOAT ALLEY

WILLOW VILLA

GIBBET WOOD
—
CULVERHOUSE FARM

CLEARING
GIBBET WOOD

GIBBET HILL

DOVECOTE
CULVERHOUSE FARM

JUBILEE FIELD

FARM LANE

ACTUAL DISTANCE
ABOUT ¾ MILE

HURNACRE FARM

ST. TANCRED'S

RIVER EFON

TO HINLEY

HIGH ROAD

NOTES:
NOT TO SCALE

FdL

The

WEED

That **STRINGS** the

HANGMAN'S

BAG

...

· O N E ·

I WAS LYING DEAD in the churchyard. An hour had crept by since the mourners had said their last sad farewells.

At twelve o'clock, just at the time we should otherwise have been sitting down to lunch, there had been the departure from Buckshaw: my polished rosewood coffin being brought out of the drawing room, carried slowly down the broad stone steps to the driveway, and slid with heartbreaking ease into the open door of the waiting hearse, crushing beneath it a little bouquet of wildflowers that had been laid gently inside by one of the grieving villagers.

Then there had been the long drive down the avenue of chestnuts to the Mulford Gates, whose rampant griffins looked away as we passed, though whether in sadness or in apathy I would never know.

Dogger, Father's devoted jack-of-all-trades, had paced

in measured step alongside the slow hearse, his head bowed, his hand resting lightly on its roof, as if to shield my remains from something that only he could see. At the gates, one of the undertaker's mutes had finally coaxed him, by using hand signals, into a hired motorcar.

And so they had brought me to the village of Bishop's Lacey, passing somberly through the same green lanes and dusty hedgerows I had bicycled every day when I was alive.

At the heaped-up churchyard of St. Tancred's, they had taken me gently from the hearse and borne me at a snail's pace up the path beneath the limes. Here, they had put me down for a moment in the new-mown grass.

Then had come the service at the gaping grave, and there had been a note of genuine grief in the voice of the vicar as he pronounced the traditional words.

It was the first time I'd heard the Order for the Burial of the Dead from this vantage point. We had attended last year, with Father, the funeral of old Mr. Dean, the village greengrocer. His grave, in fact, was just a few yards from where I was presently lying. It had already caved in, leaving not much more than a rectangular depression in the grass that was, more often than not, filled with stagnant rainwater.

My oldest sister, Ophelia, said it collapsed because Mr. Dean had been resurrected and was no longer bodily present, while Daphne, my other sister, said it was because he had plummeted through into an older grave whose occupant had disintegrated.

I thought of the soup of bones below: the soup of which I was about to become just another ingredient.

Flavia Sabina de Luce, 1939–1950, they would cause to be carved on my gravestone, a modest and tasteful gray marble thing with no room for false sentiments.

Pity. If I'd lived long enough, I'd have left written instructions calling for a touch of Wordsworth:

> *A maid whom there were none to praise*
> *And very few to love.*

And if they'd balked at that, I'd have left this as my second choice:

> *Truest hearts by deeds unkind*
> *To despair are most inclined.*

Only Feely, who had played and sung them at the piano, would recognize the lines from Thomas Campion's *Third Book of Airs*, and she would be too consumed by guilty grief to tell anyone.

My thoughts were interrupted by the vicar's voice.

". . . *earth to earth, ashes to ashes, dust to dust, in sure and certain hope of the Resurrection to eternal life, through our Lord Jesus Christ; who shall change our vile body . . .*"

And suddenly they had gone, leaving me there alone—alone to listen for the worms.

This was it: the end of the road for poor Flavia.

By now the family would already be back at Buckshaw, gathered round the long refectory table: Father seated in his usual stony silence, Daffy and Feely hugging one another with slack, tearstained faces as Mrs. Mullet, our cook, brought in a platter of baked meats.

I remembered something that Daffy had once told me when she was devouring *The Odyssey*: that baked meats, in ancient Greece, were traditional funeral fare, and I had replied that, in view of Mrs. Mullet's cooking, not much had changed in two and a half thousand years.

But now that I was dead, I thought, perhaps I ought to practice being somewhat more charitable.

Dogger, of course, would be inconsolable. Dear Dogger: butler-cum-chauffeur-cum-valet-cum-gardener-cum-estate-manager: a poor shell-shocked soul whose capabilities ebbed and flowed like the Severn tides; Dogger, who had recently saved my life and forgotten it by the next morning. I should miss him terribly.

And I should miss my chemistry laboratory. I thought of all the golden hours I'd spent there in that abandoned wing of Buckshaw, blissfully alone among the flasks, the retorts, and the cheerily bubbling tubes and beakers. And to think that I'd never see them again. It was almost too much to bear.

I listened to the rising wind as it whispered overhead in the branches of the yew trees. It was already growing cool here in the shadows of St. Tancred's tower, and it would soon be dark.

Poor Flavia! Poor, stone-cold-dead Flavia.

By now, Daffy and Feely would be wishing that they hadn't been so downright rotten to their little sister during her brief eleven years on this earth.

At the thought, a tear started down my cheek.

Would Harriet be waiting to welcome me to Heaven?

Harriet was my mother, who had died in a mountaineering accident a year after I was born. Would she recognize me after ten years? Would she still be dressed in the mountain-climbing suit she was wearing when she met her end, or would she have swapped it by now for a white robe?

Well, whatever she was wearing, I knew it would be stylish.

There was a sudden clatter of wings: a noise that echoed loudly from the stone wall of the church, amplified to an alarming volume by a half acre of stained glass and the leaning gravestones that hemmed me in. I froze.

Could it be an angel—or more likely, an archangel—coming down to return Flavia's precious soul to Paradise? If I opened my eyes the merest slit, I could see through my eyelashes, but only dimly.

No such luck: It was one of the tattered jackdaws that were always hanging round St. Tancred's. These vagabonds had been nesting in the tower since its thirteenth-century stonemasons had packed up their tools and departed.

Now the idiotic bird had landed clumsily on top of a marble finger that pointed to Heaven, and was regarding me coolly, its head cocked to one side, with its bright, ridiculous boot-button eyes.

Jackdaws never learn. No matter how many times I played this trick they always, sooner or later, came flapping down from the tower to investigate. To the primeval mind of a jackdaw, any body horizontal in a churchyard could have only one meaning: food.

As I had done a dozen times before, I leapt to my feet and flung the stone that was concealed in my curled fingers. I missed—but then I nearly always did.

With an "awk" of contempt, the thing sprang into the air and flapped off behind the church, towards the river.

Now that I was on my feet, I realized I was hungry. Of course I was! I hadn't eaten since breakfast. For a moment I wondered vaguely if I might find a few leftover jam tarts or a bit of cake in the kitchen of the parish hall. The St. Tancred's Ladies' Auxiliary had gathered the night before, and there was always the chance.

As I waded through the knee-high grass, I heard a peculiar snuffling sound, and for a moment, I thought the saucy jackdaw had come back to have the last word.

I stopped and listened.

Nothing.

And then it came again.

I find it sometimes a curse and sometimes a blessing that I have inherited Harriet's acute sense of hearing, since I am able, as I am fond of telling Feely, to hear things that would make your hair stand on end. One of the sounds to which I am particularly attuned is the sound of someone crying.

It was coming from the northwest corner of the churchyard—from somewhere near the wooden shed in which the sexton kept his grave-digging tools. As I crept slowly forward on tiptoe, the sound grew louder: Someone was having a good old-fashioned cry, of the knock-'em-down-drag-'em-out variety.

It is a simple fact of nature that while most men can walk right past a weeping woman as if their eyes are blinkered and their ears stopped up with sand, no female can ever hear the sound of another in distress without rushing instantly to her aid.

I peeped round a black marble column, and there she was, stretched out full length, facedown on the slab of a limestone tomb, her red hair flowing out across the weathered inscription like rivulets of blood. Except for the cigarette wedged stylishly erect between her fingers, she might have been a painting by one of the Pre-Raphaelites, such as Burne-Jones. I almost hated to intrude.

"Hullo," I said. "Are you all right?"

It is another simple fact of nature that one always begins such conversations with an utterly stupid remark. I was sorry the instant I'd uttered it.

"Oh! Of course I'm all right," she cried, leaping to her feet and wiping her eyes. "What do you mean by creeping up on me like that? Who are you, anyway?"

With a toss of her head she flung back her hair and stuck out her chin. She had the high cheekbones and the dramatically triangular face of a silent cinema star, and I could see by the way she bared her teeth that she was terrified.

"Flavia," I said. "My name is Flavia de Luce. I live near here—at Buckshaw."

I jerked my thumb in the general direction.

She was still staring at me like a woman in the grip of a nightmare.

"I'm sorry," I said. "I didn't mean to startle you."

She pulled herself up to her full height—which couldn't have been much more than five feet and an inch or two—and took a step towards me, like a hot-tempered version of the Botticelli *Venus* that I'd once seen on a Huntley and Palmers biscuit tin.

I stood my ground, staring at her dress. It was a creamy cotton print with a gathered bodice and a flaring skirt, covered all over with a myriad of tiny flowers, red, yellow, blue, and a bright orange the color of poppies and, I couldn't help noticing, a hem that was stained with half-dried mud.

"What's the matter?" she asked, taking an affected drag on her angled cigarette. "Never seen anyone famous before?"

Famous? I hadn't the faintest idea who she was. I had half a mind to tell her that I had indeed seen someone famous, and that it was Winston Churchill. Father had pointed him out to me from a London taxicab. Churchill had been standing in front of the Savoy with his thumbs hooked in his waistcoat pockets, talking to a man in a yellow mackintosh.

"Good old Winnie," Father had breathed, as if to himself.

"Oh, what's the use?" the woman said. "Bloody place . . . bloody people . . . bloody motorcars!" And she began to cry again.

"Is there something I can do to help?" I asked.

"Oh, go away and leave me alone," she sobbed.

Very well, then, I thought. Actually, I thought more than that, but since I'm trying to be a better person . . .

I stood there for a moment, leaning forward a bit to see if her fallen tears were reacting with the porous surface of the tombstone. Tears, I knew, were composed largely of water, sodium chloride, manganese, and potassium, while limestone was made up chiefly of calcite, which was soluble in sodium chloride—but only at high temperatures. So unless the temperature of St. Tancred's churchyard went up suddenly by several hundred degrees, it seemed unlikely that anything chemically interesting was going to be happening here.

I turned and walked away.

"Flavia . . ."

I looked back. She was reaching out a hand to me.

"I'm sorry," she said. "It's just that it's been an awfully bloody day, all round."

I stopped—then paced slowly, warily back as she wiped her eyes with the back of her hand.

"Rupert was in a foul mood to begin with—even before we left Stoatmoor this morning. We'd had rather a row, I'm afraid, and then the whole business with the van—it was simply the last straw. He's gone off to find someone to fix it, and I'm . . . well, here I am."

"I like your red hair," I said. She touched it instantly and smiled, as I somehow knew she would.

"Carrot-top, they used to call me when I was your age. Carrot-top! Fancy!"

"Carrot tops are green," I said. "Who's Rupert?"

"Who's Rupert?" she asked. "You're having me on!"

She pointed a finger and I turned to look: Parked in the lane at the corner of the churchyard was a dilapidated van—an Austin Eight. On its side panel, in showy gold circus letters, still legible through a heavy coating of mud and dust, were the words PORSON'S PUPPETS.

"Rupert Porson," she said. "Everyone knows Rupert Porson. Rupert Porson, as in Snoddy the Squirrel—*The Magic Kingdom*. Haven't you seen him on the television?"

Snoddy the Squirrel? *The Magic Kingdom*?

"We don't have the television at Buckshaw," I said. "Father says it's a filthy invention."

"Father is an uncommonly wise man," she said. "Father is undoubtedly—"

She was interrupted by the metallic rattle of a loose chain guard as the vicar came wobbling round the corner of the church. He dismounted and leaned his battered Raleigh up against a handy headstone. As he walked towards us, I reflected that Canon Denwyn Richardson was not anyone's image of a typical village vicar. He was large and bluff and hearty, and if he'd had tattoos, he might have been mistaken for the captain of one of those rusty tramp steamers that drags itself wearily from one sun-drenched port to another in whatever God-awful outposts are still left of the British Empire.

His black clerical outfit was smudged and streaked with chalky dust, as if he'd come a cropper on his bicycle.

"Blast!" he said when he spotted me. "I've lost my trouser clip and torn my cuff to ribbons," and then, dusting himself off as he walked towards us, he added, "Cynthia's going to have me on the carpet."

The woman's eyes widened and she shot me a quick glance.

"She's recently begun scratching my initials on my belongings with a needle," he went on, "but that hasn't kept me from losing things. Last week, the hectograph sheets for the parish bulletin, the week before, a brass doorknob from the vestry. Maddening, really.

"Hello, Flavia," he said. "Always nice to see you at church."

"This is our vicar, Canon Richardson," I told the red-headed woman. "Perhaps he can help."

"Denwyn," the vicar said, holding out a hand to the

stranger. "We don't stand much on ceremony since the war."

The woman stuck out two or three fingers and touched his palm, but said nothing. As she extended her hand, the short sleeve of her dress slid up, and I had a quick glimpse of the ugly green and purple bruise on her upper arm. She covered it hastily with her left hand as she tugged the cotton fabric down to hide it.

"And how may I be of service?" the vicar asked, gesturing towards the van. "It is not often that we, in our bucolic little backwater, are called upon to minister to such august theater folk."

She smiled gamely. "Our van's broken down—or as good as. Something to do with the carburetor. If it had been anything electrical, I'm sure Rupert could have mended it in a flash, but I'm afraid the fuel system is beyond him."

"Dear, dear!" the vicar said. "I'm sure Bert Archer, at the garage, can put it right for you. I'll ring him up, if you like."

"Oh, no," the woman said quickly—perhaps *too* quickly—"we wouldn't want you to go to any trouble. Rupert's gone down the high street. He's probably already found someone."

"If he had, he'd be back by now," the vicar said. "Let me ring Bert. He often slips home for a nap in the afternoon. He's not as young as he was, you know—nor are any of us, if it comes to that. Still, it is a favorite maxim of mine that, when dealing with motor mechanics—even tame ones—it never does one any harm to have the blessing of the Church."

"Oh, no. It's too much trouble. I'm sure we'll be just fine."

"Nonsense," the vicar said, already moving off among the forest of gravestones and making at full speed for the rectory. "No trouble at all. I'll be back in a jiffy."

"Vicar!" the woman called. "Please—"

He stopped in mid-stride and came reluctantly back towards us.

"It's just that . . . you see, we . . ."

"Aha! A question of money, then," the vicar said.

She nodded sadly, her head down, her red hair cascading over her face.

"I'm sure something can be arranged," the vicar said. "Ah! Here's your husband now."

A little man with an oversized head and a lopsided gait was stumping towards us across the churchyard, his right leg swinging out at each step in a wide, awkward semicircle. As he approached, I saw that his calf was caged in a heavy iron brace.

He must have been in his forties, but it was difficult to tell.

In spite of his diminutive size, his barrel chest and powerful upper arms seemed ready to burst out of the seersucker suit that confined them. By contrast, his right leg was pitiful: By the way in which his trousers clung, and flapped uselessly round what lay beneath, I could see that it was little more than a matchstick. With his huge head, he looked to me like nothing so much as a giant octopus, stalking on uneven tentacles through the churchyard.

He lurched to a halt and deferentially lifted a flat, peaked motoring cap, revealing an unruly mop of pale blond hair that matched precisely his little Vandyke goatee.

"Rupert Porson, I presume?" the vicar said, giving the newcomer a jolly, hail-fellow-well-met handshake. "I'm Denwyn Richardson—and this is my young friend Flavia de Luce."

Porson nodded at me and shot an almost invisibly quick, dark glance at the woman before turning on the full beam of a searchlight smile.

"Spot of engine trouble, I understand," the vicar went on. "Quite maddening. Still, if it has brought the creator of *The Magic Kingdom* and Snoddy the Squirrel into our midst—well, it just proves the old adage, doesn't it?"

He didn't say which old adage he was referring to, nor did anyone care enough to ask.

"I was about to remark to your good wife," the vicar said, "that St. Tancred's would be honored indeed if you might see your way clear to presenting a little entertainment in the parish hall whilst your van is being repaired? I realize, of course, how much in demand you must be, but I should be negligent if I didn't at least make the attempt on behalf of the children—and yes, the grown-ups, too!—of Bishop's Lacey. It is good, now and then, to allow children to launch an attack upon their money boxes in a worthy cultural cause, don't you agree?"

"Well, Vicar," Porson said, in a honeyed voice—too big, too resonant, too mellifluous, I thought, for such a tiny man—"we do have rather a tight timetable. Our tour has been grueling, you see, and London calls. . . ."

"I understand," said the vicar.

"But," Porson added, lifting a dramatic forefinger,

"nothing would delight us more than being allowed to sing for our supper, as it were. Isn't that so, Nialla? It shall be quite like the old days."

The woman nodded, but said nothing. She was staring off at the hills beyond.

"Well, then," the vicar said, rubbing his hands together vigorously, as if he were making fire, "it's all arranged. Come along and I'll show you the hall. It's rather tatty, but it does boast a stage, and the acoustics are said to be quite remarkable."

With that, the two men disappeared round the back of the church.

For a moment there seemed nothing to say. And then the woman spoke: "You wouldn't happen to have a cigarette, would you? I'm dying for a smoke."

I gave my head a rather idiotic shake.

"Hmmm," she said. "You look like the kind of kid who might have."

For the first time in my life, I was speechless.

"I don't smoke," I managed.

"And why is that?" she asked. "Too young or too wise?"

"I was thinking of taking it up next week," I said lamely. "I just hadn't actually got round to it yet."

She threw her head back and laughed toothily, like a film star. "I like you, Flavia de Luce," she said. "But I have the advantage, don't I? You've told me your name, but I haven't told you mine."

"It's Nialla," I said. "Mr. Porson called you Nialla."

She stuck out her hand, her face grave. "That's right," she said, "he did. But you can call me Mother Goose."

· T W O ·

MOTHER GOOSE!

I have never much cared for flippant remarks, especially when others make them, and in particular, I don't
give a frog's fundament for them when they come from an
adult. It has been my experience that facetiousness in the
mouth of someone old enough to know better is often no
more than camouflage for something far, far worse.

And yet, in spite of that, I found myself swallowing the
sharp—and deliciously nasty!—retort that was already on
the tip of my tongue, and instead, managed a diluted
smile.

"Mother Goose?" I repeated, dubiously.

She burst into tears again, and I was glad that I had
held my tongue. I was about to be instantly rewarded by
hearing something juicy.

Besides, I had already begun to detect a slight but invisible attraction between this woman and myself. Could it be pity? Or was it fear? I couldn't say: I knew only that some deep-seated chemical substance inside one of us was crying out to its long-lost complement—or was it its antidote?—in the other.

I put a hand gently on her shoulder and held out my handkerchief. She looked at it skeptically.

"It's all right," I said. "They're only grass stains."

That set her off into a remarkable contortion. She buried her face in the handkerchief, and her shoulders quaked so violently I thought for a moment she was going to fly to pieces. To allow her time to recover—and because I was rather embarrassed by her outburst—I wandered off a little distance to examine the inscription on a tall, weathered gravestone that marked the grave of one Lydia Green, who had "dyed" in 1638 at the age of "one hundred and thirty-five yeeres."

She once warr Grene but now she waxeth white, it said on the stone, *lamented by a fewe frends*.

Had Lydia lived, I reflected, she would now be four hundred and forty-seven years old, and probably a person well worth getting to know.

"Oh, I feel such a chump."

I turned to see the woman dabbing at her eyes and giving me a damp grin.

"I'm Nialla," she said, sticking out a hand. "Rupert's assistant."

I fought back my revulsion and gave her fingers a lightning-quick shake. As I had suspected, her hand was wet and sticky. As soon as I was decently able, I slid my own hand out of sight behind my back and wiped it on the back of my skirt.

"Assistant?" The word popped out of my mouth before I could stop it.

"Oh, I know the vicar assumed that I'm Rupert's wife. But it's not like that. Honestly! It's not like that at all."

I glanced over involuntarily at the Porson's Puppets van. She spotted it at once.

"Well, yes . . . we do travel together. I suppose Rupert and I have what you might call . . . a very great affection for one another. But husband and wife . . . ?"

What kind of fool did she take me for? It was no more than a week since Daffy had been reading aloud to Feely and me from *Oliver Twist*, and I knew, as surely as I knew my own name, that this woman, Nialla, was Nancy to Rupert Porson's Bill Sikes. Didn't she realize that I'd spotted the filthy great bruise on her upper arm?

"Actually, it's such jolly fun rattling about England with Rupert. He's recognized everywhere we go, you know. Just the day before yesterday, for instance, we were playing at Market Selby when we were spotted in the post office by a fat lady in a flowerpot hat.

" 'Rupert Porson!' she shrieked. 'Rupert Porson uses the Royal Mail, just like everyone else!' "

Nialla laughed. "And then she begged him for his autograph. They always do, you know. Insisted he put 'Best wishes from Snoddy the Squirrel.' When he does it that way, he always draws a couple of little nuts. She claimed she wanted it for her nephew, but I knew better. When you're on the road a lot, you develop a certain sense for these things. You can always tell."

She was prattling. If I kept quiet, it wouldn't be more than a minute before she would be confiding her size in knickers.

"Someone at the BBC told Rupert that twenty-three percent of his viewing audience is made up of childless housewives. Seems a lot, doesn't it? But there's something about *The Magic Kingdom* that satisfies one's innate desire for escape. That's the exact way they put it to Rupert: 'one's innate desire for escape.' Everyone needs to escape, don't they? In one way or another, I mean."

"Everyone but Mother Goose," I said.

She laughed. "Look, I wasn't pulling your leg. I *am* Mother Goose. At least, I am when I put on my costume. Just wait until you see it—tall witch's hat with a floppy brim and a silver buckle, a gray wig with dangling ringlets, and a great puffy dress that looks as if it once belonged to Mother Shipton. Do you know who Mother Shipton was?"

Of course I did. I knew that she was some old crone who was supposed to have lived in the sixteenth century and seen into the future, predicting, among other things, the Great Plague, the Great Fire of London, aeroplanes, battleships, and that the world would come to an end in 1881; that like those of Nostradamus, Mother Shipton's prophecies were in doggerel verse: "Fire and water shall wonders do," and all that. I also knew that there are actually still people running around loose today who believe she foresaw the use of heavy water in the making of the atomic bomb. As for myself, I didn't believe a word of it. It was nothing but a load of old tosh.

"I've heard the name," I said.

"Well, never mind. That's who I resemble when I'm all tarted up for the show."

"Brilliant," I said, not meaning it. She could see that I was a bit put off.

"What's a nice girl like you doing hanging about in a place like this?" she asked with a grin, taking in the whole of the churchyard with a wave of her hand.

"I often come here to think," I said.

This seemed to amuse her. She pursed her lips and put on an annoying, stagy voice.

"And what does Flavia de Luce think about in her quaint old country churchyard?"

"Being alone," I snapped, without meaning to be intentionally rude. I was simply being truthful.

"Being alone," she said, nodding. I could see that she was not put off by my bristling reply. "There's a lot to be said for being alone. But you and I know, don't we, Flavia, that being alone and being lonely are not at all the same thing?"

I brightened a bit. Here was someone who seemed at least to have thought through some of the same things I had.

"No," I admitted.

There was a long silence.

"Tell me about your family," Nialla said at last, quietly.

"There isn't much to tell," I said. "I have two sisters, Ophelia and Daphne. Feely's seventeen and Daffy's thirteen. Feely plays the piano and Daffy reads. Father is a philatelist. He's devoted to his stamps."

"And your mother?"

"Dead. She was killed in an accident when I was a year old."

"Good Lord!" she said. "Someone told me about a family that lived in a great rambling old mansion not far from here: an eccentric colonel and a family of girls running wild like a lot of red Indians. You're not one of *them*, are you?"

She saw instantly by the look on my face that I was.

"Oh, you poor child!" she said. "I'm sorry, I didn't mean to . . . I mean . . ."

"It's quite all right," I told her. "It's far worse than that actually, but I don't like to talk about it."

I saw the faraway look come into her eyes: the look of an adult floundering desperately to find common ground with someone younger.

"But what do you do with yourself?" she asked. "Don't you have any interests . . . or hobbies?"

"I'm keen on chemistry," I said, "and I enjoy making scrapbooks."

"Do you really?" she enthused. "Fancy that! So did I, at your age. Cigarette cards and pressed flowers: pansies, mignonettes, foxgloves, delphiniums; old buttons, valentines, poems about Granny's spinning wheel from *The Girl's Own Annual* . . . what jolly good fun it was!"

My own scrapbooks consisted of three fat purple volumes of clippings from the tide of ancient magazines and newspapers that had overflowed, and then flooded, the library and the drawing room at Buckshaw, spilling over into disused bedrooms and lumber rooms before being carted off at last to languish in damp, moldering stacks in a crypt in the cellars. From their pages, I had carefully clipped everything I could find on poisons and poisoners, until my scrapbooks were bursting at the seams with the likes of Major Herbert Rowse Armstrong, the amateur gardener and solicitor, who dispatched his wife with lovingly prepared concoctions of arsenious weed-killer; Thomas Neill Cream, Hawley Harvey Crippen, and George Chapman (remarkable, isn't it, that so many of the great poisoners' names begin with the letter C?), who with strychnine, hyoscine, and antimony respectively, sent a veritable army of wives and other women marching to their graves; Mary Ann Cotton (see what I mean?) who, after several successful trial runs on pigs, went on to poison seventeen people with arsenic; Daisy de Melker, the South African woman with a passion for poisoning plumbers: She would first marry them, and then divorce them with a dose of strychnine.

"Keeping a scrapbook is the perfect pastime for a young lady," Nialla was saying. "Genteel . . . and yet educational."

My thoughts precisely.

"My mum tossed mine in the dustbin when I ran away from home," she said with something that had it lived might have become a chuckle.

"You ran away from home?" I asked.

This fact intrigued me almost as much as her foxgloves, from which, I recalled, the vegetable alkaloid digitalin (better known to those of us who are chemists as $C_{36}H_{56}O_{14}$) could be extracted. I thought with pleasure for a moment of the several times in my laboratory I had exhausted with alcohol the leaves of foxglove plucked from the kitchen garden, watching the slender, shining needles as they crystallized, and the lovely emerald green solution that was formed when I dissolved them in hydrochloric acid and added water. The precipitated resin could, of course, be restored to its original green hue with sulfuric acid, turned light red by bromine vapor, and back to emerald green again with the addition of water. It was magical! It was also, of course, a deadly poison, and as such, was certainly far more gripping than stupid buttons and *The Girl's Own Annual*.

"Mmmm," she said. "Got tired of washing up, drying up, sweeping up, and dusting up, and listening to the people next door throwing up; tired of lying in bed at night, listening for the clatter of the prince's horse on the cobblestones."

I grinned.

"Rupert changed all that, of course," she said. " 'Come with me to the Doorway of Diarbekir,' he told me. 'Come to the Orient and I will make you a princess in liquid silks and diamonds the size of market cabbages.' "

"He did?"

"No. What he actually said was, 'My bloody assistant's run out on me. Come with me to Lyme Regis at the weekend and I'll give you a guinea, six square meals, and a bag to sleep in. I'll teach you the art of manipulation,' he said, and I was bloody fool enough to think he was talking about puppets."

Before I had time to ask for details, she had jumped to her feet and dusted off her skirt.

"Speaking of Rupert," she said, "we'd better go in and see how he and the vicar are getting on. It's ominously quiet in the parish hall. Do you suppose they might already have murdered one another?"

Her flowered dress swished gracefully off among the tombstones, and I was left to trot doggedly along in her wake.

Inside, we found the vicar standing in the middle of the hall. Rupert was up on the platform, center stage, hands on hips. Had he been taking a curtain call at the Old Vic, the lighting could not have been more dramatic. As if dispatched by Fate, an unexpected ray of sunlight shone in through a stained-glass window at the rear of the hall, fixing Rupert's upturned face dead center in its round golden beam. He struck a pose, and began spouting Shakespeare:

> *"When my love swears that she is made of truth,*
> *I do believe her though I know she lies,*
> *That she might think me some untutored youth,*
> *Unlearnèd in the world's false subtleties.*
> *Thus vainly thinking that she thinks me young,*
> *Although she knows my days are past the best,*
> *Simply I credit her false-speaking tongue:*
> *On both sides thus is simple truth suppressed."*

As the vicar had mentioned, the acoustics of the hall were quite remarkable. The Victorian builders had made its interior a conch shell of curved, polished wood paneling that served as a sounding board for the faintest noise: It was like being inside a Stradivarius violin. Rupert's warm, honey-sweet voice was everywhere, wrapping us all in its rich resonance:

> "But wherefore says she not she is unjust?
> And wherefore say not I that I am old?
> O love's best habit is in seeming trust,
> And age in love, loves not to have years told.
> Therefore I lie with her, and she with me,
> And in our faults by lies we flattered be.

"Can you hear me now, vicar?"

The spell was instantly broken. It was as if Laurence Olivier had tossed "Woof! Woof! Testing . . . one . . . two . . . three," into the middle of "To be, or not to be."

"Brilliant!" the vicar exclaimed.

What surprised me most about Rupert's speech was that I knew what he was saying. Because of the nearly imperceptible pause at the end of each line, and the singular way in which he illustrated the shades of meaning with his long white fingers, I understood the words. Every single one of them.

As if they had been sucked in through my pores by osmosis, I knew even as they swept over me that I was hearing the bitter words of an old man to a love far younger than himself.

I glanced at Nialla. Her hand was at her throat.

In the echoing wooden silence that followed, the vicar stood stock-still, as if he were carved from black and white marble.

I was witnessing something that not all of us understood.

"Bravo! Bravo!"

The vicar's cupped hands came suddenly clapping together in a series of echoing thunderbolts. "Bravo! Sonnet one hundred and thirty-eight, unless I'm badly mistaken. And, if I may offer up my own humble opinion, perhaps never more beautifully spoken."

Rupert positively preened.

Outside, the sun went behind a cloud. Its golden beam faded in an instant, and when it had gone, we were once again just four ordinary people in a dim and dusty room.

"Splendid," Rupert said. "The hall will do splendidly."

He stumped across the stage and began clambering awkwardly down the narrow steps, the fingers of one hand splayed out against the wall for support.

"Careful!" Nialla said, taking a quick step towards him.

"Get back!" he snapped, with a look of utter ferocity. "I can manage."

She stopped short in her tracks—as if he had slapped her in the face.

"Nialla thinks I'm her child." He laughed, trying to make a joke of it.

By her murderous look, I could see that Nialla didn't think any such thing.

· T H R E E ·

"WELL, THEN!" THE VICAR said brightly, rubbing his hands together, as if the moment hadn't happened. "That's settled. Where shall we begin?" He looked eagerly from one of them to the other.

"By unloading the van, I suppose," Rupert said. "I assume we can leave things here until the show?"

"Oh, of course . . . of course," said the vicar. "The parish hall's as safe as houses. Perhaps even a little safer."

"Then someone will need to have a look at the van . . . and we'll want a place to put up for a few days."

"Leave that department to me," the vicar said. "I'm sure I can manage something. Now then, up sleeves, and to work we go. Come along, Flavia, dear. I'm sure we'll find something suited to your special talents."

Something suited to my special talents? Somehow I

doubted it—unless the subject was criminal poisoning, which was my chief delight.

But still, because I didn't feel up to going home to Buckshaw just yet, I pasted on my best Girl Guide (retired) smile for the vicar, and followed him, along with Rupert and Nialla, outside into the churchyard.

As Rupert swung open the rear doors of the van, I had my first glimpse into the life of a traveling showman. The Austin's dim interior was beautifully fitted out with row upon row of varnished drawers, each one nestled snugly above, beside, and below its neighbors: very like the boxes of shoes in a well-run boot maker's shop, with each drawer capable of sliding in and out on its own track. Piled on the floor of the van were the larger boxes—shipping crates, really—with rope handles at the ends to facilitate their being pulled out and lugged to wherever they were going.

"Rupert made it all himself," Nialla said, proudly. "The drawers, the folding stage, the lighting equipment . . . made the spotlights out of old paint tins, didn't you, Rupert?"

Rupert nodded absently as he hauled away at a bundle of iron tubing.

"And that's not all. He cut the cables, made the props, painted the scenery, carved the puppets . . . everything—except *that*, of course."

She was pointing to a bulky black case with a leather handle and perforations in the side.

"What's in there? Is it an animal?"

Nialla laughed.

"Better than that. It's Rupert's pride and joy: a magnetic recorder. Had it sent him from America. Cost him a pretty penny, I can tell you. Still, it's cheaper than hiring the BBC orchestra to play the incidental music!"

Rupert had already begun to tug boxes out of the Austin, grunting as he worked. His arms were like dockyard cranes, lifting and turning . . . lifting and turning, until at last, nearly everything was piled in the grass.

"Allow me to lend a hand," the vicar said, seizing a rope handle at the end of a black coffin-shaped trunk with the word "Galligantus" stenciled upon it in white letters, as Rupert took the other end.

Nialla and I went back and forth, back and forth, with the lighter bits and pieces, and within half an hour, everything was piled up inside the parish hall in front of the stage.

"Well done!" the vicar said, dusting off the sleeves of his jacket. "Well done, indeed. Now then, would Saturday be suitable? For the show, I mean? Let me see . . . today is Thursday . . . that would give you an extra day to make ready, as well as time to have your van repaired."

"Sounds all right to me," Rupert said. Nialla nodded, even though she hadn't been asked.

"Saturday it is, then. I'll have Cynthia run off handbills on the hectograph. She can take them round the shops tomorrow . . . slap a few up in strategic places. Cynthia's such a good sport about these things."

Of the many phrases that came to mind to describe Cynthia Richardson, "good sport" was not among them; "ogress," however, was.

It was after all Cynthia, with her rodent features, who

had once caught me teetering tiptoe on the altar of St. Tancred's, using one of Father's straight razors to scrape a sample of blue zafre from a medieval stained-glass window. Zafre was an impure basic arsenate of cobalt, prepared by roasting, which the craftsmen of the Middle Ages had used for painting on glass, and I was simply dying to analyze the stuff in my laboratory to determine how successful its makers had been in the essential step of freeing it of iron.

Cynthia had seized me, upended me, and spanked me on the spot, making what I thought to be unfair use of a nearby copy of *Hymns Ancient and Modern* (Standard Edition).

"What you have done, Flavia, is not worthy of congratulation," Father said when I reported this outrage to him. "You have ruined a perfectly good Thiers-Issard hollow-ground blade."

I have to admit, though, that Cynthia was a great organizer, but then, so were the men with whips who got the pyramids built. Certainly, if anyone could manage to paper Bishop's Lacey from end to end in three days with handbills, it was Cynthia Richardson.

"Hold on!" the vicar exclaimed. "I've just had the most splendid idea! Tell me what you think. Why not present *two* shows rather than one? I don't claim to be an expert in the art of the puppet theater, by any means—knowing what is possible and what is not, and so forth—but why not put on a show Saturday afternoon for the children, and another Saturday evening, when more of the grown-ups would be free to attend?"

Rupert did not reply at once, but stood rubbing his

chin. Even I could see instantly that two performances would double the take at the box office.

"Well . . ." he said at last. "I suppose. It would have to be the same show both times, though . . ."

"Splendid!" said the vicar. "What's it to be, then . . . the program, that is?"

"Open with a short musical piece," Rupert said. "It's a new one I've been working up. No one's seen it yet, so this would be a good chance to try it out. Then *Jack and the Beanstalk*. They always clamor for *Jack and the Beanstalk*, young and old alike. Classic fare. Very popular."

"Smashing!" the vicar said. He pulled a folded sheet of paper and the nub of a pencil from an inner pocket and scribbled a few notes.

"How's this?" he asked, with a final flourish, then, with a pleased look on his face, read aloud what he had written:

"Direct from London!

"I hope you'll forgive the small fib and the exclamation point," he whispered to Nialla.

"Porson's Puppets

"(Operated by the acclaimed Rupert Porson. As seen on the BBC Television)

"Program

"I. A Musical Interlude
"II. Jack and the Beanstalk

(The former being presented for the first time on any stage; the latter declared to be universally popular with old and young alike.)
Saturday, July 22nd, 1950, at St. Tancred's Parish Hall, Bishop's Lacey.
Performances at 2:00 P.M. and 7:00 P.M. sharp!

". . . Otherwise they'll just dawdle in," he added. "I'll have Cynthia dash off a sketch of a little jointed figure with strings to put at the top. She's an exceedingly talented artist, you know—not that she's had as many opportunities as she'd like to express herself—oh, dear, I fear I'm rambling. I'd best away to my telephonic duties."

And with that he was gone.

"Peculiar old duck," Rupert remarked.

"He's all right," I told him. "He leads rather a sad life."

"Ah," Rupert said, "I know what you mean. Funerals, and all that."

"Yes," I said. "Funerals and all that."

But I was thinking more of Cynthia.

"Which way to the mains?" Rupert asked suddenly.

For a moment I was dumbfounded. I must have looked particularly unintelligent.

"The mains," he repeated. "The current. The electrical controls. But then I don't suppose you'd know where they are, would you?"

As it happened, I did. Only weeks before I had been press-ganged into standing backstage with Mrs. Witty, helping to throw the massive levers of the antique lighting control panel, as her first-year ballet students tripped across the boards in their recital of *The Golden Apples of the Sun,* in which Pomona (Deirdre Skidmore, in insect netting) wooed the reluctant Hyas (a red-faced Gerald Plunkett in improvised tights cut from a pair of winter-weight long johns), by presenting him with an ever-growing assortment of papier-mâché fruit.

"Stage right," I said. "Behind the black tormentor curtains."

Rupert blinked once or twice, shot me a barbed look, and clattered back up the narrow steps to the stage. For a few moments we could hear him muttering away to himself up there, punctuated by the metallic sounds of panels being opened and slammed, and switches clicked on and off.

"Don't mind him," Nialla whispered. "He's always nervous as a cat from the minute a show's booked until the final curtain falls. After that, he's generally as right as rain."

As Rupert tinkered with the electricity, Nialla began unfastening several bundles of smooth wooden posts, which were bound tightly together with leather straps.

"The stage," she told me. "It all fits together with bolts and butterfly nuts. Rupert designed and built it all himself. Mind your fingers."

I had stepped forward to help her with some of the longer pieces.

"I can do it myself, thanks," she said. "I've done it hundreds of times—got it down to a science. Only thing that needs two to lift is the floor."

A rustling sound behind me made me turn around. There stood the vicar with rather an unhappy look on his face.

"Not good news, I'm afraid," he said. "Mrs. Archer tells

me that Bert has gone up to London for a training course and won't be back until tomorrow, and there's no answer at Culverhouse Farm, where I had hoped to put you up. But then Mrs. I doesn't often answer the telephone when she's home alone. She'll be bringing the eggs down on Saturday, but by then it will be far too late. I'd offer the vicarage, of course, but Cynthia has quite forcibly reminded me that we're in the midst of painting the guest rooms: beds taken down and stowed in the hallways, armoires blockading the landings, and so forth. Maddening, really."

"Don't fret, Vicar," Rupert said from the stage.

I nearly jumped out of my skin. I'd forgotten he was there.

"We'll camp where we are, in the churchyard. We've a good tent in the van, with wool rugs and a rubber groundsheet, a little Primus stove, and beans in a tin for breakfast. We'll be as cozy as bugs in a blanket."

"Well," the vicar said, "if it were solely up to me, I—"

"Ah," Rupert said, raising a finger. "I know what you're thinking: Can't have gypsies camping among the graves. Respect for the dear departed, and all that."

"Well," said the vicar, "there might be a modicum of truth in that, but—"

"We'll set up in an unoccupied corner, won't we? No desecration, that way. Shan't be the first time we've slept in a churchyard, will it, Nialla?"

Nialla colored slightly and became fascinated with something on the floor.

"Well, I suppose it's settled then," the vicar said. "We don't really have a great deal of choice, do we? Besides, it's only for one night. What harm can there be in that?

"Dear me!" he said, glancing at his wristwatch. "How *tempus* does *fugit*! I gave Cynthia my solemn promise to return straightaway. She's preparing an early supper, you see. We always have an early supper on Thursdays, because of choir practice. I'd invite you to join us for potluck, but—"

"Not at all," Rupert interrupted. "We've imposed enough for one day, Vicar. Besides, believe it or not, Nialla's a dab hand with bacon and eggs over a churchyard bonfire. We shall eat like Corsican bandits and sleep like the dead."

Nialla sat down far too gently on an unopened box, and I could see that she was suddenly exhausted. Dark circles seemed to have formed under her eyes as quickly as storm clouds blow across the moon.

The vicar rubbed his chin. "Flavia, dear," he said, "I've had the most splendid idea. Why don't you come back bright and early tomorrow morning and lend a hand? I'm sure Porson's Puppets would be most grateful to acquire the services of an eager assistant.

"I have home visits for the sick and shut-ins tomorrow, as well as Altar Guild," he added. "You could serve as my *locum tenens*, so to speak. Offer our guests the freedom of the parish, as it were, besides serving as general factotum and all-round dogsbody."

"I'd be happy to," I said, making an almost imperceptible curtsy.

Nialla, at least, rewarded me with a smile.

Outside, at the back of the churchyard, I retrieved Gladys, my trusty bicycle, from the long grass, and moments later we were flying homewards through the sundappled lanes to Buckshaw.

· F O U R ·

"HELLO, ALL," I SAID to Feely's back, after I had drifted inconspicuously into the drawing room.

Without turning away from the mirror in front of which she was regarding herself, Feely glanced up at my reflection in the time-rippled glass.

"You're in for it this time," she said. "Father's been looking for you all afternoon. He's just got off the telephone with Constable Linnet, in the village. I must say he seemed rather disappointed to hear that they hadn't fished your soggy little corpse out of the duck pond."

"How do you know they didn't?" I countered shrewdly. "How do you know I'm not a ghost come back to haunt you into the grave?"

"Because your shoe's untied and your nose is running," Daffy said, looking up from her book. It was *Forever Amber* and she was reading it for the second time.

"What's it about?" I had asked her on the first go-round.

"Flies in sap," she had said with a smug grin, and I had made a mental note to put it on my reading list. I adore books about the Natural Sciences.

"Aren't you going to ask me where I've been?" I said. I was simply dying to tell them about Porson's Puppets and all about Nialla.

"No," Feely answered, fingering the point of her chin as she leaned in for a closer look at herself. "No one is the slightest bit interested in what you do. You're like an unwanted dog."

"I'm not unwanted," I said.

"Oh yes you are!" she said with a hard laugh. "Name one person in this household who wants you and I'll give you a guinea. Go ahead—name one."

"Harriet!" I said. "Harriet wanted me, or she wouldn't have had me."

Feely whirled round and spat on the floor. She actually *spat*!

"For your information, Spot, Harriet fell into a profound mental bog immediately after you were born."

"Ha!" I said. "I've got you there! You told me I was adopted."

It was true. Whenever Daffy or Feely wanted to aggravate me beyond endurance, they would renew that claim.

"And so you were," she said. "Father and Harriet made an agreement to adopt you even before you were born. But when the time came, and your natural mother delivered you, you were given out by mistake to someone else—a couple in east Kent, I believe. Unfortunately they returned you. It was said to be the first time in the two-hundred-year history of the foundling hospital that any-one had returned a baby because they didn't like it.

"Harriet didn't care for you, either, once she got you home, but the papers were already signed, and the Board of Governors refused to take you back a second time. I'll never forget the day I overheard Harriet telling Father in her dressing room that she could never love such a rat-faced mewling. But what could she do?

"Well, she did what any normal woman would do in those circumstances: She fell into a deeply troubled state—and one from which she probably never recovered. She was still in the grip of it when she fell—or was it jumped?—off that mountain in Tibet. Father has always blamed you for it—surely you must realize that?"

The room went cold as ice, and suddenly I was numb from head to toe. I opened my mouth to say something, but found that my tongue had dried up and shriveled to a curled-up flap of leather. Hot tears welled up in my eyes as I fled the room.

I'd show that bloody swine Feely a thing or two. I'd have her so tied up in knots they'd have to hire a sailor to undo her for the funeral.

There is a tree that grows in Brazil, *Carica digitata*, which the natives call *chamburu*. They believe it to be such deadly poison that simply sleeping beneath its branches will cause, first of all, ever-festering sores, followed sooner or later by a wonderfully excruciating death.

Fortunately for Feely, though, *Carica digitata* does not grow in England. Fortunately for me, fool's parsley, better known as poison hemlock, does. In fact, I knew a low and marshy corner of Seaton's Meadow, not ten minutes from

Buckshaw, where it was growing at that very moment. I could be there and back before supper.

I'd recently updated my notes on coniine, the active principle of the stuff. I would extract it by distilling with whatever alkali was handy—perhaps a bit of the sodium bicarbonate I kept on hand in my laboratory against Mrs. Mullet's culinary excesses. I would then, by freezing, remove by recrystallization the iridescent scales of the less powerful conhydrine. The resulting nearly pure coniine would have a deliciously mousy odor, and it would take less than half a drop of the oily stuff to put paid to old accounts.

Agitation, vomiting, convulsions, frothing at the mouth, horrendous spasms—I ticked off the highlights on my fingers as I went.

> *"Sanctified cyanide*
> *Super-quick arsenic*
> *Higgledy-piggledy*
> *Into the soup.*
> *Put out the mourning lamps*
> *Call for the coffin clamps*
> *Teach them to trifle with*
> *Flavia de Luce!"*

My words came echoing back to me from the high painted ceiling of the foyer and the dark polished woodwork of the galleries above. Aside from the fact that it didn't mention poison hemlock, this little poem, which I had composed for an entirely different occasion, was otherwise a perfect expression of my present feelings.

Across the black and white tiles I ran, and up the curving staircase to the east wing of the house. The "Tar" wing, as we called it, was named for Tarquin de Luce, one of Harriet's ancient uncles who had inhabited Buckshaw before us. Uncle Tar had spent the greater part of his life locked away in a magnificent Victorian chemistry laboratory at the southeast corner of the house, investigating "the crumbs of the universe," as he had written in one of his many letters to Sir James Jeans, author of *The Dynamical Theory of Gases*.

Directly below the laboratory, in the Long Gallery, there is a portrait in oils of Uncle Tar. In it, he is looking up from his microscope, his lips pressed together and his brow furrowed, as if someone with an easel, a palette, and a box of paints had rudely barged in just as he was about to discover deLucium.

"Fizz off!" his expression clearly says. "Fizz off and leave me alone!"

And so they had fizzed off—and so, eventually, had Uncle Tar.

The laboratory, and all that was in it, was now mine, and had been for a number of years. No one ever came here—which was just as well.

As I reached into my pocket and pulled out the key, something white fluttered to the floor. It was the handkerchief I had lent Nialla in the churchyard—and it was still vaguely damp to the touch.

An image rose up in my mind of Nialla as she had been when first I saw her, lying facedown upon a weathered tombstone, hair spread out like a sea of red, her hot tears sizzling in the dust.

Everything dropped into place like the tumblers in a lock. Of course!

Vengeance would have to wait.

With a pair of cuticle scissors I had pinched from Feely's vanity table, I snipped four damp disks from the linen handkerchief, taking care to avoid the green grass stains I had inflicted upon it, and cutting out only those parts diagonally opposite the stains—the spots into which Nialla had wept.

These I stuffed—with tweezers—into a test tube, which I then injected with a three-percent solution of sulfosalicylic acid to precipitate the protein. This was the so-called Ehrlich test.

As I worked, I thought with pleasure of how profoundly the great Alexander Fleming had changed the world when he accidentally sneezed into a petri dish. This was the sort of science that was dear to my heart. Who, after all, can honestly say that they have never sneezed on a culture? It could happen to anyone. It has happened to me.

After the sneeze, the magnificently observant Fleming noticed that the bacteria in the dish were shrinking back, as if in fear, from the flecks of his spattered mucus. It wasn't long before he had isolated a particular protein in his snot that repelled bacteria in much the same way that the presence of a dog foaming at the mouth keeps off burglars. He called it lysozyme, and it was this substance for which I was now testing.

Fortunately, even in high summer, the ancestral halls of Buckshaw were as cold and dank as the proverbial tomb. Room temperature in the east wing, where my laboratory was located—in spite of the heating that had been spitefully installed by warring brothers in only the west wing of the once politically divided house—was never more than sixty degrees Fahrenheit, which, as luck would have it, was precisely the temperature at which lysozyme precipitates when sulfosalicylic acid is added.

I watched, entranced, as a veil of crystals began to form, their white flakes drifting gently down in the little winter inside the test tube.

Next, I lit a Bunsen burner, and carefully warmed a beaker of water to seventy degrees. It did not take long. When the thermometer indicated that it was ready, I dipped the bottom of the test tube into the warm bath and swirled it gently.

As the newly formed precipitate dissolved, I let out a gasp of delight.

"Flavia." Father's faint voice came drifting up to the laboratory. Having traversed the front hall, floated up the curving stair, penetrated the east wing, and wended its way down the long corridor to its southernmost point, it now seeped through my closed door, its force spent, as wispy as if it had come drifting to England all the way from Ultima Thule.

"Supper," I thought I heard him call.

"It's damnably irritating," Father said.

We were seated round the long refectory table, Father at the far end, Daffy and Feely one on each side, and me at the very bottom, at Cape Horn.

"It's damnably irritating," he said again, "for one to sit here and listen to one's daughter admit that she absconded with one's eau de cologne for a bloody chemical experiment."

No matter if I denied these things or admitted my guilt, Father found it equally irritating. I simply couldn't win. I had learned that it was best to remain silent.

"Damn it, Flavia, I just bought the bloody stuff. Can't very well go up to London in this heat smelling like a shoulder of pork that's gone off, can I?"

Father was most eloquent when he was angry. I had nicked the bottle of Roger & Gallet to fill an atomizer with which I needed to spray the house after an experiment involving hydrogen sulfide had gone spectacularly wrong.

I shook my head.

"I'm sorry," I said, assuming a hangdog look and dabbing at my eye with a napkin. "I'd buy you a new bottle— but I have no money."

As if I were a tin duck in a shooting gallery, Feely glared down the long table at me in silent contempt. Daffy's nose was stuck firmly in Virginia Woolf.

"But I could make you some," I said brightly. "It's really not much more than ethanol, citrus oils, and garden herbs. I'll ask Dogger to pick me some rosemary and lavender, and I'll get some oranges and lemons and limes from Mrs. Mullet—"

"You'll do no such thing, Miss Flavia," said Mrs. Mullet, bustling—literally—into the room as she knocked open the door with one of her ample hips and dumped a large tray onto the table.

"Oh, no!" I heard Daffy whisper to Feely. "It's 'the Whiffler' again."

"The Whiffler," as we called it, was a dessert of Mrs. Mullet's own devising, which, so far as we could make out, consisted of a sort of clotted green jelly in sausage casings, topped with double Devon cream, and garnished with sprigs of mint and other assorted vegetable refuse. It sat there, quivering obscenely now and then, like some great beastly garden slug. I couldn't help shivering.

"Yummy," Father said. "How very yummy."

He meant it ironically, but Mrs. Mullet's antennae were not attuned to sarcasm.

"I knew you'd like it," she said. "It was no more than this morning I was sayin' to my Alf, 'It's been a while since the Colonel and those girls 'ave 'ad one of my lovely jells. They always remarks over my jells" (this was no more than the truth), "and I loves makin' 'em for the dears.' "

She made it sound as if her employers had antlers.

Feely made a noise like a distressed passenger at the rail of the *Queen Mary* on a November crossing of the North Atlantic.

"Eat it up, dear," said Mrs. Mullet, unfazed. "It's good for you." And with that she was gone.

Father fixed me with that gaze of his. Although he had brought the latest issue of *The London Philatelist* to the table, as he always did, he had not so much as opened it. Father was a keen, not to say rabid, collector of postage stamps, his life wholly given over to gazing through a magnifying lens at a seemingly endless supply of little colored heads and scenic views. But he was not looking at stamps now—he was looking at me. The omens did not bode well.

"Where were you all afternoon?" he asked.

"At church," I answered promptly and primly and, I hoped, a little devoutly. I was a master at this kind of deflected chitchat.

"Church?" he asked. He seemed rather surprised. "Why?"

"I was helping a woman," I said. "Her van broke down."

"Ah," he said, allowing himself a half-millimeter smile. "And there you were on the spot to offer your skills as a motor mechanic."

Daffy grinned at her book, and I knew that she was listening with pleasure to my humiliation. To give her credit, Feely remained totally absorbed in polishing her fingernails on her white silk blouse.

"She's with a traveling puppet show," I said. "The vicar asked them—Rupert Porson, I mean, and Nialla—that's her name—to put on a performance in the parish hall on Saturday, and he wants me to help."

Father deflated slightly. The vicar was one of his few friends in Bishop's Lacey, and it was unlikely he would deny my services.

"Rupert is on the television," I volunteered. "He's quite famous, actually."

"Not in my circles," Father said, looking at his wristwatch and pushing his chair back from the table.

"Eight o'clock," he said. "Thursday."

He did not have to explain himself. Without a word, Daffy and Feely and I got up and made dutifully for the drawing room, all in a scattered line like a convoy.

Thursday evenings were Wireless Night at Buckshaw. Father had recently decreed that we needed to spend more time together as a family, and so it was that Wireless

Night had been laid on as a supplement to his regular compulsory lecture series on Wednesdays. This week it was to be the fabulous Fifth Symphony by Ludwig van Beethoven, or "Larry" as I called him whenever I wanted to aggravate Feely. I remembered that Feely had once told us that, on the original printed score, Beethoven's given name had appeared as "Louis."

"Louis Beethoven" sounded to me like the name of one of the supporting gangsters in an Edward G. Robinson film, someone with a sallow, pockmarked face, an alarming twitch, and a Thompson submachine gun in a violin case.

"Play dat *Moonlight Snotta* thing by Louie B.," I'd snarl in my raspy mobster's voice, wandering into the room when she was practicing at the keyboard. A moment later I'd be in full flight, with Feely in hot pursuit and sheet music floating to the carpet.

Now, Feely was busily arranging herself in an artistic full-length pose on the chesterfield, like a film star. Daffy dropped down sideways into an overstuffed armchair with her legs hanging out over the side.

Father switched on the wireless, and sat down in a plain wooden chair, his back ramrod straight. As the valves were warming up, I did a handspring across the carpet, walked back across the room on my hands, and dropped into a cross-legged Buddha position with what I hoped was an inscrutable look on my face.

Father shot me a withering look, but with the program already beginning, he decided to say nothing.

After a long and boring spoken introduction by an announcer, which seemed likely to run on into the next century, the Fifth Symphony began at last.

Duh-duh-duh-DAH.

I cupped my chin in my hands, propped my elbows on my knees, and gave myself over to the music.

Father had told us that the appreciation of music was of paramount importance in the education of a decent woman. Those were his exact words, and I had come to appreciate that there was music suitable for meditation, music for writing, and music for relaxation.

With my eyes half closed, I turned my face towards the windows. From my vantage point on the floor, I could see both ends of the terrace reflected in the glass of the French doors, which stood ajar, and unless my eyes were playing me tricks, something had moved out there: Some dark form had passed by outside the window.

I didn't dare leap up to look, though. Father insisted on intent listening. Even so much as a tapping toe would meet instantly with a wicked glare and an accusatory downward-jabbing finger.

I leaned slightly forward, and saw that a man dressed all in black had just sat down on a bench beneath the rose bushes. He was leaning back, eyes closed, listening to the music as it came floating out through the open doors. It was Dogger.

Dogger was Father's Man with a capital M: gardener, chauffeur, valet, estate manager, and odd-job man. As I have said before, he had done it all.

Dogger's experiences as a prisoner of war had left something broken inside him: something that from time to time, with a ferocity beyond belief, went ripping and tearing at his brains like some ravenous beast, leaving him a trembling wreck.

But tonight he was at peace. Tonight he had dressed for the symphony in a dark suit and what might have been a regimental tie, and his shoes had been polished until they shone like mirrors. He sat motionless on the bench beneath the roses, his eyes closed, his face up-turned like one of the contented Coptic saints I had seen in the art pages of *Country Life*, his shock of white hair lit from behind by an unearthly beam from the setting sun. It was pleasant to know that he was there.

I stretched contentedly, and turned my attention back to Beethoven and his mighty Fifth.

Although he was a very great musician, and a wizard composer of symphonies, Beethoven was quite often a dismal failure when it came to ending them. The Fifth was a perfect case in point.

I remembered that the end of the thing, the *allegro*, was one of those times when Beethoven just couldn't seem to find the "off" switch.

Dum . . . dum . . . dum-dum-dum, it would go, and you would think it was over.

But no—

Dum, dah, dum, dah, dum, dah, dum, dah, dum, dah, dum—DAH dum.

You'd go to get up and stretch, sighing with satisfaction at the great work you'd just listened to, and suddenly:

DAH dum. DAH dum. DAH dum. And so forth. *DAH dum.*

It was like a bit of flypaper stuck to your finger that you couldn't shake off. The bloody thing clung to life like a limpet.

I remembered that Beethoven's symphonies had sometimes been given names: the *Eroica*, the *Pastorale*, and so forth. They should have called this one the *Vampire*, because it simply refused to lie down and die.

But aside from its sticky ending, I loved the Fifth, and what I loved most about it was the fact that it was what I thought of as "running music."

I pictured myself, arms outspread, running pell-mell in the warm sunshine down Goodger Hill, swooping in broad zigzags, my pigtails flying behind me in the wind, bellowing the Fifth at the top of my lungs.

My pleasant reverie was interrupted by Father's voice.

"This is the second movement, now, *andante con moto*," he was saying loudly. Father always called out the names of the movements in a voice that was better suited to the drill hall than to the drawing room. "Means 'at a walking pace, with motion,'" he added, settling back in his chair as if, for the time being, he'd done his duty.

It seemed redundant to me: How could you have a walking pace *without* motion? It defied the laws of physics, but then, composers are not like the rest of us.

Most of them, for instance, are dead.

As I thought of being dead and of churchyards, I thought of Nialla.

Nialla! I had almost forgotten about Nialla! Father's summons to supper had come just as I was completing my chemical test. I formed in my mind an image of the slight cloudiness, the swirling flakes in the test tube, and the thrilling message they bore.

Unless I was badly mistaken, Mother Goose was pregnant.

· F I V E ·

I WONDERED IF SHE knew it.

Even before she had risen up weeping from her limestone slab, I had noticed that Nialla was not wearing a
wedding ring. Not that that meant anything: Even Oliver
Twist had an unwed mother.

But then there had been the fresh mud on her dress. Although I had registered the fact in some tangled thicket of
my mind, I had given it no further thought until now.

When you stopped to think about it, though, it seemed
perfectly obvious that she had piddled in the churchyard.
Since it hadn't rained, the fresh mud on her hem would
indicate that she had done so, and hastily, at the northwest corner, away from prying eyes, behind the mound of
extra soil that the sexton, Mr. Haskins, kept handy for
grave-digging operations.

She must have been desperate, I decided.

Yes! That was it! There wasn't a woman on earth who would choose such an unwelcoming spot ("wretchedly insalubrious," Daffy would have called it) unless she had no other choice. The reasons were numerous, but the one that leapt immediately to mind was one I had recently come across in the pages of the *Australian Women's Weekly* while cooling my heels in the outer chamber of a dentist's surgery in Farringdon Street. "Ten Early Signs of a Blessed Event," the article had been called, and the need for frequent urination had been near the top of the list.

"Fourth movement. Allegro. Key of C major," Father boomed, as if he were a railway conductor calling out the next station.

I gave him a brisk nod to show I was paying attention, then dived back into my thoughts. Now then, where was I? Oh, yes—Oliver Twist.

Once, on a trip to London, Daffy had pointed out to us from the window of our taxicab the precise spot in Bloomsbury where Oliver's foundling hospital had stood. Although it was now a rather pleasant and leafy square, I had no trouble imagining myself plodding up those long-gone but nevertheless snowdrifted front steps, raising the huge brass door knocker, and applying for refuge. When I told them of my semi-orphan life at Buckshaw with Feely and Daffy, there would be no questions asked. I would be welcomed with open arms.

London! Damn and blast! I'd completely forgotten. Today was the day I was supposed to have gone up to the City with Father to be fitted for braces. No wonder he was peeved. While I was relishing death in the churchyard and chewing the fat with Nialla and the vicar, Father had almost certainly been steaming and fuming round the house like an over-stoked destroyer. I had the feeling I hadn't heard the last of it.

Well, too late now. Beethoven was—at last—winding his weary way homeward, like Thomas Gray's ploughman, leaving the world to darkness and to me—and to Father.

"Flavia, a word, if you please," he said, switching off the wireless with an ominous *click*.

Feely and Daffy got up from their respective places and went out of the room in silence, pausing only long enough at the door to shoot me a pair of their patented "Now you're in for it!" grimaces.

"Damn it all, Flavia," Father said when they had gone. "You knew as well as I that we had an appointment for your teeth this afternoon."

For my teeth! He made it sound as if the National Health were issuing me a full set of plaster dentures.

But what he said was true enough: I had recently destroyed a perfectly good set of wire braces by straightening them to pick a lock. Father had grumbled, of course, but had made another appointment to have me netted and dragged back up to London, to that third-floor ironmonger's shop in Farringdon Street, where I would be strapped to a board like Boris Karloff as various bits of ironmongery were shoved into my mouth, screwed in, and bolted to my gums.

"I forgot," I said. "I'm sorry. You should have reminded me at breakfast."

Father blinked. He had not expected such a vigorous—

or such a neatly deflected!—response. Although he had been a career army officer, when it came to household maneuvers, he was little more than a babe-in-arms.

"Perhaps we could go tomorrow," I added brightly.

Although it may not seem so at first glance, this was a masterstroke. Father despised the telephone with a passion beyond all belief. He viewed the thing—"the instrument," as he called it—not just as a letting-down of the side by the post office, but as an outright attack on the traditions of the Royal Mail in general, and the use of postage stamps in particular. Accordingly he refused, point-blank, to use it in any but the direst of circumstances. I knew that it would take him weeks, if not months, to pick the thing up again. Even if he wrote to the dentist, it would take time for the necessary back-and-forth to be completed. In the meantime, I was off the hook.

"And remember," Father said, almost as an afterthought, "that your aunt Felicity is arriving tomorrow."

My heart sank like Professor Picard's bathyscaphe.

Father's sister descended upon us every summer from her home in Hampstead. Although she had no children of her own (perhaps because she had never married) she had, nevertheless, quite startling views upon the proper upbringing of children: views that she never tired of stating in a loud voice.

"Children ought to be horsewhipped," she used to say, "unless they are going in for politics or the Bar, in which case they ought in addition to be drowned." Which quite nicely summed up her entire philosophy. Still, like all harsh and bullying tyrants, she had a few drops of sentimentality secreted somewhere inside that would come bubbling to the surface now and then (most often at Christmas but sometimes, belatedly, for birthdays), when she would inflict her handpicked gifts upon us.

Daffy, for instance, who would be devouring *Melmoth the Wanderer*, or *Nightmare Abbey*, would receive from Aunt Felicity a copy of *The Girl's Jumbo Book*, and Feely, who never gave a thought to anything much beyond cosmetics and her own pimply hide, would rip open her parcel to find a pair of gutta-percha motoring galoshes ("Ideal for Country Breakdowns").

And yet once, when we had poked fun at Aunt Felicity in front of Father, he had become instantly as angry as I had ever seen him. But he quickly gained control of himself, touching a finger to the corner of his eye to stop a twitching nerve.

"Has it ever occurred to you," he asked, in that horrible level voice, "that your aunt Felicity is not what she may seem?"

"Do you mean to say," Feely shot back, "that this whole batty business is a pose?"

I could only look on agog at her boldness.

Father fixed her for a moment in the fierce glare of that cold blue de Luce eye, then turned on his heel and strode from the room.

"Lawks-a-mercy!" Daffy had said, but only after he had gone.

And so Aunt Felicity's ghastly gifts had continued to be received in silence—at least in my presence.

Before I could even begin to recall her trespasses on my

own good nature, Father went on: "Her train gets in to Doddingsley at five past ten, and I'd like you to be there to meet her."

"But—"

"Please don't argue, Flavia. I've made plans to settle up a few accounts in the village. Ophelia is giving some sort of recital for the Women's Institute's morning tea, and Daphne simply refuses to go."

Boil me dry! I should have known that something like this would happen.

"I'll have Mundy send round a car. I'll book him when he comes tonight for Mrs. Mullet." Clarence Mundy was the owner of Bishop Lacey's only taxicab.

Mrs. Mullet was staying late to finish off the semi-annual scouring of the pots and pans: a ritual that always filled the kitchen with greasy, superheated steam, and Buckshaw's inhabitants with nausea. On these occasions, Father always insisted on sending her home afterwards by taxicab. There were various theories in circulation at Buckshaw about his reasons for doing so.

It was obvious that I couldn't be en route to or from Doddingsley with Aunt Felicity and, at the same time, be helping Rupert and Nialla set up their puppet show. I would simply have to sort out my priorities and attend to the most important matters first.

Although there was a sliver of gold in the eastern sky, the sun was not yet up as I barreled along the road to Bishop's Lacey. Gladys's tires were humming that busy, waspish sound they make when she's especially content.

Low fog floated in the fields on either side of the ditches, and I pretended that I was the ghost of Cathy Earnshaw flying to Heathcliff (except for the bicycle) across the Yorkshire moors. Now and then, a skeletal hand would reach out of the bramble hedges to snatch at my red woolen sweater, but Gladys and I were too fast for them.

As I pulled up alongside St. Tancred's, I could see Rupert's small white tent set up in the long grass, at the back of the built-up churchyard. He had pitched it in the potter's field: the plots where paupers had been laid to rest and where, consequently, there were bodies but no tombstones. I supposed that Rupert and Nialla had not been told of this, and I decided that they would not hear it from me.

Before I had waded more than a few feet through the sodden grass, my shoes and socks were soaking wet.

"Hello?" I called quietly. "Anyone home?"

There was no reply. Not a sound. I started as one of the curious jackdaws slipped down from the top of the tower and landed with a perfect aerodynamic plop on the crumbling limestone wall.

"Hello?" I called again. "Knock, knock. Anyone home?"

There was a rustling in the tent and Rupert stuck his head out, his haystack hair falling over his eyes, which were as red as if they were driven by electric dynamos.

"Christ, Flavia!" he said. "Is that you?"

"Sorry," I said. "I'm a bit early."

He withdrew his head into the tent like a turtle, and I heard him trying to rouse Nialla. After a few yawns and grumbles, the canvas began poking out at sudden odd angles, as if someone inside with a besom broom were sweeping up broken glass.

A few minutes later, Nialla came half crawling out of the tent. She was wearing the same dress as yesterday, and although the material looked uncomfortably damp, she had pulled out a Woodbine and lighted it even before she had fully straightened up.

"Cheers," she said, flapping an inclusive hand towards me, and causing her smoke to drift off and mingle with the fog that hung among the gravestones.

She coughed with a sudden horrid spasm, and the jackdaw, cocking its head, took several steps sideways on the wall, as if in disgust.

"You oughtn't to be smoking those things," I said.

"Better than smoking kippers," she replied, and laughed at her own joke. "Besides, what do you know?"

I knew that my late great-uncle, Tarquin de Luce, whose chemical laboratory I had inherited, had, in his student days, been hooted down and ejected bodily from the Oxford Union when he took the affirmative in a debate, Resolved: That Tobacco Is a Pernicious Weed.

I had, not long before, come across Uncle Tar's notes tucked into a diary. His meticulous chemical researches seemed to have confirmed the link between smoking and what was then called "general paralysis." Since he had been, by nature, a rather shy and retiring sort, his "utter and abject humiliation," as he put it, at the hands of his fellow students, had contributed greatly to his subsequent reclusive life.

I wrapped my arms around myself and took a step back. "Nothing," I said.

I had said too much. It was cold and clammy in the churchyard, and I had a sudden vision of the warm bed I'd climbed out of to come here and help.

Nialla blew a couple of what were supposed to be casual smoke rings straight up into the air. She watched them ascend until they had dissipated.

"I'm sorry," she said. "I'm not at my best at the crack of dawn. I didn't mean to be rude."

"It's all right," I said. But it wasn't.

A twig cracked, surprisingly loud in the muffling silence of the fog. The jackdaw unfolded its wings and flapped off to the top of a yew tree.

"Who's there?" Nialla called, making a sudden dash to the limestone wall and leaning over it. "Bloody kids," she said. "Trying to scare us. I heard one of them laughing."

Although I have inherited Harriet's extremely acute hearing, I had heard no more than the cracking of the twig. I did not tell Nialla that it would be strange indeed to find any of Bishop's Lacey's children in the churchyard at such an early hour.

"I'll set Rupert on them," she said. "That'll teach them a lesson. Rupert!" she called out loudly. "What are you doing in there?

"I'll bet the lazy sod's crawled back into the sack," she added with a wink.

She reached out and gave one of the guy ropes a twang, and like a parachute spilling the wind, the whole thing collapsed in a mass of slowly subsiding canvas. The tent had been pitched in the loose topsoil of the potter's field, and it crumpled at a touch.

Rupert was out of the wreckage in a flash. He seized Nialla by the wrist and twisted it up behind her back. Her cigarette fell to the grass.

"Don't ever—!" he shouted. "Don't ever—!"

Nialla motioned with her eyes towards me, and Rupert let go of her at once.

"Damn it," he said. "I was shaving. I might have cut my bloody throat."

He stuck out his chin and gave it a sideways hitch, as if he were freeing an invisible collar.

Odd, I thought. *He still has all his morning whiskers, and moreover, there's not a trace of shaving cream on his face.*

"The die is cast," said the vicar.

He had come humming across the churchyard like a spinning top, showing black and then white through the fog, rubbing his hands together and exclaiming as he came.

"Cynthia has agreed to run up some handbills in the vestry, and we'll have them distributed before lunch. Now then, about breakfast—"

"We've eaten, thanks," Rupert said, jerking a thumb back towards the tent, which now lay neatly folded in the grass. And it was true. A few wisps of smoke were still drifting up from their doused fire. Rupert had fetched a box of wood chips from the back of the van and in surprisingly short order had an admirable campfire crackling away in the churchyard. Next, he had produced a coffeepot, a loaf of bread, and a couple of sharpened sticks to make toast of it. Nialla had even managed to find a pot of Scotch marmalade somewhere in their baggage.

"Are you quite sure?" the vicar asked. "Cynthia said to tell you that if—"

"Quite sure," Rupert said. "We're quite used to—"

"—Making do," Nialla said.

"Yes, well, then," the vicar said, "shall we go in?"

He shepherded us across the grass towards the parish hall, and as he extracted a ring of keys, I turned to look back across the churchyard toward the lych-gate. If someone *had* been there, they had since run off. A misty graveyard offers an infinite number of places to hide. Someone could well be crouching behind a tombstone not ten feet away, and you'd never know it. With one last apprehensive look at the remnants of the drifting fog, I turned and went inside.

"Well, Flavia, what do you think?"

My breath was taken away. What yesterday had been a bare stage was now an exquisite little puppet theater, and such a one as might have been transported overnight by magic from eighteenth-century Salzburg.

The proscenium opening, which I guessed to be five or six feet wide, was covered with a set of red velvet draperies, richly trimmed and tasseled with gold, and embroidered with the masks of Comedy and Tragedy.

Rupert vanished backstage, and as I watched in awe, a row of footlights, red and green and amber, faded up little by little until the lower half of the curtains was a rich rainbow of velvet.

Beside me, the vicar sucked in his breath as they slowly opened. He clasped his hands in rapture.

"The Magic Kingdom," he breathed.

There, before our eyes, nestled among green hills, was a quaint country cottage, its thatched roof and half-timbered front complete in every detail, from the wooden bench beneath the window right down to the tiny tissue paper roses in the front garden.

For a moment, I wished I lived there: that I could shrink myself and crawl into that perfect little world in which every object seemed to glow as if lit from within. Once settled in the cottage, I would set up a chemical laboratory behind the tiny mullioned windows and—

The spell was broken by the sound of something falling, and a harsh "Damn!" from somewhere up in the blue painted sky.

"Nialla!" Rupert's voice said from behind the curtains. "Where's that hook for the thingumabob?"

"Sorry, Rupert," she called out, and I noticed that she took her time replying, "it must still be in the van. You were going to have it welded, remember?"

"It's the thing that holds the giant up," she explained. "But then," she added, grinning at me, "we mustn't give away too many secrets. Takes all the mystery out of things, don't you think?"

Before I could answer, the door at the back of the parish hall opened, and a woman stood silhouetted against the sunlight. It was Cynthia, the vicar's wife.

She made no move to come in, but stood waiting for the vicar to come scurrying to her, which he promptly did. As she awaited his approach, she turned her face away to the outside light and, even from where I stood, I could clearly make out her cold blue eyes.

Her mouth was as pursed as if the lips were pulled tightly shut with drawstrings, and her sparse, gray-blond hair was pulled—painfully, it appeared—into an oval bun at the nape of an exceptionally long neck. In her beige taffeta blouse, mahogany-colored skirt, and brown oxfords, she looked like nothing so much as an over-wound grandfather clock.

Aside from the sound thrashing she had given me, it was hard to put a finger on what, precisely, I disliked about Cynthia Richardson. By all reports, she was a saint, a tiger, a beacon of hope to the sick, and a comfort to the bereaved. Her good works were legendary in Bishop's Lacey.

And yet . . .

There was something about her posture that just didn't ring true: a horrid slackness, a kind of limp and tired defeat that might be seen in the faces and bodies of Blitz victims in the wartime issues of the *Picture Post*. But in a vicar's wife . . . ?

All of this ran through my mind as she carried on a whispered consultation with her husband. And then, with no more than a lightning glance inside—she was gone.

"Excellent," the vicar said, breaking into a smile as he walked slowly towards us. "The Inglebys, it seems, have returned my call."

The Inglebys, Gordon and Grace, owned Culverhouse Farm, a patchwork quilt of mixed fields and ancient woods that lay to the north and west of St. Tancred's.

"Gordon's kindly offered you a place to pitch your tent at the bottom of Jubilee Field—a lovely spot. It's on the riverbank, not far from here. Walking distance, really. You'll have plenty of fresh eggs, the shade of incomparable willows, and the company of kingfishers."

"Sounds perfect," Nialla said. "A little bit of heaven."

"Cynthia tells me that Mrs. Archer rang up, too. Not such cheerful news on that front, I'm afraid. Bert's away to Cowley, on a course at the Morris factory, and won't be home until tomorrow night. Is your van in any sort of running order?"

I knew by the worried look on the vicar's face that he was having visions of a van marked "Porson's Puppets" parked at the door of the church come Sunday morning.

"A mile or so shouldn't be a problem," Rupert said, appearing suddenly at the side of the stage. "She'll run better now she's unloaded, and I can always baby the choke."

A shadow flitted across my mind, but I let it pass.

"Splendid," said the vicar. "Flavia, dear, I wonder if you'd mind going along for the ride? You can show them the way."

· S I X ·

OF COURSE WE HAD to go the long way round.

Had we gone on foot, it would have been no more than a shady stroll across the stepping-stones behind the church, along the riverbank by way of the old towpath that marked the southern boundary of Malplaquet Farm, and over the stile into Jubilee Field.

But by road, because there was no bridge nearby, Culverhouse Farm could be reached only by driving west towards Hinley, then, a mile west of Bishop's Lacey, turning off and winding tortuously up the steep west side of Gibbet Hill on a road whose dust was now rising up behind us in white billows. We were halfway to the top, skirting Gibbet Wood in a lane so narrow that its hedgerows scratched and tore at the sides of the jolting van.

"Don't mind my hip bones," Nialla said, laughing.

We were squeezed as tightly together in the front seat as worms in an angler's tin. With Rupert driving, Nialla and I were almost sitting on one another's lap, each with an arm across the other's shoulders.

The Austin backfired fiercely as Rupert, according to some ancient and secret formula known only to him, fiddled alternately with the choke and the throttle.

"These Inglebys, now," he shouted above the incessant string of explosions. "Tell us something about them."

The Inglebys were rather morose individuals who kept mostly to themselves. From time to time I had seen Gordon Ingleby dropping off Grace, his tiny, doll-like wife, at the village market where, dressed always in black, she sold eggs and butter with little enthusiasm beneath a striped canopy. I knew, as did everyone else in Bishop's Lacey, that the Inglebys' seclusion had begun with the tragic death of their only child, Robin. Before that, they had been friendly and outgoing people, but ever since had turned inward. Even though five years had passed, the village still allowed them their grief.

"They farm," I said.

"Ah!" said Rupert, as if I had just rhymed off the entire Ingleby family history from the time of William the Conqueror.

The van bucked and jerked as we climbed ever higher, and Nialla and I had to brace our palms against the dashboard to keep from knocking our heads together.

"Grim old place, this," she said, nodding to the dense woods on our left. Even the few flecks of sunlight that did manage to penetrate the dense foliage seemed to be swallowed up in the dim world of the ancient trunks.

"It's called Gibbet Wood," I said. "There used to be a village nearby called Wapp's Hill, until about the eighteenth century, I think, but there's nothing left of it now. The gallows was at the old crossroads at the center of the wood. If you climb up that path you can still see the timbers. They're quite rotten, though."

"Ugh," Nialla said. "No, thank you."

I decided it was best, at least for the time being, not to tell her that it was at the crossroads in Gibbet Wood that Robin Ingleby had been found hanging.

"Good Lord!" Rupert said. "What in hell is that?"

He pointed to something dangling from a tree branch—something moving in the morning breeze.

"Mad Meg's been here," I said. "She picks up empty tins and rubbish along the roads and strings them on bits of cord. She likes shiny things. She's rather like a magpie."

A pie plate, a rusty Bovril tin, a bit of silver from a radiator shell, and a bent soup spoon, like some grotesque Gothic fishing lure, twisted slowly this way and that in the sun.

Rupert shook his head and turned his attention back to the choke and the throttle. As we reached the peak of Gibbet Hill, the motor emitted a most frightful bang, and with a sucking gurgle, died. The van jerked to a halt as Rupert threw on the hand brake.

I could see by the deep lines on his face that he was nearly exhausted. He pounded at the steering wheel with his fists.

"Don't say it," Nialla said. "We have company."

I thought for a moment she was referring to me, but her finger was pointing through the windscreen to the side of the lane, where a dark, grimy face peered out at us from the depths of a hedgerow.

"It's Mad Meg," I said. "She lives in there somewhere—somewhere in the wood."

As Meg came scuttling alongside the van, I felt Nialla shrink back.

"Don't worry, she's really quite harmless."

Meg, in a tattered outfit of rusty black bombazine, looked like a vulture that had been sucked up by a tornado and spat back out. A red glass cherry bobbed cheerfully from a wire on her black flowerpot hat.

"Ay, harmless," Meg said, conversationally, at the open window. " 'Be ye therefore wise as serpents, and harmless as doves.' Hello, Flavia."

"These are my friends, Meg—Rupert and Nialla."

In view of the fact that we were crammed together cheek-by-jowl in the Austin, I thought it would be all right to call Rupert by his Christian name.

Meg took her time staring at Nialla. She reached out a filthy finger and touched Nialla's lipstick. Nialla cringed slightly, but covered it nicely with a tiny counterfeit sneeze.

"It's Tangee," she said brightly. "Theatrical Red. Changes color when you put it on. Here, give it a try."

It was a magnificent job of acting, and I had to give her top marks for the way in which she disguised her fear with an open and cheery manner.

I had to shift a bit so that she could fish in her pocket for the lipstick. As she held it out, Meg's filthy fingers snapped the golden tube from her hand. Without taking her eyes from Nialla's face, Meg painted a broad swathe of the stuff across her chapped and dirty lips, pressing them together as if she were drinking from a straw.

"Lovely!" Nialla said. "Gorgeous!"

Again she reached into her pocket and extracted an enamel powder compact, an exquisite thing of flame orange cloisonné, shaped like a butterfly. She flipped it open to reveal the little round mirror in the lid, and after a quick glance at herself, handed it over to Meg.

"Here, have a look."

In a flash, Meg had seized the compact and was scrutinizing herself in the glass, turning her head animatedly from side to side. Satisfied with what she saw, she rewarded us with a broad grin that revealed the black gaps left by several missing teeth.

"Lovely!" she muttered. "Smashing!" And she shoved the orange butterfly into her pocket.

"Here!—" Rupert made a grab for it, and Meg drew back, startled, as if noticing him for the first time. Her smile vanished as suddenly as it had appeared.

"I know you," she said darkly, her eyes fixed on his goatee. "You're the Devil, you are. Aye, that's what's gone and happened—the Devil's come back to Gibbet Wood."

And with that, she stepped backwards into the hedgerow and was gone.

Rupert climbed awkwardly out of the van and slammed the door.

"Rupert—" Nialla called out. But rather than going into the bushes after Meg, as I thought he would, Rupert walked a short distance up the road, looked round a bit, and then came slowly back, his feet stirring up the dust.

"It's only a gentle slope, and we're no more than a

stone's throw from the top," he reported. "If we can push her up as far as that old chestnut, we can coast down the far side. Might even start her up again. Like to steer, Flavia?"

Although I had spent hours sitting in Harriet's old Phantom II in our coach house, it had been always for purposes of reflection or escape. I had never actually been in control of a moving motorcar. Although the idea was not unattractive at first, I quickly realized that I had no real desire to find myself hurtling out of control down the east side of Gibbet Hill, and coming to grief among the scenery.

"No," I said. "Perhaps Nialla—"

"Nialla doesn't like to drive," he snapped.

I knew at once that I had put my foot in it, so to speak. By suggesting that Nialla steer, I was at the same time suggesting that Rupert get off his backside and push—withered leg and all.

"What I meant," I said, "was that you're probably the only one of us who can get the motor started again."

It was the oldest trick in the book: Appeal to his manly vanity, and I was proud to have thought of it.

"Right," he said, clambering back into the driving seat.

Nialla scrambled out, and I behind her. Any thoughts I might have had about the wisdom of someone in her condition pushing a van uphill on a hot day were instantly put aside. And besides, I could hardly bring up the subject.

Like a flash, Nialla had darted round behind the van, pressing her back flat against the rear doors and using her powerful legs to push.

"Take off the bloody hand brake, Rupert!" she shouted.

I took up a position beside her and, with every last ounce of strength that was in me, dug in my feet and pushed.

Wonder of wonders, the stupid thing began to move. Perhaps because the puppet paraphernalia had been unloaded at the parish hall, the greatly lightened van was soon creeping, snail-like but inexorably, up towards the peak of the hill. Once we had it in motion, we turned round and shoved with our hands.

The van came to a full stop only once, and that was when Rupert threw in the clutch and turned on the ignition. A tremendous black backfire came shooting out of the tailpipe, and even without looking down, I knew that I would have to explain to Father the destruction of yet another pair of white socks.

"Don't let the clutch in now—wait until we get to the top!" Nialla shouted.

"Men!" she muttered to me. "Men and their bleeding exhaust noises."

Ten minutes later we were at the crest of Gibbet Hill. In the distance, Jubilee Field sloped away towards the river, a gently rolling blanket of flax of such electric-blue intensity that it might have caused van Gogh to weep.

"One more good heave," Nialla said, "and we're on our way."

We groaned and we grunted, pushing and shoving against the hot metal, and then suddenly, as if it had become weightless, the van began moving on its own. We were on the downside of the hill.

"Quick! Jump in!" Nialla said, and we ran alongside as the van picked up speed, bucketing and bumping down the rutted road.

We jumped onto the running board, and Nialla threw open the door. A moment later we had collapsed, hugging one another, into the seat as Rupert manipulated the engine controls. Halfway down, as the motor started at last, the van gave off an alarming backfire before settling down to an unhealthy coughing. At the bottom of the hill, Rupert touched the brakes, and we turned neatly into the lane that leads to Culverhouse Farm.

Overheated from its exertions, the Austin stood sputtering and steaming like a leaky teakettle in the farmyard, which, to all intents and purposes, seemed to be abandoned. In my experience, whenever you arrived at a farm, someone always came out of the barn to greet you, wiping his oily hands on a rag and calling to a woman with a basket of eggs to bake some scones and put the tea on. At the very least, there should have been a barking dog.

Although there were no pigs in evidence, a weathered sty at the end of a row of tumbledown sheds was full of tall nettles. Beyond that was a turreted dovecote. Assorted milk pails, all of them rusty, lay scattered about the yard, and a lone hen picked halfheartedly among the weeds, watching us with its wary yellow eye.

Rupert climbed out of the van and slammed the door loudly.

"Hello?" he called. "Anyone here?"

There was no reply. He walked past a battered chopping block to the back door of the house and gave it a thunderous knocking with his fist.

"Hello? Anyone at home?"

He cupped his hands, peering in through the grimy window of what must once have been the buttery, then motioned us out of the van.

"Odd," he whispered. "There's someone standing in the middle of the room. I can see his outline against the far window." He gave the door a couple more loud bangs.

"Mr. Ingleby," I called out, "Mrs. Ingleby, it's me, Flavia de Luce. I've brought the people from the church."

There was a long silence, and then we heard the sound of heavy boots on a wooden floor. The door creaked open upon a dark interior, and a tall blond man in overalls stood blinking in the light.

I had never seen him before in my life.

"I'm Flavia de Luce," I said, "from Buckshaw." I waved my hand vaguely in its direction to the southeast. "The vicar asked me to show these people the way to Culver-house Farm."

The blond man stepped outside, bending substantially in order to get through the low doorway without banging his head. He was what Feely would have described as "indecently gorgeous": a towering Nordic god. As this fair-haired Siegfried turned to close the door carefully behind him, I saw that there was a large, faded red circle painted on the back of his boiler suit.

It meant he was a prisoner of war.

My mind flew instantly back to the wooden block and the missing axe. Had he chopped up the Inglebys and stacked their limbs like firewood behind the kitchen stove?

What a preposterous thought. The war had been over for five years, and I had seen the Inglebys—at least Grace—as recently as last week.

Besides, I already knew that German prisoners of war were not particularly dangerous. The first ones I had seen were on my first-ever visit to a cinema, the Palace, in Hinley. As the blue-jacketed captives were marched by their armed guards into the theater and seated, Daffy had nudged me and pointed.

"The enemy!" she had whispered.

As the lights went down and the film began, Feely had leaned over and said, "Just think, you'll be sitting with them in the dark for two hours. Alone . . . if Daffy and I go for sweets."

The film was *In Which We Serve,* and I couldn't help noticing that when HMS *Torrin* was sunk in the Mediterranean by the Luftwaffe's dive-bombers, although the prisoners did not applaud the deed openly, there were nevertheless smiles among them.

"Captured Germans are to not be treated inhumanely," Father had told us when we got home, quoting something he had heard on the wireless, "but are to be shown very clearly that we regard them, officers and men, as outcasts from the society of decent men."

Although I respected Father's word—at least in principle—it was clear that the man who had greeted us at Culverhouse Farm was no outcast; not by any stretch of the imagination.

Five years after the coming of peace, he could only be wearing his bull's-eyed boiler suit out of pride.

"May I present myself? I am Dieter Schrantz," he said,

with a broad smile, shaking hands with each of us in turn, beginning with Nialla. From those four words alone, I could tell that he spoke nearly perfect English. He even pronounced his own name the way any Englishman would have done, with hard *r*s and *a*s and no unpleasant snarling of his surname.

"The vicar said that you should come."

"Bloody van broke down," Rupert said, jerking his head towards the Austin with, I thought, a certain measure of aggressiveness. As if he . . .

Dieter grinned. "Don't worry, I'll help you run it down the lane to Jubilee Field. That's where you're billeted, you know, old chap."

Old chap? Dieter had obviously been in England for quite some time.

"Is Mrs. Ingleby at home?" I asked. I thought that it was probably best if Nialla was given a tour of the amenities, as it were, before she had to ask.

The shadow of a cloud passed over Dieter's face.

"Gordon's gone off up the wood somewhere," he said, gesturing to Gibbet Hill. "He likes to work alone most of the time. He'll be down presently to help Sally in the meadow. We shall see them when we take your 'bus down to the river."

"Sally" was Sally Straw, a member of the Women's Land Army, or "Land Girl," as they were called, who had been working at Culverhouse Farm since sometime during the war.

"All right," I said. "Hullo! Here's Tick and Tock."

Mrs. Ingleby's two tortoiseshell cats came ambling out of a shed, yawning and stretching in the sun. She often took them with her, for company, to the market, as she did several of her farm creatures, including, now and then, her pet goose, Matilda.

"Tick," she had informed me once, when I inquired about their names, "because she has ticks. And Tock because she chatters like a magpie."

Tock was walking directly towards me, already well launched into a meowling conversation. Tick, meanwhile, ambled off towards the dovecote, which rose up darkly from behind the warren of shabby, overgrown sheds.

"You go on ahead," I said. "I'll come down to the field in a few minutes."

I swept Tock up into my arms. "Who's a pretty pussy, then?" I cooed, watching from the corner of my eye to see if anyone was taken in. I knew that the cat was not: She had begun to squirm immediately.

But Rupert and Nialla were already piling into the van, which still stood shuddering away to itself in the yard. Dieter gave a shove and climbed onto the running board, and a moment later, with a wave, they were bumping out of the yard and into the lane that led down the slope to Jubilee Field and the river. A gentle backfire in the middle distance confirmed their departure.

The moment they were out of sight, I put Tock down in the dusty yard.

"Where's Tick?" I said. "Go find her."

Tock resumed her long feline monologue, and stalked off to the dovecote.

Needless to say, I followed.

· S E V E N ·

THE DOVECOTE WAS A work of art. There's no other way of putting it, and I shouldn't have been in the least surprised to hear that the National Trust had its eye on it.

It was from this remarkable specimen of architecture that Culverhouse Farm had taken its name—"culverhouse" being the old word for a dovecote. This one was a tall round tower of ancient bricks, each one the shade of a faded rose, but no two of them alike. Built in the time of Queen Anne, it had once been used to breed and raise doves for the farm's dinner table. In those days, the legs of the little dovelets were snapped to keep them fattening in the nest (this fact gleaned from the kitchen chatter of Mrs. Mullet). But times had changed. Gordon Ingleby was an avid pigeon fancier, and the birds that had lived in the tower in this century were more likely to be coddled by hand than in boiling water. At the weekends, he had sent them off by rail to some far-flung flyspeck on the map of England, where they would be released to come flapping immediately back to Culverhouse Farm. Here, they would be welcomed by the slapping-off of elaborate mechanical time clocks, much petting and bragging, and a great gorging on grain by the birds.

At least, such had been the case until little Robin Ingleby had been found hanging by the neck from the rotted gallows in Gibbet Wood. Since that day, other than a few wild specimens, there had been no more doves at Culverhouse Farm.

Poor Robin, when he died, had been the same age as I was then, and I found it hard to believe that someone so young could actually be dead. Still, it was a fact.

When one lives in a village, the more things are hushed up, the more one hears, and I remembered the undercurrent of gossip that had swept through Bishop's Lacey at the time, lapping away like the tide at the timbers beneath a pier.

"They say young Robin Ingleby's gone and killed himself." "Robin Ingleby's been done in by his parents." "The little lad's been slaughtered by Satanists. Mark my words—"

Most of these theories had been leaked to me by Mrs. Mullet, and I thought of them now as I approached the tower, gazing up in wonder at its myriad of openings.

As that monk called the lector had done in the monasteries of the Middle Ages, Daffy often read aloud to us as we ate our meals. We had recently been treated to Henry

Savage Landor's description, in *Across Coveted Lands,* of the Towers of Silence, in Persia, on top of which the Parsees placed corpses in a sitting position, with a stick under the chin to keep them upright. When the crows arrived to squabble over the body, it was considered a ticket to Heaven if the right eyeball was the first one consumed. The left was not quite so auspicious.

I could not help thinking of this now, and of the author's account of the curious circular pigeon towers of Persia, each with a deep central pit for the collection of guano, whose production was the sole reason for keeping the birds.

Could there be, I wondered, some strange connection between towers, birds, death, and corruption? As I paused there for a moment, trying to think what it might be, a peculiar sound came drifting from the tower.

At first I thought it might be the muttering and cooing away to themselves of doves, high above my head in the cote. Or was it the wind?

It seemed too sustained to be either of these, rising and falling like the sound of a ghostly air-raid siren, almost at the threshold of hearing.

The sagging wooden door stood ajar, and I found that I could slip through easily into the hollow center of the tower. Tock brushed past my ankles, then vanished into the shadows in search of mice.

The sharp reek of the place slapped me in the face: the unmistakable chemical smell of dove's guano, which the great Humphry Davy had found to yield, by distillation, carbonate of ammonia, with a residuum of carbonate of lime and common salt, a finding I had once verified by experiment in my chemical laboratory at Buckshaw.

Far above my head, countless beams of sunshine slanting in through the open ports dappled the curving walls with dots of yellow light. It was as if I had stepped into the colander in which some giant strained his soup bones.

Here, inside, the wailing sound was even louder, a whirlpool of noise amplified by the circular walls, of which I was the very center. I couldn't have called out—even if I'd dared.

At the center of the room, pivoting on an ancient wooden post, was a moveable scaffold, somewhat like a library ladder, which must at one time have been used by their keepers to gain access to the doomed little birds.

The thing groaned fearsomely as I stepped onto it.

Up I went, inch by inch, hanging on for dear life, stretching my arms and legs to make impossible giant steps from one creaking crosspiece to the next. I looked down only once, and it made my head swim.

The higher I climbed, the louder the keening sound became, its echoes now coming together in a chorus of voices that seemed to congregate in some wild, high lament.

Above me, and to my left, was a vaulted opening that gave onto a niche larger than the others. By standing on tiptoe and seizing the brick ledge with my fingertips, I was able to pull myself up until my eyes were level with the floor of this grotto.

Inside, a woman knelt, her back towards me. She was singing. Her thin voice echoed from the bricks and swirled round my head:

"The robin's gone afloat.
The wind that rocks him to and fro
With a soft cradle-song and slow
Pleases him in the ebb and flow,
Rocking him in a boat."

It was Mrs. Ingleby!

In front of her, on an overturned box, a candle burned, adding its smoky odor to the stifling heat of the little brick cave. To her right was propped up a black-and-white photograph of a child: her dead son, Robin, who grinned happily at the camera, his shock of blond hair bleached nearly white by the sun of long-gone summer days. To her left, lying on its side, as if it were hauled up on the beach to be cleaned of barnacles, was a toy sailboat.

I held my breath. She mustn't know I was here. I would climb down slowly, and—

My legs began to shake. I hadn't much of a grip, and my leather soles were already slipping on the weathered wooden frame. As I started to slide back, Mrs. Ingleby began her wail again, this time another song and, oddly, in another voice: a harsh, swashbuckling, piratical gargle:

"So, though bold Robin's gone,
Yet his heart lives on,
And we drink to him with three times three."

And she let out a horrible, snuffling laugh.

I pulled myself up on tiptoe again, just in time to see her twist the cork from a tall clear bottle, and take a quick, bobbing swig. It looked to me like gin, and it was plain to see that she had been at it for some time.

With a long, shuddering sigh, she pushed the bottle back under a pile of straw and lit a new candle from the dwindling flame of the one that was dying. With drips of flowing wax, she stuck it in place beside its exhausted fellow.

And now she began another song, this one in a darker minor key; sung more slowly, and more like a dirge, pronouncing every word with an awful, exaggerated clarity:

> "Robin-Bad-fellow, wanting such a supper,
> Shall have his breakfast with a rope and butter
> To which let all his fellows be invited
> That with such deeds of darkness are delighted."

Rope and butter? Deeds of darkness?

I suddenly realized that my hair was standing completely on end, the way it did when Feely stroked her black ebonite comb on her cashmere sweater and brought it close to the nape of my neck. But while I was still trying to calculate how quickly I could scramble back down the wooden frame and make a run for it, the woman spoke: "Come up, Flavia," she said. "Come up and join in my little requiem."

Requiem? I thought. *Do I really want to scramble up into a brick cell with a woman who is at best more than a little inebriated, and at worst a homicidal maniac?*

I hauled myself up into the gloom.

As my eyes became accustomed to the candlelight, I saw that she wore a white cotton blouse with short puffed sleeves and a low peasant-girl neckline. With her raven black hair and her brightly colored dirndl skirt, she might easily be taken for a gypsy fortune-teller.

"Robin's gone," she said.

Those two words nearly broke my heart. Like everyone else in Bishop's Lacey, I had always thought that Grace Ingleby lived in her own private, insulated world: a world where Robin still played in the dusty dooryard, chasing flustered hens from fence to fence, dashing into the kitchen now and then to beg a sweet.

But it was not true: She had stood as I had done, beside the small gravestone in the churchyard of St. Tancred's, and read its simple inscription: *Robin Tennyson Ingleby, 1939–1945, Asleep in the Lamb.*

"Robin's gone," she said again, and now it was almost a moan.

"Yes," I said, "I know."

Motes of dust floated like little worlds in the pencil beams of sunlight that penetrated the chamber's gloom. I sat down in the straw.

As I did so, a pigeon clattered up from its nest, and out through the little arched window. My heart almost stopped. I had thought the pigeons long gone, and I almost sat on the stupid thing.

"I took him to the seaside," Grace went on, caressing the sailboat, oblivious to the bird. "Robin loved the seaside, you know."

I pulled my knees up under my chin and wrapped my arms around them.

"He played in the sand. Built a sand castle."

There was a long silence, and I saw that she had drifted off somewhere.

"Did you have ice cream?" I asked, as if it were the most important question in the world. I couldn't think of anything else.

"Ice cream?" She nodded her head. "They gave it to us in paper cups . . . little pointed paper cups. We wanted vanilla—we both loved vanilla, Robin and I. Funny thing, though . . ." She sighed. "When we ate it, there was a taste of chocolate . . . as if they hadn't rinsed the scoop properly."

I nodded wisely.

"That sometimes happens," I said.

She reached out and touched the sailboat again, running her fingertips over its smooth painted hull. And then she blew out the candle.

We sat for a while in silence among the spatterings of sunshine that seeped into the red brick cave. *This must be what the womb is like*, I thought.

Hot. Waiting for something to happen.

"Why are you here?" she said at last. I noticed that she was not slurring her words as much as before.

"The vicar sent some people to camp in Jubilee Field. He asked me to show them the way." She seized my arm.

"Does Gordon know?" she demanded.

"I think he does," I said. "He told the vicar it would be all right if they camped at the bottom of the lane."

"The bottom of the lane . . ." She let out a long, slow breath. "Yes, that would be all right, wouldn't it?"

"It's a traveling puppet show," I said. "Porson's Puppets. They're putting on a performance Saturday. The vicar's asked them. Their van's broken down, you see, and . . ."

I was gripped by a sudden inspiration.

"Why don't you come?" I asked. "Everyone in the village will be there. You could sit with me, and—"

Mrs. Ingleby was staring at me with horror.

"No!" she said. "No! I couldn't do that."

"Perhaps you and Mr. Ingleby could both come, and—"

"No!"

She scrambled to her feet, raising a thick cloud of chaff, and for a few moments, as the stuff swirled round us, we stood perfectly still, like figures in a snow-globe paperweight.

"You'd better go," she said suddenly, in a throaty voice. "Please go now."

Without a word I groped my way to the opening, my eyes streaming from the dust. With surprisingly little effort, I found myself able to drop down onto the wooden vane, and begin the long climb down.

I have to admit that Jack and the Beanstalk crossed my mind.

The farmyard was deserted. Dieter had gone down the lane with Rupert and Nialla to the river, and by now they had probably already made camp. If I was lucky, I might be just in time for a cup of tea. I felt as if I'd been up all night.

What was the time, anyway?

God blind me with a fish fork! Aunt Felicity's train was due to arrive at five past ten and I'd completely forgotten about her! Father would have my guts for garters.

Even if Aunt Felicity wasn't already fuming on the platform and frothing at the mouth, how on earth was I ever going to get to Doddingsley? It was a good six miles from Culverhouse Farm, even as the crow flies, and as far as I knew, I wasn't about to sprout wings.

Down the lane I ran, windmilling my arms as if that could propel me to a greater speed. Fortunately, it was downhill all the way, and at the bottom, I could see Rupert's van parked beneath the willows.

Dieter had the Austin's hood open and was poking around in its innards. Nialla was hanging a shirt on the bushes to dry. Gordon Ingleby was nowhere in sight, nor was Sally Straw.

"First chance I've had to break out the old Sunlight," Nialla told me. "Dieter's having a peek at the motor. Whatever took you so long?"

"What time is it?" I pleaded.

"Search me," she replied. "Rupert's the only one who owns a watch, and he's taken himself off somewhere."

As he always does. She did not actually speak the words, but her meaning was as clear as if she'd shouted them from the top of Big Ben.

"Dieter?" I asked.

Dieter shook his head. "Sorry. It was for such a long time forbidden to possess one. . . ."

"Excuse me," I interrupted, "but I have to meet a train."

Before they could answer, I was off along the towpath at top speed. It was an easy run along the old embankment, which skirted the southern edge of Jubilee Field, and within surprisingly few minutes, I was leaping across the stepping-stones to the churchyard.

The clock on the church tower showed twenty minutes to four, which was impossible: The stupid thing had probably stopped in the reign of Henry the Eighth and nobody had cared enough to set it going again.

Gladys, my trusty BSA, was exactly where I had left her at the side of the parish hall. I pushed off for Buckshaw.

As I raced past the corner of Spindle Lane, the clock set into the wall of the Thirteen Drakes showed that the time was either noon or midnight. I'm afraid I let slip rather a rude word.

Out of the village I went like the wind, southwestwards towards Buckshaw, until I came at last to the Mulford Gates, where Clarence Mundy sat waiting, perched on one of the wings of his taxicab, dragging thirstily at a cigarette. By the snowfall of butts on the road, I could tell that it was not his first.

"Hullo, Clarence," I said. "How's the time?"

"Ten hundred hours," he said, glancing at his elaborate military wristwatch. "Better climb aboard."

He let in the clutch as I did so, and we were off like a skyrocket.

As we tore along through lanes and hedgerows, Clarence worked the gear stick like a snake charmer grappling with a wilful cobra, seizing its head every few seconds and shoving it to some new quarter of the compass. Outside the windows, the countryside streamed past in an ever-accelerating blur of green, until I wanted to scream "Yarooh!"—but I restrained myself.

During the war, Clarence had flown the jumbo-sized Sunderland flying boats, endlessly patrolling the vast Atlantic for German U-boats, and, as we fairly flew along between the pressing hedgerows, he seemed still to imagine himself at the controls of one of these behemoths. At any moment, I thought, he would pull back on the steering wheel and we would lift off into the air. Perhaps, during our ascent into the summer sky, we might even catch a glimpse of Harriet.

Before she had married Father, Harriet had piloted her own de Havilland Gipsy Moth, which she had named *Blithe Spirit,* and I sometimes imagined her floating alone up there in the sunshine, dipping in and out of the puffy valleys of cumulus, with no one to answer to except the wind.

Clarence skidded to a stop at one end of the Doddingsley railway platform as the train steamed in at the other.

"Ten-oh-five," he said, glancing at wristwatch. "On the dot."

As I knew she would be, the first passenger to step down from the carriage was Aunt Felicity. In spite of the heat, she was wearing a long, light-colored motoring coat and a great solar topee, which was tied under her chin with a broad blue ribbon. Various bits protruded from her person in all directions: hatpins, umbrella handles, rolled-up magazines, newspapers, shooting sticks, and so forth. She looked like a walking bird's nest, or, rather, more like an ambulatory haystack.

"Fetch my luggage, Clarence," she said, "and mind the alligator."

"Alligator?" Clarence said, his eyebrows shooting up.

"The bag," said Aunt Felicity. "It's new from Harrods, and I won't have it ruined by a clumsy rustic on some godforsaken railway platform.

"Flavia," she said, "you may carry my hot-water bottle."

· E I G H T ·

DOGGER MET US AT the front door. He fished a cloth change purse from his pocket and raised his eyebrows at Clarence.

"Two bob," Clarence said, "going and coming—including the wait."

As Dogger counted out the coins, Aunt Felicity leaned back and ran her eyes over the façade of the house.

"Shocking," she said. "The place grows shabbier before one's very eyes."

I did not feel it my place to tell her that, when it came to expenses, Father was nearly at his wit's end. The house had actually belonged to Harriet, who had died young, unexpectedly, and without troubling to make a will. Now, because of what Father called "complications," it seemed unlikely that we would be able to remain at Buckshaw for much longer.

"Take my bags to my room, Dogger," Aunt Felicity said, returning her gaze to earth, "and mind the alligator."

"Yes, Miss Felicity," Dogger said, a wicker hamper already under each arm and a suitcase in each hand. "Harrods, I believe."

"Aunt Felicity's arrived," I said, slouching into the kitchen. "I'm suddenly not very hungry. I think I'll just have a lettuce sandwich and eat it in my room."

"You'll do no such thing," Mrs. Mullet said. "I've gone and made a nice aspic salad, with beets and that."

I pulled a horrid face, but when she glanced at me unexpectedly, I remembered Nialla's dodge and cleverly transformed my grimace into a yawn, covering my mouth with my hand.

"Sorry. I was up early this morning," I said.

"So was I. More's the pity."

"I was at Ingleby's farm," I volunteered.

"So I heard," she said.

Petrify the woman! Was there nothing that escaped her ears?

"Mrs. Richardson told me you was helpin' them puppet people, her with her Judas hair, like, and him with his gampy leg."

Cynthia Richardson. I should have guessed. Obviously, the presence of the puppeteers had loosened the purse-string mouth.

"Her name's Nialla," I said, "and his is Rupert. She's quite a nice person, actually. She makes scrapbooks—or she used to, at least."

"That's all very well, I'm sure, dear, but you'll have to—"

"I met Mrs. Ingleby, too," I persisted. "In fact, we had quite an interesting chat."

Mrs. Mullet's polishing of the salad plates slowed—and stopped. She had taken the bait.

"A chat? Her? Ha! That'll be the thirsty Friday!"

"Poor soul," she added, as a quick afterthought.

"She talked about Robin, her son," I said, with a crumb of truth.

"Get away with you!"

"She said that Robin's gone."

This was too much even for Mrs. Mullet.

"Gone? I should say he is. He's deader than a doorknob these five years or more. Dead and buried. I mind the day they found him, hangin' by 'is neck in Gibbet Wood. It was a washday Monday, and I'd just hung a load on the line when Tom Batts the postman come to the gate. 'Mrs. M,' he says to me, he says, 'you'd best get ready to hear some bad news.' 'It's my Alf!' I says, and he says, 'No, it's young Robin, Gordon Ingleby's boy,' and *phoosh*! The wind went out of me just like that. I thought I was going to—"

"Who found him?" I interrupted. "Young Robin, I mean."

"Why, Mad Meg it was. Her as lives up there in Gibbet Wood. She spotted a bit of bright under a tree—that's what she calls any old bit of 'mongery she comes across: 'a bit of bright'—and when she goes to pick it up, she sees it's one of them toy shovels, them as you'd take to the beach, like, and the tin sand pail, too, lyin' right there in the woods."

"Robin's mother took him to the seaside," I was about

to say, but I stopped myself just in time. I remembered that gossip withheld draws more gossip: "like flies to a magnet," as Mrs. Mullet herself had once remarked about another matter entirely.

"And then she saw 'im, swingin' by the neck from that there old scaffold," she went on. "'Is face was awful, she said—like a blackened melon."

I was beginning to regret that I hadn't brought my notebook.

"Who killed him?" I asked bluntly.

"Ah," she said, "that's the thing. Nobody knows."

"Was he murdered?"

"Might have been, for all that. But like I said, nobody knows for sure. They had what they call an ink-quest at the library—it's the same thing as a poet's mortem, Alf says. Dr. Darby got up and told them the little lad was hanged, and that's all he could rightly say. Mad Meg claimed the Devil took 'im, but you know what she's like. They called up the Inglebys, and that German what drives their tractor—Dieter, 'is name is—as well as Sally Straw. Dumb as Dorothy's donkey, the lot of 'em. Including the police."

The police? Of course!

The police would certainly have investigated Robin Ingleby's death, and if my guess was right, my old friend Inspector Hewitt would have had a hand in it.

Well, the Inspector wasn't *exactly* an old friend, but I had recently assisted him with an investigation in which he and his colleagues were completely baffled.

Rather than rely on Mrs. Mullet's village hearsay, I'd get the facts straight from the horse's mouth, so to speak.

All I needed was an opportunity to bicycle over to the police station in Hinley. I would drop in casually, just in time for tea.

As I cycled past St. Tancred's, I couldn't help wondering how Rupert and Nialla were getting on. Well, I thought, as I braked and circled back, it wouldn't take long to find out.

But the door to the parish hall was locked. I gave it a good old shaking and more than a few hard knocks, but no one came to let me in. Could they still be at Culverhouse Farm?

I pushed Gladys through the churchyard to the riverbank, and lifted her across the stepping-stones. Although it was overgrown in places with weeds, and deeply rutted, the towpath brought me quickly back to Jubilee Field.

Nialla was sitting under a tree, smoking, with Dieter at her side. He scrambled to his feet as soon as he saw me.

"Well, well," she said. "Look what the cat dragged in."

"I thought you'd be at the church."

Nialla twisted the butt of her cigarette fiercely against a tree trunk. "I suppose we should be," she said, "but Rupert hasn't found his way back yet."

This struck me as rather odd, since Rupert presumably didn't know anyone in the neighborhood of Bishop's Lacey. What—or who—could have kept him away so long?

"Perhaps he's gone off to see about the van," I said, noticing that the Austin's hood was now closed and latched.

"More likely he's just gone off to have a good sulk," Nialla said. "He does that, now and again. Sometimes he just wants to be alone for a while. But he's been gone for hours.

"Dieter thought he saw him heading off in that direction," she added, pointing a finger over her shoulder.

I turned, and found myself staring up with renewed interest at Gibbet Wood.

"Flavia," Nialla said, "leave him be."

But it wasn't Rupert I wanted to see.

By keeping to the grassy headlands at the edge of the field, I was able to stay clear of the growing flax as I trudged steadily on upwards. It wasn't much of a climb for me, but for Rupert, with his leg in an iron brace, it must have been torture.

What on earth would possess the man to climb back up to the top of Gibbet Hill? Did he have some notion of flushing Meg from the dense thickets, and demanding that she hand over Nialla's butterfly compact? Or was he in a sulk, threatened by Dieter's blond good looks?

I could think of a dozen more reasons, yet not one of them made perfect sense.

Above me, Gibbet Wood clung to the top of Gibbet Hill like a green skullcap. As I approached, and then entered beneath the branches of this ancient forest, it was like stepping into a painting by Arthur Rackham. Here, in the dim green gloom, the air was sharp with the smell of decay: of funguses and leaf mold, of black humus, of slithering muck, and of bark gnawed away to dust by beetles.

Bright cobwebs hung suspended like little portcullises of light between the rotted tree stumps. Beneath the ancient oaks and lichen-coated hornbeams, bluebells peeped out from the deep shadows among the ferns, and there on the far side of the glade I spotted the serrated leaves of the poisonous dog's mercury that, when steeped in water, produced a gorgeous indigo poison that I had once transformed into the bright red color of arterial blood simply by adding a two-percent solution of hydrochloric acid.

I thought with pleasure of how the ammonia and amides given off by the deep compost on the forest floor provided a perfect feast for omnivorous molds that converted it to nitrogen, which they then stored in their protoplasm, where it would be fed upon by bacteria. It seemed to me a perfect world: a world in which cooperation was a fact of life.

I drew in a deep breath, sucking the sour tang into my lungs and savoring the chemical smell of decay.

But this was no time for pleasant reflections. The day was hurrying on, and I had still to find my way to the heart of Gibbet Wood.

The farther I went in among the trees, the more silent it became. Now, even the birds had become eerily still. This wood, Daffy had told me, was once a royal forest in which, many centuries ago, kings of England had hunted the wild boar. Later, the Black Death had taken most of the inhabitants of the little village that had grown up beneath its skirts.

I shivered a bit as, high in the branches above me, the leaves stirred fitfully, though whether it was from the swift passage of the ghostly royal hunters or the restless spirits of the plague victims—surely they were buried somewhere nearby?—I could not tell.

I tripped on a hummock and threw out my arms to save myself. A rotted stump of moss-covered wood was all that stood between the muck and me, and I grabbed at it instinctively.

As I regained my balance, I saw that the wood had once been square, not round. This was no branch or tree trunk, but a cut timber that had weathered and been eaten away to something that looked like gray coral. Or petrified brain matter.

My mind recognized it before I did: Only slowly did I realize that I was hanging on for dear life to the rotted remains of the old gallows.

This was the place where Robin Ingleby had died.

The backs of my upper arms bristled, as if they were being stroked with icicles.

I released my grip on the thing and took a step backwards.

Except for its frame and a shattered set of stairs, there was little left of the structure. Time and weather had crumbled all but one or two of its floorboards, reducing the platform to a few skeletal remains that stuck up out of the brambles like the bones of a dead giant's ribcage.

It was then that I heard the voices.

I have, as I have said before, an acute sense of hearing, and as I stood there under the ruined gallows, I became aware that someone was talking, although the sound was coming from some distance away.

By rotating slowly on the spot and cupping my hands behind my ears as makeshift reflectors, I quickly determined that the voices were coming from somewhere on my left, and with careful steps, I crept towards them, slipping quietly from tree to tree.

Suddenly the wood began to thin, and I had to take great care to keep out of sight. Peering round the trunk of an ash, I found myself at the edge of a large clearing that lay at the very heart of Gibbet Wood.

Here, a garden had been cultivated, and a man with a battered hat and working clothes, was hoeing away industriously among the rows of widely spaced plants.

"Well, they're all over the bloody place," he was saying to someone I could not yet see.

". . . Behind every fence post . . . hiding under every bloody hayrick."

As he removed his hat to mop his face and the top of his head with a colored handkerchief, I saw that the speaker was Gordon Ingleby.

His lips, set in a weathered face, were the startling crimson hue of what Father called "the sanguine temperament," and as I watched, he wiped away the spittle that had come with his angry words.

"Ah! 'The heavens set spies upon us,'" said the other person in a dramatic voice: a voice I recognized at once as Rupert's.

He was lounging in the shade beneath a bush, smoking a cigarette.

My heart nearly stopped in my chest! Had he spotted me?

Best to keep still, I decided. *Don't move a muscle. If I'm caught, I'll pretend I came looking for Rupert and became lost in the woods, like Goldilocks.* Because there was something in them that had the ring of truth, people always fell for fairy-tale excuses.

"Squire Morton was round again last week talking a lot of rubbish to Dieter. Prying's more like it."

"You're smarter than the lot of them, Gordon. They've all got bricks for brains."

"Maybe so," Gordon replied, "and maybe not. But like I told you, this is the end of the line. This is where Gordon gets off."

"But what about me, Gord? What about the rest of us? Are we just to be left hanging?"

"You *bastard!*" Gordon shouted, raising his hoe in the air like a battle-ax, and taking a couple of threatening steps. He was instantly livid.

Rupert scrambled awkwardly to his feet, holding out one hand defensively in front of him. "I'm sorry, Gord. I didn't mean it. It's just an expression. I didn't think."

"No, you didn't think, did you? You never do. You don't know what it's like living in my skin day and night—living with a dead woman, and the ghost of a dangling kid."

A dead woman? Could he be talking about Mrs. Ingleby?

Well, whatever the case, one thing seemed perfectly clear: This was not a conversation between two men who had met for the first time this morning. By the sound of it, Gordon and Rupert had known one another for a very long time indeed.

They stood there for a few moments, staring at one another, not knowing what to say.

"Best be getting back," Rupert said at last. "Nialla

frets." He turned and walked to the far side of the clearing, then vanished into the wood.

When he had gone, Gordon wiped his face again, and I saw that his hands were shaking as he pulled a sack of tobacco and a packet of cigarette papers from his shirt pocket. He rolled a clumsy cigarette, spilling shreds of tobacco in his haste, then dug into his trouser pocket for a brass lighter, and lit up, inhaling the smoke with a deep sucking and exhaling so slowly I was sure he must be suffocating.

In a surprisingly short time he had finished. Grinding the butt into the soil with the heel of his boot, he shouldered his hoe and was gone.

I waited for about ten minutes to be sure that he wasn't coming back, then went quickly to the spot where he had been standing. From the earth beneath his heel print, I had no difficulty in retrieving the soggy remains of his cigarette. I broke a couple of leaves from one of the plants and, using them as a makeshift pot holder, picked up the butt, double-rolled it in a fresh leaf, and shoved the thing into the bottom of my pocket. Rupert, too, had left several fag ends beneath the bush where he had been sitting. These I retrieved also, and added to the others. Only then did I retrace my steps through the wood and back across the shoulder of Gibbet Hill.

Nialla and Rupert were perched on a couple of rotted pilings, letting the flowing water cool their bare feet. Dieter was nowhere in sight.

"Oh, there you are!" I said brightly. "I was looking for you everywhere."

I undid my shoes, peeled off my socks, and joined them. The sun was well down in the afternoon sky. It was probably now too late to bicycle to Hinley. By the time I got there, it would be past five o'clock, and Inspector Hewitt would be gone for the day.

My curiosity would have to wait.

For a man who had recently been threatened with the blade of a sharp hoe, Rupert was in remarkably good spirits. I could see his shriveled foot, swimming round like a pale little fish, just below the water's surface.

He reached down, dipped two fingers in the river, and flicked a couple of drops of water playfully in my direction.

"You'd better beetle off home for a decent meal and a good night's sleep. Tomorrow's the big day."

"Righty-ho," I said, scrambling to my feet. "I wouldn't miss it for the world. I'm frightfully keen on puppet shows."

· N I N E ·

SUPPER HAD SOMEHOW BEEN survived, and the table cleared. We were sitting round it just waiting for someone to think of an excuse for us to go our separate ways: Father to his stamps, Daffy to the library, Feely to her mirror, Aunt Felicity to one of the far-flung guest bedrooms, and I to my laboratory.

"And how's London these days, Lissy?" Father asked.

Since there was hardly a fortnight that passed without his traveling up there for one stamp show or another, he knew perfectly well how London was. These journeys, though, he always treated as top secret military operations. Father would rather be roasted than let Aunt Felicity know he was in the City.

"She still has all her own teeth," he used to tell us, "—and she knows how to use 'em."

Which meant, Feely said, that she wanted things her

own way. Daffy said it meant she was a blood-soaked tyrant.

"London?" Aunt Felicity said. "London is always the same: all soot and pigeons and Clement Attlee. Just one damnable deprivation after another. They ought to have men with nets to capture those children one sees in Kensington and train them to run the power plants at Battersea and Bankside. With a better class of people at the switches, the current mightn't go off so frequently."

Daffy, who because of company was not allowed to read at supper, was sitting directly across the table from me, letting her eyeballs slowly and agonizingly drift towards one another, as if her brain had just died and the optic nerves and muscles were in their last throes. I would not allow her the satisfaction of a smile.

"I don't know what the world is coming to," Aunt Felicity went on. "I shudder to think of the people one meets nowadays—that man on the train, for instance. Did you see him on the platform, Flavia?"

I shook my head.

"Neither did I," she went on, "but I believe he kept back because he thought I'd whistle for the guard. Kept sticking his head into the compartment all the way down from London—asking if we were at Doddingsley yet. A rum-looking individual he was, too. Leather patches on his elbows and a bandanna round his neck like some brute of an apache dancer from Paris. It oughtn't to be allowed. I had, at last, to put him in his place.

" 'When the train comes to a full stop and the signboard outside the window says "Doddingsley," ' I told him, 'we shall be at Doddingsley—and not a moment sooner.' "

Now it seemed that Daffy's brain had not only died, but that it had begun to curdle. Her right eye rolled off into one corner, while the other looked as if it were about to explode clean out of her head.

This was an effect she had been working on for years: the ability to bulge her eyes out in two different directions at the same time.

"A touch of the old exophthalmia," she had called it once, and I had begged her to teach me the trick. I had practiced in front of a looking glass until my head was splitting, but I could never manage more than a slight lateral googly.

"God moves in mysterious ways, His wonders to perform," she had said, when I reported my failure.

He did indeed. The very thought of Daffy's words had given me an idea.

"May I be excused?" I asked, already pushing back my chair. "I forgot to say my prayers this morning. I'd better see to them now."

Daffy's eyes uncrossed and her jaw dropped—I should like to think in admiration.

As I unlocked the door and walked into my laboratory, the Leitz microscope that had once belonged to Great-Uncle Tar shot me a welcoming gleam of brass. Here, close to the window, I would be able to adjust its reflecting mirror to focus a late beam of sunlight up through the specimen stage to the eyepiece.

I snipped a lozenge-shaped sample from one of the leaves I had brought from what I now thought of as the

Secret Garden in Gibbet Wood, and placed it on a glass slide beneath the lens.

As I twiddled the focus, with the instrument set at one hundred times magnification, I found almost instantly what I was looking for: the barbed cystoliths that projected like thorns from the leaf's surface. I flipped the leaf over with a pair of tweezers I had pinched from Feely's mother-of-pearl vanity set. If I was correct, there would be an even greater number of these clawlike hairs on the underside—and there they were!—shifting in and out of focus beneath the snout of the lens. I sat for a few moments, staring at those stony hairs of calcium carbonate which, I remembered, had first been described by Hugh Algernon Weddell, the great botanist and globe-trotter.

More for my own amusement than anything, I placed the leaf in a test tube, into which I decanted a few ounces of dilute hydrochloric acid, then corked it and gave it a vigorous shaking. Holding it up to the light, I could see the tiny bubbles of carbon dioxide form and rise to the surface as the acid reacted with the calcium carbonate of the tiny spurs.

This test was not conclusive, though, since cystoliths were sometimes present in certain nettles, for instance. In order to confirm my findings, I would need to go a little further.

I was eternally grateful to Uncle Tar who, before his death in 1928, had bought a lifetime subscription to *Chemical Abstracts & Transactions*, which, perhaps because the editors had never been informed of his death, still arrived faithfully each month on the hall table at Buckshaw.

Piles of these enticing journals, each issue with a cover the exact blue of a mid-March sky, were now stacked in every corner of my laboratory, and it was among these—in one of the issues from 1941, in fact—that I had found a description of the then newly discovered Duquenois-Levine test. It was my own variation of this procedure that I was about to perform.

First I would need a small quantity of chloroform. Since I had used the last available bottle for a failed fireworks display on Buckshaw's south lawn to celebrate Joseph Priestley's birthday in March, I would first have to manufacture a fresh supply.

A quick raid below-stairs produced (from Mrs. Mullet's cleaning cupboard) a tin of chlorine bleaching powder, and from her pantry, a bottle of pure vanilla extract.

Safely back upstairs in the laboratory, I locked the door and rolled up my sleeves.

The tin of Bleachitol was, in reality, no more than calcium hypochlorite. Would calcium hypochlorite, I wondered, by any other name smell as sweet? Heated with acetone to a temperature of somewhere between 400 and 500 degrees Fahrenheit—or until the haloform reaction occurs—a quite decent chloroform may afterwards be extracted from the resulting acetate salts by simple distillation. This part of it was, as they say, a piece of cake.

"Yarooh!" I shouted, as I poured the results into a brown bottle and shoved home the cork.

Next, I stirred a half teaspoon of vanilla extract into a few drops of acetaldehyde (which, because the stuff is volatile and boils at room temperature, Uncle Tar had thoughtfully stored beneath a layer of argon in a sealed bottle), then tipped the mixture into a clean beaker into which I had already measured six and a half tablespoons of ethanol—plain old C_2H_5OH. This I had pinched from Father's sideboard, where it had lain unopened for ages after being brought him as a gift from a fellow philatelist who had been posted to Russia by the Foreign Office.

And now the stage was set.

Placing a fresh sample of one of the leaves into a clean test tube, I added a few drops of my alcoholic vanillin preparation (which I thought of calling the Duquenois-Levine-de-Luce reagent), and after waiting for a minute, just a nibbins of concentrated hydrochloric acid.

Again, as in my previous test, small bubbles arose in the tube as the carbon dioxide was formed, but this time, the liquid in the test tube turned quickly to a shade of blueish purple.

Excitedly, I added to the mixture a couple of drops of my homemade chloroform, which, since chloroform is not miscible in water, sank promptly to the bottom.

When the stuff had stratified into two distinct layers (the clear chloroform on the bottom and the blueish purple of the Duquenois reagent floating on top of it), I gave it a jolly good mixing up with a glass stirring rod and, holding my breath, waited for it to settle one last time.

It didn't take long: Now the chloroform layer had taken on the color of its upper blanket, the mauve of a hidden bruise.

Because I had already suspected the outcome, I didn't bother to cry "Eureka."

It wasn't parsnips Gordon Ingleby was growing in his secret glade: It was Indian hemp!

I had read about the stuff in an offprint of O'Shaugh-
nessy's *On the Preparations of the Indian Hemp, or Gunjah;
Their Effects on the Animal System in Health, and Their
Utility in the Treatment of Tetanus and Other Convulsive
Diseases,* a copy of which I had found tucked away in one
of Uncle Tar's desk drawers.

Had Uncle Tar been using Indian hemp? Would that
further explain his sudden and spectacular departure from
Oxford as a young man?

Gunjah, or bhang, had long been known as an opium
substitute, and Dr. O'Shaughnessy himself had reported
great success in using it to treat a case of infantile convulsions.

And what more was Rupert's infantile paralysis, I
thought, than muscular convulsions that would drag on
cruelly, all day every day, until the last day of his life?

Testing the ends of the cigarettes that Gordon and Rupert had smoked was almost an anticlimax. The results
were as I knew they would be. When I had washed up and
put away the glassware (ughh!—how I loathe washing
up!), I wrote in my notebook:

Friday, 21st of July 1950, 9:50 P.M.
*Duquenois-Levine test of leaves and cigarette remnants
from Gibbet Wood indicates presence of Indian hemp
(Cannabis sativa). Gordon Ingleby growing—and
smoking—the stuff. Overheard his remark that it was
"the end of the line" for him. What did he mean? Who
are the "rest of us" Rupert spoke of? Who is "the dead
woman"? Could it be Mrs. Ingleby? Whatever is going
on at Culverhouse Farm, Rupert Porson is part of it.*

"And so . . ." as that man Pepys would have written: "to bed."

But I could not sleep. For a long while I lay staring at the ceiling, listening to the curtains as they whispered quietly to one another in the night breeze.

At Buckshaw, time does not pass as it does in other places. At Buckshaw, time seems to be controlled not by those frantic, scurrying little cogs in the hall clock that spin like hamsters in their shuttered cages, but rather by the solemn great gears that manage to creep through just one complete turn each year.

How could I be so contented, I suddenly wondered, when someone I knew personally was hiding out in the dark tower of a dovecote?

Which made me think at once, of course, of *King Lear*. Father had taken us to see John Gielgud in the title role at Stratford-upon-Avon, and although Gielgud was marvelous, it was the words of Poor Tom, the Bedlam beggar on the stormy heath (actually Edgar, in disguise), that still rang in my ears:

Child Rowland to the dark tower came;
His word was still, Fie, foh, and fum,
I smell the blood of a British man.

"Did Shakespeare steal that from *Jack and the Bean-stalk?*" I had whispered in Daffy's ear. Or had the fairy tale borrowed the words from Shakespeare? "Neither," she whispered back: Both had cribbed from Thomas Nashe's

Have With You to Saffron-Walden, which, having been staged in 1596, predated them.

Good old Daffy. There were times when I could almost forgive her for hating me.

Well, Rupert would be presenting his own version of *Jack and the Beanstalk* in just a few hours' time. I might even learn something from it.

After a while I got up, dressed, and crept outside.

I found Dogger sitting on a bench that overlooked the ornamental lake and the folly.

He was dressed as he had been the previous evening: dark suit, polished shoes, and a tie that probably spoke volumes to those in the know.

The full moon was rolling up the sky like a great silver cheese, and Dogger sat bolt upright, his face upturned, as if he were basking in its rays, holding a black umbrella open above his head.

I slid quietly onto the bench beside him. He did not look at me, nor I at him, and we sat, for a time, like a couple of grave ancient astronomers studying the moon.

After a while, I said, "It's not raining, Dogger."

Somewhere, during the war, Dogger had been exposed to torrential rains: rains without mercy; rains from which there could be no shelter and no escape. Or so Mrs. Mullet had told me.

"'E takes great comfort in 'is brolly, dear," she had said. "Even when the dogs is pantin' in the dust."

Slowly, like a clockwork figure, Dogger reached up and released the lock on the umbrella's handle, allowing the ribs and the waterproof cloth to fold down like bats' wings, until his upper hand was enveloped in black.

"Do you know anything about polio?" I asked at last.

Without removing his eyes from the moon, Dogger said: "Infantile paralysis. Heine-Medin disease. Morning paralysis. Complete bed rest.

"Or so I've been told," he added, looking at me for the first time.

"Anything else?"

"Agony," he said. "Absolute agony."

"Thank you, Dogger," I said. "The roses are beautiful this year. You've put a great deal of work into them."

"Thank you for saying so, miss," he said. "The roses are beautiful every year, Dogger or no Dogger."

"Good night," I said, as I got up from the bench.

"Good night, Miss Flavia."

Halfway across the lawn, I stopped and looked back. Dogger had raised the umbrella again, and was sitting beneath it, straight-backed as Mary Poppins, smiling at the summer moon.

· T E N ·

"PLEASE DON'T GO WANDERING off today, Flavia," Father said after breakfast. I had encountered him rather unexpectedly on the stairs.

"Your aunt Felicity wants to go through some family papers, and she's particularly asked that you be with her to help lift down the boxes."

"Why can't Daffy do it?" I asked. "She's the expert on libraries and so forth."

This was not entirely true, since I had charge of a magnificent Victorian chemistry library, to say nothing of Uncle Tar's papers by the ton.

I was simply hoping I wouldn't have to mention the puppet show, which was now just hours away. But Duty trumped Entertainment.

"Daphne and Ophelia have gone to the village to post

some letters. They're lunching there, and going on to Foster's to look at Sheila's pony."

The dogs! Those scheming wretches!

"But I've promised the vicar," I said. "He's counting on me. They're trying to raise money for something or other—oh, I don't know. If I'm not at the church by nine, Cynthia—Mrs. Richardson, I mean—will have to come for me in her Oxford."

As I expected it would, this rather low blow gave Father real pause.

I could see his eyebrows pucker as he weighed his options, which were few: Either concede gracefully or risk coming face-to-face with the Wreck of the Hesperus.

"You are unreliable, Flavia," he said. "Utterly unreliable."

Of course I was! It was one of the things I loved most about myself.

Eleven-year-olds are supposed to be unreliable. We're past the age of being poppets: the age where people bend over and poke us in the tum with their fingers and make idiotic noises that sound like "boof-boof"—just the thought of which is enough to make me bring up my Bovril. And yet we're still not at the age where anyone ever mistakes us for a grown-up. The fact is, we're invisible—except when we choose not to be.

At the moment, I was not. I was fixed in the beam of Father's fierce-eyed tiger stare. I batted my eyelids twice: just enough not to be disrespectful.

I knew the instant he relented. I could see it in his eyes.

"Oh, very well," he said, gracious even in his defeat. "Run along. And give my compliments to the vicar."

Paint me with polka dots! I was free! Just like that!

Gladys's tires hummed their loud song of contentment as we sped along the tarmac.

"*Summer is icumen in,*" I warbled to the world. "*Lhude sing cuccu!*"

A Jersey cow looked up from her grazing, and I stood on the pedals and gave her a shaky curtsy in passing.

I pulled up outside the parish hall just as Nialla and Rupert were coming through the long grass at the back of the churchyard.

"Did you sleep well?" I called out to them, waving.

"Like the dead," Rupert replied.

Which described perfectly what Nialla looked like. Her hair hung in long, unwashed strings, and the black circles under her red eyes reminded me of something I'd rather not think about. Either she'd ridden with witches all night from steeple to steeple, or she and Rupert had had a filthy great row.

Her silence told me it was Rupert.

"Fresh bacon . . . fresh eggs," Rupert went on, giving his chest a hearty pounding, like Tarzan, with his fists. "Sets a man up for the day."

Without so much as a glance at me, Nialla darted past and ducked into the parish hall—to the ladies' W.C., I expected.

Naturally, I followed.

Nialla was on her knees, shouting "Rope!" into the porcelain, crying and vomiting at the same time. I bolted the door.

"You're having a baby, aren't you?" I asked.

She looked up at me, her mouth gaping open, her face white. "How did you know?" she gasped.

I wanted to say "Elementary," but I knew this was no time for cheek.

"I did a lysozome test on the handkerchief you used."

Nialla scrambled to her feet and seized me by the shoulders. "Flavia, you mustn't breathe a word of this! Not a word! Nobody knows but you."

"Not even Rupert?" I asked. I could hardly believe it.

"*Especially* Rupert," she said. "He'd kill me if he knew. Promise me. Please, Flavia . . . promise me!"

"On my honor," I said, holding up three fingers in the Girl Guide salute. Although I had been chucked from that organization for insubordination (among other things), I felt it was hardly necessary to share the gruesome details with Nialla.

"Bloody good job we're camped in the country. They must have heard us for miles around, the way the two of us went at one another's throats. It was about a woman, of course. It's always about a woman, isn't it?"

This was beyond my field of expertise, but still, I tried to look attentive.

"It never takes long for Rupert to zero in on the skirt. You saw it; we weren't in Jubilee Field for half a tick when he was off up the wood with that Land Girl, Sarah, or whatever her name is."

"Sally," I said.

Although it was an interesting idea, I knew that Rupert had, in actual fact, been smoking Indian hemp in Gibbet Wood with Gordon Ingleby. But I could hardly tell Nialla that. Sally Straw had been nowhere in sight.

"I thought you said he went to see about the van."

"Oh, Flavia, you're such a—" She bit off the word in the nick of time. "Of course I said that. I didn't want to air our dirty laundry in front of a stranger."

Did she mean me—or was she referring to Dieter?

"Rupert always smudges himself with smoke, trying to cover up the scent of his tarts. I smell it on him.

"But I went a bit too far," she added ruefully. "I opened up the van and threw the first thing at him that came to hand. I shouldn't have. It was his new Jack puppet: He's been working on it for weeks. The old one's getting tatty, you see, and it tends to come apart at the worst possible moment.

"Like me," she wailed, and threw up again.

I wished that I could make myself useful, but this was one of those situations in which a bystander can do nothing to help.

"Up all the night he was, trying to fix the thing."

By the fresh marks on her neck, I could see that Rupert had done more in the night than patch up a puppet.

"Oh, I wish I were dead," she moaned.

There was a banging at the door: a sharp, rapid volley of *rat-a-tat-tat* knocks.

"Who's in there?" a woman's voice demanded, and my heart cringed. It was Cynthia Richardson.

"There may be others wishing to use the facilities," she called. "Please try to be more considerate of other people's needs."

"Just coming, Mrs. Richardson," I called out. "It's me, Flavia."

Damn the woman! How could I quickly feign illness?

I grabbed the cotton hand towel from the ring beside the sink, and gave my face a rough scrubbing. I could feel the blood rising even as I worked. I messed up my hair, ran a bit of water from the tap and mopped it across my reddening brow, and let loose a thread of spit to dangle horribly from the corner of my mouth.

Then I flushed the toilet and unbolted the door.

As I waited for Cynthia to open it, as I knew she would, I caught a glimpse of myself in the mirror: I was the very image of a malaria victim whose doctor had just stepped out to ring the undertaker.

As the knob turned and the door swung inwards, I took a couple of unsteady steps out into the hallway, puffing out my cheeks as if I were about to vomit. Cynthia shrank back against the wall.

"I'm sorry, Mrs. Richardson," I said shakily. "I've just sicked up. It must have been something I ate. Nialla's been very kind . . . but I think, with a bit of fresh air, I'll be all right."

And I tottered past her with Nialla in my wake; Cynthia didn't give her so much as a glance.

"You *are* terrifying," Nialla said. "You really are. Do you know that?"

We were sitting on a slab tomb in the churchyard as I waited for the sun to dry my feverish face. Nialla put away her lipstick and rummaged in her bag for a comb.

"Yes," I said, matter-of-factly. It was true—and there was no use denying it.

"Aha!" said a voice. "*Here* you are, then!"

A dapper little man in slacks and jacket with a yellow silk shirt was coming rapidly towards us. His neck was swathed in a mauve ascot, and an unlit pipe protruded from between his teeth. He stepped gingerly from side to side, trying not to tread directly on some of the more sunken graves.

"Oh, God!" Nialla groaned without moving her mouth, and then to him: "Hello, Mutt. Half-holiday at the monkey house, is it?"

"Where's Rupert?" he demanded. "Inside?"

"How lovely to see you, Nialla," Nialla said. "How perfectly lovely you're looking today, Nialla. Forgotten your manners, Mutt?"

Mutt—or whoever he was—turned on his heel in the grass and trod off towards the parish hall, still minding where he stepped.

"Mutt Wilmott," Nialla told me. "Rupert's producer at the BBC. They had a flaming row last week and Rupert walked out right in the middle of it. Left Mutt holding the bag with Auntie—the Corporation, I mean. But how on earth did he find us? Rupert thought we'd be quite safe here. 'Rusticating in the outback,' he called it."

"He got off the train at Doddingsley yesterday morning," I said, making a leap of deduction, but knowing I was right.

Nialla sighed. "I'd better go in. There's bound to be fireworks."

Even before we reached the door, I could hear Rupert's voice rising furiously inside the echoing hall.

"I don't care what Tony said. Tony can go sit on a paintbrush, and so can you, Mutt, come to think of it. You've shat on Rupert Porson for the last time—the lot of you."

As we entered, Rupert was halfway up the little staircase that led to the stage. Mutt stood in the middle of the hall with his hands on his hips. Neither seemed to notice we were there.

"Oh, come off it, Rupert. Tony has every right to tell you when you've overstepped the mark. And hearken unto me, Rupert, this time you *have* overstepped the mark, and by quite a long chalk at that. It's all very well for you to stir up a hornet's nest and then dodge the flak by taking your little show on the road. That's what you always do, don't you? But this time you at least owe him the courtesy of a hearing."

"I don't owe Tony a parson's whistle."

"That's where you're wrong, old boy. How many binds has he extracted you from?"

Rupert said nothing as Mutt ticked them off on his fingers.

"Well, let's see: There was the little incident with Marco. Then there was the one with Sandra Paisley—a nasty business, that. Then the thing with Sparkman and Blondel—cost the BBC a bundle, that one did. To say nothing of—"

"Shut your gob, Mutt!"

Mutt went on counting. "To say nothing of that girl in Beckenham . . . what was her name . . . Lulu? *Lulu*, for God's sake!"

"Shut up! Shut up! Shut up!"

Rupert was into a full-fledged tantrum. He came storming stiff-legged down the steps, his brace clattering dreadfully. I glanced over at Nialla, who had suddenly become as pale and as still as a painted Madonna. Her hand was at her mouth.

"Go get in your bloody Jaguar, little man, and drive it straight to hell!" Rupert snarled. "Leave me alone!"

Mutt was not intimidated. Even though they were now nose to nose, he didn't give an inch. Rather, he plucked an imaginary bit of lint from the sleeve of his jacket and pretended to watch it float to the floor.

"Didn't drive down, old boy. Came by British Rail. You know as well as I that the BBC's cutting back on expenses, what with the Festival of Britain next year, and all that."

Rupert's eyes widened as he spotted Nialla.

"Who told you we were here?" he shouted, pointing. "Her?"

"Hold on, hold on," Mutt said, his voice rising for the first time. "Don't go blaming Nialla. As a matter of fact it was a Mrs. Something right here in Bishop's Lacey. Her boy saw your van by the church and scooted off home to tell Mummy he'd hold his breath and pop if he couldn't have Porson's Puppets for his birthday party, but by the time he dragged her back, you were gone. She made a long-distance call to the BBC, and the switchboard put her through to Tony's secretary. Tony told me to come and fetch you straightaway. And here I am. End of story. So don't go blaming Nialla."

"All snug with Nialla, are you?" Rupert fumed. "Sneaking round on—"

Mutt placed the palm of his hand on Rupert's chest. "And while we're at it, Rupert, I might as well tell you that if you lay so much as a fingerprint on her again, I'll—"

Rupert shoved Mutt's hand away roughly. "Don't threaten me, you vile little snail. Not if you value living!"

"Gentlemen! Gentlemen! What on earth? You must stop this at once."

It was the vicar. He stood in the open doorway, a dark figure against the daylight.

Nialla ducked past him and fled. I quickly followed.

"Dear lady," the vicar said, holding out an engraved brass collection plate. "Try a cucumber and lettuce sandwich. They're said to be remarkably soothing. I made them myself." *Made them himself?* Had domestic warfare been declared at the vicarage?

We were outside in the churchyard again, quite near the spot where I had first seen Nialla weeping facedown on the gravestone. Had it been only two days ago? It seemed an eternity.

"No, thank you, Vicar," Nialla said. "I'm quite myself again, and I have things to do."

Lunch was a trial. Because the windows of the hall had been covered with heavy blackout curtains for the performance, we sat in near darkness as the vicar fussed with sandwiches and a jug of lemonade he must have conjured from thin air. Nialla and I sat at one end of the front row of chairs, with Mutt at the other. Rupert had vanished backstage some time before.

"We shall soon have to open the doors," said the vicar, drawing back the edge of a curtain for a peek outside. "Our public has already begun to queue up, their pockets heavy with coins of the realm."

He consulted his watch. "Ninety minutes to curtain time," he called through cupped hands. "Ninety minutes."

"Flavia," Nialla said, "be a dear—run backstage and tell Rupert to fade the music down when I begin speaking. He botched it in Fringford, and I don't want it to happen again."

I looked at her questioningly.

"Please—as a favor. I've my costume to get ready, and I don't much want to see him right now."

Actually, I didn't much want to see Rupert either. As I plodded up the steps to the stage, I thought of Sydney Carton ascending the scaffold to meet Madame Guillotine. I found the opening in the black tormentor drapes that hung on either side of the puppet stage, and stepped through into another world.

Little pools of light were everywhere, illuminating rows of electrical switches and controls, their wires and cables snaking off in all directions. Behind the stage, everything fell away into darkness, and the glow of the little lamps, gentle as it was, made it impossible to see beyond the shadows.

"Come up," said a voice from the darkness above me. It was Rupert.

"There's a ladder on the other side. Watch your step."

I felt my way round the back of the stage and found the rungs with my hands. A few steps up and I found myself standing on a raised wooden platform that ran across and above the back of the puppet stage.

A sturdy rail of black metal piping provided support for Rupert's waist as he leaned forward to operate his puppets. Although they were turned away so that I could not see their faces, several of these jointed characters were hanging from a rod behind me: an old woman, a man, and a boy, judging from their peasant clothing.

To one side, and within easy reach, the magnetic tape recorder was mounted, its two spools loaded with a shiny brown ribbon which, judging by its color, I thought must be coated with an emulsion of iron oxide.

"Nialla said to remember to lower the music volume when she starts speaking," I whispered, as if telling him a secret.

"All right," he said. "No need to whisper. The curtains absorb the sound. No one can hear us up here."

This was not a particularly comforting thought. If he were so inclined, Rupert could put his powerful hands around my neck and strangle me in luxurious silence. No one out front would be any the wiser until there was nothing left of me but a limp corpse.

"Well, I'd better be getting back," I said. "I'm helping with the tickets."

"Right," Rupert said, "but have a look at this before you go. Not many kids get a chance to come backstage."

As he spoke, he reached out and rotated a large knob, and the lights faded up on the stage below us. I nearly lost my balance as the little world seemed to materialize from nothingness beneath my feet. I found myself suddenly gazing down, like God, into a dreamy countryside of blue sky and green painted hills. Nestled in a valley was a thatched cottage with a bench in the yard, and a ramshackle cowshed.

It took my breath away.

"You made all this?"

Rupert smiled and reached for another control. As he moved it, the daylight faded away to darkness and the lights came on in the windows of the cottage.

Even though I was looking at it upside down, as it were, from above, I felt a pang—a strange and inexplicable pang that I had never felt before.

It was homesickness.

Now, even more than I had earlier when I'd first glimpsed it, I longed to be transported into that quiet little landscape, to walk up the path, to take a key from my pocket and open the cottage door, to sit down by the fireplace, to wrap my arms around myself, and to stay there forever and ever.

Rupert had been transformed, too. I could see it in his face. Lit from below, his features completely at peace, his broad features relaxed in a gentle and benevolent smile.

Leaning against the piping of the rail, he reached forward and pulled a black cotton hood from a bulky object at the side of the stage.

"Meet Galligantus the giant," he said. "Last chance before he gets his comeuppance."

It was the face of a monster, its features twisted into a look of perpetual anger and spotted with boils, its chin covered with grizzled black whiskers like carpet tacks.

I let out a squeak and took a step backwards.

"He's only papier-mâché," Rupert said. "Don't be alarmed—he's not as horrid as he looks. Poor old Galligantus—I'm quite fond of him, actually. We spend a lot of time together up here, waiting for the end of the show."

"He's . . . marvelous," I said, swallowing. "But he has no strings."

"No, he's not actually a marionette—no more than a head and shoulders, really. He has no legs. He's hinged where his waist should be, held upright out of sight just offstage, and—promise you won't repeat this: It's a trade secret."

"I promise," I said.

"At the end of the play, as Jack is chopping down the beanstalk, I only have to lift this bar—he's spring-loaded, you see, and—"

As he touched one end of it, a little metal bar flew up like a railway signal, and Galligantus tumbled forward, crashing down in front of the cottage, nearly filling the opening of the stage.

"Never fails to get a gasp from out front," Rupert said. "Always makes me laugh to hear it. I have to take care, though, that Jack and his poor old mother don't get in his way. Can't have them being smashed by a falling giant."

Reaching down and seizing Galligantus by the hair, Rupert pulled him upright and locked him back into position.

What bubbled up inexplicably from the bottom of my memory at that moment was a sermon the vicar had preached at the beginning of the year. Part of his text, taken from Genesis, was the phrase *"There were giants in the earth in those days."* In the original Hebrew, the vicar told us, the word for giants was *nephilim,* which, he said, meant cruel bullies or fierce tyrants: not physically large, but sinister. Not monsters, but human beings filled with malevolence.

"I'd better be getting back," I said. "Thank you for showing me Galligantus."

Nialla was nowhere in sight, and I had no time to look for her.

"Dear, dear," the vicar had said. "I don't know what to tell you to do. Just make yourself generally useful, I expect."

And so I did. For the next hour, I looked at tickets and ushered people (mostly children) to their seats. I glared at Bobby Broxton and motioned for him to take his feet off the rungs of the chair in front of him.

"It's reserved for me," I hissed menacingly.

I clambered up onto the kitchen counter and found the second teapot, which had somehow been shoved to the very back of the top shelf, and helped Mrs. Delaney place empty cups and saucers on a tea tray. I even ran up the high street to the post office to swap a ten-pound note for loose change.

"If the vicar needs coins," said Miss Cool, the postmistress, "why doesn't he break into those paper collection boxes from the Sunday school? I know the money's for missions, but he could always stuff in banknotes to replace what he's taken. Save him from imposing on His Majesty for pennies, wouldn't it? But then, vicars are not always as practical as you might think, are they, dear?"

By two o'clock, I was completely fagged out.

As I took my seat at last—front row, center—the eager buzz of the audience rose to a climax. We had a full house.

Somewhere backstage, the vicar switched off the house lights, and for a few moments we were left sitting in utter darkness.

I settled back in my chair—and the music began.

· E L E V E N ·

IT WAS A LITTLE thing by Mozart: one of those melodies that make you think you've heard it before, even if you haven't.

I could imagine the reels of Rupert's tape machine winding away backstage, the strains of music being summoned up, by magnetism, from the subatomic world of iron oxide. As it had likely been nearly two hundred years since Mozart first heard them in his head, it seemed somehow appropriate that the sounds of the symphony orchestra should be stored in nothing more than particles of rust.

As the curtains opened, I was taken by surprise: Rather than the cottage and the idyllic hills I had been expecting, the stage was now totally black. Rupert had obviously masked the country setting with a dark throw-cloth.

A spotlight faded up, and in the very center of the

stage there stood a miniature harpsichord, the ivories of its two keyboards starkly white against the surrounding blackness.

The music faded down, and an expectant hush fell upon the audience. We were all of us leaning forward, anticipating. . . .

A stir at one side of the stage caught our attention, and then a figure strode confidently out towards the harpsichord—it was Mozart!

Dressed in a suit of green silk, with lace at his throat, white knee-stockings, and buckled shoes, he looked as if he had stepped straight through a window from the eighteenth century and into our own. His perfectly powdered white wig framed a pink and insolent face, and he put a hand up to shade his eyes, peering out into the darkness to see who it was that had the audacity to be giggling.

Shaking his head, he went to his instrument, pulled a match from his pocket, and lit the candles: one at each end of the harpsichord's keyboards.

It was an astonishing performance! The audience erupted in applause. Every one of us knew, I think, that we were witnessing the work of a master showman.

The little Mozart seated himself on the spindled chair that stood before the keyboard, raised his hands, as if to begin—then loudly cracked his knuckles.

A great gust of laughter went up from the audience. Rupert must have recorded the close-up sound of a wooden nutcracker cracking walnuts, I thought: It sounded as if the little puppet had crushed every bone in his hands.

And then he began to play, his hands flitting easily

over the keys like the shuttles in a loom. The music was the Turkish March: a lilting, driving, lively tune that made me grin.

There's no need to describe it all: From the collapsing chair to the twin keyboards that snapped at the puppet's fingers like shark's teeth, the whole thing, from beginning to end, had all of us rocking with laughter.

When at last the little figure had managed, in spite of it all, to fight his way to the final, triumphant chord, the harpsichord reared up, took a bow, and folded itself neatly up into a suitcase, which the puppet picked up. Then he strode off the stage to a storm of applause. A few of us even leapt to our feet.

The lights went down again.

There was a pause—a silence.

When the audience had settled, a strain of music—different music—came floating to our ears.

I recognized the melody at once. It was "Morning," from Edvard Grieg's *Peer Gynt* suite, and it seemed to me the perfect choice.

"Welcome to the Land of Fairy Tales," said a woman's voice as the music faded down, and a spotlight came up to reveal the most strange and remarkable character!

Seated to the right of the stage—she must have taken her place during the moments of darkness, I thought—she wore a ruff of Elizabethan lace, a black Pilgrim dress with a laced bodice, black shoes with square silver buckles, and a tiny pair of spectacles that perched precariously on the end of her nose. Her hair was a mass of gray curls, spilling out from under a tall pointed hat.

"My name is Mother Goose."

It was Nialla!

There were *oohs* and *aahs* from the audience, and she sat, smiling patiently, until the excitement died down.

"Would you like me to tell you a story?" she asked, in a voice that was not Nialla's, yet at the same time, not anyone else's.

"Yes!" everyone shouted, including the vicar.

"Very well, then," said Mother Goose. "I shall begin at the beginning, and go on till I come to the end. And then I shall stop."

You could have heard a pin drop.

"Once upon a time," she said, "in a village not far away . . ."

And as she spoke those words, the red velvet curtains with their gold tassels opened slowly to reveal the cozy cottage I had glimpsed from behind the scenes, but now I could see it in far greater detail: the diamond-paned windows, the painted hollyhocks, the three-legged milking stool . . .

". . . there lived a poor widow with a son whose name was Jack."

At that, a boy in short leather pants and an embroidered jacket and jerkin came strolling into the scene, whistling off-key to the music.

"Mother," he shouted, "are you at home? I want my supper."

As he turned to look around, his hand shielding his eyes from the light of the painted sun, the audience let out a collective gasp.

Jack's carved wooden face was a face we all recognized: It was as if Rupert had deliberately modeled the puppet's head from a photograph of Robin, the Inglebys' dead son. The likeness was uncanny.

Like a wind in the cold November woods, a wave of uneasy whispers swept through the hall.

"Shhh!" someone said at last. I think it was the vicar.

I wondered how *he* must feel at being confronted with the face of a child he had buried in the churchyard.

"Jack was a very lazy boy," Mother Goose went on. "And because he refused to work, it was not long before his mother's small savings were completely gone. There was nothing to eat in the house, and not so much as a farthing left for food."

Now the poor widow appeared, coming round the side of the cottage with a rope in her hand, and at the other end of the rope, a cow. Both of them were little more than skin and bones, but the cow had the advantage of a gorgeous pair of huge brown eyes.

"We shall have to sell the cow to the butcher," the widow said.

At this, the cow's enormous eyes turned sadly towards the widow, then towards Jack, and finally towards the audience. "*Help me!*" they seemed to say.

"Ahhhh," everyone said at once, on a rising note of sympathy.

The widow turned her back on the poor creature and walked away, leaving Jack to do the dirty work. No sooner was she gone than a peddler appeared at the gate.

"Marnin', Squire," he said to Jack. "You looks like a sharpish lad—the kind o' lad what might be needin' some beans."

"I might," said Jack.

"Jack thought of himself as a shrewd trader," Mother Goose said, "and before you could say '*Llanfairpwllgwyngyllgogerychwyrndrobwyllllantysiliogogogoch*'—which is the name of a place in Wales—he had traded the cow for a handful of beans."

The cow went all stiff-legged and dug in its heels as the peddler dragged it off, and Jack was left standing, looking at the little pile of beans in his palm.

Then suddenly his mother was back.

"Where's the cow?" she demanded. Jack pointed to the road, and held out his hand.

"You dunderhead!" the widow shrieked. "You stupid dunderhead!"

And she kicked him in the pants.

At this, a great laugh went up from the children in the audience, and I have to admit I chuckled a little myself. I'm at that age where I watch such things with two minds, one that cackles at these capers and another that never gets much beyond a rather jaded and self-conscious smile, like the Mona Lisa.

At the kick, Jack actually flew right up into the air, scattering beans everywhere.

Now, the whole audience was rocking with laughter.

"You shall sleep in the chicken coop," the widow said. "If you're hungry, you can peck for corn."

And with that, she was gone.

"Poor old I," Jack said, and stretched himself out on the bench at the cottage door.

The sunlight faded rather quickly, and suddenly it was night. A full moon shone above the folded hills. The lights in the cottage were on, their warm orange light spilling out into the yard. Jack twitched in his sleep—shifted position—and began to snore.

"But look!" said Mother Goose. "Something is stirring in the garden!"

Now the music had become mystical—the sound of a flute in an oriental bazaar.

Something was stirring in the garden! As if by magic, a thing that looked at first like a green string, and then like a green rope, began to snake up from the soil, twisting and twining like a cobra in a fakir's basket, until the top was out of sight.

As it rose into the sky, and night changed quickly to day, the stalk grew thicker and thicker, until at last it stood like a tree of emerald green, dwarfing the cottage.

Again, the music was "Morning."

Jack stretched and yawned and rolled clumsily off the bench. With hands on hips, he bent back impossibly far at the waist, trying to loosen his stiff joints. And then he spotted the beanstalk.

He reeled back as if he had been punched, fighting to keep his balance, his feet stumbling, his arms going like windmills.

"Mother!" he shouted. "Mother! Mother! Mother! Mother!"

The old lady appeared directly, broom in hand, and Jack danced crazily round her in circles, pointing.

"The beans, you see," said Mother Goose, "were magic beans, and in the night they had grown into a beanstalk that reached higher than the clouds."

Well, everyone knows the story of Jack and the Beanstalk, so there's no need for me to repeat it here. For the next hour, the tale unrolled as it has done for hundreds of years: Jack's climb, the castle in the clouds, the giant's wife and how she hid Jack in the oven, the magic harp, the bags of silver and gold—all of it was there, brought to brilliant life by Rupert's genius.

He held us captive in the palm of his hand from beginning to end, as if he were the giant, and all of us were Jack. He made us laugh and he made us cry, and sometimes both at the same time. I had never seen anything like it.

My head was buzzing with questions. How could Rupert operate lights, sound effects, music, and stage settings at the same time he was manipulating several marionettes and providing all the voices? How had he made the beanstalk grow? How could Jack and the giant run such a merry chase without their strings becoming entangled? How did the sun come up? And the moon?

Mother Goose was right: The beans *had* been magic, and they had entranced us all.

And now the end was near. Jack was scrambling down the beanstalk, bags of gold and silver at his waist. The giant wasn't far behind.

"Stop!" roared the voice of the giant. "Stop, thief, stop!"

Even before Jack reached the ground, he was calling down to his mother:

"Mother! Mother! Fetch the axe!" he cried, and taking it from her hands as he jumped to the ground, he began chopping furiously at the beanstalk, which seemed to recoil as if in pain from the sharp blade.

The music swelled to a crescendo, and there was a

strange instant during which time seemed frozen. Then the beanstalk collapsed and a moment later the giant came crashing down to earth.

He landed in the front yard of the cottage, his huge torso dwarfing the dwelling, his glassy eyes staring blankly out over our heads. The giant was stone-cold dead.

The children shrieked—even some of the parents leapt to their feet.

It was, of course, Galligantus, the hinged monster I had seen before the show. But I'd had no idea how terrifying his fall and his death would be when seen from this point of view.

My heart was pounding at my ribcage. It was glorious!

"And so died Galligantus," said Mother Goose, "the cruel giant. After a time, his wife grew lonely in the sky, and found another giant to marry. Jack and his mother, now rich beyond their wildest dreams, lived, as all good people do, happily ever after.

"And we know that all of you will, too—each and every one of you."

Jack dusted off his hands, carelessly, as if killing a giant was an everyday affair.

The red curtains swept slowly closed, and as they did, all hell broke loose in the parish hall.

"It's the Devil!" shrieked a woman's voice at the back of the hall. "The Devil's took the little boy and shrinked him up! God help us! It's the Devil!"

I turned and saw someone flapping about in the open doorway. It was Mad Meg. She was pointing, jabbing her finger at the stage, but then she threw her hands up to cover her face. At that moment, the house lights came on.

The vicar was quickly at her side.

"No! No!" she shrieked. "Don't take old Meg! Leave her be!"

He somehow managed to get an arm around her shoulder, and led her gently but firmly off into the hall's kitchen where, for a minute or so, her poor cracked voice could be heard whimpering, "The Devil! The Devil! The Devil got poor Robin!"

A hush fell on the place. Parents began shepherding their children—all of them now subdued—towards the exits.

The women from the Ladies' Auxiliary did a bit of aimless tidying, then scurried away—probably to gossip, hands over mouths, I thought.

I found myself alone.

Nialla seemed to have vanished, although I had not seen her leave. Since I could hear the soft murmur of voices backstage, Rupert was presumably still up on the bridge of his puppet stage.

It was then that I thought of putting physics to work. As I have said, the hall's Victorian designers had made a perfect sound reflector of its interior. The vast expanses of the room's dark varnished paneling picked up the slightest sounds, and focused them wonderfully. By standing at the very center of the room, I found that, with my acute hearing, I could easily make out every word. One of the voices I had heard was Rupert's.

"Bloody hell!" he was saying, in a loud whisper. "Bloody hell, Nialla!"

Nialla said nothing, although I thought I heard a sob.

"Well, we shall have to put a stop to it. That's plain."

Put a stop to what? Had she told him she was pregnant? Or was he talking about his quarrel with Mutt Wilmott? Or with Gordon Ingleby?

Before I could overhear another word, the door to the kitchen opened, and the vicar came out into the hall with Mad Meg leaning on his arm, followed by Cynthia and two members of the Ladies' Auxiliary.

"It's out of the question," Cynthia was saying, "quite out of the question. The place is simply reeking with paint fumes. Furthermore, we don't have—"

"I'm afraid I must overrule you on this occasion, my dear. This poor woman needs somewhere to rest, and we can hardly send her packing back to—"

"A hovel in the woods?" Cynthia asked, a red flush rising in her cheeks.

"Flavia, dear girl," the vicar said as he spotted me. "Would you mind running ahead to the vicarage? The door is open. If you'll be kind enough to clear the books off the couch in my study . . . it doesn't much matter where you put them. We shall be along directly."

Nialla appeared suddenly from behind the curtains. "Just a moment, Vicar," she said. "I'm coming with you."

I could see that she was holding herself together, but only just.

The vicarage study looked as if Charles Kingsley had just put down his pen and stepped out of the room. The bookcases, floor to ceiling, were jammed cheek-by-jowl with volumes which, to judge by their solemn bindings, could only have been of ecclesiastical interest. A cluttered, overflowing desk covered most of the room's single window, and a black horsehair sofa—an Everest of dusty books—leaned at a crazy angle on a threadbare Turkish carpet.

No sooner had I shifted the books to the floor than Nialla and the vicar arrived, leading Meg solicitously to the sofa. She seemed dazed, managing only a few vague mutters as Nialla helped her to recline and smoothed her filthy clothing.

A moment later, Dr. Darby's portly presence filled the doorway. Someone must have run up the high street to fetch him from his surgery.

"Um," he ventured, as he put down his black medical bag, opened the clasp, and had a good dig round inside. With a noisy rustle, he brought forth a paper bag and extracted a crystal mint, which he popped into his mouth.

With that detail out of the way, he bent over Meg for a closer look.

"Um," he said again, and reached into the bag for a syringe. He filled the thing from a little bottle of clear liquid, rolled up Meg's sleeve, and slid the needle into her arm.

Meg made not a sound, but looked up at him with eyes like a sledgehammered horse.

From a tall wardrobe in the corner—as if by magic—the vicar produced a pillow and a brightly colored afghan.

"Afternoon naps." He smiled, covering her gently, and Meg was snoring even before the last one of us had stepped softly from the room.

"Vicar," Nialla said abruptly, "I know you'll think it awful of me, but I have a very great favor to ask."

"Ask away," the vicar said, with a worried glance at Cynthia, who was hovering at the far end of the hall.

"I'd be eternally grateful if you could permit me a hot bath. I haven't had one for so long, I feel like something that lives under a stone."

"Of course, my dear," the vicar said. "It's upstairs at the end of the hall. Help yourself to soap and towels.

"And don't mind the little yacht," he added with a smile. "It's mine."

As Nialla climbed the stairs, a rubber heel squeaked on waxed floorboards, and Cynthia was gone.

"Cynthia has offered to run you over to Buckshaw," the vicar said, turning to me, and I knew instantly that he was fibbing. "I expect you'll be back this evening with your family?"

"Oh, of course," I said. "They're all jolly keen on Jack and the Beanstalk."

With Gladys strapped precariously to the roof, we crept slowly along the lane in the tired, dusty Oxford. Cynthia, like vicar's wives in general, had a tendency to over-control, steering from side to side in a series of pie crust scallops between the hedges.

Sitting beside her in the front seat, I had a good opportunity to examine her overbite, close-up and in profile. Even with her mouth shut, she showed a remarkable amount of tooth, and I found myself seriously rethinking my rebellion against braces.

"There's always something, isn't there?" she said suddenly, her face still on fire from her recent humiliation.

"One is forever being rousted out of one's own house by someone more needy—not that I mind, of course. First, it was the Gypsies. Then, during the war, the evacuees. Then, last year, the Gypsies came again. Denwyn went to them in Gibbet Wood, and invited them personally, each and every one, to attend the Holy Eucharist. Not a single man jack of them ever showed up, of course. Gypsies are savages, essentially, or perhaps Roman Catholics. Not that they don't have souls—they do, naturally—but one always feels that theirs are so much shadier than one's own."

"I wonder how Nialla's getting on with her bath?" I remarked brightly, as we drove up the avenue of chestnuts to Buckshaw.

Cynthia stared straight ahead, gripping the wheel.

"Nonsense!" Aunt Felicity declared. "We shall go as a family."

We were in the drawing room, spread as widely apart as was humanly possible.

Father muttered something about stamp albums, and I could see that Daffy was already holding her breath in an attempt to feign a fever.

"You and your girls need to get out more, Haviland. You're all of you as pale as jellyfish. It will be my treat. I shall have Clarence bring round his car as soon as we've eaten."

"But—" Father managed.

"I shall brook no buts, Haviland."

Outside, Dogger was weeding at the edge of the terrace. Aunt Felicity rapped sharply on the windowpane to get his attention.

"Yes, miss?" he said, coming to the French doors, straw hat in hand.

"Ring up Clarence and tell him we shall require a taxi for seven at six-thirty."

"Six-thirty, miss?" Dogger asked, his brow furrowed.

"Of course," Aunt Felicity said. "He'll have to make two trips. I expect you and Mrs. Mullet would both have your noses out of joint if you were left behind. Puppet shows are not just for bluebloods, you know."

"Thank you, miss," Dogger said.

I tried to catch his eye, but he was gone.

· TWELVE ·

CLARENCE PULLED UP AT the lych-gate at twenty minutes to seven. He came round the taxicab to hold the door open for Aunt Felicity, who had insisted on sitting in the front seat with him in order to, as she put it, "keep a sharp eye out for road hogs."

She had dressed herself in a sort of comic-opera cape over a voluminous red silk suit that might have been pinched from a Persian harem. Her hat was a collapsed black bag with a peacock's feather billowing out behind like smoke from the *Flying Scotsman*; on her feet were a pair of medieval slippers in mustard yellow, with long upturned points like a pair of icing bags. When we arrived at the parish hall, Father and Feely got out on the far side of the taxicab.

"Now off you go to fetch the others, Clarence," Aunt Felicity commanded, "and don't dawdle."

Clarence raised a forefinger to the peak of his cap and, with an impertinent shifting of gears, was gone.

Inside the parish hall, we found that the entire front row of chairs had been reserved for us. Aunt Felicity had certainly not skimped on the cost of tickets. She and Father were to sit front and center, with Feely and Daffy on their left. I was on Father's right, with Dogger and Mrs. Mullet (when they arrived) on our flank.

All was in readiness. The house lights had already been lowered to a level of delicious expectation. Incidental music floated from backstage, and from time to time, the red velvet curtains on the puppet stage gave an enticing twitch.

The entire population of Bishop's Lacey seemed to be there. Mutt Wilmott, I saw, had taken a seat against the wall near the back. Miss Cool was in the row behind him, listening to Cynthia Richardson, who had her ear, and behind her sat Miss Mountjoy, the niece of the late Dr. Twining, Father's old schoolmaster. To Miss Mountjoy's right, from Culverhouse Farm, Dieter Schrantz and Sally Straw, the Land Girl, sat side by side. I gave them a little wave, and both of them grinned.

"*Haroo, mon vieux*—Flavia!"

It was Maximilian Wight, our diminutive neighbor who, after several triumphant world tours as a concert pianist, had settled down at last in our village to teach music. Feely had been one of his pupils, but had begged off her lessons when Max began asking too many intrusive questions about her "paramours."

Max waved a white glove, and I waved back.

As I scanned the rows of faces, my eyes skidded to a

stop on a dark-haired woman in a sage green sweater set. She was no one I had seen before, and must be, I thought, a stranger to Bishop's Lacey. Perhaps a visiting relative.

The man beside her saw me staring, and gave me a pleasant smile: Inspector Hewitt. It was not so long since I had assisted him in bringing a murderer to justice.

In a flash I was standing before them, shifting awkwardly from foot to foot as I realized I was probably intruding.

"Fancy meeting you here," the Inspector said. It was not a particularly original comment, but it neatly covered what might have been an awkward moment.

"Antigone," he told the dark-haired woman, "I'd like you to meet Flavia de Luce."

I knew for a fact that she was going to say, "Oh, yes, my husband has mentioned you," and she would say it with that little smirk that tells so much about the amused conversation that had followed.

"I'm so pleased to meet you, Flavia," she said, putting out the most beautiful hand in the world and giving me a good solid shake, "and to find that you share my love of marionettes."

If she'd told me to "fetch" I would have done it.

"I love your name," I managed.

"Do you? My father was Greek and my mother Italian. She was a ballet teacher and he was a fishmonger, so I grew up dancing in the streets of Billingsgate."

With her dark hair and sea green eyes, she was the image of Botticelli's *Flora*, whose features adorned the back of a hand mirror at Buckshaw that Father had once given to Harriet.

I wanted to ask "In what far isle is your shrine? that I might worship there," but I settled for shuffling my feet and a mumbled, "Nice to meet you, Mrs. Hewitt. I hope you and Inspector Hewitt enjoy the show."

As I slipped into my seat, the vicar strode purposefully to the front of the hall and took up a position in front of the stage. He smiled indulgently, waiting, as Daffy, Mrs. Mullet, and Dogger slid into their seats.

"Ladies and gentlemen, boys and girls, parishioners of St. Tancred's and otherwise, thank you for coming. We are honored, this evening, to welcome to our midst, the renowned puppet-showman—if he will allow me to make use of that illustrious nomenclature—Rupert Porson."

(*Applause*)

"Although Mr. Porson, or Rupert, if I may, is best known nowadays for his performances on the BBC Television of *The Magic Kingdom* which, as I'm sure all of you know, is the realm of Snoddy the Squirrel . . ."

(*Applause*)

". . . I am told on good authority that he has traveled widely, presenting his puppet artistry in all of its many forms, and has, on at least one occasion, performed before one of the crowned heads of Europe."

(*Applause*)

"But before Jack sells his mother's cow for a handful of beans—"

"Hssst! Don't give away the plot, Vicar!"

(*Tully Stoker, the proprietor and landlord of the Thirteen Drakes, greeted with hoots of laughter, including his own.*)

". . . and while the maestro prepares his enchanted

strings, the Ladies' Auxiliary of St. Tancred's is pleased to present, for your musical entertainment, the Misses Puddock, Lavinia and Aurelia."

Oh, Lord! Spare us! Please spare us!

We had been saved from having to listen to them during the matinee performance only because their St. Nicholas Tea Room kept them too busy to attend.

The Misses Puddock had a death grip on public events at St. Tancred's parish hall. No matter if it was a tea put on by the Ladies' League, a whist drive by the Altar Guild, a white elephant sale by the Ladies' Auxiliary, or a spring flower show by the Vestry Guild, the Misses Puddock would perform, winter or summer, rain or shine.

Miss Lavinia would seat herself at the upright piano, rummage in her string bag, and fish out at last a tattered piece of sheet music: "Napoleon's Last Charge."

After an interminable wait—during which she would thrust her face forward until her nose was touching the music—she would sit back, her spine stiff as a poker, raise her hands above the keyboard, drop them, take a second squint at the music, and then tear into it like a grizzly bear clawing at a salmon in the Pathé newsreels.

When she was finished, her sister, Miss Aurelia, would take up her position, her white-gloved fingertips idly brushing the dusty piano top, and warble (there's no other word for what she did) "Bendemeer's Stream."

Afterwards, the chairman would announce that the Vestry Guild had voted unanimously to present the Misses Puddock with an honorarium: "a purse of appreciation," as he always put it.

And they're off!

Miss Lavinia, her eyes riveted to the music, was into "Napoleon's Last Charge," and I noticed for the first time that, as she read the music, her lips were moving. I couldn't help wondering what she was saying. There were no lyrics to the piece—could she be naming the chords? Or praying?

Mercifully, she took it at a somewhat faster gallop than usual, and the thing was soon over—at least, relatively speaking. I noticed that Feely's jaw muscles were twitching, and that Max looked as if he were biting down on a stainless-steel humbug.

Now it was Miss Aurelia's turn. Miss Lavinia pounded out the first few bars as an introduction before her sister joined in:

> *"There's a bower of roses by Bendemeer's Stream*
> *And the nightingale sings round it all the day long.*
> *At the time of my childhood 'twas like a sweet dream."*

(Miss Aurelia's childhood, to look at her, must have been during George the Third.)

> *"To sit in the roses and hear the bird's song."*

When she finished, there was a smattering of polite applause, and Miss Aurelia stood with her head cocked for a few moments, checking the piano with her fingers for dust, waiting to be coaxed into an encore. But the audience, knowing better than to encourage her, settled quickly back into their seats, and some of us crossed our arms.

As the house lights went down, I turned round for one last look at the audience. A couple of latecomers were just taking their seats on the aisle. To my horror, I saw that they were Gordon and Grace Ingleby, she in her usual dreadful black outfit, he with a bowler hat, for God's sake! And both of them looking less than happy to be there.

At first, I felt anger rushing up and fluttering within my chest. Why had no one warned them? Why had no one cared enough to keep them away?

Why hadn't I?

Crazily, the thing that popped into my mind was something Daffy once told me: It is the duty of a constitutional monarch to warn and advise.

If His Royal Majesty, King George the Sixth, had been among us this evening, he would be bound to take them aside and say something about the puppet with their dead child's face. But he was not.

Besides, it was already too late. . . . The hall was in total darkness. No one but me seemed to have noticed the Inglebys.

And then the show began. Because of the interminable Misses Puddock, I suppose, Rupert had decided to cut out the Mozart sketch and go straight for the main feature.

The red velvet curtains opened, just as they had in the afternoon, revealing the widow's cottage. The spotlight came up to illuminate Nialla in her Mother Goose costume. Grieg's "Morning" floated in the air, painting haunting images in the mind of dark forests and icy fjords.

"Once upon a time, in a village not far away," Nialla

began, "there lived a widow with a son, whose name was Jack."

And in came Jack: the Jack with Robin Ingleby's face.

Again, the audible sucking-in of breath as some of the audience recognized the dead boy's features. I scarcely dared turn and look, but by pretending my skirt had become pinched in the folding mechanism of the chair, I was able to twist round in my seat just far enough to sneak a look at the Inglebys. Grace's eyes were wide and staring, but she did not cry out; she seemed frozen to the spot. Gordon was clutching at her hand, but she took no notice.

On the stage, the puppet Jack shouted: "Mother, are you at home? I want my supper."

"Jack was a very lazy boy," said Mother Goose. "And because he refused to work, it was not long before his mother's small savings were completely gone. There was nothing to eat in the house, and not so much as a farthing left for food."

As the gasps and the murmurs died down, the show went on. Rupert was in fine form, the puppets so convincing in their movements and so perfectly voiced that the audience soon fell under his enchantment—as the vicar had suggested they would.

Lighted by the colored lamps of the stage, the faces of the people around me were the faces in a painting by Toulouse-Lautrec, red, overheated, and fiercely intent upon the little wooden actors. As Aunt Felicity crunched excitedly on a digestive mint, I noticed that even Father had a half-amused look on his face, though whether it was caused by the puppets or his sister, I could not decide.

The business of the cow and the beans and the kick in the pants was greeted with even more raucous laughter than it had been at the afternoon performance.

Mouths (including even Daffy's) fell open as the beanstalk grew while Jack slept, and the audience began nudging one another with delight. By the time Jack climbed the beanstalk into the giant's kingdom, Rupert had all of Bishop's Lacey eating out of his hand.

How was Mutt Wilmott reacting to this success? I wondered. Here was Rupert, obviously at his best in a live (so to speak) performance, with no television apparatus— wonderful as it was—standing between him and his audience. When I turned to look, I saw that Mutt was gone, and the vicar had taken his chair.

More oddly, Gordon Ingleby, too, was no longer present. His chair stood empty, but Grace still sat motionless, her vacant eyes fixed on the stage, where the giant's wife had just hidden Jack in her great stone oven.

"Fee! Fie! Fo! Fum!" the giant roared as he came into the kitchen. "I smell the blood of an Englishman!"

"Jack leapt out of the oven . . . ," said Mother Goose.

"Master! Master!" cried the charming puppet harp, plucking at its own strings in agitation. This was the part I liked best.

". . . grabbed the golden harp, and took to his heels, with the giant close behind!"

Down the beanstalk came Jack, the green leaves billowing round him. When the vegetation thinned out at last, the scene had changed to his mother's cottage. It was a marvelous effect, and I couldn't for the life of me see how Rupert had done it. I would have to ask him.

"Mother! Mother! Fetch the axe!" Jack shrieked, and the old lady came hobbling round from the garden—oh, so slowly!—with the hatchet in her hand.

Jack threw himself at the beanstalk with all his might, the axe flying fast and furious, the beanstalk shrinking back again and again as if in agony from the wickedly glinting blade.

And then, as it had done before, the beanstalk sagged, and crumpled to the ground.

Jack seemed to be looking up as, with a sound like thunder, the giant came crashing down from the sky.

For a few moments, the monster lay twitching horribly, a trickle of ruby blood oozing from the corner of its mouth, its ghastly head and shoulders filling the stage with flying sparks, as smoke and little flames rose in acrid tendrils from its burning hair and goatee. But the blank eyes that stared out unseeing into mine were not those of the hinged giant, Galligantus—they were the glazed and dying eyes of Rupert Porson.

And then the lights went out.

·THIRTEEN·

Plunged suddenly into darkness, the audience sucked in a collective breath and released a collective gasp.

In the kitchen, someone had the presence of mind to switch on a flashlight, and after a moment brought it out, like a darting will-o'-the-wisp, into the main part of the parish hall.

How quick-witted it was of the vicar to think of closing the curtains! At least, that was what he was trying to do when he was stopped in his tracks by a loud, commanding voice: "No! No! Stand back. Don't touch anything."

It was Dogger. He had risen to his feet and was blocking the vicar's way, his arms fully extended, and seeming to be as surprised as the rest of us at his own boldness. Nialla, who had jumped up and taken a single step towards the proscenium, froze abruptly in her tracks.

All of this took place in the moving beam of the flashlight, making the scene seem like some ghastly drama played out during an air raid, illuminated by a raking searchlight.

A second voice came out of the darkness at the back of the hall: the voice of Inspector Hewitt.

"Stand still, everyone—please stay where you are. Don't move until I tell you to move."

He walked quickly to the front of the auditorium and vanished backstage as someone near the door vainly flicked a few switches, but the incandescent bulbs in their frosted glass wall sconces remained dark.

There were a few grumbles of protest until Constable Linnet—out of uniform for the evening—came to the front row of chairs, holding a hand high in the air for attention. He had brought a second flashlight, which he shone upwards upon his own face, giving him an appalling and cadaverous look.

"Please do as the Inspector says," he told the audience. "He's in charge here now."

Dr. Darby, I noticed, was already shoving his way up the crowded side aisle towards the stage.

Nialla, when I caught a glimpse of her, seemed rooted to the spot; she had not moved a muscle. Her tall Mother Goose hat was askew and, had the situation not been what it was, I might have laughed out loud at the sight of her.

My first reaction, of course, was to go to her, but I found I was being restrained by one of Father's hands, heavy on my arm.

As Rupert's body crashed to the stage, both Daffy and

Feely had leapt to their feet. Father was still motioning them to sit down, but they were too excited to pay him any attention.

The Inspector reappeared in the doorway at the left of the stage. There were two of these hallways—one on either side—each leading to an exit and a short set of steps up to the stage. It was in these pens that choirs of giggling angels were usually marshaled for St. Tancred's annual Christmas Pageant.

"Constable Linnet, may I have your flashlight, please?"

PC Linnet handed over his five-cell Ever Ready, which looked like one of the sort that you see being used to search the foggy moors in the cinema. He had probably brought it along to illuminate his way home through the lanes after the show, never thinking it would come in so handy.

"May I have your attention, please," Inspector Hewitt said. "We are making every attempt to restore the lights, but it may be some time before we're able to turn them back on permanently. It may be necessary, for safety's sake, to switch the current on and off several times. I would ask you to resume your seats, and to remain there until such time as I am able to give you further instructions. There is absolutely no cause for alarm, so please remain calm."

I heard him say quietly to Constable Linnet, "Cover the stage. That banner on the balcony will do." He pointed to a wide swath of canvas that stretched across the front of the balcony, above the main door: *St. Tancred's Women's Institute*, it said, with a red and white Cross of St. George, *One Hundred Years of Service 1850–1950*.

"And when you've done that," the Inspector added, "ring up Graves and Woolmer. Give them my compliments, and ask them to come as quickly as possible."

"It's their evening for cricket, sir," said PC Linnet.

"So it is. In that case, give them my compliments *and* my regrets. I'm sure the vicar will permit you the use of the telephone?"

"Dear me!" said the vicar, looking round the hall in puzzlement. "We do have one, of course . . . for the use of the Ladies' Auxiliary and the Women's Institute, you know . . . but I fear we've been forced to keep it in a locked cupboard in the kitchen . . . so many people making long-distance calls to their friends in Devon—or even Scotland, in one instance."

"And the key?" asked Inspector Hewitt.

"I handed it to a gentleman from London, just before the performance—from the BBC, he said he was—needed to make an urgent call . . . said he'd reimburse me from his own pocket as soon as the central operator rang back with the charges. How odd, I don't see him here now.

"Still, there's always the vicarage telephone," he added.

My first impulse was to offer to pick the lock, but before I could say a word, Inspector Hewitt shook his head.

"I'm sure we can have the hinges off with no damage."

He crooked a finger at George Carew, the village carpenter, who was out of his chair like a shot.

Aside from the occasional dull glow from the backstage flashlight, we sat in darkness for what seemed like an eternity.

And then suddenly, the lights came back on, causing

us all to blink and rub our eyes, and to look round at one another rather foolishly.

And there was Rupert, his dead face, frozen in a look of surprise, still occupying center stage. They would soon be covering his body with the banner, and I realized that if I were to remember the scene for future reference, I needed to make a series of indelible mental snapshots. I wouldn't have long to work.

Click!

The eyes: The pupils were hugely dilated, so much so that if I had been able to get a bit closer, I was quite sure I should have been able to see myself reflected in their convex surfaces as clearly as Jan van Eyck was reflected in the bedroom mirror in his painting of the Arnolfinis' wedding day.

Not for long, though: Rupert's corneas had already begun to film over and the whites to lose their luster.

Click!

The body was no longer twitching. The skin had taken on a milky bluish tinge. The corner of the mouth seemed to have stopped bleeding, and what little blood was still visible now appeared very slightly darker and thicker, although the red, green, and amber bulbs of the footlights might be influencing my color perception.

Click!

On the forehead, just below the scalp, was a dark discoloration the size and shape of a sixpence. Although the hair was still smoldering, filling the hall with the acrid odor one would expect whenever the sulfur-rich amino acid keratin is burnt, it was not enough to account for the smoke that was still gathering—still hanging heavily—

about the lights. I could see that the curtains and the scenery were quite intact, so it must be something else that was still combusting backstage. Judging by the smell of burning grass, I guessed that it was linen—probably seersucker.

Click!

When Rupert first came crashing down, Nialla had leapt to her feet and moved towards the stage, but she then had stopped, hovering in her tracks. Oddly, no one, including me, had gone to her, and now that minutes had passed, she was walking slowly towards the kitchen with both hands cupped over her face. *Was it a delayed reaction?* I wondered. *Or something more?*

PC Linnet came clomping to the front of the auditorium, the rolled-up banner under his arm and the large jackknife with which he had cut its cords still clutched in his hand. He and the vicar made quick work of draping the canvas between two coat trees, and in so doing, blocked our view of the deceased.

Well, I was *assuming* that Rupert was deceased. Although Inspector Hewitt must surely have checked for signs of life when he first went backstage, I hadn't heard him call for an ambulance. No one, as far as I knew, had yet attempted resuscitation. No one, in fact, had seemed anxious to touch the body. Even Dr. Darby had not exactly galloped to the rescue.

All of this happened, of course, in much less time than it takes to tell about it: In actual fact, it couldn't have taken more than five minutes.

Then, as the Inspector had said they might, the lights went out again.

At first there was that sense of being plunged into what Daffy describes as "Stygian blackness," and Mrs. Mullet calls "a blind man's holiday." Mrs. Mullet, by the way, was still sitting as she had been since the show began, like a waxwork figure with a half smile on her face. I could only assume that she was still smiling zanily into the darkness.

It was that kind of darkness that seems, at first, to paralyze all of the senses.

But then one realizes that things are not quite so black as they look, nor are they as silent as they seem. Pinpoints of light, for instance, penetrated the shabby blackout curtains that had been used to cover the windows since before the war, and although there was little daylight left outside, it was enough to create a faint impression of the hall's larger features.

From behind the curtains came the sound of deliberate footsteps, and the banner, which had been draped in front of the puppet stage, was suddenly illuminated from behind by a slash of yellow light from a powerful torch.

Now began the ghastly shadow show. The outline of Dr. Darby was seen to reach down and touch the body, no doubt searching for signs of life. I could have saved him the trouble.

The shadow shook its head and a great sigh went up from the audience. It seemed clear to me that, with Rupert pronounced dead, Inspector Hewitt would now want to leave things untouched until Detective Sergeant Woolmer arrived from Hinley with his plate camera.

Aunt Felicity, meanwhile, was rummaging in her purse for more mints, and I could hear her inhaling and exhaling through her nose. To my left, Daffy was whispering to

Feely, but since Father, who sat between us, was clearing his throat at regular intervals, as he does whenever he's nervous or upset, I could not quite make out her words.

After what seemed like another eternity, the lights suddenly came back on, and again, we were all left blinking.

Mrs. Mullet was dabbing at her eyes with a handkerchief, her shoulders shaking, and I realized that she was quietly crying. Dogger noticed, too. He offered her his arm, which she took without raising her eyes, and he led her off into the kitchen.

He was back in less than a minute.

"She'll be more at ease among the pots and pans," he whispered to me as he resumed his seat.

A great flash of light bleached the hall of all color for an instant, and I, along with everyone else, turned round to see that Detective Sergeant Woolmer had arrived. He had set up his bulky camera and tripod on the balcony, and had just captured all of us on film. As the flash fired a second time, it occurred to me that this second exposure would show no more than a sea of upturned white faces. Which, perhaps, was precisely what he wanted.

"Please—may I have your attention?" Inspector Hewitt had stepped out from behind the black curtains and was now standing center stage. "I'm sorry to have to tell you that there has been an unfortunate accident, and that Mr. Porson is dead."

Even though the fact should have been evident, its confirmation caused a wave of sound to break from the audience: a mixture of gasps, cries, and excited whispers. The Inspector waited patiently for it to die down.

"I'm afraid I'm going to have to ask you to remain in your seats a little longer, until we are able to take names and addresses as well as a brief statement from each one of you. This process will take some time, and for that I must apologize. When you have been interviewed, you will be free to go, although we may wish to speak with you again at some later time. Thank you for your attention."

He beckoned to someone behind me, and I saw that it was Detective Sergeant Graves. I wondered if the sergeant would remember me. I had first met him at Buckshaw during the police investigation into the death of Father's old school chum Horace Bonepenny. I kept my eyes fixed on his face as he came to the front of the hall, and at last I was rewarded with an ever-so-slight but distinct grin.

"Schoolboys!" Aunt Felicity huffed. "The police recruiters are ransacking the cradles of England."

"He's extremely experienced," I whispered. "He's already a detective sergeant."

"Poppycock!" she said, and dug for another mint.

Since the corpse had been hidden from view, there was nothing left for me to do but study the people around me.

Dieter, I noticed, was staring fixedly at Feely. Although he was sitting with Sally Straw—whose face was a petulant thundercloud—he was gazing at my sister's profile as if her hair were an altar of beaten gold.

Daffy had noticed it, too. When she saw the look of puzzlement on my face, she leaned over in front of Father and whispered, "The phrase you're fishing for is 'reverent infatuation.'" Then she leaned back and resumed not speaking to me.

Father paid us no attention. He had already retreated into his own world: a world of colored inks and perforations-per-inch; a world of albums and gum arabic; a world where our Gracious Majesty, King George the Sixth, was firmly ensconced on both the throne and the postage stamps of Great Britain; a world in which sadness—and reality—had no place.

At last the interviews began. As Inspector Hewitt and Sergeant Woolmer took on one side of the hall, Sergeant Graves and Constable Linnet attended to the other.

It was a long and weary old process. Time, as they say, hung heavily on our hands, or, to be more exact, on our behinds. Even Aunt Felicity was shifting uneasily on her more-than-ample padding.

"You may stand up and stretch," Inspector Hewitt had said at one point, "but please do not move from your places."

It was probably no more than about an hour before they got round to us, but it seemed to take forever. Father went first, to the corner where a plain wooden table with a couple of chairs had been set up. I could not hear what the Inspector asked him, nor could I hear any of his responses, which seemed to consist mainly of shaking his head in the negative.

It was not so very long since Inspector Hewitt had charged Father with the murder of Horace Bonepenny, and although Father had never said it in so many words, he still felt a certain coolness towards the constabulary. He was quickly back, and I waited patiently as Aunt Felicity, then Feely, then Daffy went up to speak quietly with the Inspector.

As each one returned to their seat, I tried to catch their eye, to get some hint of what they had been asked or what they had replied, but it was no use. Feely and Daffy both had that smarmy, sanctimonious look they get after partaking of Holy Communion, their eyes downcast and hands clasped at their waists in humbug humility. Father and Aunt Felicity were inscrutable, too.

Dogger was another matter.

Although he had borne up well under the Inspector's grilling, I noticed that he went back to his seat like a man walking a tightrope. A twitch had appeared at the corner of one eye, and his face had that strained yet vacant look that invariably preceded his attacks. Whatever it was that had happened to Dogger during the war, it had left him with an inability to be confronted close-up by any sort of officialdom.

Damn the consequences! I got up from my chair and knelt at his feet. Although Inspector Hewitt glanced in my direction, he made no move to stop me.

"Dogger," I whispered, "have you seen what I've seen?"

As I slipped into the chair beside him vacated by Mrs. Mullet, he looked at me as if he'd never seen me before in his life and then, like a pearl diver fighting his way slowly back to the surface from some great depth, he re-entered the real world, nodding his head in slow motion.

"Yes, Miss Flavia. Murder—I fear we have seen murder."

As my turn at the table approached, I suddenly became aware of my own heartbeat. I wished that I were a Tibetan lama, so that I could control its racing valves.

But before I could think about it further, Inspector Hewitt beckoned me. He was messing about with a stack of papers and forms, waiting until I had seated myself. For an idle instant, I found myself wondering where the blank forms had come from. *Woolmer and Graves must have brought them,* I decided. The Inspector certainly hadn't been carrying a briefcase before the performance.

I twisted round for a look at his wife, Antigone. Yes, there she was, sitting quietly among the villagers in her seat, radiant in spite of the situation.

"She's very beautiful," I whispered.

"Thank you," he said, not looking up from his papers, but I could tell by the corners of his mouth that he was pleased.

"Now then—name and address?"

Name and address? What was the man playing at?

"You know that already," I said.

"Of course I do"—he smiled—"but it's not official until you say it."

"Flavia de Luce—Buckshaw," I replied rather icily, and he wrote it down.

"Thank you," he said. "Now then, Flavia, what time did you arrive this evening?"

"Six-forty," I said, "on the dot. With my family. In a taxicab. Clarence Mundy's taxicab."

"And you were in the hall the whole evening?"

"Of course I was. I came over and spoke to you—don't you remember?"

"Yes. Answer the question, please."

"Yes."

I must admit that the Inspector was making me quite

cross. I had hoped to be able to collaborate with him: to provide him with a richly described, minute-by-minute account of the horror that had taken place—almost in my lap—this evening. Now I could see that I was going to be treated as if I were just another gawking spectator.

"Did you see or speak to Mr. Porson before the performance?"

What did he mean by that? I had seen and spoken to Mr. Porson on several occasions over the past three days. I had driven with Mr. Porson to Culverhouse Farm and had overheard his quarrel with Gordon Ingleby in Gibbet Wood. And that was not all that I knew about Rupert Porson. Not by a long chalk.

"No," I said.

Two could play at this game.

"I see," he said. "Well, thank you. That will be all."

I had just been checkmated.

"You're free to go," he added, glancing at his wristwatch. "It's probably past your bedtime."

The nerve of the man! Past my bedtime indeed! Who did he think he was talking to?

"May I ask a question?"

"You may," he said, "although I might not be able to answer it."

"Was Rupert—Mr. Porson, I mean—electrocuted?"

He looked at me narrowly, and I could see that he was thinking carefully about his reply.

"There is that possibility. Good night, Flavia."

The man was fobbing me off. Rupert had fried like a flounder, and the Inspector knew it as well as I did.

Flashbulbs were still going off behind the puppet stage

as I rejoined Father in the front row. Feely and Daffy were nowhere in sight.

"Mundy has already taken them home," he said.

"I'll be ready in a jiff," I said, walking towards the W.C. No one, anywhere, at any time in history, has ever stopped a female en route to the Baffins.

At the last moment, I changed direction and slipped into the kitchen, where I found Mrs. Mullet in full command. She had made a huge pot of tea, and had placed steaming cups in front of Nialla and Sergeant Woolmer, who sat at a side table.

Nialla saw me before the sergeant did, and her eyes flashed—but only for an instant—like a startled animal. She gave me an almost imperceptible shake of the head, but its meaning was clear.

Women's wireless at work. I rubbed my nose casually to let her know that the message had been received.

"Thank you, Miss Gilfoyle," the sergeant said. "You've been most helpful."

Gilfoyle? Was that Nialla's name? It was the first time I'd heard it.

Sergeant Woolmer drained his cup in a single draught, with no apparent ill effects.

"Champion tea, Mrs. Mullet," he said, closing his notebook. He gathered his papers, and with a pleasant nod in my direction, walked back out into the auditorium.

The man must have a stomach like a ship's boiler, I thought.

"Now then, dear, as I was saying," Mrs. Mullet said, "there's no use you goin' back to Culverhouse Farm tonight. It's rainin' cats and dogs—has been for an hour or more. The river will be mortal high—not safe to cross. 'Sides, no one would expect you to sleep in a tent in a wet field with the situation bein' what it is, if you take my meanin'. Alf's brought a brolly that's big enough for the three of us, and we're just across the way. Our Agnes's room hasn't been slept in since she left home to take up Pitman shorthand six years ago come November thirteenth. Alf and me have kept it a kind of a shrine, like. Has its own hot plate and a goose-down mattress. And don't say no, 'cause I won't hear you."

Nialla's eyes were suddenly brimming with tears, and for the life of me, I could not tell if they were tears of grief or joy.

I'd have given a guinea to know what words passed between Father and Dogger in the backseat of the taxicab, but the simple truth is that I dropped off. With the heater turned full up against the chill of the cold night rain, and the windscreen wipers making their quiet *swish-swash* in the darkness, the urge to sleep was irresistible. Not even an owl could have stayed awake.

When Father roused me at the door of Buckshaw, I stumbled into the house and up the stairs to bed—too tired even to bother undressing.

I must have fallen asleep with my eyes open.

· F O U R T E E N ·

THE SUN WAS STREAMING splendidly in at my casement window; the birds in the chestnuts were singing their little throats out. The first thought that came flashing into my mind was of Rupert's face: his lips pulled slightly back, his teeth showing obscenely.

I rolled over onto my back and stared at the ceiling. I always find that a blank screen helps clarify one's thoughts marvelously; helps bring them into focus.

In death Rupert had looked, I decided, remarkably like the dead dog I had once almost stepped on in a field behind the Thirteen Drakes, its fog-filled eyes staring, its yellowed fangs bared in a frozen grimace. (Although with Rupert, there had been no flies, and his teeth were quite presentable, actually.)

Somehow, the dog reminded me of something—but what?

Of course! Mutt Wilmott! The Thirteen Drakes! Mutt Wilmott would be staying at the Thirteen Drakes!

If Mrs. Mullet were to be believed, it had begun raining shortly after the evening performance began. Mutt had been there at about six-forty—say, six forty-five—I had seen him with my own eyes. He would hardly have set out for London in such a downpour. No, had he planned to leave, he would have done so before the show. It seemed obvious that he still had business to conclude with Rupert.

Ergo: He was, at this very instant, eating bacon and eggs at the Thirteen Drakes, Bishop Lacey's sole hostelry.

Fortunately, I was already dressed.

There was a cryptlike silence in the house as I crept down the east staircase. Last night's excitement had drained everyone of their energy and they were, I guessed, still snoring away in their respective rooms like a pack of convalescent vampires.

As I was slipping out the kitchen door, however, I came to an abrupt halt. On the wooden stand beside the door, tucked between the two full bottles the milk float had left on our doorstep at dawn, was a package.

It was a pustulent purple color, with projecting top and bottom rims. The clear cellophane in which it was wrapped had protected it from last night's rain. On the lid, in gold letters, were the words *Milady Chocolates—Finest Assorted—2 lb. Duchess Selection*. Wrapped around it lengthwise was a ribbon the color of a faded red rose. The label was still attached like the Mad Hatter's hat: 10/6.

I had seen this box before. In fact, I had seen it just a few days ago in the flyblown window of Miss Cool's confectionery shop cum post office in the high street, where it had languished since time immemorial—perhaps since the war, or even longer. And I realized at once how it had made its way to the back door at Buckshaw: Ned Cropper.

Ned earned £7 a week doing chores for Tully Stoker at the Thirteen Drakes, and he was smitten with, among others, my sister Ophelia. Even though he had accompanied Tully's daughter, Mary, to *Jack and the Beanstalk* last night, it had not kept him from leaving his midnight love token on our doorstep, as an adoring tomcat drops a mouse at its owner's feet.

The chocolates were so old, I thought, they were most likely full to bursting with countless varieties of interesting molds, but unfortunately there was no time to investigate. Reluctantly, I returned to the kitchen and stuffed the box in the top compartment of the ice cabinet. I would deal with Feely later.

"Ned!"

I gave him a smile, and a wave with my fingers spread generously apart, the way royalty is taught to do. With his sleeves rolled up and brilliantined hair like a wet haystack, Ned was high atop the steep-pitched roof of the Thirteen Drakes, his heels braced against a chimney pot, using a brush to slather hot pitch onto tiles that looked as if they'd been up there since King Alfred burned the cakes.

"Come down!" I shouted.

"Can't, Flavia. Got a leak in the kitchen. Tully wants this done before the Inspector shows up. Said he'd be here bright and early.

"Tully says he's counting on the early part, anyhow," he added. ". . . Whatever that means."

"I have to talk to you," I said, dropping my voice to a loud stage whisper. "I can't very well go shouting it up to the housetops."

"You'll have to come up." He pointed to a ladder that leaned against the wall. "Mind your step."

The ladder was as old as the inn, or so it seemed to me. It tottered and twisted as I climbed, creaking and groaning horribly. The ascent seemed to take forever, and I tried not to look down.

"It's about last night, isn't it?" Ned asked, as I neared the top.

Double damnation! If I was so transparent that even someone like Ned could see through me, I might as well leave it to the police.

"No," I said, "as a matter of fact it isn't, Mister Smart-Pants. A certain person asked me to thank you for your lovely gift."

"She did?" Ned said, his features broadening into a classic village idiot grin. The Folklore Society would have had him in front of a cine-camera before you could turn round three times and spit across the wind.

"She'd have come herself, but she's being detained in her tower by her wicked father who feeds her on floor sweepings and disgusting table scraps."

"Haw!" Ned said. "She didn't look too underfed last night." His features darkened, as if he had only just re-membered what had taken place.

"Pretty sad, that puppet man," he said. "I feel sorry for him."

"I'm glad you do, Ned. He hadn't many friends in the world, you know. It might be nice if you expressed your condolences to Mr. Wilmott. Someone said he's staying here."

This was a lie, but a well-intentioned one.

"Is he? Dunno. All I know right now is 'Roof! Roof! Roof!'—sounds like a dog when you say it like that, doesn't it? 'Roof! Roof! Roof!' "

I shook my head and started down the shaky ladder.

"Look at yourself!" Ned said. "You're covered with tar."

"Like a roof," I said, getting a look at my filthy hands and my dress. Ned hooted with laughter and I managed a pathetic grin.

I could cheerfully have fed him to the pigs.

"It won't come off, you know. You'll still have it plastered all over you when you're an old lady."

I wondered where Ned had picked up this rustic folklore—it was probably from Tully. I knew for a fact that Michael Faraday had synthesized tetrachloroethene in the 1820s by heating hexachloroethane and piping off the chlorine as it decomposed. The resulting solvent would remove tar from fabric like stink. Unfortunately—much as I should like to have done—I hadn't the time to repeat Faraday's discovery. Instead, I would have to fall back on mayonnaise, as recommended in *The Butler and Footman's Vade Mecum*, which I had come across one rainy day while snooping through the pantry at Buckshaw.

"Perhaps Mary would know. Is she somewhere about?"

I didn't dare barge in and ask Tully about a paying guest. To be perfectly honest, I was afraid of him, although it's difficult to say why with any certainty.

"Mary? She's taken the week's wash to the laundry, then she'll most likely be off to church."

Church! Baste me with butter! I'd forgotten all about church. Father would be going purple!

"Thanks, Ned," I shouted, grabbing Gladys from the bicycle stand. "See you!"

"Not if I see you first." Ned laughed, and like Santa Claus, turned to his work.

As I had feared, Father was standing at the front door glaring at his watch as I slid to a stop.

"Sorry!" I said. He didn't even bother asking.

Through the open door I flew and into the front hall. Daffy was sitting halfway up the west staircase with a book open in her lap. Feely wasn't down yet.

I charged up the east staircase to my bedroom, threw on my Sunday dress like a quick-change artist, scrubbed my face with a cloth, and within two minutes by the clock—barring a bit of tar on the end of my pigtails—I was ready for morning prayer.

It was then that I remembered the chocolates. I'd better retrieve them before Mrs. Mullet began to concoct her dreadful Sunday ices. If I didn't, there would be a host of cheeky questions to answer.

I tiptoed down the back stairs to the kitchen, and peered around the corner. Something nasty was just coming to the boil on the back of the cooker, but there was no one in sight.

I retrieved the chocolates from the ice cabinet and was back upstairs before you could say "Jack and the Beanstalk."

As I opened my laboratory door, my eye was arrested by a glint of glassware, which was reflecting a wayward sunbeam from the window. It was a lovely device called a Kipp's apparatus: one of Tar de Luce's splendid pieces of Victorian laboratory glass.

"A thing of beauty is a joy forever," the poet Keats had once written—or so Daffy had told me. There couldn't be a shred of doubt that Keats had written the line while contemplating a Kipp's apparatus: a device used to extract the gas resulting from a chemical reaction.

In form, it was essentially two clear glass balls mounted one above the other, a short tube connecting them, with a stoppered glass gooseneck projecting from the top globe, and a vent tube with a glass stopcock sticking out of the bottom one.

My plan took form instantly: a sure sign of divine inspiration. But I had only minutes to work before Father would come storming in to drag me down the stairs.

First, I took from a drawer one of Father's old razors—one I had nicked for an earlier experiment. I carefully slipped the faded ribbon from the chocolate box, turned it upside down, and made a careful, dead straight incision in the cellophane along the line where the ribbon had lain. A slit in the bottom and each end was all that was needed for the wrapping to open up like an oyster shell. Replacing it would be child's play.

That done, I carefully lifted the lid on the box and peered inside.

Perfect! The creams looked to be in pristine condition. I had suspected that age might have taken its toll—that opening the box might yield a sight similar to the one I had once seen in the churchyard when Mr. Haskins, the sexton, while digging a new grave, had accidentally broken through into another that was already occupied.

But then it had occurred to me that the chocolates, having been hermetically sealed—to say nothing of the preservatives that might have been added—might still seem fresh to the naked eye. Luck was on my side.

I had chosen my method because of its ability to take place at normal temperatures. Although there were other procedures that would have resulted in the same product, the one I selected was this: Into the bottom sphere of the Kipp's apparatus, I measured a quantity of ordinary iron sulfide. Into the top bulb, I carefully tipped a dilute sulfuric acid, using a glass rod to make sure that the liquid went straight into the target vessel.

I watched as the reaction began in the bottom container: a lovely chemical hubbub that invariably takes place when anything containing sulfur—including the human body—decomposes. When I judged it complete, I opened the bottom valve and let the gas escape into a rubber-stoppered flask.

Next came the part I loved best: Taking a large brass-bound glass syringe from one of Uncle Tar's desk drawers (I had often wondered if he used it to inject himself with a seven-percent solution of cocaine, like Sherlock Holmes), I shoved its needle through the rubber stopper, depressed the plunger, and then pulled it up again.

I now had a needle charged with hydrogen sulfide gas. Just one more step to go.

Sticking the needle through the rubber stopper of a test tube, I rammed the plunger down as hard as I could with both thumbs. Only fourteen atmospheric pressures were required to precipitate the gas into a liquid and, as I knew it would, it worked the first time.

I now had a test tube containing perfectly clear hydrogen sulfide in its liquid form. All that remained was to retract the plunger again, and watch it rise up into the glass of the syringe.

Carefully, I injected each chocolate with a drop or two of the stuff, touching the injection site with the glass rod (slightly warmed in the Bunsen burner) to smooth over the little hole.

I had carried out the procedure so perfectly that only the faintest whiff of rotten egg reached my nostrils. Safe inside the gooey centers, the hydrogen sulfide would remain cocooned, invisible, unsuspected, until Feely—

"Flavia!"

It was Father, shouting from the front hall.

"Coming!" I called. "I'll be there in a jiff!"

I replaced the lid of the box and then the cellophane wrapping, giving it two quick dabs of mucilage on the bottom to tack down the almost invisible incision. Then I replaced the ribbon.

As I slowly descended the curving staircase, trying desperately to look sedate and demure, I found the family gathered, waiting, in a knot at the bottom.

"I expect these are for you," I said, holding the box out to Feely. "Someone left them at the door."

She blushed a bit.

"And I have a confession to make," I added. All eyes were on me in a flash: Father's, Aunt Felicity's, Feely's, Daffy's—even Dogger's.

"I was tempted to keep them for myself," I said, eyes downcast, "but it's Sunday, and I really *am* trying hard to be a better person."

Eager hands outstretched, Feely rose to the bait like a shark to a swimmer's foot.

· F I F T E E N ·

WITH FATHER AND AUNT FELICITY leading the way,
and Dogger in the rear wearing a black bowler hat, we
straggled, as we always did, single file across the fields like
ducks to a pond. The green countryside in which we were
enfolded seemed as ancient and as settled in the morning
light as a canvas by Constable, and I shouldn't have been
a bit surprised to find that we were really no more than
tiny figures in the background of one of his paintings,
such as *The Hay Wain*, or *Dedham Vale*.

It was a perfect day. Bright prisms of dew glittered like
diamonds in the grass, although I knew that, as the day
went on, they would be vaporized by the sun.

Vaporized by the sun! Wasn't that what the universe
had in store for all of us? There would come a day when
the sun exploded like a red balloon, and everyone on
earth would be reduced in less than a camera flash to car-

bon. Didn't Genesis say as much? *For dust thou art, and unto dust shalt thou return.* This was far more than dull old theology: It was precise scientific observation! Carbon was the Great Leveler—the Grim Reaper.

Diamonds were nothing more than carbon, but carbon in a crystal lattice that made it the hardest known mineral in nature. That was the way we all were headed. I was sure of it. We were destined to be diamonds!

How exciting it was to think that, long after the world had ended, whatever was left of our bodies would be transformed into a dazzling blizzard of diamond dust, blowing out towards eternity in the red glow of a dying sun.

And for Rupert Porson, the process had already begun.

"I doubt very much, Haviland," Aunt Felicity was saying, "if they'll go ahead with the service. It seems hardly right in view of what's happened."

"The Church of England, Lissy," Father replied, "like time and tide, waits for no man. Besides, the fellow died in the parish hall—not in the church proper, as it were."

"Perhaps so," she said with a sniff. "Still, I shall be put out if all this walking is for nothing."

But Father was right. As we walked alongside the stone wall that ran like a tightened belt round the banked-up churchyard, I could see the hood of Inspector Hewitt's blue Vauxhall saloon peeking out discreetly at the end of the lane. The Inspector himself was nowhere in sight as we stepped onto the porch and entered the church.

Morning Prayer was as solemn as a Requiem High Mass. I know that for a fact because we de Luces are Roman Catholics—we are in fact, virtually charter members of the club. We have seen our share of bobbing and ducking. But we regularly attend St. Tancred's because of its proximity, and because the vicar is one of Father's great friends.

"Besides," Father says, "it is one's bounden duty to trade with local firms."

This morning, the church was packed to the rafters. Even the balcony beneath the bell tower was filled to overflowing with people from the village who wanted to be as close as possible, without being unseemly, to the Scene of the Crime.

Nialla was nowhere in sight. I noticed that at once. Nor were Mrs. Mullet, or Alf, her husband. If I knew our Mrs. M, she would, at this very moment, be bombarding Nialla with sausages and questions. "Plying and prying," Daffy called it.

Cynthia was already on her knees, front and center, praying to whatever gods she wanted to bribe before the service began. She was always the first to kneel and always the first to spring to her feet again. I sometimes thought of her as St. Tancred's spiritual coxswain.

For once, because it would be about someone I had known personally, I was quite looking forward to the sermon. The vicar, I expected, would deliver something inspired by Rupert's demise—tasteful but instructional. "In the midst of life we are in death," was my guess.

But when he climbed up into the pulpit at last, the vicar was strangely subdued, and it wasn't entirely due to the fact that Cynthia was running a white-gloved forefinger along the wooden rack that held scattered copies of the Hymnary and the *Book of Common Prayer*. In fact, the vicar made no reference to the matter at all, until he had finished the sermon.

"In view of the tragic circumstances of last evening," he said in a hushed and solemn voice, "the police have requested that the parish hall be made available to them until their work is complete. Consequently, our customary refreshments, for this morning only, will be served at the vicarage. Those of you who wish to do so are cordially invited to join us after the service. And now may God the Father, God the Son, and God the Holy Ghost . . ."

Just like that! No thoughts on "the stranger in our midst," such as he had delivered when Horace Bonepenny was murdered at Buckshaw. No ruminations on the immortality of the soul . . . Nothing.

To be perfectly honest, I felt more than a little cheated.

It is never possible, at least at St. Tancred's, to burst forth from the church into the sunshine like a cork from a bottle. One must always pause at the door to shake hands with the vicar, and to make some obligatory remark about the sermon, the weather, or the crops.

Father chose the sermon, and Daffy and Feely both chose the weather—the swine!—with Daffy commenting on the remarkable clarity of the air and Feely on its warmth. That left me with little choice, and the vicar was already clasping my hand.

"How's Meg getting on?" I asked. To tell the truth, I'd forgotten all about Mad Meg until that very moment, and the question just popped into my head.

Did the vicar's face go slightly white, or had I just fancied it?

He looked to the left and then to the right, very quickly. Cynthia was hovering outside among the gravestones, already halfway along the path to the vicarage.

"I'm afraid I can't tell you," he said. "You see, she was—"

"Vicar! I have a bone to pick with you, you know!"

It was Bunny Spirling. Bunny was one of the Spirlings of Nautilus Old Hall who, as Father once remarked, had gone to the dogs by way of the horses.

Because Bunny was shaped rather like the capital letter *D*, no one could get past him, and the vicar was now wedged firmly between Bunny's ample tummy and the Gothic door frame. Aunt Felicity and Dogger, I supposed, were still penned up somewhere inside the vestibule, queuing like crewmen on a sunken submarine for their turn at the escape hatch.

As Bunny proceeded to pick his bone (something about tithing and the shocking disrepair of the padding in the kneeling benches), I saw my opportunity to escape.

"Oh, dear," I remarked to Father, "it looks as though the vicar has been detained. I'll run ahead to the vicarage and see if I can make myself useful with the cups and saucers."

There's not a father on earth who has it in him to refuse such a charitable child, and I was off like a hare.

"Morning!" I shouted to Cynthia as I flew past.

I vaulted over the stile and ran round to the front of the vicarage. The door stood open, and I could hear voices in the kitchen at the back of the house. The Women's Institute, I decided: Several of them would have slipped out of the service early to put the kettle on.

I stood in the dim hallway, listening. Time was short,

but it would never do to be caught snooping. With one last look down the stretch of polished brown linoleum, I stepped into the vicar's study and closed the door behind me.

Meg, of course, was long gone, but the afghan with which the vicar had covered her yesterday still lay crumpled on the horsehair sofa, as if Meg had only just tossed it aside, got up, and left the room, leaving in her wake— to put it nicely—a woodsy smell: the smell of damp leaves, dark earth, and something-less-than-perfect personal hygiene.

But before I could put my mind to work, the door was flung open.

"What are you doing in here?"

Needless to say, it was Cynthia. She closed the door craftily behind her.

"Oh, hello, Mrs. Richardson," I said. "I just looked in to see if Meg was still here. Not that she would be, of course, but I worry about her, you see, and . . ."

When you're stumped for words, use your hands. This was a dodge that had never failed me in the past, and I hoped that it would not now.

I snatched at the wadded afghan and began to fold it. As I did so, something dropped with a barely audible plop to the carpet.

"I just thought I'd help tidy up, then see if they can put me to work in the kitchen.

"Drat!" I said, as I let a corner of the afghan escape my fingers. "Oh, sorry, Mrs. Richardson, I'm afraid I'm quite clumsy. We're so spoiled at Buckshaw, you know."

Awkwardly, I spread out the afghan on the floor,

crouched in front of it, and began folding again. Under cover of its colorful woolen squares—and using my body to block Cynthia's view—I ran my fingers across the carpet.

I felt it at once: a cold, flat, metallic object. Using my thumb as a clamp, I pressed it firmly into my palm. As long as I kept my hands moving, all would be well. That was the way the sleight-of-hand magicians worked. I could always pocket the thing later.

"Here, give me that," Cynthia said.

I panicked! She had caught me out after all.

As she stepped into the room, I began a frantic jitter-bug, kicking up my legs and throwing my elbows out like pikestaffs.

"Oh!" I said. "That afghan's making me itchy all over. I have a nasty allergy to wool."

I began scratching myself furiously: my arms, the back of my hands, my calves . . . anywhere, just as long as I didn't let my hands come to rest.

When I got to my neck, I shoved my hand into the top of my dress and let go the object from my palm. I felt it fall inside—and stop at my waist.

"Give me that," she repeated, snatching the afghan from my hands.

I breathed a sigh of relief as I realized that she hadn't seen whatever it was I'd retrieved. It was the afghan she wanted, and I held it out cheerily, giving myself several more houndlike scratches for insurance purposes.

"I'll go help in the kitchen," I said, moving towards the door.

"Flavia—" Cynthia said, stepping in front of the door and seizing my wrist in one rapid motion.

I looked into her pale blue watery eyes and they did not waver.

But at that instant, there was laughter outside in the hallway as the first parishioners arrived from the church.

"One thing we de Luce girls *are* good at"—I grinned into her face as I slipped round her and out the door—"is making tea!"

I had no more intention of making tea than of signing on as a coal pit donkey.

Still, I made a beeline down the hall and into the kitchen.

"Good morning, Mrs. Roberts! Good morning, Miss Roper! Just checking to see if you have enough cups and saucers?"

"Plenty, thank you, Flavia, dear," Mrs. Roberts said. She had been doing this since the dawn of time.

"But you can put the eggs in the bottom of the fridge on your way out," Miss Roper told me. "The egg lady must have left them on the kitchen counter yesterday. Nothing keeps in this weather, not the way it used to, at any rate. And while you're at it, dear, you can fill that pitcher with lemonade. Mr. Spirling likes a nice glass of lemonade after church, and as he's always so generous when the collection plate goes round, we wouldn't want to get into his bad books, would we?"

Before they could devise another task, I flew busily out the kitchen door. Later, when they had a moment—when they were washing up, perhaps—Mrs. Roberts and Miss Roper would remark to one another what a nice girl I was—and how unlike my sisters.

Outside in the churchyard, Father still stood on the

cobbled walk, listening patiently to Bunny Spirling, who was telling him, word for word, what he had just said to the vicar. Father nodded from time to time, probably to keep his neck from going to sleep.

I stepped off the path and into the grass, pretending to inspect the inscription on a weathered gravestone that jutted up like a yellowed tooth from a green gum (*Hezekiah Huff 1672–1746, At Peece In Paradice*). Turning my back on the gossiping stragglers, I extracted the metal object I had dropped down the front of my dress: It was, as I knew it would be, Nialla's orange cloisonné butterfly compact. It lay cradled in the flat of my hand, gleaming softly in the warm sunlight. Meg must have dropped it while sleeping on the couch in the vicar's study.

I'd return it to Nialla later, I thought, shoving it into my pocket. She'd be happy to have it back.

As I rejoined the family, I saw that Daffy was perched on the stone wall at the front of the churchyard with her nose stuck in Robert Burton's *Anatomy of Melancholy*, her latest grand enthusiasm. How she had managed to slip such a fat volume in and out of church I could not even begin to imagine, until I came close enough to spot the neatly made tinfoil cross she had glued to its black cover. Oh, what a fraud she was! Well done, Daff!

Feely stood laughing under an oak, letting her hair fall forward to cover her face, the way she does when she wants to look like Veronica Lake. Basking in her attention, and dressed in a rough wool suit, was a tall, blond Nordic god. It took me a moment to recognize him as Dieter Schrantz, and I realized, not without a sinking feeling, that he was already completely in Feely's thrall, hanging on her every word like a ball on a rubber string, nodding like a demented woodpecker, and grinning like a fool.

They did not even notice my look of disgust.

Aunt Felicity was talking to an elderly person with a hearing trumpet. It seemed, from their conversation, that they were old friends.

"But one mustn't arch one's back and spit!" the old lady was saying, curling her red-nailed fingers into a claw, at which they both cackled obscenely.

Dogger, meanwhile, sat patiently on a bench beneath a yew tree, his eyes closed, a slight smile on his lips, and his face upturned towards the summer sun, looking for all the world like one of those modern brass sculptures called *Sunday*.

No one paid me the slightest attention. I was on my own.

The double doors in the porch of the parish hall were draped with a rope, from which hung a notice: *Police Line—Do Not Cross*.

I didn't: I walked round the back of the building and went in by one of the exits.

It was pitch dark inside. At the far end of the corridor, I knew, was the door that opened into the auditorium. To my right were the several steps that led up to the stage.

I could hear the rumble of men's voices, and although I strained my ears to the utmost, I could not make out what they were saying. The black velvet curtains that lined the stage must be absorbing their words.

Unable to make any sense of the murmur, and because I didn't want to risk being caught eavesdropping, I clattered noisily up the stairs.

"Hullo!" I shouted. "Anyone for tea?"

Inspector Hewitt was standing in a pool of light talking to sergeants Woolmer and Graves. At the sight of me, he broke off at once and came striding across the stage behind the puppet theater.

"You oughtn't to be in here. Didn't you see the signs?"

"Sorry," I said, without answering his question. "I came in the back way."

"No signs in the rear, Sergeant?" the Inspector asked Graves.

"Sorry, sir," the sergeant said with a sheepish grin. "I'll see to it right away."

"Too late now," the Inspector said. "The damage is done."

Sergeant Graves lost the grin and his brow furrowed. "Sorry, sir," he said. "Entirely my fault."

"Well," the Inspector went on, "since we're almost finished, it's not a *complete* disaster. But keep it in mind for next time."

"Yes, sir."

"Now, then," the Inspector said, turning to me, "what are you doing here? And don't give me any guff about tea."

I had learned from past experience that it was best to be frank with the Inspector—at least in replying to direct questions. One could always be helpful, I reminded myself, without spilling one's guts.

"I was making notes upon a few points."

I hadn't made notes, in fact, but now that I'd thought of it, I realized it was a good idea. I'd see to it tonight.

"Notes? Why on earth would you do that?"

Because I could think of nothing to say, I said nothing. I could hardly tell the man that Dogger thought it was murder.

"And now, I'm afraid, I'm going to have to ask you to leave, Flavia."

As he spoke, I looked round desperately for something— anything!—to seize upon.

And suddenly I saw it! I almost whooped with joy. My heart welled up inside me and I could hardly keep from laughing as I spoke.

"Edgar Allan Poe!" I said aloud. *"The Purloined Letter."*

The Inspector stared at me as if I'd gone mad.

"Are you familiar with the story, Inspector?" I asked. Daffy had read it aloud to us on Christmas Eve.

"Isn't everyone?" he said. "Now, please, if you'll be so good—"

"Then you'll remember where the letter was hidden: on the mantelpiece—in plain sight—dangling from a dirty blue ribbon."

"Of course," he said, with a brief but indulgent smile.

I pointed to the wooden rail of the puppet stage, which was no more than a foot above his head.

"Has the current been switched off?" I asked.

"We're not idiots, Flavia."

"Then," I said, reaching up and almost touching the thing, "perhaps we should tell the vicar we've found his lost bicycle clip."

· S I X T E E N ·

IT WAS DIFFICULT, AT first, to see the thing. Black metal on black painted wood was nearly invisible. If it hadn't been for the patterned spray of carbon, I shouldn't have noticed it at all.

Black on black on black. I was proud of myself.

The bicycle clip was pushed down over a wooden strut, as if the strut were an ankle. Beneath it ran a length of electric flex, which connected a row of toggle switches above the stage to the colored footlights below. Even from where I stood, I could see the glint of copper wire where a section of the flex had been stripped of its insulation.

"Good Lord!" the Inspector said. "Whatever makes you think this belongs to the vicar?"

"Several things," I told him, ticking them off on my fingers. "In the first place, I heard him say on Thursday afternoon that he had lost his bicycle clip. In the second place, I know for a fact that it wasn't here yesterday afternoon before the show. Rupert let me have a good look round just before the matinee. And finally, it has the vicar's initials on it. Look here: If you squat a bit and look edge-on, you can see them: *D.R.*—Denwyn Richardson. Cynthia scratched them on with a needle because he's forever losing things."

"And you're quite sure the clip wasn't here on Saturday afternoon?"

"Positive. I was holding on to that very spot on the railing when Rupert took me up on the bridge—to show me how Galligantus worked."

"I beg your pardon?" The look on the Inspector's face was a puzzle.

"Galligantus. That's the name of the giant in *Jack and the Beanstalk*. Here, I'll show you. Is it all right to climb up there?" I asked, pointing to the bridge.

"It's extremely irregular, but carry on."

I scrambled up the ladder to the catwalk behind the puppet stage, with the Inspector hot on my heels.

Galligantus was still firmly in position.

"In the third act, as Jack is hacking away at the beanstalk, Rupert pulls this iron lever, which releases Galligantus. He's spring-loaded, you see."

There was a very long silence. Then the Inspector took out his notebook and unscrewed the cap of his biro.

"All right, Flavia," he said with a sigh, "tell me more."

"When Jack chops down the beanstalk, the giant's supposed to come crashing down from the sky. But he didn't, of course . . . Rupert did instead."

"Therefore Rupert couldn't have operated the lever. Is that what you're saying?"

"Exactly! If he had, Galligantus would have been triggered. But he wasn't, of course, because the vicar's bicycle clip was clamped over the end of the lever. Black on black. Rupert mustn't have noticed it."

"Good Lord!" the Inspector exclaimed, realizing what I was saying. "Then it wasn't—"

"A tragic accident? No, Inspector. I should hardly say so."

He let out a low whistle.

"See this? Someone's cut away the insulation from this cable," I went on, "right down to the bare wire, then shoved the bicycle clip down on top to cover it. The other end of the bicycle clip is clamped over the end of Galligantus's lever."

"Forming an electrical jumper," he said. "A deliberate short circuit."

"Precisely," I said. "Here—you can see the deposit of carbon where it arced. See where the wood beneath it is a little charred?"

Inspector Hewitt leaned in for a closer look, but said nothing.

"It seems to me," I added, " that the bicycle clip couldn't have been put there until sometime after the first performance. Otherwise, Galligantus couldn't have fallen."

"Flavia," the Inspector said, "you must promise me you will discuss this with no one. Not a word. Do you understand?"

I stared at him for a moment, as if the very thought of doing so were highly offensive.

"He was electrocuted, wasn't he?" I asked.

The Inspector nodded. "Dr. Darby thinks it most likely. We'll have the autopsy results later today."

We'll have the autopsy results? Was the Inspector including me? Did he count me as part of his team? I needed to choose my words carefully.

"My lips are sealed," I said. "Cross my heart and—"

"Thank you, Flavia," he said firmly. "A simple promise is sufficient. Now run along and let me get on with it."

Run along? What jolly cheek! What utter gall!

I'm afraid I made a rude noise on my way out.

As I suspected she would be, Feely was still flirting with Dieter beneath the oaks.

Father stood near the door of the church with the perplexed look on his face of a man trying to decide if he should rush to the aid of someone who has unwittingly wandered into the tiger's cage, but can't quite make up his mind about which of the cage's two occupants is in greater need of saving from the other.

"Feely," he called out at last, "we mustn't keep Mrs. Mullet waiting."

My stomach curdled instantly. Today was Sunday, the day of the week upon which we were force-fed, like Strasbourg geese, upon one of Mrs. Mullet's failed culinary experiments, such as stuffed sow's liver brought whole to the table and passed off as Mock Denbighshire Sweet Loaf.

"Father," Feely said, taking the bull by the horns, "I'd like you to meet Dieter Schrantz."

Father, of course, like everyone else in Bishop's Lacey,

was aware that there were German prisoners of war working in the neighbourhood. But until that moment, he had
never been put in the position of having to converse with
someone he always referred to, at home in Buckshaw's
drawing room, as the Enemy.

He offered his hand.

"It's a pleasure to meet you, sir," Dieter said, and I
could see that Father was taken aback by Dieter's perfect
English. But before he could respond, Feely fired off the
next round: "I've invited Dieter to tea," she said. "And
he's accepted."

"Providing you approve, of course, sir," Dieter added.

Father seemed flustered. He pulled his spectacles from
his waistcoat pocket and began polishing them on his
handkerchief. Fortunately, Aunt Felicity arrived in time
to intervene.

"Of course he approves!" she said. "Haviland's never
been one to hold a grudge, have you, Havvie?"

Like a man in a dream, Father looked round him and
remarked, to no one in particular, "Interesting weather."

I took immediate advantage of his momentary confu-
sion.

"Go on ahead without me," I said. "I just want to pop
in and make sure Nialla's all right. I'll be home directly."

And no one lifted a finger to stop me.

Mrs. Mullet's cottage was nestled at the far end of Cob-
bler's Lane, a narrow, dusty track that ran south from the
high street and ended at a stile. It was a cozy little place
with hollyhocks and a ginger cat dozing in the sun. Her

husband, Alf, was sitting on a bench in the yard, carving a willow whistle.

"Well, well," he said when he saw me at his gate, "to what do we owe this most prodigious great pleasure?"

"Good morning, Mr. Mullet," I said, falling effortlessly into my best prunes-and-prisms voice, "I hope you're keeping well?"

"Fair . . . fair to troublesome digestion. Sometimes kicks like a kangaroo—elsewise, burns like Rome."

"I'm sorry to hear that," I said, meaning every word of it. We de Luces were not the only ones subjected to Mrs. Mullet's culinary concoctions.

"Here," Alf said, handing me the wooden whistle. "Give 'er a blow. See if you can fetch up an elf."

I took the slender piece of wood and raised it to my lips.

"Perhaps I'd better not," I said. "I don't want to wake Nialla."

"Ha!" he said. "No fear o' that. She's gone afore the sun."

"Gone?"

I was astonished. How could she be gone?

"Where?" I asked.

"God only knows." He shrugged. "Back to Culverhouse Farm, maybe—maybe not. That's all I know. Now give us a toot."

I blew into the whistle, producing a high, shrill, piercing wail.

"Wizard tone," I said, handing it back.

"Keep it," Alf said. "I made it for you. I thought you'd be round before long."

"Smashing!" I said, because I knew it was expected of me.

As I walked back to Buckshaw, I thought how similar my life was to the lives of those swarming clerics in Anthony Trollope who seemed to spend their days buzzing from cloister to vicarage and from village to the bishop's palace like black clockwork beetles scuttling to and fro in a green maze. I had dipped into *The Warden* during one of our compulsory Sunday afternoon reading periods, and followed it a few weeks later by skimming bits of *Barchester Towers*.

I must confess that, since there was no one of my own age group in his writings, I did not care much for Trollope. Most of his fossilized clergymen, for instance, quite frankly made me want to spew my sausages. The character with whom I most identified was Mrs. Proudie, the tyrant wife of the rabbity bishop, who knew what she wanted and, for the most part, knew how to get it. Had Mrs. Proudie been keen on poisons, she might have become my favorite character in all of literature.

Although Trollope had not specifically mentioned it, there was no doubt in my mind that Mrs. Proudie had been brought up in a home with two older sisters who treated her like dirt.

Why did Ophelia and Daphne despise me so? Was it because Harriet had hated me, as they claimed? Had she, while suffering from "the baby blues," stepped off into thin air from a mountain in Tibet?

In short, the question was this: Had I killed her?

Did Father hold me responsible for her death?

Somehow the sparkle had gone out of the day as I plodded glumly along the lanes. Even the thought of Rupert's murder and its messy aftermath did little to cheer me.

I gave a couple of toots on the willow whistle, but it sounded like a baby cuckoo, fallen from its nest, crying woefully for its mother. I shoved the thing into the bottom of my pocket and trudged on.

I needed some time alone—some time to think.

Seen from the Mulford Gates, Buckshaw always had about it a rather sad and abandoned air, as if some vital essence were missing. But now, as I walked along beneath the chestnuts, something was different. I spotted it at once. Several people were standing on the gravel sweep in the forecourt, and one of them was Father, who was pointing at the roof. I broke into a run, dashing across the lawn like a sprinter, chest out, fists going like pistons at my side.

I needn't have bothered. As I drew closer, I saw that it was only Aunt Felicity and Daffy, both standing on one side of Father, with Feely at the other.

At her right hand stood Dieter. I couldn't believe my eyes!

Feely's eyes were sparkling, her hair was shining in the summer sun, and her smile was dazzlingly perfect. In her gray skirt and canary yellow sweater set, with a single strand of Harriet's cultured pearls draped round her neck, she was more than vibrant . . . she was *beautiful*—I could have throttled her.

"Ruskin found square drip moldings abominable," Father was saying, "but he was being facetious, of course. Even the best of our British sandstone is but a pale mockery of the fine-grained marble one finds in Greece."

"Quite true, sir," Dieter agreed. "Although, was it not your Charles Dickens who thought that the Greeks used marble only because of the way it took paint and color? Still, the style and the material mean nothing when the molding is placed under a portico. It is the architect's joke, isn't it?"

Father considered for a moment, rubbing his hands together behind his back as he stood staring at the front of the house.

"By Jove!" he said at last. "You may have hit on something."

"Ah, Flavia!" Aunt Felicity said as she spotted me. "Think of the Devil and she shall appear. I should like to paint presently and you shall be my assistant. I relish the brushwork but I simply can't bear the sticky tubes and the dirty rags."

Daffy rolled her eyes and edged slowly away from her mad old aunt, fearing, I think, that she was going to be put to work as well. I relented enough to ask her one question. There were times when curiosity trumped even pride.

"What's *he* doing here?" I whispered into her ear, giving a slight tip of my head towards Dieter.

Of course I already knew, but it was a rare opportunity to talk sister-to-sister without rancor.

"Aunt Felicity insisted. Said he should walk us home and stay to tea.

"I think she's got her eye on him," she added with a coarse snicker.

Although I'm quite accustomed to Daffy's excesses, I must admit that I was shocked.

"For Feely," she explained.

Of course! No wonder Father was exercising his rusty charm! One daughter fewer would mean a one-third reduction in the number of surplus mouths he had to feed. Not that Feely ate that much—she didn't—but coupled with a similar reduction in the dose of daily insolence he would need to put up with, palming her off on Dieter was well worth the effort.

Then, too, I thought, there would be an end to the vast outlays of cash for the constant re-silvering of Buckshaw's looking glasses. Feely was hell on mirrors.

"And your father . . ." Father was saying to Dieter.

I knew it! He was already greasing the skids!

". . . I believe you said something about books?"

"He's a publisher, sir," Dieter said. "He's the 'Schrantz' of Schrantz and Markel. You may not have heard of them but they publish in German, editions of—"

"Of course! The *Luxus Ausgaben Schrantz und Markel*. Their Pliny—the one with the Dürer plates—is quite remarkable."

"Come along, Flavia," Aunt Felicity said. "You know how tiresome it is to paint brickwork once it's in shadow."

From a distance, I must have looked like a sinking galleon as, with Aunt Felicity's easel over my shoulder, a stretched canvas under each arm, and a wooden box of paints and brushes in each hand, I waded barefoot through the shallow waters of the ornamental lake, towards the island upon which the folly was situated. Aunt Felicity brought up the rear, carrying a three-legged stool. In her tweed suit, floppy hat, and smock, she reminded me of photos I had seen in *Country Life* of Winston Churchill dabbling with his paints at Chartwell. The only thing missing was the cigar.

"I've wanted for ages to render the south front as it was in the days of dear Uncle Tar," she shouted, as if I were on the far side of the world.

"Now, then, dear," she said, when I had finally set up the painting gear to her satisfaction, "it's time for a quiet talk. Out here, at least, we shall not be overheard—save by the bees and the water rats."

I looked at her in astonishment.

"I expect you think I know nothing about the kind of life you lead."

This was the sort of statement of which I had learned to be exceptionally wary: Its implications were immense and, until I saw which way the conversational wind was blowing, I knew that it was best to keep quiet.

"On the contrary," she went on, "I know a great deal about what you must feel: your loneliness, your isolation, your older sisters, your preoccupied father . . ."

I was about to say that she must be mistaken, when I suddenly saw that the coming chat could be turned to my advantage.

"Yes," I said, staring off over the water and blinking, as if to stop a tear, "it *can* be difficult at times. . . ."

"That's precisely what your mother used to say about living at Buckshaw. I remember her coming here summers, as a girl, as had I before her."

Picturing Aunt Felicity as a girl was not an easy task.

"Oh, don't look so shocked, Flavia. In my youth, I used to run wild here on the island like a Pawnee princess. 'Moo-noo-tonowa,' I called myself. Pinched nice bits of beef from the larder and pretended I was cooking dog over a campfire lighted with rubbing sticks and snuff.

"Later, even in spite of the great difference in our ages, Harriet and I were always the greatest of chums. 'The Wretched Outcasts' we used to call ourselves. We would come out here to the island to talk. Once, when we hadn't seen one another for a very long time, we sat out all night in the folly, wrapped in blankets, jabbering away until the sun came up. Uncle Tar sent Pierrepoint, the old butler, to bring us Plasmon biscuits and calf's-foot jelly. He had spotted us from the windows of his laboratory, you see, and—"

"What was she like," I interrupted. "Harriet, I mean."

Aunt Felicity made a dark slash of color on her canvas, which I guessed was supposed to represent the trunk of one of the chestnuts in the drive.

"She was exactly like you," she answered. "As you very well know."

I gulped. "She was?"

"Of course she was! How could you not be aware of it?"

I could have filled her ears with the horrid tales that Feely and Daffy had told me, but I chose not to.

"*Zipped lips save ships.*"

Dogger had said that to me once when I asked him a

rather personal question about Father. "Zipped lips save ships," he had answered, turning back to his deadheading, and I hadn't the nerve to ask which of the three of us were the mutes and which the vessels.

I had mumbled something unsatisfactory then, and now I found myself doing it again.

"Good heavens, child! If you want to see your mother, you have no more than to look in the glass. If you want to know her character, look inside yourself. You're so much like her it gives me the willies."

Well, then.

"Uncle Tar used to invite us down to Buckshaw for the summer," she went on, either unaware of or choosing to ignore my burning face.

"He had some extraordinary idea that the presence of young females in the house held it together in some abstruse chemical fashion—something about bonds and the unsuspected dual gender of the carbon molecule. Mad as a March hare, Tar de Luce was, but a lovely old gentleman, for all that.

"Harriet, of course, was his favorite; perhaps because she never grew weary of sitting on a tall stool in that stinking laboratory, and taking down notes as he dictated them. 'My whiz-bang assistant,' he used to call her. It was a private joke: Harriet told me once that he was referring to a spectacular experiment gone awry that might have wiped Buckshaw off the map—to say nothing of Bishop's Lacey and beyond. But she swore me to silence. I don't know why I'm telling you this."

"He was investigating the first-order decomposition of nitrogen pentoxide," I said. "It was work that led eventually to the development of the atomic bomb. There are some letters among his papers from Professor Arrhenius of Stockholm that make it quite clear what they were onto."

"And you, as it were, are left to carry the torch."

"I beg your pardon?"

"To carry on the glorious name of de Luce," she said. "Wherever it may lead you."

This was an interesting thought; it had never occurred to me that one's name could be a compass.

"And where might that be?" I asked, somewhat slyly.

"You must listen to your inspiration. You must let your inner vision be your Pole Star."

"I try," I said. I must sound to Aunt Felicity like the village idiot.

"I know you do, dear. I've heard several reports of your doings. For instance there was that horrid business with Bunpenny, or whatever his name was."

"Bonepenny," I said. "Horace. He died just over there."

I pointed across the lake to the wall of the kitchen garden.

Aunt Felicity plowed on regardless. "You must never be deflected by unpleasantness. I want you to remember that. Although it may not be apparent to others, your duty will become as clear to you as if it were a white line painted down the middle of the road. You must follow it, Flavia."

"Even when it leads to murder?" I asked, suddenly bold.

With her brush extended to arm's length, she painted in the dark shadow of a tree. "Even when it leads to murder."

We sat for a few moments in silence, Aunt Felicity dabbing away at her canvas with no particularly exciting results, and then she spoke again: "If you remember nothing else, remember this: Inspiration from outside one's self is like the heat in an oven. It makes passable Bath buns. But inspiration from *within* is like a volcano: It changes the face of the world."

I wanted to throw my arms around this dotty old bat in her George Bernard Shaw costume and hug her until the juices ran out. But I didn't. I couldn't.

I was a de Luce.

"Thank you, Aunt Felicity," I said, scrambling to my feet. "You're a brick."

· S E V E N T E E N ·

WE WERE AT TEA in the library. Mrs. Mullet had come in and gone out, leaving behind a vast tray of Jenny Lind cake and currant scones. To my whispered question about Nialla, she had replied with a shrug, and wrinkled her brow to remind me that she was on duty.

Feely was at the piano. It hadn't taken more than three minutes for Dieter to ask politely which of us played, and Feely had replied with her blushes. Now, sufficiently coaxed and implored, she was just beginning the second movement of Beethoven's *Pathétique* sonata.

It was a lovely piece and, as the music faded away and then welled up again, like longings in the heart, I remembered that it was the music Laurie Laurence had played in *Little Women*, as Jo, who had refused his proposal, walked away outside his window, and I wondered if Feely had chosen it subconsciously.

Father was dreamily tapping a forefinger against the edge of his saucer, which he held beautifully balanced in his hands. There were times when, for no apparent reason, I felt a huge tidal wave of love—or at least respect—for him, and this was one of them.

In the corner, Daffy was curled up like a cat in an armchair, still in the clutches of *The Anatomy of Melancholy*, and Aunt Felicity sat contentedly near the window, doing something intricate with a pair of needles and a ball of sulfur yellow wool.

Suddenly I noticed that Dieter was biting the corner of his lip, and there was a glistening at the corner of his eye. He was almost in tears, and trying not to show it.

How cruel it was of that witch, Feely, to choose something so sad and so evocative: a melody by Beethoven that could only serve as a bitter reminder to our German guest of the homeland he had left behind.

But at that instant, Feely broke off abruptly and leapt up from the keyboard.

"Oh!" she gasped, "I'm so sorry! I didn't mean to—"

And I could see that for probably the first time in her life, she was genuinely distressed. She flew to Dieter's side and held out her handkerchief—and to his eternal credit, he took it.

"No. It is I who should be sorry," he said, wiping at his eyes. "It's just that—"

"Dieter," I found my mouth suddenly blurting, "tell us how you came to be a prisoner of war. I've been simply dying to ask you. I'm frightfully keen on history, you know."

You could have heard a pin drop in Antarctica.

"Flavia!" Father finally managed—but only when it was far too late to have the effect that he intended.

But Dieter was already smiling. It seemed to me he was relieved to have got past the dampness.

"But of course!" he said. "For five years I have been waiting for someone to ask me—but no one ever has. You English are all such perfect gentlemen—even the ladies!"

Aunt Felicity shot him a look of beaming approval.

"But," Dieter added, "I must warn you—it's a long story. Are you sure you want to hear it?"

Daffy closed her book and set it aside. "I adore long stories," she said. "In fact, the longer, the better."

Dieter took up a stance on the rug in front of the fire-place, his elbow on the mantelpiece. You could almost picture him at a hunting lodge in the Black Forest.

"Well," he said, "I think you could safely say that I was shot down in England because of the Brontë sisters."

Shot down? This was something new! I was all agog.

Daffy's eyes were instantly like china doorknobs, and even Father sat up straight.

"Good Lord!" he muttered.

"I was spoiled, as a boy," Dieter began, "and I must admit to it. I was an only child, brought up in a well-to-do household by a *Kinderpflegerin*—a nursery governess.

"My father, as I have said, was a publisher, and my mother an archaeologist. Although they loved me well enough, I suppose, they were both so wrapped up in their own worlds that everything having to do with 'the boy' was left up to Drusilla. That was the governess's name—Drusilla.

"Drusilla was a very great reader of English novels. She consumed books like a whale eats krill. You never saw her without a book in her hand—in fact, she taught me to read while I was still sucking my thumb.

"Drusilla had read all of the Brontë sisters' books, of course: *Wuthering Heights, Jane Eyre, Shirley, The Tenant of Wildfell Hall*—she had them almost by heart.

"I was half in love with her, I think, and I thought that I could make her love me by reading aloud in English from her favorites.

"And that was how I became an Anglophile. From that time on, I wanted nothing more than to read English books: Dickens, of course, and Conan Doyle; Jane Austen and Thomas Hardy. When I was a bit older, Drusilla gave me for Christmas subscriptions to *The Boy's Own Annual* and *Chums*. By the time I was twelve, I was more British than many a boy from Brixton!

"Then came the wireless. From the articles in *Chums*, and with the help of a schoolboy friend who lived next door—his name was Wolfgang Zander—I was able to put together a simple single-valve wireless receiver with which we could tune in to the broadcasts of the BBC.

"We were mad about electrical gadgets, Wolfgang and I. The first thing we made was a battery-operated doorbell; the next was a telephone between my bedroom and his, with the wire strung over the rooftops and through the trees.

"Long after our families were asleep, that cotton-covered wire high in the branches buzzed long into the night with our feverish speculations. We would talk away the night, about wireless, of course, but also about English books, for Wolfgang, you see, also had been bitten by the English—and particularly the Brontë—bug.

"The adolescent imagination is a powerful force, and I suppose we saw ourselves, Wolfgang and I, as Knights of the Round Table who would come riding out from our Teutonic stronghold to rescue these Brontë sisters: these three fair, pale maidens—whose very names identify them as daughters of the Thunder-god—who were being held hostage by a monster in their cold stone tower in the north.

"Besides," he added, "there is something about young, helpless damsels in damp climates that makes every adolescent boy want to carry them off and marry them."

He paused to let his words have their effect, looking keenly from one of us to another, and as he did, I saw with a sudden shock that in Feely and Daffy and me, Dieter fancied he had found his Brontës; and in Buckshaw, his cold stone tower. We were his Charlotte, Emily, and Anne!

And there we sat, the three of us, our mouths hanging open like dogs.

My mind was reeling as Dieter went on: "But too soon we grow up," he said with a sigh. "Too soon we take on the joys of the grown-up world, but also its troubles.

"Always, there is an age when boys discover flying, and it came early to me. My parents enrolled me in the NSFK—the National Socialist Flying Corps—and when I was fourteen, I found myself suddenly alone at the controls of a *Schulgleiter*, soaring like a hawk high above the Wasserkuppe, in the hills of the Hessian Rhön.

"From the air, these mountains, even though they are of quite a different geology, bear in some places a startling resemblance to the moors of North Yorkshire."

"How do you know that?" Daffy interrupted.

"Daphne!" Father said. His pointed look added the word *manners*.

"Is it because you've bombed Sheffield?"

There was a shocked silence at her question. How bold she was! Even I would not have asked Dieter about his aerial activities over England, although I will admit that, just minutes before, that very point had crossed my mind.

"Because," Daffy added, "if you have, you must say so."

"I was coming to that," Dieter said quietly.

He continued without batting an eye.

"When the war came, and I was transferred to the Luftwaffe, I always kept the small English 'Everyman' editions of *Jane Eyre* and *Wuthering Heights* wrapped carefully in a white silk flying scarf at the bottom of my rucksack, cheek to cheek with Lord Byron and Shelley.

"I decided that when the war was over, I would enroll at a university—perhaps even Oxford, since I already had the language—where I would read English Literature. I would take a double first, and accept a teaching post at one of the great public schools, and would end my days as an honored and respected schoolmaster, somewhat like your Mr. Chips.

" 'Goodbye, Herr Schrantz,' I used to say. But Fate had not yet finished with me. An order was received that I was to proceed at once to France.

"My father, it seemed, had run into an old acquaintance in Berlin: someone who was high up in the Ministry and could arrange almost anything one might desire. Father wanted to have a son who flew a fighter: one whose name was in all the headlines, not one who mooned about with his nose in a book—and an English book at that!

"Before I could protest, I found myself posted to a reconnaissance group, Luftflotte III, based in France, near Lille.

"Our aircraft were the Messerschmitt Bf 110, a twin-engine machine nicknamed the *Zerstörer*."

"The *Destroyer*," said Daffy sourly. There were times when she could be quite snappish.

"Yes," Dieter replied. "The Destroyer. These ones, though, were specially modified for reconnaissance duties. We carried no bombs."

"Spying," Daffy said. Her cheeks were a little flushed, though whether from anger or excitement, I could not tell.

"Yes, spying, if you like," Dieter agreed. "In the war, there was reconnaissance on both sides."

"He's right, you know, Daphne," Father said.

"As I was saying," Dieter went on, with a glance at Daffy, "the *Zerstörer* was a twin-engine machine with a crew of two: a pilot and a second member, who could be a wireless operator, a navigator, or a rear gunner, depending upon the mission.

"My first day on the line, as I walked towards the briefing hut, an *Oberfeldwebel*—a flight sergeant—in flying boots, clicked his heels and called out 'Herr Hauptmann! Heathcliff!' Of course it was my old chum, Wolfgang Zander.

"I looked round quickly to see if anyone had heard him, since such familiarity between ranks would not be tolerated. But no one else was within earshot.

"We shook hands happily. 'I'm your navigator,' Wolfgang said, laughing. 'Did they tell you that? Of all the navigators in the land, my name alone was chosen to be carried aloft to the wars in your tin dragon!'

"Although it was wonderful to see him again, we had to be discreet. It was a complicated situation. We developed a whole set of stratagems—rather like lovers in a Regency romance.

"We would walk to the aircraft, pointing here and there with our fingers and ducking under the fuselage, as if we were discussing the tension of cables, but our talk, of course, was of little but English novels. If anyone came close, we would switch quickly from Hardy to Hitler.

"It was during one of these inspections that the great scheme was born. I don't remember now if it was Wolfgang or I who first came up with the idea.

"We were walking around *Kathi*'s tail—*Kathi* was the thinly disguised name painted on the nose of our aircraft—when suddenly one of us, I think it might have been Wolfgang . . . or it might have been me . . . said, 'Do you suppose the heather is in bloom today on Haworth Moor?'

"It was that simple. In just those few moments, the die, as Julius Caesar remarked, was cast.

"And then, as if she had been listening at the door, Fate again stepped in. Two days later we were given an objective in South Yorkshire: a railway yard and a bicycle factory thought to be producing Rolls-Royce engines.

Photographs only. 'A piece of cake,' as the RAF blokes used to say. A perfect opportunity to deliver, in person, our little gift.

"The flight across the Channel was uneventful, and for once, we were not bounced by Spitfires. The weather was beautiful, and *Kathi*'s engines were purring away like a pair of huge, contented cats.

"We arrived over the target on time—'on the dot,' as you say—and took our photographs. *Snap! Snap! Snap!* and we were finished. Mission accomplished! The next quarter of an hour belonged to us.

"The parsonage at Haworth now lay less than ten miles to the northwest, and at our speed, which was three hundred miles an hour, it was no more than two minutes away.

"The problem was that we were too high. Although we had descended to seventeen thousand feet for the photographs, for our personal mission, we needed to lose more altitude quickly. A Messerschmitt with black crosses on its wings swooping down like a hawk upon a quiet English village would hardly go unnoticed.

"I shoved the control column forward, and down and down we circled in a giant spiral, our ears popping like champagne corks. Beneath us, the heather on the moor was a sea of purple billows.

"At a thousand feet I began to pull out and dropped nearly to hedge level.

" 'Get ready!' I shouted to Wolfgang.

"We came in from the east, and suddenly there it was atop its hill: the village of Haworth! We roared along, skimming the fields, barely clearing the farmhouse chimney pots.

"As we came in over the Haworth road, I caught my first glimpse of the church at the top of the steep high street: then, a hundred yards behind it, beyond the churchyard, the familiar shape of the Brontës' parsonage. It was exactly as I had always imagined it: the dark stained stones and the empty windows.

" 'Now!' I shouted, and Wolfgang shoved our gift out the open port in the canopy and into the slipstream. Although I couldn't see it, I could picture our wreath arcing down through the air, tumbling over and over, its purple ribbon streaming out behind it as it fell. Later, someone would retrieve it from among the old tombstones near the parsonage door, and read the message: gold letters the color of gorse on heather-colored silk, saying *All the World Loves You——Rest in Peace*.

"It was too risky to climb back to cruising altitude. We should have to go home by hedgehopping from point to point, keeping to the open countryside. Of course, we would burn more fuel that way, but both of us were young and foolish, and we had done what we had come to do. As soon as we were spotted, we knew, all the hounds of Hell, the Hurricanes and Spitfires, would be on our tail.

"But it was a perfect August day. With a bit of luck and a tailwind, I was telling Wolfgang, we might even manage to overfly Thomas Hardy's house on the way home at no additional cost to the Reich.

"It was at that precise moment that the canopy in front of my face shattered in a rain of exploding bullets. We were hit!

" 'Spitfire!' Wolfgang shouted. But it was too late. A dark shadow shot past us, then banked and turned, its red, white, and blue roundels flashing like mad eyes in the summer sun.

" 'Watch out,' I yelled. 'He's coming round for another pass!'

"It was then that I noticed that our port engine temperature gauge was pinned to the top. It was overheating. I glanced to the side and, to my horror, saw the black smoke and orange flames that were billowing out from beneath the cowling. I feathered the prop and switched off the engine.

"By now the Spitfire was behind us again. In what was left of my rearview mirror, I could see his fragmented image rocking gently from side to side, riding our slipstream. He had us in his sights.

"But he held his fire. It was most unnerving.

"*Come on*, I thought. *Get it over with*. He was playing with us like a terrier with a rat.

"I don't know how long it went on. You cannot judge time when you are about to die.

" 'Why doesn't he shoot?' I called out to Wolfgang, but there was no answer. With my shoulder harness locked, I could not twist round far enough in my seat to see him.

"But even on one engine, *Kathi* was easily able to stay aloft, and for what seemed like an eternity, that British hound chased the German hare across the green countryside.

"The shattered windscreen had reduced forward visibility to zero, and I had to tack sharply from side to side in order to see what lay ahead. It was a dicey situation.

"And then the other engine died. *Phut!* Just like that! I had only seconds to make a decision. The trees on a wooded hill were rushing by beneath the wings. At the edge of the wood was a sloping field. It was there that I would put her down. No wheels, I thought. Better to make a belly landing and come to a stop more quickly.

"The sound of the crash was louder than I ever could have imagined. The aircraft slewed from side to side as the earth tore at her belly, battering and banging along, lurching, bucking—it was like being thrown alive into a millrace.

"And then the unearthly silence. It took a moment to realize that we were no longer moving. I unbuckled my harness, threw back the front canopy, and jumped out onto the wing, then ran back and peered in at Wolfgang.

" 'Get out!' I shouted. 'Quickly! Get out!'

"But there was no reply.

"Inside the glass canopy, in a sea of blood, Wolfgang sat with a happy smile on his face. His dead eyes were staring out almost feverishly at the green English countryside.

"I jumped down from the wing and vomited into the long grass.

"We had come to rest at the far side of the field. Now, from higher up the hillside, two men, one tall, the other short, had emerged from the trees and were clumping slowly, warily, down towards me. One of them was carrying a shotgun, the other a pitchfork.

"I stood there, not moving. As they drew near, I put one hand in the air, slowly pulled my pistol from its holster and threw it away, making sure they saw what I was doing. Then I put up the other hand.

" 'You're a German,' the tall man called out as they approached.

" 'Yes,' I shouted back. 'But I speak English.'

"He seemed a little taken aback.

" 'Perhaps you should call the police,' I suggested, jerking my head towards the battered Messerschmitt. 'My friend is dead in there.'

"The tall man edged cautiously over to the aircraft and peered inside. The other stood his ground, staring at me as if I had landed from another planet. He drew the pitchfork back, as if he were about to jab me in the stomach.

" 'Let him be, Rupert,' the man with the shotgun said. 'He's just had a bad crash.'

"Before the other man could respond, there was a high-pitched screaming in the sky, and the Spitfire shot past, lifting at the end of the field into a victory roll.

"I watched it climb straight up into the blue air, and then I said:

" *'He rises and begins to round,*

" *'He drops the silver chain of sound.'*

"The two men looked at me as if I had suddenly fallen into shock—and perhaps I had. Not until later would it come crashing home to me that poor Wolfgang was dead.

"George Meredith," I told them. " 'The Lark Ascending.' "

"Later, at the police station in the village, the Spitfire pilot paid me a visit. He was with a squadron based at Catterick, and had taken his machine up to check the controls after the mechanics had made a few adjustments. He had not the slightest intention of getting into a scrap that day, he told me, but there we were, Wolfgang and I, suddenly in his gunsights over Haworth. What else could he do?

" 'Hell of a prang. Bad luck, old chap,' he said. 'Damned sorry about your friend.'

"All of that was six years ago," Dieter said with a sigh. "The tall man in the field with the shotgun, as I was to find out later, was Gordon Ingleby. The other one, the man with the pitchfork, as perhaps you have already guessed, was Rupert Porson."

· EIGHTEEN ·

RUPERT PORSON? BUT HOW could the man with the pitchfork have been Rupert?

My mind was spinning like a painted tin top.

The last place on earth I had ever expected Dieter's tale to end was in Jubilee Field at the Ingleby farm. But one thing now became perfectly clear: If Rupert *had* been at Culverhouse Farm six years ago, during the war, it would explain, at least in part, how the wooden face of his puppet Jack had come to be carved in the image of Robin Ingleby.

Father let out a sigh.

"I remember it well," he said. "Your machine was brought down in Jubilee Field, just below Gibbet Wood."

Dieter nodded. "I was sent for a short time to a prisoner-of-war camp with thirty or forty other Luftwaffe officers and men, where our days were spent ditching and hedging. It was backbreaking work, but at least I was still in England. Most German pilots who were captured were sent abroad to camps in Canada, where there was little hope of escape.

"When I was offered a chance to live and work on a farm, I jumped at it; although it was not compulsory, many of us did. Those who did not called us traitors, among other things.

"But the war was moving towards its end, and a lot of us knew it. Better to begin paving my own personal road to Oxford, I thought, than to leave my future to chance.

"No one was more surprised than I was to find I had been assigned to the Inglebys' farm. It amused me to think that Gordon, who only a short time before had had me at the end of a shotgun, was now helping Grace fry my kippers in the farmhouse kitchen."

"That was six years ago, you say—in 1944?" I asked.

"It was." Dieter nodded. "In September."

I couldn't help it. Before I could stifle the words, I found myself blurting, "Then you must have been at Culverhouse Farm when Robin was found hanging in Gibbet Wood."

"Flavia!" Father said, putting his cup and saucer down with a clatter. "We will have *no* gossiping about the grief of others."

Dieter's face went suddenly grim, and a fire—could it have been anger?—came into his eyes.

"It was I," he said, "who found him."

You who found him? I thought. *Impossible!* Mrs. Mullet had made it perfectly clear that it was Mad Meg who had discovered Robin's body.

There was a remarkably long silence, and then Feely leapt to her feet to refresh Dieter's teacup.

"You must excuse my little sister," she said with a brittle laugh. "She has rather an unhealthy fascination with death."

Full points, Feely, I thought. But although she had hit the nail on the head, she didn't know the half of it.

The rest of the afternoon was pretty much a thud. Father had made what I admit was a noble attempt to switch the conversation to the weather and the flax crops, while Daffy, sensing that little else was worthy of her attention, had crawled back into her book.

One by one, we made our excuses: Father to tend to his stamps, Aunt Felicity to have a nap before supper, and Daffy to the library. After a while, I grew bored with listening to Feely prattle on to Dieter about various balls and outings in the country, and made my escape to the laboratory.

I chewed on the end of my pencil for a while, and then I wrote:

Sunday, 23rd of July, 1950
   WHERE IS EVERYONE? That is the burning question.
   WHERE IS NIALLA? After spending the night at Mrs. Mullet's cottage, she simply disappears. (Does Inspector Hewitt know she's gone?)
   WHERE IS MAD MEG? After erupting at the afternoon performance of Jack and the Beanstalk, *she is taken to rest on the vicar's couch. And then she vanishes.*
   WHERE IS MUTT WILMOTT? He seems to have slunk off sometime during the fatal performance.

WHAT WAS RUPERT DOING AT CULVERHOUSE FARM 6 YEARS AGO? Why, when he and Dieter met at the farm on Friday, did they not admit that they already knew one another?

AND WHY, ABOVE ALL, DOES DIETER CLAIM TO BE THE ONE WHO FOUND ROBIN INGLEBY'S BODY HANGING IN GIBBET WOOD? Mrs. Mullet says it was Mad Meg, and Mrs. M is seldom wrong when it comes to village chin-wagging. *YET WHY WOULD DIETER LIE ABOUT A THING LIKE THAT?*

Where to begin? If this were a chemical experiment, the procedure would be obvious: I would start with those materials most closely to hand.

Mrs. Mullet! With any luck, she would still be puttering in the kitchen before plundering the pantry and carting off her daily booty to Alf. I ran to the top of the stairs and peered through the balustrades. Nobody in the hall.

I slid down the banister and dashed into the kitchen.

Dogger looked up from the table where, with clinical accuracy, he was excising the skin from a couple of cucumbers.

"She's gone," he said, before I could ask. "A good half hour ago."

He's a devil, that Dogger! I don't know how he does it!

"Did she say anything before she left? Anything interesting, that is?"

With Dogger in the kitchen as an audience, Mrs. M would hardly have been able to resist blathering on about how she took Nialla in (poor waif!), tucked her into a cozy bed with a hot-water bottle and a glass of watered-down sherry, and so forth, with a full account of how she slept, what they had for breakfast, and what she left on her plate.

"No." Dogger picked up a serrated bread knife and applied its edge to a loaf of new bread. "Just that the joint is in the warming oven, apple pie and clotted cream in the pantry."

Bugger!

Well, then, there was nothing for it but to make a fresh start in the morning. I'd set my alarm for sunrise, then strike out for Culverhouse Farm and Gibbet Wood beyond. It was unlikely that there would be any clues left after all these years, but Rupert and Nialla had camped at the bottom of Jubilee Field on Friday night. If my plan were properly executed, I could be there and back before anyone at Buckshaw even knew that I was gone.

Dogger tore off a perfect square of waxed paper, and wrapped the cucumber sandwiches with hospital bed corners.

"I thought I'd make these tonight," he said, handing me the package. "I knew you'd want to get away early in the morning."

Curtains of wet mist hung in the fields. The morning air was damp and chill, and I breathed in deeply, trying to come fully awake, filling my nostrils and then my lungs with the rich aroma of dark soil and sodden grass.

As I bicycled into St. Tancred's churchyard, I saw that the Inspector's Vauxhall was gone, and so, I reasoned, was

Rupert's body. Not that they would have left him crumpled on the puppet stage from Saturday evening until Monday morning, but I realized that the corpse would no longer be there inside the parish hall, its eyes bugging, its string of saliva congealed by now into a stalactite of spit. . . .

If I thought it had been, I might have been tempted to barge in for another look.

Behind the church, I removed my shoes and socks and wheeled Gladys through the deeper water beside the submerged stepping-stones. Saturday night's rain had increased the flow of water, which roiled about her spokes and tires, washing clean the accumulated mud and clay from my ride into Bishop's Lacey. By the time I reached the other bank, Gladys's livery was as fresh as a lady's painted carriage.

I gave my feet a final rinse, sat down on a stile, and restored my footwear.

Here, along the river, visibility was even less than it had been on the road. Trees and hedges loomed like pale shadows as I cycled along the grassy verge in a gray, wooly fog that blotted all the sound and color from the world. Except for the muted grumble of the water, all was silence.

At the bottom of Jubilee Field, Rupert's van stood forlorn beneath the willows, its gaily painted sign, "Porson's Puppets," jarringly out of place with both the location and the circumstances. There wasn't a sign of life.

I laid Gladys carefully down in the grass and tiptoed alongside the van. Perhaps Nialla had crept back and was now asleep inside, and I wouldn't want to frighten her. But the lack of condensation on the windscreen told me what I had already begun to feel: that no one was breathing inside the cold Austin.

I peered in at the windows but saw nothing unusual. I went round to the back door and gave the handle a twist. It was locked.

I walked in ever-widening circles through the grass, looking for any trace of a fire, but there was none. The campsite was as I had left it on Saturday.

As I reached the bottom of the farm lane, I was stopped in my tracks by a rope hung across the road, from which a sign was suspended. I ducked underneath to read its message.

Police Investigation——No Admittance by Order—— Hinley Constabulary

Inspector Hewitt and his detectives *had* been here. But in posting their sign, they had obviously not thought of anyone coming across the swollen river. In spite of his promise to the Inspector, Sergeant Graves had still not learned his lesson about people slipping in by way of the back door.

Very well, then. Since there was nothing to see here anyway, I would move on to my next objective. Although I could not see it in the fog, I knew that Gibbet Wood lay not far ahead at the top of Gibbet Hill. It would be wet and soggy in among the trees, but I was willing to bet that the police had not been there before me.

I dragged Gladys under the barricade and pushed her slowly up the lane, which was far too steep to pedal. Halfway to the top, I shoved her behind a hawthorn hedge, and continued my climb, hemmed in on all sides with misty glimpses of blue flax.

Then suddenly the dark trees of the wood loomed out of the mist immediately in front of me. I had come upon it without realizing how close I was.

A weathered wooden sign was nailed to a tree, bearing the red words: KEEP OUT— —TRESP— —

The rest of it had been shot away by poachers.

As I had known it would be, everything in the wood was wet. I gave a shiver at the clammy coldness, steeled myself, and waded into the vegetation. Before I had gone half a dozen steps into the ferns and bracken, I was thoroughly soaked to the knees.

Something snapped in the underbrush. I froze as a dark form swooped on silent wings across my path: an owl, perhaps, mistaking the heavy morning mist for its twilight hunting time. Although it had startled me, its very presence was comforting: It meant that no one else was with me in the wood.

I pushed on, trying to follow the faint paths, any one of which, I knew, would lead me to the clearing at the very center.

Between two ancient, gnarled trees, the way was barred with what seemed to be a mossy gate, its gray wood twisted with rot. I was halfway over the crumbling barrier before I realized that I was once again at the steps of the old gallows. How many doomed souls had climbed these very stairs before being turned off the platform overhead? With a gulp, I looked up at the remnants of the structure, which now was open to the sky.

A leathery hand seized my wrist like a band of hot iron.

"What you up to, then? What you doin' snoopin' round this place?"

It was Mad Meg.

She shoved her sooty face so close to mine I could see the sandy bristles on the end of her chin. *The witch in the wood*, I thought, for one panicky moment, before I regained my senses.

"Oh, hullo, Meg," I said, as calmly as I could, trying to tame my pounding heart. "I'm glad I found you. You gave me quite a fright."

My voice was shakier than I had hoped.

"Frights as lives in Gibbet Wood," Meg said darkly. "Frights as lives here an' not elsewhere."

"Exactly," I agreed, not having the faintest idea what she was on about. "I'm glad you're here with me. Now I shan't be afraid."

"No Devil now," Meg said, rubbing her hands together. "Devil's dead and jolly good."

I remembered how frightened she had been at Rupert's performance of *Jack and the Beanstalk*. To Meg, Rupert was the Devil, who had killed Robin Ingleby, shrunk him to a wooden doll, and put him on the stage. Better to approach this indirectly.

"Did you have a nice rest at the vicarage, Meg?" I asked.

She spat on the trunk of an oak as if she were spitting in a rival witch's eye.

"Her turned me out," she said. "Took old Meg's bracelet and turned her out, so she did. 'Dirty, dirty.' "

"Mrs. Richardson?" I asked. "The vicar's wife? She turned you out?"

Meg grinned a horrid grin and set off through the trees at a near-gallop. I followed at her heels, through underbrush and ferns, deadfall, and the snags of thorns. Five minutes later and breathless, we were back where we had begun, at the foot of the rotted gallows.

"See there," she said, pointing. "That's where 'e took 'im."

"Took who, Meg?"

Robin Ingleby, she meant. I was sure of it.

"The Devil took Robin right here?" I asked.

"Turned 'im into wood, 'e did," she confided, looking over her shoulder. "Wood to wood."

"Did you actually see him? The Devil, I mean."

This was something that hadn't occurred to me before. Was there a chance that Meg had seen someone in the wood with Robin? She lived, after all, in a shack among the trees, and it seemed unlikely that much happened within the bounds of Gibbet Wood that escaped her scrutiny.

"Meg saw," she said knowingly.

"What did he look like?"

"Meg saw. Old Meg sees plenty."

"Can you draw?" I asked, with sudden inspiration. I pulled my notebook from my pocket and handed her a stubby pencil.

"Here," I said, flipping to a blank page, "draw me the Devil. Draw him in Gibbet Wood. Draw the Devil taking Robin."

Meg gave something that I can describe only as a wet snicker. And then she squatted down, flattened the open notebook against her knee, and began to draw.

I think I was expecting something childish—nothing more than scrawled stick figures—but in Meg's sooty fingers, the pencil sprang to life. On the page, the glade in Gibbet Wood slowly appeared: a tree here, a tree there; now the rotted wood of the gallows, instantly recognizable. She had started at the margins and was working in towards the center of the page.

From time to time she clucked over her work, turning the pencil over and erasing a line. She was quite good, I have to give her that. Her sketch was probably better than I might have done myself.

And then she drew Robin.

I scarcely dared breathe as I looked on over her shoulder. Little by little, the dead boy took shape before my eyes.

He was hanging quite peacefully in midair, his neck canted to one side, a look of slightly surprised contentment on his face, as if he had suddenly and unexpectedly walked into a room full of angels. In spite of the subdued light of the wood, his neatly parted hair gave off a healthy, and therefore rather unnerving, shine. He wore a striped sweater and dark britches, their legs tucked carelessly into a pair of rubber boots. He must have died quickly, I thought.

Only then did she draw the noose that cramped his neck: a dark braided thing that dangled from the gallows into the space beneath. She shaded the rope with angry slashes of the pencil.

I breathed in deeply. Meg looked up at me triumphantly, seeking approval.

"And now the Devil," I whispered. "Draw the Devil, Meg."

She looked me straight in the eye, relishing the attention. A canny smile appeared at the corner of her mouth.

"Please, Meg—draw the Devil."

Without taking her eyes from mine, she licked a finger and thumb and turned elaborately to a fresh page. She began again, and as she drew, Gibbet Wood appeared once more at her fingertips. This second sketch grew darker than the first as Meg scrubbed at the pencil marks, smearing them to suggest the half-light of the glade. Then came the gallows, viewed this time from a slightly different angle.

How odd, I thought, *that she didn't begin with the Devil,* as most people would be tempted to do. But only when she had set the stage to her own satisfaction with trees and bushes did she begin to rough in the figure that was to be the focus of her creation.

In an approximate oval that she had left blank upon the page until now, a sketchy figure began to emerge: arms and shoulders first, followed by knees, legs, arms, hands, and feet.

It wore a black jacket, and stood on one leg in the clearing, as if captured in the midst of a frenzied dance.

Its trousers were hung by their suspenders from a low-hanging branch.

Meg shielded the paper with her left hand as she penciled in the features. When she was finished, she thrust it at me roughly, as if the paper were contaminated.

It took me a moment to recognize the face: to recognize that the figure in the glade—the Devil—was the vicar, Denwyn Richardson.

The vicar? It was too ridiculous for words. Or was it?

Just minutes earlier Meg had told me the Devil was dead, and now she was sketching him as the vicar.

What was going on in her poor addled mind?

"Are you quite sure, Meg?" I asked, tapping the notebook. "Is that the Devil?"

"Hsssst!" she said, cocking her head and putting her fingers to my lips. "Someone's comin'!"

I looked round the glade, which, even to my heightened sense of hearing, seemed perfectly silent. When I looked back, my notebook and pencil lay at my feet, and Meg had vanished among the trees. I knew there was little point in calling her back.

I stood there motionless for a few moments, listening, waiting for something, although I'm not sure what it was.

The woodland, I remembered, is an ever-changing world. From minute to minute, the shadows shift, and from hour to hour the vegetation moves with the sun. Insects tunnel in the soil, heaving it up, at first in little hummocks, and then in larger ones. From month to month, leaves grow and fall, and from year to year, the trees. Daffy once said that you can't step into the same river twice, and it's the same with forests. Five winters had come and gone since Robin Ingleby died here, and now there was nothing left to see.

I walked slowly back past the crumbling gallows and plunged into the woods. Within minutes, I was out into the open at the top of Jubilee Field.

Not twenty yards away, almost invisible in the fog, a gray Ferguson tractor was stopped in the field, and someone in a green overall and rubber boots was bending over the engine. That must have been what Meg had heard.

"Hullo!" I shouted. It's always best to announce one's self heartily when trespassing. (Even though I had invented it on the spot, this seemed to be a good general rule.)

As the figure straightened up and turned round, I realized that it was Sally Straw, the Land Army girl.

"Hello," she said, wiping her oily hands on a rag. "You're Flavia de Luce, aren't you?"

"Yes." I stuck out my hand. "And you're Sally. I've seen you at the market. I've always admired your freckles and your ginger hair."

To be most effective, flattery is always best applied with a trowel.

She gave me a broad, honest grin and a handshake that nearly crushed my fingers.

"It's all right to call me Sal," she said. "All my best friends do."

She reminded me somewhat of Joyce Grenfell, the actress: a bit mannish in the way she moved, but otherwise decidedly female.

"My Fergie's gone bust," she said, pointing to the tractor. "Might be the ignition coil. They do that sometimes, you know: get overheated and go open circuit. Then there's nothing for it but to wait for the ruddy thing to cool."

Since motors were not my forte, I nodded wisely and kept my mouth shut.

"What are you doing away out here?"

"Just rambling," I said. "I like to get away, sometimes. Go for a walk—that sort of thing."

"Lucky you," she said. "I never get away. Well, hardly ever. Dieter's taken me for a pint of half-and-half at the Thirteen Drakes a couple of times, but then there was a most god-awful flap about it. The POWs are not allowed to do that, you know. At least they weren't during the war."

"Dieter told me your sister Ophelia had him to tea yesterday," she added, somewhat cagily. I realized at once that she was fishing.

"Yes," I said, kicking carelessly at a clod of dirt, gazing off into the distance, and pretending I wasn't remotely interested. Friend or not, if she wanted gossip from me, it would have to be tit for tat.

"I saw you at the puppet show," I said. "At the church, on Saturday night. Wasn't that a corker? About Mr. Porson, I mean?"

"It was horrid," she said.

"Did you know him?"

It probably wasn't a fair question, and I fired it at her without warning: straight out of the blue.

Sally's expression became instantly guarded, and she hesitated a bit too long before answering.

"I—I've seen him around." Her lie was obvious.

"On the telly, perhaps?" I asked, perhaps too innocently. "*The Magic Kingdom*? Snoddy the Squirrel?"

I knew as soon as I said it that I'd pushed things too far.

"All right," she said, "what are you up to? Come on—out with it."

She planted her hands on her hips and fixed me with an unwavering stare.

"I don't know what you mean," I said.

"Oh, come off it. Don't give me that. Everyone for fifty miles around knows that Flavia de Luce doesn't go walking in the woods just to put roses in her cheeks."

Could that be true? Fifty miles? Her answer rather surprised me: I should have thought a hundred.

"Gordon'd have your hide if he caught you in that wood," she said, pointing to the sign.

I put on my best sheepish look, but kept quiet.

"How much do you know about all this?" Sally demanded, sweeping her hand round in a large half-circle to take in the farm. Her meaning was clear.

I took a deep breath. I had to trust her.

"I know that Rupert has been coming here to get cannabis for quite a long time. I know that Gordon grows it in a patch in Gibbet Wood—not far from where Robin was found hanging."

"And you think that Dieter and I are somehow mixed up in all this?"

"I don't know," I replied. "I hope not."

"So do I," Sally said. "So do I."

· N I N E T E E N ·

"RUPERT WAS—A LADIES' man," Sally said slowly, as if reluctant to put her thoughts into words, "but then, you've probably found that out by now."

I nodded, careful not to interrupt. I had learned by observing Inspector Hewitt that silence is the best primer for a conversational pump.

"He's been coming to Culverhouse Farm off and on, for years—since well before the war. And Rupert's not the only one, you know. Gordon has a regular little army of others just like him. He supplies them with something to help manage the pain."

"Bhang," I said. I couldn't help myself. "Gunjah . . . Indian hemp, cannabis."

She looked at me with narrowed eyes, and then went on. "Some, like Rupert, come because they once had infantile paralysis—polio, they call it now—others, well, God only knows.

"You see, Gordon considers himself a kind of herbalist: someone who helps to blot out the sufferings that the doctors can't, or won't. He's very discreet about it, but then he has to be, doesn't he? Other than you, I really don't think anyone in Bishop's Lacey has ever guessed that the occasional travelers who stop by Culverhouse Farm are anything other than lost—or perhaps selling agricultural supplies.

"I've been here for eight years," Sally went on. "And don't even bother asking me: The answer is no—I'm not one of Gordon's smokers."

"I didn't expect you were," I said, fawning a little. It worked.

"I grew up in a good home," she went on, a little more eagerly. "My parents were what they used to call, in the old double-decker novels, 'poor but honest.' My mam was sick all the time, but she never would tell us what was wrong with her. Even my father didn't know. Meanwhile, I plodded on at school, got myself a bit of an education, and then the war came.

"Of course, I wanted to help out a bit with the medical bills, so I joined the WLA. Sounds simple, doesn't it? And so it was—there was no more to it than that. I was just a girl from Kent who wanted to fight Adolf Hitler, and see her mother well again.

"I was billeted, along with about forty other girls, at a Land Army hostel between here and Hinley, and that was where I first laid eyes on Rupert. Like a bee to honey that man was, make no mistake about it. He was rambling hither and yon about the countryside every summer with his little puppet show—getting back to his roots, he called it—and whenever I saw him, he seemed to have a new assistant. And she was always a bit of a knockout, if you get my meaning."

"Not long after I came to work at Culverhouse Farm, Rupert showed up for a fresh supply of smoking material. I recognized him at once as the little lame chap who was always chatting us up at the hostel, or the pub, of a weekend.

"I swore from the outset that I wouldn't get involved with him myself; I'd leave it to the other girls to take him down a notch or two. But then—"

Her gaze drifted off into another time.

So Nialla had been right! Rupert *had* gone off in search of Sally on the day they arrived. The pieces were beginning to fall into place.

Although the fog had now thinned a little, it was still quite dense, wrapping Sally and me in a misty cocoon of oddly reassuring silence. Unless they had come across us by accident, no one would know we were up here at the top of Jubilee Field. No one could have overheard us unless they had come up the length of the field from the bottom, or crept stealthily down from the wood above.

"Oh, Rupert was a charmer, make no mistake about that," Sally went on. "He could charm the—no, I mustn't say that in polite company, must I? He could charm the chickens out of the trees—and especially the hens.

"He'd start with Shakespeare, and then move on to things he'd heard in music halls. If *Romeo and Juliet* didn't do the job, he'd try his naughty recitations.

"And he got away with it, too—at least, mostly he did. Until he tried it on with Gordon's wife."

Grace Ingleby? I let out an involuntary whistle.

"That must have been quite a long time ago," I said. I knew that it sounded callous, although I didn't mean it that way.

"Years ago," Sally said. "Before Robin died. Before she went all strange. Although you wouldn't think it to look at her now, she used to be quite a stunner."

"She seems very sad," I said.

"Sad? Sad's not the word for it, Flavia. Broken is more like it. That little boy was her whole world, and the day he died, the sun went out."

"You were here then?" I asked gently. "It must have been very difficult for you."

She went on as if she hadn't heard me. "Gordon and Grace had told Robin more than once about their idyllic honeymoon by the sea, and it was something he'd always wanted to do: the sand, the seashells, the pail, the shovel, the sandcastles, the ices, the bathing machines.

"He used to dream about it. 'I dreamed the tide was coming in, Sally!' he told me once, 'and I was bobbing on the sea like a pink balloon!' Poor little tyke."

She wiped away a tear with the rough sleeve of her overall. "God! Why am I telling you all this? I must be daft."

"It's all right," I said. "I promise I won't breathe a word. I'm very good at keeping things to myself."

As a token of goodwill, I went through the motions of cross-my-heart-and-hope-to-die, but without actually saying the words.

After a quick and oddly shy glance at me, Sally went on with her story:

"Somehow they'd managed to put a bit aside for Robin's birthday. Because the harvest was so near, Gordon couldn't get away, but they agreed that Grace would take Robin to the seaside for a few days. It was the first time the two of them, mother and son, had ever been anywhere together without Gordon, and the first time Grace had taken a holiday since she was a girl.

"The weather was hot, even for late August. Grace hired a beach chair and bought a magazine. She watched Robin with his little pail, mudlarking along the water's edge. He was quite safe, she knew. She had warned him about the danger of the tides, and Robin was a most obedient little boy.

"She drifted off to sleep and slept for ages. She hadn't realized how utterly exhausted she was until she awoke and saw how far the sun had moved. The tide had gone out, and Robin was nowhere in sight. Had he disobeyed her warnings and been swept out to sea? Surely someone would have seen him. Surely someone would have wakened her."

"Did Grace tell you this?" I asked.

"Good God, no! It all came out at the inquest. They had to pry it out of her in tiny, broken pieces. Her nerves were something shocking.

"She'd wasted too much time, she said, running up and down the beach, calling out Robin's name. She ran along the edge of the water, hoping for a glimpse of his little red bathing suit; hoping to see his face among the children who were dabbling near the shore.

"Then up and down the beach again, begging the bathers to tell her if they'd seen a little boy with blond hair. It was hopeless, of course. There might have been dozens of children on the beach who answered to that description.

"And then, through sun-dazzled eyes, she saw it: a crowd gathered in the shade beneath the promenade. She burst into tears and began walking towards them, knowing what she would find: Robin had drowned, and the knot of people had gathered round to gawk. She had already begun to hate them.

"But as she drew closer, a wave of laughter went up, and she shoved her way through to the center of the crowd, not caring what they thought.

"It was a Punch and Judy show. And there, seated on the sand, tears of laughter running down his face, was her Robin. She grabbed him up and hugged him, not trusting herself to say a word. After all, it had been her fault: She had fallen asleep, and Robin had been attracted to the Punch and Judy pitch as any child would be.

"She carried him along the beach and bought him an ice, and another. Then she ran back with him to the little booth, to watch the next performance, and she joined in when he roared with laughter, and she shouted out with him 'No! No!' when Punch grabbed the policeman's stick to beat Judy on the head.

"They laughed with the rest of the crowd when Punch tricked Jack Ketch, the hangman, into sticking his own head into the noose, and—"

I had seen the traditional Punch and Judy shows nearly every year at the church fête, and I was all too familiar with the plot.

" *'I don't know how to be hanged,'* " I said, quoting Punch's famous words. " *'You'll have to show me, then I shall do it directly.'* "

" 'I don't know how to be hanged,' " Sally echoed, " 'You'll have to show me.' That's what Grace told the jury later, when an inquest was called into Robin's death, and those were likely her last sane words.

"Worse than that was the fact that, at the inquest, she spoke those words in that awful, strangled, quacking voice that the puppet show men use for Punch: *'I don't know how to be hanged. You'll have to show me.'*

"It was ghastly. The coroner called for a glass of water, and someone on the jury lost their nerve and laughed. Grace broke down completely. The doctor insisted that she be excused from further questioning.

"The rest of what happened that awful day at the beach, and later at the farm, had to be pieced together; each of us knew a little. I had seen Robin dragging about a length of rope he'd found in the machine shed. Later, Gordon had seen him playing cowboy at the edge of Jubilee Field. It was Dieter who found him hanging in Gibbet Wood."

"Dieter? I thought it was Mad Meg." It slipped out before I could stop myself.

Sally looked instantly away, and I realized that it was one of those times when I needed to keep my mouth shut and wait things out.

Suddenly she seemed to come to a decision. "You must remember," she said, "that we were only just out of the war. If it was known in Bishop's Lacey that Robin's body had been found hanging in the wood by a German prisoner of war, well . . . just think."

"It might have been like that scene from *Frankenstein*: furious villagers with torches, and so forth."

"Exactly," she said. "Besides, the police believed that Meg actually *had* been there before Dieter, but that she hadn't told anyone."

"How do you know that?" I asked. "What the police believed, I mean?"

Without realizing what she was doing, Sally was suddenly fluffing up her hair.

"There was a certain young police constable," she said, "whose name I am not at liberty to mention, who used to take me, of an evening, to watch the moon rise over Goodger Hill."

"I see," I said, and I did. "They didn't want Meg to be called up at the inquest."

"Funny, isn't it," she said, "how the law can have a soft spot like that? No, someone had seen her in the village at the time Robin went missing, so she wasn't really a suspect. It was decided that because of her . . . because she was . . . well, not to put too fine a point on it, that Meg was best left out of things entirely, and that's how it was done."

"So it *was* Dieter who found the body then."

"Yes. He told me about it that same evening. He was still in shock—hardly making sense: all about how he had come racing down from Gibbet Wood, yelling himself hoarse . . . leaping fences, sliding in the mud . . . running into the yard, looking up at the empty windows. Like dead eyes, they were, he kept saying, like the windows of the Brontës' parsonage. But as I said, poor Dieter was in shock. He didn't know what he was saying."

I felt a vague stirring in my stomach, but I put it down to Mrs. Mullet's Jenny Lind cake. "And where was Rupert all this time?"

"Strange you should ask. Nobody seems to remember. Rupert came and went, often at night. As time passed, he seemed to become more and more addicted to the stuff Gordon was providing him, and his visits became more frequent. If he wasn't here when Robin died, he wasn't far away."

"I'll bet the police were all over the place."

"Of course they were! At the outset, they didn't know if it was an accident, or if Robin had been murdered."

"Murdered?" The thought had never crossed my mind. "Who on earth would murder a little boy?"

"It's been done before," Sally answered sadly. "Children have always been murdered for no good reason."

"And Robin?"

"In the end, they decided there was no evidence to support that idea. Aside from Gordon and Dieter and me—and Mad Meg, of course—no one else had been in Gibbet Wood. Robin's footprints leading up Jubilee Field and round the old scaffold made it quite clear that he had gone there alone."

"And acted out the scaffold scene from Punch and Judy," I said. "Pretending he was first Punch—and then the hangman."

"Yes. That's what they thought."

"Still," I said, "the police must have had a jolly good look round the wood."

"Almost uprooted it," she said. "Measuring tapes, plaster casts, photographs, little bags of this and that."

"Isn't it odd," I said, "that they didn't spot the patch of cannabis? It's hard to believe Inspector Hewitt would have missed it."

"This must have been before his time," Sally said. "If my memory serves me rightly, it was an Inspector Gully who was in charge of the investigation."

Aha! So *that* was who decided to keep mum about Meg. In spite of his lack of vigilance, the man must have had at least a rudimentary heart.

"And what was the outcome?" I asked. "Of the inquest, I mean."

I knew that I could look it up later, in the newspaper archive at the library, but for now I wanted to hear it in Sally's own words. She had, after all, been on the spot.

"The coroner told the jury it must reach one of three verdicts: death by unlawful killing, death by misadventure, or an open verdict."

"And?"

"They settled on 'death by misadventure,' although they had the very dickens of a time reaching an agreement."

Suddenly, I realized that the fog was lifting, and so did Sally. Although a light mist still capped the trees in the wood above us, the river and the full sloping length of Jubilee Field, looking like a hand-tinted aerial photograph, were now laid out below us in weak sunlight.

We would be clearly visible from the farmhouse.

Without another word, Sally clambered up onto the tractor's seat and engaged the starter. The engine caught at once, roared briefly, then settled into a steady ticking hum.

"I've said too much," she told me. "I don't know what I was thinking. Mind you keep your promise, Flavia. I'm going to hold you to it."

Her eyes met mine, and I saw in them a kind of pleading.

"I could get into a lot of trouble, you know," she said.

I bobbed my head but didn't actually say yes. With any luck, I could wedge in one last question.

"What do *you* think happened to Robin and to Rupert?"

With a toss of her head, Sally clenched her jaw, let in the clutch, and lurched away across the field, clods of black mud flying up from the tractor's tires before falling back to the ground like shot birds.

· TWENTY ·

I RETRIEVED GLADYS FROM behind the hedge where I had left her, removed the cucumber sandwiches from her carrier, and sat on a grassy bank to eat and think about the dead.

I pulled the notebook from my pocket and flipped it open to Meg's drawing: There was Robin, hanging by the neck from the gnarled timbers of the old scaffold. The expression on his face was that of a child sleeping peacefully, a slight smile at the corner of his lips.

Something in my mind went *click!* and I knew that I could put it off no longer: I would have to pay a visit to the village library—or at least the Pit Shed, the outbuilding where the back issues of newspapers were stored.

The Pit Shed was a long-defunct motorcar repair shop, which stood, surrounded by weeds, in Cow Lane, a short and rather neglected pathway that ran from Bishop Lacey's high street down to the river. The sudden recollection of my recent captivity in that moldering mausoleum gave me goose bumps.

Part of me (my quieter voice) was saying, *Give it up. Don't meddle. Go home and be with your family.* But another part was more insistent: *The library isn't open until Thursday,* it seemed to whisper. *No one will see you.*

"But the lock," I said aloud. "The place is locked."

Since when did a locked door ever stop you? replied the voice.

The Pit Shed, as I have said, was easily reached from the riverbank. I re-crossed the water on the stepping-stones behind the church (still no sign of police cars) and followed the old towpath, which took me quickly, and with little risk of being seen, to Cow Lane.

There was no one in sight as I tried to walk nonchalantly up the path to the entrance.

I gave the door a shake, but as I had expected, it was locked. A new lock, in fact—one of the Yale design—had recently been fitted, and a hand-lettered sign placed in the window. *Positively no admittance unless accompanied by the Librarian* it said. Both the sign and the lock, I thought, had likely been put in place because of my recent escapades.

Although Dogger had given me several tutorials on the art of lock picking, the intricacies of the Yale required special tools that I did not have with me.

The door's hinges were on the inside, so there wasn't a chance of removing the pins. Even if that had been possible, it would have been foolhardy to attempt such a thing in full view of anyone passing in the high street at the end of the lane.

Round the back I went. In the long grass, directly beneath a window, lay a monster piece of rusty scrap metal, which looked as if it might have seen better days as a motor in a Daimler. I climbed on top of the things and peered in through the dirt-fogged glass.

The newspapers lay stacked in their wooden bunks as they had done for eons, and the interior had been cleared of the wreckage caused by my last visit.

As I stood on tiptoe, my foot slipped, and I nearly pitched headfirst through the windowpane. As I clutched at the sill to steady myself, something crumbled beneath my fingertips and a river of tiny grains trickled to the ground.

Wood rot, I thought. *But wait! Hang on a minute—wood rot isn't gray. This is rotten putty!*

I jumped down and within seconds was back at the window with an open-end wrench from Gladys's tool kit in my hand. As I picked away at the edges of the glass, hard wedges of putty broke off with surprisingly little effort. It was almost too easy.

When I had chipped my way round the pane, I pressed my mouth hard against the glass, and sucked for all I was worth to create a vacuum. Then I pulled my head slowly back.

Success! As the pane came free of its frame and leaned out towards me, I grasped the glass by its rough edges and lifted it carefully to the ground. In less time than it takes to tell, I had wiggled through the frame and dropped to the floor inside.

Although the broken glass from my earlier rescue had been cleared away, the place still gave me the shivers. I wasted no time in finding the issues of *The Hinley Chronicle* for the latter part of 1945.

Although Robin's exact dates hadn't been carved on his headstone, Sally's story indicated that he had died sometime after the harvest in that year. *The Hinley Chronicle* had been—and still was—published weekly, on Fridays. Consequently, there were only a couple of dozen issues covering the time between the end of June and the end of the year. I knew, though, that I would most likely find the story in an earlier issue than a later one. And so it was: Friday, 7 September, 1945.

> *An inquest will be held today at Almoner's Hall in Bishop's Lacey into the death of Robin Ingleby, five years of age, whose body was found on Monday in Gibbet Wood, near that village. Inspector Josiah Gully of the Hinley constabulary has declined comment at this time, but strongly urges any member of the public who may have information about the child's death to contact police authorities immediately at Hinley 5272.*

Directly below this was printed the notice:

> *Patrons are informed that the post office and confectionery located in the high street, Bishop's Lacey, will close today (Friday, 7th inst.) at noon. Both will be open as usual on Saturday morning. Your patronage is appreciated. Letitia Cool, Proprietress.*

Miss Cool was the postmistress and purveyor of sweets to the village, and there was only one reason I could think of that she would have closed her shop on a Friday.

I turned eagerly to the following week: the issue of 14 September.

> An inquest convened to inquire into the death of Robin Ingleby, aged five years, of Culverhouse Farm, near Bishop's Lacey was adjourned Friday last at 3:15 P.M. after forty minutes of deliberation. The coroner recorded a verdict of Death by Misadventure, and expressed his sympathy to the bereaved parents.

And that was all. It seemed obvious that the village wanted to spare Robin's parents the grief of seeing the horrid details in print.

A quick look through the remaining papers turned up nothing more than a brief notice of the funeral, at which the pallbearers had been Gordon Ingleby, Bartram Tennyson (Robin's grandfather, who had come down from London), Dieter Schrantz, and Clarence Mundy, the taxi-cab proprietor. Rupert's name was not mentioned.

I replaced the newspapers in their cradle and, with no more damage to myself than a scuffed knee, shoehorned myself back out of the window.

Curses! It was beginning to rain. A black-bottomed cloud had drifted across the sun, bringing a sudden chill to the air.

I ran across the weeded lot to the river, where fat raindrops were already pocking the water with perfectly formed little craters. I scrambled down the slope and, with my bare hands, scooped out a gob of the sticky clay that formed the bank.

Then back to the Pit Shed again, where I dumped the muck in a mound on the windowsill. Taking care not to get any of it on my clothing, I rolled handfuls of the stuff between my palms, making a family of long stringy gray snakes. Then, clambering up onto the rusty motor once again, I seized the edges of the windowpane, and hoisted it gingerly back into position. With my forefinger as a makeshift putty knife, I pressed the stuff all round the edges of the glass into what looked, at least, like a tight and sturdy seal.

How long it would last was anybody's guess. If the rain didn't wash it away, it might well last forever. Not that it would need to: At the first opportunity, I thought, I would replace it by pinching some bona fide putty and the proper knife from Buckshaw, where Dogger was forever using the stuff to shore up loose panes in the decaying greenhouse.

"*The Mad Putty-Knifer has struck again!*" the villagers would whisper.

After a quick dash to the river to scrub the caked clay from my hands, I was, aside from being soaked through, almost presentable.

I picked up Gladys from the grass and strolled in a carefree manner up Cow Lane to the high street, as if butter wouldn't melt in my mouth.

Miss Cool's confectionery, which incorporated the village post office, was a narrow Georgian relic, hemmed in by a tearoom and an undertaker's establishment to the east and a fish shop to the west. Its flyblown display windows were sparsely strewn with faded chocolate boxes, their lids picturing plump ladies in striped stockings and feathers who grinned brazenly as they sat half astride cumbersome three-wheeled tricycles.

This was where Ned had bought the chocolates he had left on our doorstep. I was sure of it, for there on the right was the dark rectangular mark where the box had reposed since horse-drawn charabancs had rumbled past it in the high street.

For a fleeting instant I wondered if Feely had sampled my handiwork yet, but I banished the thought at once. Such pleasures would have to wait.

The bell over the door tinkled to announce my entrance, and Miss Cool looked up from behind the post office counter.

"Flavia, dear!" she said. "What a pleasant surprise. Why, you're all wet! I was just thinking about you not ten minutes ago, and here you are. Actually, it was your father I was thinking of, but it's all the same, isn't it? I've a strip of stamps here that might interest him: four Georges with an extra perforation clean through his face. Hardly seems right, does it? Quite disrespectful. Miss Reynolds over at Glebe House bought them last Friday and returned them on Saturday.

" 'Too many holes in them!' she said. 'I won't have my letters to Hannah—' (that's her niece in Shropshire, dear)—'being seized for infringement of the Postal Act.' "

She handed me a glassine envelope.

"Thank you, Miss Cool," I said. "I'm sure Father will

appreciate having these in his collection, and I know he'd want me to thank you for your thoughtfulness."

"You're such a good girl, Flavia," she said, blushing. "He must be very proud of you."

"Yes," I said, "he is. Very."

Actually, it was a thought that had never crossed my mind.

"You really mustn't stand around like that in wet clothing, dear. Go into my little room in the back and take off your things. I'll hang them in the kitchen to dry. You'll find a quilt at the bottom of my bed—wrap yourself up in it and we shall have a nice cozy chat."

Five minutes later, we were back in the shop, me like a blanketed Blackfoot and Miss Cool, with her tiny spectacles looking for all the world like the Factor at a Hudson's Bay trading post.

She was already moving across the shop towards the tall jar of horehound sticks.

"How many would you like today, my dear?"

"None, thank you, Miss Cool. I left home in rather a rush this morning and came away without my purse."

"Take one anyway," she said, holding out the jar. "I think I shall have one, too. Horehound sticks are meant to be shared with friends, don't you think?"

She was dead wrong about that: Horehound sticks were meant to be gobbled down in solitary gluttony, and preferably in a locked room, but I didn't dare say so. I was too busy setting my trap.

For a few minutes we sat in companionable silence, sucking on our sweets. Gray, watery light from the window seeped into the shop, illuminating from within the rows of glass sweet jars, lending them a pallid and unhealthy glow. *We must look*, I thought, *for all the world like a couple of alchemists plotting our next attack upon the elements.*

"Did Robin Ingleby like horehound sticks, Miss Cool?"

"Why, what a strange question! Whatever made you think of that?"

"Oh, I don't know," I said carelessly, running my finger along the edge of a glass display case. "I suppose it was seeing poor Robin's face on that puppet at the church hall. It was such a shock. I haven't been able to get him out of my mind."

This was true enough.

"Oh, you poor thing!" she said. "I'm sure none of us can, but no one wanted to mention it. It was almost . . . what's the word? *Obscene.* And that poor man! What a tragedy. I couldn't sleep a wink after what happened. But then, I expect it gave all of us quite a turn, didn't it?"

"You were on the jury at Robin's inquest, weren't you?"

I was becoming rather good at this. The air went out of her sails in an instant.

"Why . . . why, yes, so I was. But how on earth could you know that?"

"I think Father might have mentioned it at some time or another. He has a great deal of respect for you, Miss Cool. But surely you know that."

"A respect that is entirely mutual, I assure you," she said. "Yes, I was a member of the jury. Why do you ask?"

"Well, to be honest, my sister Ophelia and I were having an argument about it. She said that at one time, it was thought that Robin had been murdered. I disagreed. It was an accident, wasn't it?"

"I'm not sure that I'm allowed to discuss it, dear," she said. "But it was years ago, wasn't it? I think I can tell you—just among friends, mind—that the police did consider that possibility. But there was nothing in it. Not a shred of evidence. The little boy went up to the wood alone and hanged himself alone. It was an accident. We said so in our verdict—Death by Misadventure, they called it."

"But how did you know he was alone? You must be awfully clever to figure that out!"

"Why, because of his footprints, love! Because of his footprints! There were no others anywhere near that old scaffold. He went up to the wood alone."

My gaze shifted to the shop window. The downpour had begun to slacken.

"Had it rained?" I asked with sudden inspiration. "Before they found him?"

"It had, in fact," she answered. "In great bloomin' buckets."

"Ah," I said, noncommittally. "Has a Mr. Mutt Wilmott been in to pick up his mail? It would probably be poste restante."

I knew at once that I had gone too far.

"I'm sorry, dear," Miss Cool said, with a barely detectable sniff. "We are not permitted to give out information like that."

"He's a BBC producer," I said, putting on my best slightly crushed look. "Quite a famous one, actually. He's in charge of—at least he used to be—poor Mr. Porson's television program, *The Magic Kingdom*. I was hoping to get his autograph."

"If he comes in, I'll tell him you were asking," Miss Cool said, softening. "I don't believe I've had the pleasure of meeting the gentleman yet."

"Oh, thank you, Miss Cool," I babbled. "I'm frightfully keen on adding a few BBC personalities to my little collection."

Sometimes I hated myself. But not for long.

"Well, it looks as if the rain has stopped," I said. "I must really be getting along. I expect my clothes are dry enough to get me home, and I wouldn't want Father to be worried. He has so much on his mind nowadays."

I was well aware that everyone in Bishop's Lacey knew about Father's financial difficulties. Late-paid bills in a village were as good as a signal rocket in the night. I might as well chalk up a few points for deportment.

"Such a thoughtful child, you are, Flavia," she said. "Have another horehound."

Minutes later, I was dressed and at the door. Outside, the sun had come out, and a perfect rainbow arched across the sky.

"Thank you for a lovely chat, Miss Cool, and for the horehound. It will be my treat next time—I insist."

"Ride home safely, dear," she told me. "Mind the puddles. And keep it under your hat—about the stamps, I mean. We're not supposed to let the defectives circulate."

I gave her a ghastly conspiratorial wink and a twiddle of the fingers.

She hadn't answered my question about whether Robin was fond of horehound sticks, but then it didn't really matter, did it?

· T W E N T Y · O N E ·

I GAVE GLADYS A jolly good shaking, and raindrops went flying off her frame like water from a shaggy dog. I was about to shove off for home when something in the window of the undertaker's shop caught my eye: no more than a slight movement, really.

Although it had been in business at the same location since the time of George the Third, the shop of Sowbell & Sons stood as discreet and aloof in the high street as if it were waiting for an omnibus. It was quite unusual, actually, to see anyone enter or leave the place.

I sauntered a little closer for a look, feigning a great interest in the black-edged obituary cards that were on display in the plate-glass window. Although none of the dead (*Dennison Chatfield, Arthur Bronson-Willowes, Margaret Beatrice Peddle*) were people whose names I recognized, I pored over their names intently, giving each one a rueful shake of my head.

By moving my eyes from left to right, as if I were reading the small print on the cards, and yet shifting my focus through to the shop's dim interior, I could see someone inside waving his hands as he talked. His yellow silk shirt and mauve cravat were what had caught my eye: It was Mutt Wilmott!

Before reason could apply the brakes, I had burst into the shop.

"Oh, hello, Mr. Sowbell," I said. "I hope I'm not interrupting anything. I just wanted to stop by and let you know that our little chemical experiment worked out quite admirably in the end."

I'm afraid this was varnishing the facts a little. The truth was that I had buttonholed him in St. Tancred's churchyard one Sunday after Morning Prayer, to ask his professional opinion—as an expert in preservatives, as it were—about whether a reliable embalming fluid could be inexpensively obtained by collecting, macerating, boiling, and distilling the formic acid from large numbers of red ants (*formica rufa*).

He had fingered his long jaw, scratched his head, and stared up into the branches of the yew trees for quite some time before saying he'd never really thought about it.

"It's something I'd have to look up, Miss Flavia," he said.

But I knew he would never actually do so, and I was right. The older craftsmen can be awfully tight-lipped when it comes to discussing the tricks of the trade.

He was standing now in the shadows near a dark-paneled door that led to some undoubtedly grisly back room: a room I'd give a guinea to see.

"Flavia." He nodded—somewhat warily, I thought.

"I'm afraid you'll have to excuse us," he said. "We're in the midst of rather a—"

"Well, well," Mutt Wilmott interrupted, "I do believe it's Rupert's ubiquitous young protégée, Miss . . ."

"De Luce," I said.

"Yes, of course—de Luce." He smiled condescendingly, as if he'd known it all along; as if he were only teasing.

I have to admit that, like Rupert, the man had an absolutely marvelous professional speaking voice: a rich, mellifluous flow of words that came forth as if he had a wooden organ pipe for a larynx. The BBC must breed these people on a secret farm.

"As one of Rupert's young protégées, so to speak," Mutt went on, "you'll perhaps be comforted to learn that Auntie—as we insiders call the British Broadcasting Corporation—is laying on the sort of funeral that one of her brightest stars deserves. Not quite Westminster Abbey, you understand, but the next best thing. Once Mr. Sowbell here, gets the . . . ah . . . remains back to London, the public grieving can begin: the lying in state, the floral tributes, the ruddy-faced mother of ten from Weston-super-Mare, kneeling at the bier alongside her tear-drenched children, and all with the television cameras looking on. No less a personage than the Director General himself has suggested that it might be a poignant touch to have Snoddy the Squirrel stand vigil at the foot of the coffin, mounted upon an empty glove."

"He's here?" I asked, with a gesture towards the back room. "Rupert's still here?"

"He's in good hands." Mutt Wilmott nodded, and Mr. Sowbell, with a smirk, made a humble little bow of acknowledgment.

I have never wanted anything more in my life than I wanted at that moment to ask if I could have a look at the corpse, but for once, my normally nimble mind failed me. I could not think of a single plausible reason for having a squint at Rupert's remains—as Mutt Wilmott had called them—nor could I think of an implausible one.

"How's Nialla taking it?" I asked, making a wild stab in the dark.

Mutt frowned.

"Nialla? She's taken herself off somewhere," he said. "No one seems to know where."

"Perhaps she took a room at the Thirteen Drakes," I suggested. "She might have needed a hot bath."

I was hoping Mutt would take the bait, and he did.

"She's not at the Thirteen Drakes," he replied. "I've been bivouacked there myself since I first arrived."

So! As I had suspected, Mutt Wilmott *had* been within walking distance of St. Tancred's, before, during, and perhaps after Rupert was murdered.

"Well," I said, "sorry to have bothered you."

They had their heads together before I was out the door.

As they so often do in summer, the skies had quickly cleared. The dark overcast had moved off to the east and the birds were singing like billy-oh. Although it was still quite early in the day, and in spite of the fresh air and the warm sunshine, I found myself yawning like a cat as I rode along the lanes towards Buckshaw. Perhaps it was because I had been up before dawn; perhaps because I had been up too late the night before.

Whatever the case, I was suddenly quite fagged out. Daffy had once remarked that Samuel Pepys, the diarist, was forever climbing into bed, and Father was always going on about the remarkable restorative power of a brief nap. For once, I understood how they felt.

But how to get into the house unseen? Mrs. Mullet guarded the kitchen like a Foo Dog at the tomb of a Chinese emperor, yet if I used the front door, I ran the risk of being set upon by Aunt Felicity and assigned unwelcome duties for whatever remained of the day.

The coach house was the only place where one could easily come and go without being seen or disturbed.

I parked Gladys behind one of the great chestnut trees that lined the drive, and made my way stealthily round the side of the house.

A door in the far side of the coach house opened into what had once been a small paddock. I scaled the fence, lifted the wrought-iron latch, and slipped noiselessly inside.

Although my eyes were somewhat dazzled from the light outside, I could still make out the dark, looming form of Harriet's vintage Rolls-Royce, a Phantom II, its nickel radiator gleaming dully in the gloom. No more than a diffused and feeble light managed to find its way in through the small, dusty windows, and I knew I would have to watch my step.

Sometimes I came here to brood. I would climb aboard this palace on wheels, and in its comforting interior, I would sit in creamy leather, pretending I was Harriet, just about to engage the gears and drive off to a better life.

I took hold of the door handle and turned it quietly. If Dogger was nearby, I knew he'd be alerted by the slightest sound, and would come running to see who was burgling the coach house. *God bless the good ship Rolls-Royce, and all who sail in her,* I thought as the heavy door swung open in utter silence, and I hauled myself up into the driver's seat.

I inhaled the plush motorcar scent, as Harriet must once have done, and prepared to curl myself up into a ball. With any luck, and the near-darkness, I'd be asleep in less than a minute. There would be time enough later to think about murder.

As I stretched luxuriously, my fingers touched something: the skin of a human leg, by the feel of it. Before I could let out a scream, someone clapped a hand tightly over my mouth.

"Keep still!" a voice hissed into my ear.

My eyes rolled like a horse's in a slaughterhouse. Even in that dim light I could see the face of the person who was stifling me.

It was Nialla.

My first inclination was to bite off one of her fingers: I have a phobia about being physically restrained, and there are times when my reflexes are faster than reason.

"Don't make a sound!" she whispered, giving me a little shake. "I need your help."

Damn! She had given the female password—spoken

those magic words that stretched back through the mists of time to a bond made in some primordial swamp. I was in her power. I went instantly limp and nodded my head. She removed her hand.

"Are the police looking for me?" she asked.

"I—I don't think so. I don't know," I said. "I'm not exactly one of their confidantes."

I was still a little miffed at being seized and shaken.

"Oh, come off it, Flavia," she said. "Don't go all shirty on me. I need to know. Are they looking for me?"

"I haven't seen the police since Saturday night, right after Rupert was—after Rupert—"

Although I have no qualms about the word, I couldn't bring myself to say it to Nialla's face.

"Murdered," she said, falling back into her seat. "Nor have I. That Inspector simply wouldn't stop asking me questions. It was horrid."

"Murdered?" I spat out the word as if the thought had never crossed my mind. "What makes you think Rupert was murdered?"

"It's what everyone thinks: the police, and now you. You just said 'right after Rupert was—' That implies something, doesn't it? Murdered . . . killed, what difference does it make? You certainly weren't about to say 'right after Rupert died,' and don't pretend you were. I'm not a fool, Flavia, so please don't keep treating me as if I were."

"Perhaps it was an accident," I said, stalling to get my thoughts organized.

"Would the police have spent half the night grilling the audience, if they thought it was an accident?"

She had a point.

"What's worse," she went on, "is they think I did it."

"I can see why," I said.

"What? Whose side are you on, anyway? I told you I needed help and suddenly you're accusing me of murder!"

"I am not accusing you of murder," I said. "I'm merely stating the obvious."

"Which is?"

She was becoming angrier by the minute.

"Which is," I said, taking a deep breath, "that you've been in hiding, that Rupert had been beating you, that there was Another Woman, and that you're pregnant."

In these waters, I was well in over my head, but still, determined to swim like a dog tossed off the end of a pier. Even so, the effect of my words on Nialla was quite remarkable. I thought for an instant that she was going to slap my face.

"Is it that obvious?" she asked, her lip trembling.

"It is to me," I replied. "I can't speak for anyone else."

"Do you think I did it? Killed Rupert, I mean?"

"I don't know," I said. "I shouldn't have judged you capable of such a thing, but then I'm no Spilsbury."

Although Sir Bernard had been a dab hand at fingering murderers, including those two great poisoners Dr. Crippen and Major Armstrong, he had, oddly enough, taken his own life by gassing himself in his laboratory. Still, I thought, if Spilsbury were alive, he would be the first to point out that Nialla had the means, the motive, and the opportunity.

"Stop prattling on like that," she snapped. "Do *you* think I murdered Rupert?"

"Did you?" I shot back.

"I can't answer that," she said. "You mustn't ask me."

I was no stranger to such female sparring: Eleven years under the same roof as Feely and Daffy had made me quite immune to that sort of ducking and dodging.

"All right," I persisted, "but if you didn't, then who did?"

By now, I had become accustomed to the dusky light of the coach house, and I watched as Nialla's eyes widened like luminous twin moons.

There was a long, and rather unpleasant, silence.

"If it wasn't you," I said at last, "then why are you hiding out here?"

"I'm not hiding out! I needed to get away. I told you that. The police, the Mullets—"

"I understand about the Mullets," I told her. "I'd rather spend a morning in the dentist's chair than listen to an hour of Mrs. Mullet's rattling on."

"You mustn't say things like that," Nialla said. "They were both very sweet, especially Alf. He's a lovely old gentleman—puts me in mind of my grandfather. But I needed to get away somewhere to think, to pull myself together. You don't know what it's like to come flying apart at the seams."

"Yes, I do. More than you might think. I quite often come here myself when I need to be alone."

"I must have sensed that. I thought of Buckshaw at once. No one would ever think to look for me here. The place wasn't actually that hard to find."

"You'd better get back," I said, "before they notice you're gone. The Inspector wasn't at the church when I came past. I expect they had rather a late night. Since he's already questioned you, there's no reason you shouldn't be taking a long walk in the country, is there?"

"No . . ." she said, tentatively.

"Besides," I added, getting back to my usual cheerful self, "no one but me knows you were here."

Nialla reached into the side pocket on the door of the Rolls-Royce and pulled something out. It came free with a rustle of wax paper. As she opened it out into her lap, I couldn't help noticing the razor-sharp creases in the paper.

"No one knows," she said, handing me a cucumber sandwich, ". . . but you—and one other person. Here, eat this. You must be famished."

· T W E N T Y · T W O ·

"Go on! Go on!" Dogger growled, his hands trembling like the last two leaves of autumn. He did not see me standing there, in the doorway of the greenhouse.

With one blade of his pocketknife opened at a near right angle, he was clumsily trying to hone it on a whetstone. The blade skittered crazily here and there, making ghastly grating noises on the black surface.

Poor Dogger. These episodes came upon him without warning, and almost anything could trigger them: a spoken word, a smell, or a drifting snatch of melody. He was at the mercy of his broken memory.

I backed away slowly until I was behind the garden wall. Then I began whistling softly, only gradually increasing the volume. It would sound as if I were just coming across the lawn towards the kitchen garden. Halfway to the greenhouse, I broke into song: a campfire ditty I had learned just before I was excommunicated from the Girl Guides:

> *"Once a jolly swagman camped by a billabong,*
> *Under the shade of a coolibah tree,*
> *And he sang as he watched and waited till his billy boiled,*
> *'Who'll come a-waltzing Matilda with me?'*"

I strolled square-shouldered into the greenhouse.

"G'day, mate!" I said, with a hearty, Down-Under grin.

"McCorquedale? Is that you?" Dogger called out, his voice as thin and wispy as the wind in the strings of an old harp. "Is Bennett with you? Have you got your tongues back?"

His head was cocked to one side, listening, his wrist held up to shield his eyes, which were turned blindly up to the glare of the greenhouse glass.

I felt as if I had blundered into a sanctuary, and the flesh crawled on the back of my neck.

"It's me, Dogger—Flavia," I managed.

His brows knitted themselves into a look of puzzlement. "Flavia?"

My name issued from his throat like a whisper from an abandoned well.

I could see that he was already fighting his way back from whatever had seized him, the light in his eyes coming back only warily from the depths to the surface, like golden fish in an ornamental pool.

"Miss Flavia?"

"I'm sorry," I said, taking the knife from his shaking hands. "Have I broken it? I borrowed it yesterday to cut a bit of twine, and I might have jammed the blade. If I did, I'll buy you a new one."

This was sheer fantasy—I hadn't touched the thing—but I have learned that under certain circumstances, a fib is not only permissible, but can even be an act of perfect grace. I took the knife from his hands, opened it fully, and began rubbing it in smooth circles on the surface of the stone.

"No, it's fine," I said. "Phew! I'd have been in big trouble if I'd jiggered your best knife, wouldn't I?"

I snapped the blade shut and handed it back. Dogger took it from me, his fingers now much more sure of themselves.

I turned over an empty pail and sat on it as we shared a silence.

"It was good of you to think of feeding Nialla," I said, after a while.

"She needs a friend," he said. "She's—"

"Pregnant," I blurted.

"Yes."

"But how did you know that? Surely she didn't tell you?"

"Excessive salivation," Dogger said, ". . . and telangiectasia."

"Tel- *what?*"

"Telangiectasia," he said in a mechanical voice, as if he were reading from an invisible book. ". . . Spider veins in proximity to the mouth, nose, and chin. Uncommon, but not unknown in early pregnancy."

"You amaze me, Dogger," I said. "How on earth do you know these things?"

"They float in my head," he replied quietly, "like corks

upon the sea. I've read books, I think. I've had a lot of time on my hands."

"Ah!" I said. It was the most I'd heard him say in ages.

But Dogger's former captivity was not a topic for open discussion, and I knew that it was time to change the subject.

"Do you think she did it?" I asked. "Killed Rupert, I mean?"

Dogger knitted his eyebrows, as if thinking came to him only with the greatest effort.

"The police will think that," he said, nodding slowly. "Yes, that's what the police will think. They'll soon be along."

As it turned out, he was right.

"It is a well-known fact," Aunt Felicity trumpeted, "that the Black Death was brought into England by lawyers. Shakespeare said we ought to have hanged the lot of them, and in light of modern sanitary reform, we now know that he was right. This will never do, Haviland!"

She stuffed a handful of papers into a dusty hatbox and clapped the lid on. "It's a perfect disgrace," she added, "the way you've let things slide. Unless something turns up, you'll soon have no option but to sell up Buckshaw and take a cold-water flat in Battersea."

"Hello, all," I said, strolling into the library, pretending for the second time in less than half an hour that I was oblivious to what was going on.

"Ah, Flavia," Father said. "I think Mrs. Mullet requires an extra pair of hands in the kitchen."

"Of course," I said. "And shall I then be allowed to go to the ball?"

Father looked puzzled. My witty repartee was completely lost on him.

"Flavia!" Aunt Felicity said. "That's no way for a child to speak to a parent. I should have thought that you'd outgrown that saucy attitude by now. I don't know why you let these girls get away with it, Haviland."

Father moved towards the window and stared out across the ornamental lake towards the folly. He was taking refuge, as he often does, in letting his eyes, at least, escape an unpleasant situation.

Suddenly he whirled round to face her.

"Damn it all, Lissy," he said, in a voice so strong I think it surprised even him. "It isn't always easy for them. No . . . it isn't always easy for them."

I think my mouth fell open as his closed.

Dear old Father! I could have hugged him, and if either of us had been other than who we were, I think I might have.

Aunt Felicity went back to rummaging among the papers.

"Statutory legacies . . . personal chattels," she said with a sniff. "Where will it all end?"

"Flavia," Feely said, as I passed the open door of the drawing room, "a moment?"

She sounded suspiciously civil. She was up to something.

As I stepped inside, Daffy, who had been standing near the door, closed it softly behind me.

"We've been waiting for you," Feely said. "Please sit down."

"I'd rather not," I said. They had both remained standing, putting me at a disadvantage when it came to sudden flight.

"As you wish," Feely said, sitting down behind a small table and putting on her eyeglasses. Daffy stood with her back pressed against the door.

"I'm afraid we have some rather bad news for you," Feely said, toying with her spectacles like a judge at the Old Bailey.

I said nothing.

"While you've been gadding about the countryside, we've held a meeting, and we've all of us decided that you must go."

"In short, we've voted you out of the family," Daffy said. "It was unanimous."

"Unanimous?" I said. "This is just another of your stupid—"

"Dogger, of course, pleaded for leniency, but he was overruled by Aunt Felicity, who has more weight in these matters. He wanted you to be allowed to stay until the end of the week, but I'm afraid we can't permit it. It's been decided that you're to be gone by sundown."

"But—"

"Father has given instructions to Mr. Pringle, his solicitor, to draw up a Covenant of Reversion, which means, of course, that you will be returned to the Home for

Unwed Mothers, who will have no option but to take you back."

"Because of the Covenant, you see," Daffy said. "It's in their Constitution. They can't say no. They can't refuse."

I clenched my fists as I felt the tears beginning to well up in my eyes. It was no good waiting upon reason.

I shoved Daffy roughly away from the door.

"Have you eaten those chocolates yet?" I demanded of Feely.

She was somewhat taken aback by the harshness in my voice.

"Well, no . . . ," she said.

"Better not," I spat. "They might be *poisoned*."

As soon as the words were out of my mouth, I knew I'd done the wrong thing.

Blast it! I'd given myself away. All that work in my laboratory wasted!

Flavia, I thought, *sometimes you're no brighter than a lightning-struck lizard.*

Angry with myself for being angry, I stalked out of the room on general principles, and nobody tried to stop me.

I took a deep breath, relaxed my shoulders, and opened the kitchen door.

"Flavia," Mrs. Mullet called, "be a dear and fetch me a glass of sherry from the pantry. I've gone all-over strange. Not too much, mind, or else I shall be tipsy."

She was stretched full length in a chair by the window, her heels on the tiles, fanning herself with a small frying pan.

I did as I was bidden, and she gulped down the drink in a flash.

"What is it, Mrs. M?" I asked. "What's happened?"

"The police, dearie. They gave me such a turn, comin' for that young woman like they did."

"What young woman? You mean Nialla?"

She nodded glumly, waggling her empty glass. I refilled it.

"Such a dear, she is. Never done nobody no harm. She rapped at the kitchen door to thank me, and Alf, of course, for puttin' her up the night. Said she was movin' on—didn't want us to think she was ungrateful, like. No more the words were out of her mouth than that there Inspector whatsis—"

"Hewitt," I said.

"Hewitt. That's 'im—that's the one . . . 'E shows up in the doorway right behind 'er. Spotted 'er comin' across from the coach house, 'e did."

"And then?"

" 'E asked if 'e might have a word outside. Next thing I knows, poor girl's off in the car with 'im. I 'ad to run round the front to get a good look. Proper fagged me out, so it did."

I refilled her glass.

"I shouldn't ought to, dearie," she said, "but my poor old heart's not up to such a muddlederumpus."

"You're looking better already, Mrs. M," I told her. "Is there anything I can do to help?"

"I was just about to put them things in the oven," she said, pointing to an array of dough-filled pans on the table, and heaving herself to her feet. "Open the oven door for me—that's a good girl."

Much of my life was given over to holding the oven door of the Aga as Mrs. M fed heaps of baking into its open maw. Hell, in Milton's *Paradise Lost*, had nothing to compare with my drudgery.

"Clean out of pastries, we were," she said. "When it comes to dainties, that young man of Miss Ophelia's seems to have a bottomless stomach."

Miss Ophelia's young man? Had it come to that already? Had my rambles round the village caused me to miss some sensational scene of courtship?

"Dieter?" I asked.

"Even if 'e *is* a German," she said with a nod, " 'e's ever so much more refined than that rooster as keeps leavin' 'is rubbishy gifts on the kitchen doorstep."

Poor Ned! I thought. Even Mrs. Mullet was against him.

"I just 'appened to overhear a bit of what 'e said while I was dustin' the hall—about 'Eathcliff, an' all that. I mind the time me and my friend, Mrs. Waller, took the bus over to Hinley to see 'im in the cinema. *Wuthering Heights*, it was called, and a good name for it, too! That there 'Eathcliff, why, 'e kept 'is wife 'id up in the attic as if she was an old dresser! No wonder she went barmy. I know I should 'ave! Now then, what you laughin' at, miss?"

"At the idea," I said, "of Dieter mucking across Jubilee Field through rain and lightning to carry off the Fair Ophelia."

"Well, 'e might do," she said, "but not without a right fuss from Sally Straw—and, some say, the old missus herself."

"The old missus? Grace Ingleby? Surely you don't mean Grace Ingleby?"

Mrs. Mullet had suddenly gone as red as a pot of boiling beets.

"I've said too much," she said, flustered. "It's the sherry, you see. Alf always says as 'ow sherry coshes the guard what's supposed to be keepin' watch on my tongue. Now then, not another word. Off you go, dearie. And mind you—I've said nothing."

Well! I thought. *Well, well, well, well, well!*

· T W E N T Y · T H R E E ·

THERE'S SOMETHING ABOUT pottering with poisons that clarifies the mind. When the slightest slip of the hand could prove fatal, one's attention is forced to focus like a burning-glass upon the experiment, and it is then that the answers to half-formed questions so often come swarming to mind as readily as bees coming home to the hive.

With a good dollop of sulfuric acid already decanted into a freshly washed flask and warmed slightly, I gingerly added a glob of crystalline jelly, and watched in awe as it slowly dissolved, quivering and squirming in the acid bath like a translucent squidling.

I had extracted the stuff, with water and alcohol, from the roots of a Carolina jessamine plant (*Gelsemium sempervirens*) that, to my delight, I had discovered blooming blissfully away in the corner of the greenhouse, its flowers like little trumpets sculpted from fresh butter.

The plant was native to the Americas, Dogger had told me, but had been brought home to English greenhouses by travelers; this particular specimen by my mother, Harriet.

I had asked if I could have it for my laboratory, and Dogger had readily agreed.

The root contained a lovely alkaloid called gelsemine, which had lurked undetected inside the plant since the Creation, until it was teased out in 1870 by a man from Philadelphia with the charming name of Wormley, who administered the bitter poison to a rabbit, which turned a complete backwards somersault and perished in twenty minutes.

Gelsemine was a killer whose company I much enjoyed.

And now came the magic!

Into the liquid I introduced, on the tip of a knife, a small dose of $K_2Cr_2O_7$, or potassium dichromate, whose red salts, illuminated by a fortuitous beam of sunlight from the casement window, turned it the livid cherry red hue of a carbon monoxide victim's blood.

But this was only the beginning! There was more to come.

Already the cherry brilliance was fading, and the solution was taking on the impressive violet color of an old bruise. I held my breath, and—*yes!*—here it was, the final phase of yellow-green.

Gelsemine was one of chemistry's chameleons, shifting

color with delicious abandon, and all without a trace of its former hue.

People were like that, too.

Nialla, for instance.

On the one hand, she was captive to a traveling pup-peteer; a young woman who, other than the baby she was now carrying, had no family to speak of; a young woman who allowed herself to be beaten by a semi-invalid lover; a young woman now left with no money and no visible means of support. And yet, in rather a complicated way that I did not entirely understand, she did not have my complete sympathy.

Was it because she had run away from the scene of the crime, so to speak, and hidden in the coach house at Buckshaw? I could see her wanting to be alone, but she had hardly chosen the best time to do so.

Where was she now? I wondered. Had Inspector He-witt arrested her and dragged her to a cell in Hinley?

I wrote *Nialla* on a scrap of paper.

And then there was Mutt Wilmott: a larger-than-life character, who seemed to have stepped right out of an Orson Welles film. Not to put too fine a point on it: Mutt had arrived, Rupert had died; Mutt had vanished after quarreling with Rupert, and was next seen arranging to have the body in question shipped up to London for a state funeral.

Was Mutt an assassin, hired by the BBC? Had Rupert's set-to with the mysterious Tony pushed "Auntie"—and her Director General—too far? Was Rupert's messy end on the stage of a rustic puppet theater really no more than the conclusion of a bitter contractual dispute?

What about Grace Ingleby? To be honest, the dark little woman gave me the creeps. Her shrine to a dead child in an abandoned birdhouse was enough to spook anyone—and now Mrs. Mullet was hinting that the farmer's wife was more than just a landlady to Dieter.

And Dieter! For all his Nordic godliness and passion for English literature, it seemed that he had conspired with his captors to grow and supply cannabis to what Sally Straw had called "a regular little army of others." Who were they? I wondered.

Rupert, of course, had been chief among them, and had visited the Ingleby farm with the regularity of a tramcar for many years. He had been a ladies' man—there was no doubt about it (Sally again). Of whom had he run afoul? Who wanted him dead badly enough to actually do him in?

As for Sally, both Rupert and Dieter had been keen on her. Had Rupert been shoved off into eternity by a rival in love?

Sally seemed central: She had been at the Ingleby farm for years. It was clear that she had a crush on Dieter, although whether her passions were wholly returned was another matter entirely.

And then there was Gordon Ingleby. Gordon the linen-draped saint who did for those in pain what no doctor was willing to do; Gordon the market gardener; Gordon the father of the dead child in the woods.

To say nothing of Mad Meg, who had been in Gibbet Wood when Robin died, or at least, not long afterwards.

And Cynthia—dear Cynthia Richardson, the vicar's wife, whose only passion was her hatred of sin. The sudden appearance of a pair of promiscuous puppeteers who proposed to put on a show in her husband's parish hall must have seared her soul like the lake of fire in the Book of Revelation.

In spite of all that, Cynthia's soul was no hotbed of Christian charity. What was it Meg had said when I asked about her nap at the vicarage? That Cynthia had taken away her bracelet and then turned her out because she was dirty. No doubt she was referring to Nialla's butterfly compact, but if that were the case, why had I found it tangled in the afghan in the study? Had Cynthia taken the compact from Meg and then, caught in the act by one of the dozens of villagers milling about the vicarage, hidden it away to be retrieved for her own later use?

It seemed unlikely: If there was one sin of which Cynthia Richardson was not guilty, that sin was vanity. Just one look at her was enough to know that makeup had never soiled that pale ferret face; jewelry had never dangled from that scrawny neck or brightened up those matchstick wrists. To put it politely, the woman was as plain as a pudding.

I sharpened my pencil and added six names to my list: *Mutt Wilmott, Grace Ingleby, Dieter Schrantz, Sally Straw, Mad Meg (Daffy had once told me that Meg's surname was Grosvenor, but I didn't believe her) . . . and Cynthia Richardson.*

I drew a line, and below it, printed in capital letters: AFFAIRS——LOOK UP!!!

Although I had a sketchy idea of what went on between two people having an affair, I did not actually know the precise mechanical details. Once, when Father had gone away for several days to a stamp exhibition in Glasgow, Daffy had insisted upon reading *Madame Bovary* aloud to us at every meal, morning, noon, and night, including tea, and finished on the third day just as Father was walking in the door.

At the time, I had nearly died of boredom, although it has since become one of my favorite books, containing, as it does in its final chapters, what must be the finest and most exciting description of death by arsenic in all of literature. I had particularly relished the way in which the poisoned Emma had "raised herself like a galvanized corpse." But now I realized that I had been so gripped by the excitement of poor Madame Bovary's suicide that I had failed to take in the fine points of her several affairs. All I could remember was that, alone with Rodolphe by the lily pond, surrounded by duckweeds and jumping frogs, Emma Bovary—in tears, hiding her face, and with a long shudder—"gave herself up to him."

Whatever that meant. I would ask Dogger.

"Dogger," I said, when I found him at last, hacking away at the weeds in the kitchen garden with a long-handled hoe, "have you read *Madame Bovary*?"

Dogger paused in his work and extracted a handkerchief from the bib pocket of his overalls. He gave his face a thorough mopping before he replied.

"A French novel, is it not?" he asked.

"Flaubert."

"Ah," Dogger said, and shoved the handkerchief back into his pocket. "The one in which a most unhappy person poisons herself with arsenic."

"Arsenic from a blue jar!" I blurted, hopping from one foot to the other with excitement.

"Yes," Dogger said, "from a blue jar. Blue, not because of any danger of decomposition or oxidation of the contents, but rather—"

"To keep it from being confused with a bottle containing a harmless substance."

"Exactly," Dogger said.

"Emma Bovary swallows the stuff due to several unhappy affairs," I said.

Dogger studiously scraped a clod of mud from the sole of his shoe with the hoe.

"She had an affair with a man named Rodolphe," I added, "and then with another, named Léon. Not at the same time, of course."

"Of course," Dogger said, and then fell silent.

"What does an affair entail, precisely?" I asked, hoping my choice of words would imply, even slightly, that I already knew the answer.

I thought for a moment that I could outwait him, even though my heart knew that trying to outwait Dogger was a mug's game.

"What did Flaubert mean," I asked at last, "when he said that Madame Bovary gave herself up to Rodolphe?"

"He meant," Dogger said, "that they became the greatest of friends. The very greatest of friends."

"Ah!" I said. "Just as I thought."

"Dogger! Come up here at once before I do mysel

some grave internal injury!" Aunt Felicity's voice came trumpeting down from an upstairs window.

"Coming, Miss Felicity," he called out, and then in an aside to me he said, "Miss Felicity requires assistance with her luggage."

"Her luggage?" I asked. "She's leaving?"

Dogger nodded noncommittally.

"Cheese!" I exclaimed. It was a secret prayer, whose meaning was known only to God and to me.

Aunt Felicity was already halfway down the west staircase in a canvas outfit that suggested Africa, rather than the wilds of Hampstead. Clarence Mundy's taxicab was at the door, and Dogger was helping Bert hoist Aunt Felicity's cargo aboard.

"We're going to miss you, Aunt Fee," Feely said.

Aunt Fee? It seemed that in my absence Feely had been ingratiating herself with Father's sister, most likely, I thought, in the hope of inheriting the de Luce family jewels: that ghastly collection of gewgaws that my grandfather de Luce (on Father's and Aunt Felicity's side) had foisted upon my grandmother who, as she received each piece, had dropped it, with thumb and forefinger, into a pasteboard box as casually as if it were a grass snake, and never looked at it again.

Feely had wasted the entire afternoon slavering over this rubbish the last time we had gone up to Hampstead for one of Aunt Felicity's compulsory teas.

"So romantic!" she had breathed, when Aunt Felicity had, rather grudgingly, I thought, lent her a pink glass pendant that would not have been out of place on a cow's udder. "I shall wear it to Rosalind Norton's coming-out, and all eyes will be on yours truly. Poor Rosalind, she's such an awful sweat!"

"I'm sorry it's turned out this way, Haviland," Aunt Felicity bellowed from the landing, "but you've well and truly botched it. All the king's horses and all the king's men couldn't put your accounts together again. I should, of course, be more than happy to rescue you from your excesses if I weren't so heavily invested in consols. There's nothing for it now but to sell those ridiculous postage stamps."

Father had drifted so silently into the hall that I had not noticed him until now. He stood, one hand holding Daffy's arm, his eyes downcast, as if he were intently studying the black and white tiles beneath his feet.

"Thank you for coming, Felicity," he said quietly, without looking up. "It was most kind of you."

I wanted to swat the woman's face!

I had actually taken half a step forward before a firm hand fell on my shoulder, stopping me in my tracks. It was Dogger.

"Will there be anything else, Miss Felicity?" he asked.

"No, thank you, Dogger," she said, rummaging in her reticule with two fingers. From its depths, like a stork pulling a fish from a pond, she extracted what looked like a shilling and handed it to him with a sigh.

"Thank you, miss," he said, pocketing the insult with ease—and without looking at it—as if it were something he did every day.

And with that Aunt Felicity was gone. A moment

later, Father had stepped into the shadows of the great hall, followed closely by Daffy and Feely, and Dogger had vanished without a word into his little corridor behind the stairs.

It was like one of those electric moments just before the final curtain in a West End play: that moment when all the supporting characters have faded into the wings, leaving the heroine alone at center stage to deliver her magnificent closing line to a silent house that awaited her words with bated breath.

"Bloody hell!" I said, and stepped outdoors for a breath of fresh air.

The problem with we de Luces, I decided, *is that we are infested with history in much the same way that other people are infested with lice.* There have been de Luces at Buckshaw since King Harold stopped an arrow with his eye at the Battle of Hastings, and most of them have been unhappy in one complicated way or another. We seem to be born with wisps of both glory and gloom in our veins, and we can never be certain at any given moment which of the two is driving us.

On the one hand, I knew, I would never be like Aunt Felicity, but on the other, would I ever become like Harriet? Eight years after her death, Harriet was still as much a part of me as my toenails, although that's probably not the best way of putting it.

I read the books that she had owned, rode her bicycle, sat in her Rolls-Royce; Father had once, in a distracted moment, called me by her name. Even Aunt Felicity had put aside her gorgon manner long enough to tell me how much like Harriet I was.

But had she meant it as a compliment? Or a warning?

Most of the time I felt like an imposter; a changeling; a sackcloth-and-ashes stand-in for that golden girl who had been snatched up by Fate and dashed down a mountainside in an impossibly distant land. Everyone, it seemed, would be so much happier if Harriet were brought back to life and I were done away with.

These thoughts, and others, tumbled in my mind like autumn leaves in a millstream as I walked along the dusty lane towards the village. Without even noticing them, I had passed the carved griffins of the Mulford Gates, which marked the entrance to Buckshaw, and I was now within sight of Bishop's Lacey.

As I slouched along, a bit dejectedly (all right, I admit it—I was furious at Aunt Felicity for making such a chump of Dogger!) I shoved my hand into my pocket and my fingers came in contact with a round, metallic object: something that hadn't been there before—a coin.

"Hullo!" I said. "What's this?"

I pulled it out and looked at it. As soon as I saw the thing, I knew what it was and how it had made its way into my pocket. I turned it over and had a jolly good squint at the reverse.

Yes, there could be no doubt about it—no doubt whatsoever.

· TWENTY·FOUR ·

As I LOOKED AT it from across the high street, the St. Nicholas Tea Room was like a picture postcard of Ye Olde England. Its upstairs rooms, with their tiny-paned bow windows, had been the residence of the present Mr. Sowbell's grandparents, in the days when they had lived above their coffin and furniture manufactory.

The Sowbell tables, sideboards, and commodes, once known far and wide for the ferocity of their black shine and the gleam of their ornate silver knobs and drawer pulls, had now fallen out of favor, and were often to be found at estate sales, standing sullen and alone in the driveway until being knocked down at the end of the day for little more than a pound or two.

"By unscrupulous sharpers who use the wood to turn Woolworth's dressers into antiques," Daffy had once told me.

The undertaker's shop, I noticed, now had a cardboard clock stuck in its window, suspended from an inverted V of black cord. The minute hand pointed to twelve, and the hour hand was missing. Mr. Sowbell had obviously gone to the Thirteen Drakes for his afternoon pint.

I crossed the street and, opening the tearoom door, stepped inside. To my right was a steep wooden staircase, with a painted blue hand pointing upwards: *Tea Room Upstairs*. Beside the stairs, a dim, narrow passageway vanished into the gloom at the rear of the building. On the wall, another helpful painted hand—this one in red, and marked *Gentlemen's and Ladies' Water Closets*—pointed the way discreetly.

I knew that the tea shop and the undertaker's shared the W.C. Feely had insisted on dragging us here for tea one autumn afternoon, and I had been gobsmacked at the sight of three women in black dresses and black veils, chattering happily away at the door to the toilet like a congress of toothy crows, before resuming their grim demeanors and slipping back into Mr. Sowbell's premises. The door through which they had vanished opened directly into the undertaker's rooms.

I was right! A discreet *Sowbell & Sons*, lettered in gold upon the dark varnish, must have been meant to remind mourners not to go blundering off into the tea shop's corridor after they had "soaped their 'ands," as Mrs. Mullet put it.

The black paneled door swung open on silent hinges.

I found myself in a dark Victorian parlor, with flocked wallpaper of black and yellow-cream. On three sides of the room were spindly wooden chairs and a small round table with a spray of artificial baby's breath. The place smelled of dust, with an underlying chemical base.

The wall at the far end of the room was bare, save for a dark framed print of Millet's *Angelus*, in which a man and a woman, obviously Flemish peasants, stand alone in a field at sunset. The woman's huge hands, which are those of a laborer, are clasped at her breast in prayer. The man has removed his hat, which he holds clutched uncomfortably in front of him. He has set aside his fork and stuck it half into the loose earth. As crows congregate above them like vultures, the couple stands with downcast eyes. Between them, half-empty on the ground, lies a wicker basket.

Max Wight had once told me that when the original of Millet's painting was exhibited in America, the sale of prints had been sluggish at best until someone thought of changing the name from *Angelus* to *Burying the Baby*.

It was beneath this print, I guessed, that the coffins were customarily parked. Since the spot was empty, it was obvious that Rupert's body, if it were still on the premises, must be in another room.

To my right was an L-shaped partition. There had to be another door behind it.

I peered round behind the half-wall and found myself looking into a room that was nearly the twin of the first. The only difference that I could see was that the flocked wallpaper was black and pink-cream, and the print on the far wall was Holman Hunt's *Light of the World*, in which Jesus stands at the door like Diogenes seeking an honest man, with a tin lantern in His hand.

Beneath its dark frame, on trestles, was a coffin.

I crept towards it on tiptoe, my ears tuned for the slightest sound.

I ran my fingers along the highly polished woodwork, the way one might caress a piano lid before lifting it to reveal the keys. I put my thumbs under the join and felt it lift slightly.

I was in luck! The lid was not screwed down. I lifted it and looked inside.

There, like a doll in a box, lay Rupert. In life, his personality had made him seem so much larger, I had forgotten how small he really was.

Was I frightened out of my wits? I'm afraid not. Since the day I had found a body in the kitchen garden at Buckshaw, I had developed a fascination with death, with a particular emphasis on the chemistry of putrefaction.

In fact, I had already begun making notes for a definitive work which I would call *De Luce on Decomposition*, in which I would outline, step by step, the process of human cadaveric decay.

How exciting it was to reflect upon the fact that, within minutes of death, the organs of the body, lacking oxygen, begin to digest themselves! Ammonia levels start to rise and, with the assistance of bacterial action, methane (better known as marsh gas) is produced, along with hydrogen sulfide, carbon dioxide, and mercaptan, a captivating sulfur-alcohol in whose structure sulfur takes the place of oxygen—which accounts for its putrid smell.

How curious it was, I thought, that we humans had taken millions of years to crawl up out of the swamps and yet, within minutes of death, we were already tobogganing back down the slope.

My keen sense of smell told me that Mr. Sowbell had used a formalin-based embalming fluid on Rupert (a two-percent solution of formaldehyde seemed most likely, with a slight bouquet of something else: chloroform, by the smell of it) and by the slight green tint at the end of Rupert's nose, I could tell that the undertaker had skimped on the ingredients. One could only hope that the lying-in-state at the BBC would be a closed-coffin affair.

Better hurry up, though, I thought. Mr. Sowbell might walk in at any moment.

Rupert's pale hands were folded across his abdomen, with the right hand uppermost. I took hold of his fingers (it was like lifting linked sausages from the icebox) and pulled upwards.

To my amazement, his left hand came with it, and I saw at once that they had been cunningly sewn together. By twisting the cold hands and bending down for a better look beneath them, I saw what I was looking for: a blackened channel that ran from the base of his left thumb to the tips of his first and second fingers.

In spite of Mr. Sowbell's embalming efforts, Rupert was still giving off rather a scorched smell. And there could be no doubt about it: The burn on the palm of his left hand was the precise width of the lever that operated Galligantus.

A floorboard creaked.

As I closed the coffin lid, the door opened and Mr. Sowbell walked into the room. I hadn't heard him coming.

Because I was still in a half-crouch from inspecting Rupert's burned fingers, I was able to come slowly to a standing position.

"Amen," I said, crossing myself extravagantly.

"What on earth—?" said Mr. Sowbell.

"Oh, hello, Mr. Sowbell," I said in an appropriately hushed tone. "I just dropped in to pay my respects. There was no one here, but I thought a quiet prayer would be in order.

"Mr. Porson had no friends in Bishop's Lacey, you know," I added, pulling a handkerchief from my pocket and wiping away an imaginary tear. "It seemed such a shame, and I thought it would do no harm if I—I'm sorry if—"

"There, there," he said. "Death comes to us all, you know, old and young alike. . . ."

Was he threatening me, or was my imagination over-heated?

"And even though we expect it," he went on, "it always comes as a shock in the end."

It certainly had for Rupert—but was the man being facetious?

Evidently not, for his long face maintained its professional polish.

"And now if you will excuse me," he said. "I must prepare him for his final journey."

Final journey? Where did they get this claptrap? Was there a phrasebook published for the undertaking trade?

I gave him my ten-years-old-going-on-eleven smile, and faked a flustered exit.

The bell above the door of the St. Nicholas Tea Room jangled merrily as I stepped inside. The establishment, a bit of a climb at the top of the stairs, was owned by none other than Miss Lavinia and Miss Aurelia, the Puddock sisters: those same two relics who had provided the musical prelude to Rupert's spectacular demise.

Miss Lavinia, in a nook at the far side of the room, seemed to be locked in mortal combat with a large silver samovar. In spite of the simplicity of its task, which was the boiling of water, this Heath Robinson contraption was a bulbous squid of tubes, valves, and gauges, which spat hot water as it gurgled and hissed away like a cornered dragon.

"No tea, I'm afraid," she said over her shoulder. She could not yet see who had entered the shop.

"Anything I can do to help, Miss Puddock?" I offered cheerily.

She let out a little shriek as her hand strayed accidentally into a jet of hot steam, and the china cup she was holding crashed to the floor, where it flew into a hundred pale pieces.

"Oh, it's the little de Luce girl," she said, spinning round. "My goodness! You gave me quite a fright. I wasn't expecting to hear your voice."

Because I could see that she'd scalded her hand, I fought back my baser urges.

"Anything I can do to help?" I repeated.

"Oh, dear," she said, flustered beyond reason. "Peter always chooses to act up when Aurelia's not here. She's so much better with him than I am."

"Peter?" I asked.

"The samovar," she said, wiping her wet red hands on a tea towel. "Peter the Great."

"Here," I said, "let me—"

Without another word I took up a bowl of lemon wedges from one of the round tables and squeezed each of them into a jug of iced water. Then I grabbed a clean white table napkin, immersed it until it was soaked, wrung it out, and wrapped it around Miss Puddock's hand. She flinched as I touched her, and then relaxed.

"May I?" I asked, removing an opal brooch from her lapel and using it to pin the ends of the makeshift bandage.

"Oh! It feels better already," she said with a pained smile. "Wherever did you learn that trick?"

"Girl Guides," I lied.

Experience has taught me that an expected answer is often better than the truth. I had, in fact, quite painfully looked up the remedy in one of Mrs. Mullet's household reference books after a superheated test tube seared most of the flesh from a couple of my fingers.

"Miss Cool has always spoken so highly of you," she said. "I shall tell her she was 'bang-on,' as those nice bomber boys from the RAF used to say."

I gave her my most modest smile. "It's nothing, Miss Puddock—just jolly good luck I got here when I did. I was next door, at Mr. Sowbell's, you see, saying a prayer or two at Mr. Porson's coffin. You don't suppose it will do any harm, do you?"

I realized that I was gilding the lily with a string mop for a paintbrush, but business was business.

"Why no, dear," she said. "I think Mr. Porson would be touched."

She didn't know the half of it!

"It was so sad." I lowered my voice to a conspiratorial whisper and touched her good arm. "But I must tell you,

Miss Puddock, that in spite of the tragedy on Saturday evening, my family and I enjoyed 'Napoleon's Last Charge' and 'Bendemeer's Stream.' Father said that you don't often hear music like that nowadays."

"Why, thank you, dear," she murmured damply. "It's kind of you to say so. Of course, mercifully, we didn't actually see what happened to poor Mr. Porson, being busy in the kitchen, as it were. As proprietresses of Bishop Lacey's sole tearoom, certain expectations attach, I'm afraid. Not that we resent—"

"No, of course not," I said. "But surely you must have tons of people offering to help out."

She gave a little bark. "Help? Most people don't know the meaning of the word. No, Aurelia and I were left alone in the kitchen from start to finish. Two hundred and sixty-three cups of tea we poured, but of course that's counting the ones we served after the police took charge."

"And no one offered to help?" I asked, giving her an incredulous look.

"No one. As I said, Aurelia and I were alone in the kitchen the whole while. And I was left completely on my own when Aurelia took a cup of tea to the puppeteer."

My ears went up like a flag on a pole. "She took Rupert a cup of tea?"

"Well, she tried to, dear, but the door was locked."

"The door to the stage? Across from the kitchen?"

"No, no . . . she didn't want to use that one. She'd have had to brush right past that Mother Goose, that woman who was in the spotlight, telling the story. No, Aurelia took the tea all the way round the back of the hall and down to the other door."

296 · ALAN BRADLEY

"The one in the opposite passage?"

"Well, yes. It's the only other one, isn't it, dear? But as I've already told you, it was locked."

"During the puppet show?"

"Why, yes. Odd, isn't it? Mr. Porson had asked us before he began if we could bring him a nice cup of tea during the show. 'Just leave it on the little table behind the stage,' he said. 'I'll find it. Puppetry's dry work, you know,' and he gave us a little wink. So why on earth would he lock the door?"

As she went on, I could already feel the facts beginning to marshal themselves in my mind.

"Those were Aurelia's exact words when she'd come all the way back with his cup of tea still in her hand. 'Whatever would possess him to lock the door?' "

"Perhaps he didn't," I said, with sudden inspiration. "Perhaps someone else did. Who has the key, do you know?"

"There are two keys to the stage door, dear. They each open the ones on either side of the stage. The vicar keeps one on his keychain, and the duplicate on a nail in his study at the vicarage. It's all because of that time he went off to Brighton for the C and S—that's the Churchwardens' and Sidesmen's—cricket match, and took Tom Stoddart with him. Tom's the locksmith, you know, and with the two of them gone, no one could get on or off the stage without a stepladder. It played havoc with the Little Theater Group's production of *King Lear*, let me tell you!"

"And there was no one else about?"

"No one, dear. Aurelia and I were in the kitchen the

whole time. We had the door half closed so the light from the kitchen wouldn't spoil the darkness in the hall."

"There was no one in the passageway?"

"No, of course not. They should have had to walk through the beam of light from the kitchen door, right under our noses so to speak. Once we had the water on to boil, Aurelia and I stood right there at the crack of the door so that we could at least hear the puppet show. 'Fee! Fi! Fo! Fum.' Oh! It gives me the goose bumps just to think about it now!"

I stood perfectly still and held my breath, not moving a muscle. I kept my mouth shut and let the silence lengthen.

"Except—" she said, her gaze wavering. "I thought—"

"Yes?"

"I thought I heard a footstep in the hall. I'd just glanced over at the wall clock, and my eyes were a little dazzled by the light above the stove. I looked out and saw—"

"Do you remember the time?"

"It was twenty-five past seven. We had the tea laid on for eight o'clock, and it takes those big electric urns a long time to come to the boil. How odd that you should ask. That nice young policeman—what's his name?—the little blond fellow with the dimples and the lovely smile?"

"Detective Sergeant Graves," I said.

"Yes, that's him: Detective Sergeant Graves. Funny, isn't it? He asked me the same question, and I gave him the same answer I am going to give you."

"Which is?"

"It was the vicar's wife—Cynthia Richardson."

TWENTY FIVE

CYNTHIA, THE RODENT-FACED avenger! I should have known! Cynthia, who doled out good works in the parish of St. Tancred's with the hand of a Herod. I could easily see her taking it upon herself to punish Rupert, the notorious womanizer. The parish hall was part of her kingdom; the spare key to the stage doors was kept on a nail in her husband's study.

How she might have come into possession of the vicar's missing bicycle clip remained something of a mystery, but mightn't it have been in the vicarage all along?

By his own admission, the vicar's absentmindedness was becoming a problem. Hence the engraved initials. Perhaps he had left home without the clip last Thursday and shredded his trouser cuff because he wasn't wearing it.

The details were unimportant. One thing I was sure of: There was more going on in the vicarage than met the eye, and whatever it was (husband dancing naked in the woods, and so forth), it seemed likely that Cynthia was at the heart of it all.

"What are you thinking, dear?" Miss Puddock's voice interrupted my thoughts. "You've suddenly gone so quiet!"

I needed time to get to the bottom of things, and I needed it now. I was unlikely to have a second chance to plumb the depths of Miss Puddock's village knowledge.

"I—I suddenly don't feel very well," I said, snatching at the edge of a table and lowering myself into one of the wire-backed chairs. "It might have been the sight of your poor scalded hand, Miss Puddock. A delayed reaction, perhaps. A touch of shock."

I suppose there must have been times when I hated myself for practicing such deceits, but I could not think of any at the moment. It was Fate, after all, who thrust me into these things, and Fate would jolly well have to stand the blame.

"Oh, you poor thing!" Miss Puddock said. "You stay right where you are, and I shall fetch you a nice cup of tea and a scone. You do like scones, don't you?"

"I l-love scones," I said, remembering suddenly that shock victims were known to shiver and shake. By the time she came back with the scones, my teeth were chattering like marbles shaken in a jar.

She removed a vase of lily of the valley (*Convallaria majalis*), whisked the starched linen cloth from one of the tables, and wrapped it round my shoulders. As the sweet smell of the flowers wafted across my nostrils, I remembered with pleasure that the plant contained a witch's brew of cardioactive glycosides, including convallatoxin and glucoconvalloside, and that even the water in which the flowers had stood was poisonous. Our ancestors had called it Our Lady's tears, or Ladder-to-Heaven, and with good reason!

"You mustn't take a chill." Miss Puddock clucked solicitously as she poured me a cup of tea from the hulking samovar.

"Peter the Great seems to be behaving himself now," I observed with a calculated tremor and a nod towards the gleaming machine.

"He's very naughty sometimes." She smiled. "It comes of his being Russian, I expect."

"Is he really Russian?" I asked, priming the pump.

"From his distinguished heads," she said, pointing to the double-headed black eagle that functioned as a hot water tap, "to his royally rounded bottom. He was manufactured in the shops of the brothers Martiniuk, the celebrated silversmiths of Odessa, and it was said that he was once used to make tea for Tsar Nicholas and his unfortunate daughters. When the city was occupied by the Reds after the Revolution, the youngest of the Martiniuks, Vladimir, who was just sixteen at the time, bundled Peter up in a wolf skin, roped him to a handcart, and fled with him on foot—on foot, fancy!—to the Netherlands, where he set up shop in one of Amsterdam's cobbled alleys, and changed his name to van den Maarten.

"Peter," she said, giving the samovar a light but affectionate pat, "was his sole possession, other than the handcart, of course. He planned to make his fortune by producing endless copies, and selling them to Dutch aristocrats, who were said to be mad about Russian tea."

"And were they?" I asked.

"I don't know," she replied, "and nor did Vladimir. He died of influenza in the great epidemic of 1918, leaving his shop and all that was in it to his landlady, Margriet van Rijn. Margriet married a farm boy from Bishop's Lacey, Arthur Elkins, who had fought in Flanders, and he brought her back with him to England not long after the end of the Great War.

"Arthur was killed when a factory chimney collapsed on him in 1924, and Margriet died of shock when they brought her the news. After her death, my sister and I found that she had willed us Peter the Great—and there was nothing for it but to open the St. Nicholas Tea Room. Twenty-five years ago, that was, and as you can see, we're still here.

"He's a very temperamental old samovar, you know," she went on, moving as if to caress his silver surface, but thinking better of it. "Of course, he's an awful old fraud. Oh, he spits boiling water and blows out fuses on occasion, but underneath it all he has a heart of gold—or at least, of silver."

"He's quite magnificent," I said.

"And doesn't he know it! Well, well, here I am talking about him as if he were a cat. When Grace was with us, she used to call him 'the Tyrant.' Imagine that! 'The Tyrant wants his polishing,' she'd say. 'The Tyrant wants his electrical contacts cleaned.' "

"Grace?" I asked.

"Grace Tennyson. Or Ingleby, as she is now."

"Grace Ingleby used to work here?"

"Oh, yes! Until she left to marry Gordon, she was our star waitress. You wouldn't think it to look at her, but she was as strong as an ox. You don't often see that in such a tiny bit of a thing.

"And she wasn't the slightest bit intimidated by Peter and his moods. Spark and spit as he may, Grace was never afraid to roll up her sleeves and have a good rummage round his innards."

"She sounds very clever," I said.

"She was all of that." Miss Puddock laughed. "All of that and more. And no wonder! One of our customers once told us—an RAF Squadron Leader, I think he was—and in confidence, of course—that Grace had the highest IQ he'd ever seen in 'the fairer sex,' as he put it: that if the people in Special Operations hadn't whisked her off to do top secret work, she might well have spent the rest of the war installing wireless sets in Spitfires."

"Top secret work?" I gasped. The thought of Grace Ingleby doing anything other than cringing in her dovecote tower, like a captive maiden waiting to be rescued by Sir Lancelot, was almost laughable.

"Of course, she would never breathe a word about it." Miss Puddock lowered her voice, in the way that people often do when they talk about the war. "They're not allowed to, you know. But then, we seldom see her nowadays. Since that tragedy with her little boy—"

"Robin," I said.

"Yes. Since then, she keeps to herself. I'm afraid she's not at all the same laughing girl who used to put Peter the Great in his place."

"Was Gordon a member of Special Operations, too?" I asked.

"Gordon?" She laughed. "Good lord, no. Gordon's 'a

farmer born and a farmer he shall die,' as Shakespeare wrote, or was it Harry Lauder, or George Formby, or someone like that? My memory's gone all wormholes, and so will yours, in time."

I couldn't think what to say, and I saw at once she thought she'd offended me.

"But not for many a year, dear. No, I'm quite sure *your* memory will still be going strong when the rest of us are in our graves and paved over for parking at the bowling palaces."

"Have you seen Mrs. Ingleby recently?" I asked.

"Not since Saturday night at the parish hall. Of course I had no opportunity to chat, what with our little musicale on my mind. The rest of the evening was a nightmare, wasn't it: the death of that poor man—the puppet that was carved with Robin's face? I don't know what Gordon was thinking, bringing Grace there when she's so fragile. But then, he had no way of knowing, did he?"

"No," I said. "I don't suppose he did."

By the time I set out for Buckshaw, it was well past lunchtime. Fortunately, Miss Puddock had wrapped a couple of buttered scones in paper and insisted upon tucking them into my pocket. I nibbled at them absently as I pedaled along the road, lost in thought.

At the end of the high street, the road made a gentle angle to the southwest as it skirted the southern perimeter of St. Tancred's churchyard.

If I hadn't glanced to my right, I mightn't have seen it: the Austin van, with "Porson's Puppets" in gold letters on its panels, parked at the side of the parish hall. Gladys's tires skidded in the dust as I applied her hand brakes and swerved into the churchyard.

As I pulled up, Nialla was stowing odds and ends in the van's interior.

"You've got it running!" I shouted. She gave me the kind of look that you might give to a bit of dog dirt in your porridge, and went on with her packing.

"It's me, Flavia," I said. "Have you forgotten me already?"

"Piss off, you little traitor," she snapped. "Leave me alone."

For an instant, I thought I was back at Buckshaw, talking to Feely. It was the kind of dismissal I've lived through a thousand times—and survived, I thought. I decided to stand my ground.

"Why? What have I done to you?"

"Oh, come off it, Flavia. You know as well as I do. You told the police I was at Buckshaw. They thought I was hiding out, or running away, or whatever you want to call it."

"I did no such thing!" I protested. "I haven't laid eyes on a policeman since I saw you in the coach house."

"But you were the only one who knew I was there."

As it always did when I was angry, my mind burned with crystal clarity.

"I knew you were there, Dogger knew you were there, and so did Mrs. Mullet, to name but three."

"I can hardly believe Dogger would peach on me."

"And nor would Mrs. Mullet," I said.

Good Lord! Was I actually defending Mrs. M?

"She may be a bloody gossip, but she's not mean," I

said. "She'd never rat on you. Inspector Hewitt came to Buckshaw—probably to ask me a few more questions about Saturday night—and happened to see you walking from the coach house to the kitchen. There's no more to it than that. I'm sure of it."

I could see that Nialla was thinking about it. I wanted nothing more than to take her by the shoulders and give her a good shaking, but I had to keep in mind the fact that her emotions were being stoked by a storm of hormones: fierce clouds of hydrogen, nitrogen, oxygen, carbon, and sulfur, combining and recombining in the eternal dances of life.

It almost made me forgive her.

"Here," I said, pulling the butterfly compact dramatically from my pocket and holding it out towards her. "I believe this belongs to you."

I hugged myself in anticipation of a tidal wave of gratitude and praise. But none came.

"Thanks," Nialla said, and pocketed the thing.

Thanks? Just *thanks*? The nerve! I'd show her: I'd pretend she hadn't hurt me; pretend I didn't care.

"I can't help noticing," I remarked casually, "that you're packing the van, which means that Bert Archer's repaired it and you're about to be on your way. Since Inspector Hewitt is nowhere in sight, I expect that means you're free to go."

"Free?" she repeated, and spat in the dirt. "Free? The vicar's given me four pounds, six shillings, and eightpence from the show. Bert Archer's bill comes to seven pounds ten. It's only because the vicar put in a word for me that he's willing to let me drive to Overton to pawn whatever

I can. If you call that free, then I'm free. It's all bloody well and good for Little Miss Nabob, who lives in a country house the size of Buckingham Palace, to make her smart-pants deductions. So think what you like, but don't bloody well patronize me!"

"All right," I said. "I didn't mean to. Here, take this, please."

I dug into my pocket again and pulled out the coin, the one Aunt Felicity had foisted upon Dogger, thinking it was a shilling. Dogger, in turn, had planted it in my pocket, believing, perhaps, that it would soon be spent on horehound sticks at Miss Cool's shop.

I handed it to Nialla, who looked at it with disbelief.

"Fourpence!" she said. "Bloody fourpence!"

Her tears were flowing freely as she flung it away among the tombstones.

"Yes, it *is* only fourpence," I said. "But it's fourpence in Maundy money. The coins are produced by the Royal Mint, to be handed out by the Sovereign—"

"Blow the Sovereign!" she shouted. "And blow the Royal Mint!"

"—on Maundy Thursday. They're quite rare. If I remember correctly, Bert Archer is a coin collector, and I think you'll find the Maundy fourpence will more than pay for the van."

With all the righteous dignity I could muster, I grabbed Gladys by the handlebars and shoved off for home. When I looked back from the corner of the church, Nialla was already on her hands and knees, scrabbling in the churchyard grass, and I couldn't tell whether the tears she was wiping away were tears of anger or of happiness.

· T W E N T Y · S I X ·

"ALL RIGHT, DOGGER," I SAID, "the jig is up."

I had found him in the butler's pantry, polishing Father's shoes.

Dogger's duties at Buckshaw varied in direct proportion to his present capabilities, his participation in our daily life rising and descending, rather like those colored balls in Galileo's thermometer that float at different levels in a glass tube, depending on the temperature. The fact that he was doing shoes was a good sign. It indicated clearly that he had advanced once again from gardener to butler.

He looked up from his work.

"Is it?" he asked.

"Cast your mind, if you please, back to Saturday evening at the parish hall. You're sitting beside me watching *Jack and the Beanstalk* when suddenly something goes wrong backstage. Rupert comes crashing down dead, and within minutes you are telling me that you fear we have seen murder. How did you know that? How did you know it wasn't an accident?"

This question had been gnawing away at my subconscious like a rat at a rope, but until that very moment, I had not been fully aware of it.

Dogger breathed on the upper of one of Father's regimental half-wellingtons before he answered, giving the glassy black surface a final loving rub with his shirtsleeve.

"The circumstances spoke against it," he said. "Mr. Porson was a perfectionist. He manufactured all his own equipment. A puppeteer works in the dark. There's no room for error. A frayed electrical wire was out of the question."

"It wasn't frayed," I said. "I spotted it when I was backstage with Inspector Hewitt. The insulation was scraped away."

"I should have been surprised if it wasn't," he said.

"Congratulations on a brilliant deduction," I said, "although it's one that didn't occur to me."

And it certainly hadn't, because the female mind doesn't work that way.

Seen from the air, the male mind must look rather like the canals of Europe, with ideas being towed along well-worn towpaths by heavy-footed dray horses. There is never any doubt that they will, despite wind and weather, reach their destinations by following a simple series of connected lines.

But the female mind, even in my limited experience, seems more of a vast and teeming swamp, but a swamp that knows in an instant whenever a stranger—even miles away—has so much as dipped a single toe into her waters. People who talk about this phenomenon, most of whom know nothing whatsoever about it, call it "woman's intuition."

Although I had arrived at much the same conclusion as Dogger, it had been by a very different route.

In the first place, although it was obvious that Rupert had been murdered for what he had done to a woman, I think I had known almost from the moment of his death that Nialla was not his killer.

"The instant he came crashing down onto the stage," I said, "Nialla leaped to her feet and moved towards him. Her first, and automatic, impulse was to go to his aid."

Dogger rubbed his chin and nodded.

"But she forced herself to stop," I went on, "as soon as she saw the smoke and the sparks. She quickly realized that touching any part of his body could mean instant death. For her—and her baby."

"Yes," Dogger said. "I noticed that, too."

"Therefore, Nialla is not the murderer."

"I believe you can safely remove her from your list," said Dogger.

It wasn't until I was halfway along the road to Culverhouse Farm that I realized how tired I was. I'd been up before the sun and had been going flat out ever since. But time was of the essence: If I didn't get there before Inspector Hewitt, I wouldn't know the gruesome details until I read about them in the *News of the World*.

This time, rather than crossing the river behind the church, I had decided to go round by the Hinley road and approach the farm from the west. By doing so, I would have the advantage of height to survey the terrain, as well as keeping to the cover of Gibbet Wood. Now that the noose was tightening, so to speak, it would never do to be ambushed by a cold-blooded killer.

By the time I was halfway up the chalky road of Gibbet Hill, I felt as if my blood were mud, and my shoes were made of lead. Under any other circumstances, I might have crawled into a quiet thicket for a nap, but it was not to be. Time was running out and, as Father was so fond of saying, "Tired is a mucker's excuse."

As I listened to the wind sighing and whispering in the treetops of Gibbet Wood, I found myself half hoping that Mad Meg would leap out and divert me from my mission. But this, too, was not to be: Aside from a yellowhammer tapping away like a busy shoemaker at the far side of the wood, there were no signs of life.

When I reached the top of the hill, Jubilee Field sloped away from me towards the river, a blanket of electric blue. At the outbreak of war, Gordon had been made to grow flax, or so Mrs. Mullet had told me, by order of HM Government, who required the stuff to manufacture parachutes. But the Battle of Britain had been years ago, and parachutes were no longer required in anywhere near the same quantity.

Still, working under the cloak of wartime necessity, it seemed that Gordon had managed to keep his secret crop of cannabis tucked handily away among the trees of Gibbet Wood, its very existence known to no more than a handful of people.

Which one of them, I wondered—if it was one of them—besides hating him passionately enough to kill, possessed sufficient electrical knowledge to have put the jolt to Rupert Porson?

A flash of light caught my eye: a reflection from the side of the road. I saw at once that it was one of Mad Meg's roadside junk ornaments, dangling by a string from a bramble bush. It was no more than a jagged bit of chrome trim, jarred loose from the radiator of some passing motorcar by the roughness of the road. Hanging beneath it, and twisting idly in the sun (it was this that had caught my eye) was a small ridged circular disk of silver which, judging by its red stains, had once been the lid on a half-pint tin of paint.

It reminded me, oddly enough, of something I had experienced the previous year when Father had taken Ophelia, Daphne, and me up to London for midnight mass at the Brompton Oratory. At the elevation of the Host, as the priest held the round white wafer (which some of us believed to be the Body of Christ) above his head for an inordinately long time, it had for just an instant caught the light from the candles and the colored reflections of the chancel, glowing with an unearthly iridescent sheen that was neither solid nor vaporous. At the time, it had seemed to me a signal that something momentous was about to happen.

Now, at the verge of Gibbet Wood, the oiled teeth of some mental cogwheel fell into place with a series of almost audible clicks.

Church. *Click!* Vicar. *Click!* Circle suspended. *Click!*
Bicycle clip. *Click!* Paint lid. *Click!* Meg. *Click!*

And I saw as if in a blinding vision: The vicar had been
here at Culverhouse Farm last Thursday. It was here that
he had caught his trouser leg in the bicycle chain and lost
his clip. He *had* been wearing it after all! And it was here
in the chalky dust that he had taken a tumble. The white
smudges on his black clerical garb had come from this
very road.

Mad Meg, the perennial magpie, had found the clip—
as she did with all shiny metallic objects dropped in the
vicinity of Gibbet Wood—and Meg had picked it up and
brought it with her to the vicarage.

*Her turned me out. Took old Meg's bracelet and turned her
out. Dirty, dirty!*

Meg's words echoed in my memory. She had been talking about the vicar's wife.

It was Cynthia Richardson who had taken the bicycle
clip—Meg's "bracelet"—away from her, and shooed her
out of the vicarage.

From the vicarage, it was only a hop, step, and jump to
the parish hall, where the thing turned up backstage, as
the murder weapon, in Rupert's puppet theater.

That's the way it must have happened. I was sure of it:
as sure as my name is Flavia de Luce. And I could hardly
wait to tell Inspector Hewitt!

Below me, in the distance, on the far shore of a sea of
blue flax, a gray Ferguson tractor was creeping slowly
alongside a stone wall, towing a flatbed trailer in its wake.
A flash of blond hair in the sunlight told me that the man
on foot, unloading stones for wall-mending, must be

Dieter, and there was no doubt that the person in overalls at the tractor's wheel was Sally. Even if they had been paying attention—which they weren't—they were too far away to spot me slinking down towards the farmhouse.

As I moved cautiously across the courtyard, the place seemed sunken in shadow: old stone piled upon old stone, with dead-eyed windows (as Sally had said) staring out blindly upon nothing. Which of the blank panes, I wondered, had been Robin's bedroom? Which of the empty windows had framed his lonely little face before that unthinkable Monday in September of 1945, when his short life had ended so abruptly at the end of a rope?

I gave a token knock at the door, and waited a respectful thirty seconds. At the end of that time I turned the knob and stepped inside.

"Mrs. Ingleby?" I called. "Mr. Ingleby? It's me, Flavia. I've come to see if you have any extra-large eggs."

I didn't think there would be a reply, and I was right. Gordon Ingleby was far too hardworking to be mooning about his house while there was still a trace of daylight outside, and Grace—well, Grace was either in her dovecote tower or wandering the hills. The inquisitive Mrs. Mullet had once asked me if I ever came upon her in my rambles about the shire.

"She's a queer one, that Grace Ingleby," she'd said. "My friend Edith—that's Edith Crowly, dear—her as was Edith Fisher before she married Jack—was walkin' over to her choir-practor's appointment in Nether Stowell— she'd missed the bus, you see—and she spotted Grace Ingleby comin' out of a copse at the bottom of Biddy's Lane which goes over the hill to nowhere.

" 'Grace!' she called out to her. 'Yoo-hoo, Grace Ingleby!' but Grace slithered through a stile—those are her very words: 'slithered through a stile,' if you can picture it, and by the time she got there herself, Grace was gone. 'Gone like a dog's breath in December.' That's what she said."

When it came to village gossip, Mrs. M was infallible, like Pope Pius IX.

I moved slowly along the corridor, fairly confident that I was alone in the house. At the end of the hall, beside a round window, a grandfather clock was "tocking" away to itself, the only sound in the otherwise silent farmhouse.

I looked quickly into each room: parlor, cloakroom, kitchen, pantry . . .

Beside the clock, two steps led up to a small square landing, and by peering round the corner, I could see that a narrow stairway continued upwards to the first floor.

Tucked in beneath the stairs was a cupboard, its oddly angled door of dovetailed boards fitted out with a splendid doorknob of green and white china that could only have been Wedgwood. I would have a jolly good dig through it later.

Each step gave out its own distinctive wooden groan as I ascended: like a series of old coffin lids being pried open, I thought with a pleasant shudder.

Steady on, Flave, old girl. No sense getting the wind up.

At the top of the stairs was a second small landing, from which, at right angles, another three steps led to the upstairs corridor.

It seemed obvious that all the rooms up here were bedrooms, and I was right: A glance into each of the first two revealed cold, spartan chambers, each with a single bed, a washstand, a wardrobe, and nothing more.

The large bedroom at the front of the house was Gordon and Grace's—no doubt about it. Aside from a double dresser and a double bed with a shabby quilt, this room was as cold and sterile as the others.

I had a quick snoop in the dresser drawers: on his side socks, underwear, a wristwatch with no strap, and a greasy, much-thumbed deck of playing cards bearing the crest of the Scots Greys; on hers, slips, knickers, a bottle of prescription sleeping ampules (my old friend chloral hydrate, I noted: $C_2H_3Cl_3O_2$—a powerful hypnotic that when slipped in alcohol to American thugs was called a "Mickey Finn." In England, it was slipped to high-strung housewives by country doctors and called "something to help you sleep.").

I couldn't keep back a quick smile as I thought of the time that, using no more than alcohol, lavatory cleaner, and a bottle of chlorine bleach, I had synthesized a batch of the stuff and given it, inside a doctored apple, to Phoebe Snow, a prize pig belonging to our neighbor Max Wight. Phoebe had taken five days and seventeen hours to sleep it off and, for a while, "The Remarkable Sleeping Pig" had been the eighth wonder of the British agricultural world. Max had graciously lent her for the fête at St. Tancred's, where Phoebe could be viewed, for sixpence a time, snoring in the back of a lorry marked "Sleeping Beauty." In the end, she had raised nearly five pounds for the choir's surplice fund.

With a sigh I returned to my work.

At the back of Grace's drawer, tucked beneath a soiled

linen handkerchief, was a well-thumbed Bible. I flipped open the cover and read the words on its flyleaf: *Please return to the parish church of St. Tancred's, Bishop's Lacey.*

As I was putting it back into the drawer, a slip of paper fell out and fluttered to the floor. I picked it up with my fingernails, taking great care not to leave my dabs on the thing.

The words were written in purple ink: *Grace——— Please call if I may provide any further solace.* And it was signed *Denwyn.*

Denwyn Richardson—the vicar. Whom Mad Meg had seen dancing naked in nearby Gibbet Wood.

I pocketed the evidence.

All that was left now was the small bedroom at the back of the house. Robin's bedroom. It had to be. I made my way across the silent landing and stopped in front of the closed door. It was only then that I began to feel a little apprehension. What if Gordon or Grace suddenly stormed into the house and up the stairs? How could I possibly explain my invasion of their bedrooms?

I put an ear to the door's dark paneling and listened. Not a sound.

I turned the knob and stepped inside.

As I had suspected, the room was Robin's, but it was the room of a little boy who had been dead five years: a pathetically small bed, folded blankets, an empty wardrobe, and linoleum on the floor. No shrine, no candles, no framed pictures of the deceased astride a rocking horse or hanging from his knees in an apple tree. What a bitter disappointment!

It was as bare and simple as van Gogh's *Bedroom in Arles*, but without the warmth; the room was as cold and impersonal as the winter moon.

After a quick look round, there was no more to see, and I stepped outside, closing the door respectfully—almost tenderly—behind me.

And then I heard a footstep downstairs.

What was I to do? The possibilities flashed across my brain. I could gallop down the stairs in tears, pretending I had become lost and disorientated while sleepwalking. I could claim I was suffering a nervous breakdown and didn't know where I was; that I had seen, from the farmyard, a face at an upstairs window, beckoning me with a long finger: that I had thought it was Grace Ingleby in distress.

Interesting though they were, these actions would all come with consequences, and if there was one thing I did not need, it was to introduce complications to my life. No, I thought, I would sneak down the stairs and hope like mad that I would not be caught.

But the idea died almost before it was born. The instant I put my foot on it, the top step gave out a ghastly groan.

There was a flapping near the bottom of the stairs, as if a large bird were trapped in the house. I went slowly, but steadily, down the rest of the staircase. At the bottom, I stuck my head round the corner and my blood ran cold.

A beam of bright sunlight illuminated the end of the hallway. In it, a little boy in rubber boots and a sailor suit was vanishing through the open door.

·TWENTY·SEVEN·

I WAS SURE OF IT.

He had been in the cupboard beneath the stairs all along. I stood there, stock-still at the open door, faced with a dilemma. What should I do? I knew for certain that once I stepped outside this farmhouse, I would not be likely to enter it ever again. Best to have a quick look behind the angled door now, before setting off in pursuit of the sailor-suited apparition.

Inside the dim cupboard, a length of string dangled from a naked bulb. I gave it a tug and the space sprang to feeble light. It was empty.

Empty, that is, except for a pair of child's rubber boots, very much like the ones I had just seen on the feet of the figure in the doorway.

The chief difference was that this pair of Dunlops was clodded with clay, still wet from the morning's rain.

Or the grave.

As I dashed through the open front door, I caught a glimpse of the navy blue sailor suit, just disappearing behind the machine shed. Beyond those rusty galvanized walls, I knew, was a bewildering warren of outbuildings: a maze of sagging sheds, any one of which could easily provide a dozen hiding places.

Off I loped in pursuit, like a hound on the scent. It never occurred to me to be afraid.

But then I slid to a sudden stop. Behind the machine shed, a narrow alley led off to the right. Had the fugitive darted down it to throw me off the track? I edged along the narrow passage, taking great care not to touch the neglected walls on either side. A single scratch from any one of the razor-sharp flaps of ripped tin would almost certainly end in tetanus, and I would end up hog-tied in a hospital ward, foaming at the mouth and wracked by bone-breaking spasms.

How happy Daffy and Feely would be!

"I told you she would come to no good end," Daffy would tell Father. "She should never have been allowed to run loose."

Accordingly, I inched slowly, crab-wise, along the narrow passage. When I finally reached the end, I found my way blocked on the left by a stack of battered petrol drums; on my right by a nettle-ridden pigpen.

As I edged back along the Passage of Death, which seemed, if anything, even more narrow on the return journey, I stopped to listen, but other than the distant sound of clucking hens, I could hear nothing but my own breathing.

I tiptoed softly along between the tumbledown sheds, paying close attention to my peripheral vision, aware that, at any moment, something could pounce upon me from a darkened doorway.

It wasn't until then that I noticed the tracks on the ground: tiny footprints that could only have been made by the waffle-patterned soles of a child's Dunlop rubber boot.

With all of my senses on high alert, I followed their trail.

On past the machine shed they led me; past the rusting hulk of an ancient tractor that leaned crazily to one side, missing a back wheel, looking for all the world like something half sunk in the sands, some ancient engine cast up by the sea.

Another jog to the left and I found myself at the foot of the dovecote, which towered above me like a fairy-tale castle, its piebald bricks stained almost golden by the late light of day.

Although I had been here before, it had been by a different route, and I slowly crept round it to the decrepit wooden door, the sharp pong of pigeon droppings already beginning to fill my nostrils.

Perhaps I had been wrong, I thought for a moment: Perhaps the boy in the sailor suit had run straight on past the tower, and was, by now, well away across the fields. But the footprints in the soil proved otherwise: They led straight to the dovecote door.

Something brushed against my leg and my heart nearly stopped.

"*Yow!*" said a voice.

It was Tock, the more vocal of the Inglebys' cats.

I put a finger to my lips to shush her, before I remembered that cats don't read sign language. But perhaps they do, for without another sound, she crouched low to the ground and slunk off into the shadows of the dovecote's interior.

Hesitantly, I followed her.

Inside, the place was as I remembered it: the myriad lights beaming in through chinks in the ancient brickwork; the claustrophobic, dust-choked air. This time, though, there was no banshee keening spilling out from the room above. The place was as silent as the crypt that lies beneath Death's own castle.

I put one foot onto the scaffolding and peered up to where it disappeared into the gloom above my head. The old wood let out a baleful croak, and I paused. Whoever—or whatever—was above me in the near-darkness, knew now that I had them cornered.

"Hallo!" I called out, as much to cheer myself as anything. "Hallo! It's me—Flavia! Anyone up there?"

The only sound from above was the buzzing of bees round the upper windows of the dovecote, grotesquely amplified by the tower's hollow structure.

"Don't be frightened," I called. "I'm coming up."

Little by little, one small step at a time, I began my precarious ascent. Again, I felt like Jack, this time climbing the beanstalk; dragging myself up, inch by inch, to face some unknown horror. The old wood creaked horribly, and I knew that it could crumble at any moment, dashing me down to certain death on the flagstones below, in much the same way that the giant—and Rupert—had come crashing down upon the puppet stage.

The climb seemed to go on forever. I stopped to listen: There was still no sound but that of the bees.

Up and up I went again, shifting my feet carefully from one wooden rung to the next, clutching at the crosspieces with fingers that were already beginning to grow numb.

As my eyes at last came level with the arched opening, the interior of the upper chamber came into view. A figure was hunched over the shrine to Robin Ingleby: the same figure that had fled the farmhouse.

On its knees, its back turned to me, the small apparition was dressed in a white and navy sailor suit with a middy collar and short trousers; the waffle soles of its Dunlop rubber boots were almost in my face. I could have reached out and touched them.

My knees began to tremble violently—threatening to buckle and send me plummeting down into the stony abyss.

"Help me," I said, the words brought up suddenly, inexplicably, and surprisingly, from some ancient and reptilian part of my brain.

A hand reached out, white fingers seized mine, and with surprising strength, hauled me up to safety. A moment later I found myself crouched, safe but trembling, face-to-face with the specter.

While the white sailor suit, with its crown-and-anchored jacket, and the Dunlop boots undoubtedly belonged to the dead Robin Ingleby, the strained and haggard face that stared back at me from beneath the beribboned HMS *Hood* hat was that of his tiny mother, Grace.

"You," I said, unable to restrain myself. "It was you."

Her face was sad, and suddenly very, very old. It was hard to believe that there remained in this woman a single atom of Grace Tennyson, that happy, outgoing girl who had once so cheerfully conquered the wired innards of Peter the Great, the silver samovar at the St. Nicholas Tea Room.

"Robin's gone," she said with a cough. "The Devil took him."

The Devil took him! Almost the same words Mad Meg had used in Gibbet Wood.

"And who was the Devil, Mrs. Ingleby? I thought for a while it was Rupert, but it wasn't. It was you, wasn't it?"

"Rupert's dead now," she said, touching her fingers to her temples as if she were dazed.

"Yes," I said. "Rupert's dead. He was the Punch and Judy man at the seaside, wasn't he? You had arranged to meet him there, and Robin saw you together. You were afraid he would tell Gordon."

She gave me a half-canny smile.

"At the seaside?" she said with a chuckling cough. "No, no—not at the seaside. Here . . . in the dovecote."

I had suspected for some time that the single set of footprints—the ones that had been found five years ago, leading up Jubilee Field to Gibbet Wood—had been those of Grace Ingleby, carrying the dead Robin in her arms. In order to leave only his footprints, she had put on her child's rubber boots. They were, after all, the same size as her own. As if to prove it, she was wearing them now.

Five years after his death, she was still dressing up in Robin's clothing, trying desperately to conjure her son back from the dead. Or to atone for what she had done.

"You carried him to the wood and hung him from a tree. But Robin died *here*, didn't he? That's why you've made this his shrine, and not his bedroom."

How matter-of-fact it sounded, this nightmare conversation with a madwoman! I knew that if ever I made it safely home to Buckshaw, I was going to be in need of a long, hot, steaming bath.

"I told him to stay down," she said rather petulantly. " 'Go back to the house, Robin,' I called out. 'You mustn't come up here.' But he wouldn't listen. Little boys are like that sometimes. Disobedient."

She coughed again, and shook her head ruefully. " 'I can do a trick with the rope!' he shouted back. He'd been playing cowboy all day with a rope he'd found in a shed."

Just as Sally had said. Grace must be telling me the truth.

"He climbed up here before we could stop him. Rupert was furious. He grabbed at Robin to give him a shake, but his iron brace slipped on the bricks. Robin—"

Now, silent tears were coursing down her face.

"Fell," I said. There was no need to elaborate.

"Fell," she repeated, and the way she dragged out the word made it echo from the bricks, hovering grotesquely in the round chamber: a sound I would never forget.

With it came an idea.

"Was it Rupert who thought of the Punch and Judy

story? That Robin had been playing out the scene with Punch and the hangman?"

"Where did you hear that?" she demanded, suddenly lucid, canny. I thought of Mad Meg's smile in Gibbet Wood; these two women had so much in common.

"Your evidence to the jury at the inquest," I answered. "It's public knowledge."

I did not think it necessary to add that I had heard it from Sally.

"He made me do it," she said, wiping her eyes on the sleeve of the sailor suit, and I realized for the first time how much she looked like Robin. Once noticed, the resemblance was eerie.

"Rupert told me no one would ever know. Robin's neck was broken in the fall, and if we . . . if I . . ."

A shudder ran through her entire body.

"If I wouldn't do as he ordered, he'd tell Gordon what had been going on between us. I'd be the one to be punished. Gordon's quick with his fists, you know."

As was Rupert. I'd seen the bruises he left on Nialla's arm. Two quick-tempered men. And rather than fighting it out between them, they both had made punching bags of their women.

"Was there no one you could talk to? The vicar, for instance?"

This seemed to set her off, and she was racked by a siege of coughing. I waited until she had finished.

"The vicar," she said, gasping for breath, "is the only one who has made these past five years bearable."

"He knew about Robin?" I could hardly believe it!

"A clergyman's lips are sealed," she said. "He's never

breathed a word. He tried to come to Culverhouse Farm once a week, just to let me talk. The man's a saint. His wife thought he was—"

"In love with you."

She nodded, squeezing her eyes tight shut, as if she were in excruciating pain.

"Are you all right?" I asked.

"Wait a few minutes," she said, "and I shall be fine."

Her body was crumbling before my eyes, tipping towards the opening into the shaft.

I grabbed at her arm, and as I did so, a glass bottle that she had been clutching in her fist fell to the brick floor and bounced away, clinking, into the corner, sending a pigeon clattering up towards the opening. I dragged Grace into the center of the chamber and sprang after the bottle, which had come to rest in a mound of ancient guano.

The label told me all I needed to know: *Calcium Cyanide*, it said. *Poison*.

Rat poison! The stuff was in common farm use, particularly on those farms whose henhouses attracted vermin. There was still one of the white tablets in the bottom. I removed the stopper and smelled it. Nothing.

Grace was now flat on the floor, twitching, her limbs flailing.

I dropped to my knees and sniffed her lips. The scent of bitter almonds.

The tablets of calcium cyanide, I knew, as soon as they met the moisture of her mouth, throat, and stomach, would produce hydrogen cyanide, a toxic gas that could kill in five minutes.

There was no time to waste. Her life was in my hands. I almost panicked at the thought—but I didn't.

I took a careful look round, registering every detail. Aside from the candle, the shrine, the photograph of Robin, and his toy sailboat, there was nothing in the chamber but rubble.

Well, not quite nothing. On one wall was an ancient watering device for the birds: an inverted glass bulb and tube whose gravity feed kept a dish full for the pigeons to dip their beaks into. From the clarity of the water, it seemed as if Grace had recently filled it.

A glass cock allowed the gravity feed to be turned off. I gave it a twist and pulled the full dish carefully out of its spring clips.

Grace moaned horribly on the floor, apparently no longer aware of my presence.

Treading carefully, I moved to the spot from which the pigeon had flown. Feeling gingerly in the straw with my fingertips, I was quickly rewarded. An egg. No, two little eggs!

Putting them down gently beside the dish, I picked up the sailboat. At the bottom of its tin keel was a lead weight. Damn!

I wedged the thing into the crack between two bricks in the windowsill and pulled for all I was worth—then pulled again. The third time, the weight snapped off.

Using the sharp bottom edge of the keel as a makeshift putty knife, I leaned out the opening to the wide shelf that had served for centuries as a perch.

Below me, the farmyard was empty. No sense wasting time by yelling for help.

I ground the thin keel along the ledge until I had gathered what I needed, then scraped it off, with a reluctant finger, into the water dish.

One step left.

Although their small size made it a tricky bit of work, I cracked the eggs, one at a time, the way Mrs. Mullet had taught me: a sharp rap in the middle, then using the two halves of the shell like twin egg cups, tipping the yolk back and forth from one to the other until the last of the whites had oozed away into the waiting water dish.

Taking up the glass pill bottle, I used it as a pestle: twisting, grinding, and stirring until I had perhaps half a teacup of grayish curded mud, with the slightest tinge of yellow.

So that neither of us would knock it over—Grace was now kicking feebly and pink in the face from lack of oxygen—I sat down beside her, cross-legged on the floor, and pulled her head into my lap, face upwards. She was too weak to resist.

Then seizing her nose between my thumb and forefinger, I pulled open her mouth, hoping that, in her spasms, she wouldn't bite me.

She snapped it shut at once. This was not going to be as easy as I had thought.

I pinched her nose a little tighter. Now, if she wanted to breathe at all, it was going to have to be through her mouth. I hated myself for what I was doing to her.

She struggled, her eyes bulging—and then her mouth flew open and she sucked in a breath of air—then snapped it shut again.

As slowly and as gently as I could, I leaned over and

picked up the brimming dish, awaiting the proper moment.

It came sooner than I expected. With a gasp, Grace's mouth flew open, and as she sucked in air again, I dumped the contents of the dish into her mouth and slammed it shut with the heel of my hand under her chin. The empty dish fell to the floor with a crash.

But Grace was fighting me; I could see that. Some part of her was so dead set on dying that she was keeping the stuff in her mouth, refusing to swallow.

With the little finger of my right hand, I began prodding at her gullet, like a seabird digging in the sand.

We must have looked like Greek wrestlers: she with her head locked tightly in the crook of my arm, me bending over her, trembling with the sheer physical effort of trying to keep her from spitting out the nauseating mixture.

And then, just before she went limp, I heard her swallow. She was no longer resisting. I carefully pried open her mouth. Aside from a faint and distasteful glistening of foreign matter, it was empty.

I raced to the window, leaning out as far as I could into the sunshine.

My heart sank. The farmyard was still empty.

Then suddenly there was a noise of machinery in the lane, and a moment later, the gray Fergie came clattering into view, Sally bouncing at the wheel and Dieter dangling his long legs over the gate of the trailer.

"Sally! Dieter!" I shouted.

At first they didn't know where my voice was coming from. They were looking everywhere round the yard, perplexed.

"Up here—in the dovecote!"

I dug in my pocket, fished out Alf's willow whistle, and blew into it like a demented bobby.

At last they spotted me. Sally gave a wave.

"It's Grace!" I hollered. "She's taken poison! Telephone Dr. Darby and tell him to come at once."

Dieter was already dashing for the farmhouse, running full tilt, the way he must once have done when scrambling for his Messerschmitt.

"And tell him to make sure he's got amyl nitrite and sodium thiosulfate in his bag!" I shouted, in spite of a couple of wayward tears. "He's going to need them!"

· T W E N T Y · E I G H T ·

"Pigeon droppings?" Inspector Hewitt said, for perhaps the third time. "You're telling me that you concocted an antidote from *pigeon droppings?*"

We were sitting in the vicar's study, sizing one another up.

"Yes," I said. "I had no other choice. Pigeon guano, when it's left outdoors in the sunlight, is remarkably high in $NaNO_3$—sodium nitrate—which is why I had to scrape it from the outside perch, rather than using the older stuff that was in the chamber. Sodium nitrate is an antidote to cyanide poisoning. I used the whites of pigeons' eggs to produce the suspension. I hope she's all right."

"She's fine," the Inspector said, "although we're seeking an opinion about whether to charge you with practicing medicine without a license."

I studied his face to see if he was teasing, but he didn't seem to be.

"But," I protested, "Dr. Darby said he couldn't have done better himself."

"Which isn't saying much," the Inspector said, looking away from me and out the window.

I saw that I had him beaten.

Inspector Hewitt had flagged me down on my way back to Buckshaw, and asked me to account for my presence at Culverhouse Farm.

A hastily fabricated story about fetching eggs for Mrs. Mullet, who wanted to make an angel food cake, seemed to have got me off the hook. At least for now.

The Inspector had assured me that Grace Ingleby was still alive; that she had been taken to the hospital at Hinley.

He did not say that my antidote had saved her life. I supposed only time would tell.

The vicar, having given up his desk and chair to Inspector Hewitt, stood like a black stork in the corner, rubbing at his eyeglasses with a linen handkerchief.

As Detective Sergeant Woolmer stood at one of the windows, pretending to polish an anastigmat lens from his precious camera, Detective Sergeant Graves glanced up from his notes just long enough to give me a beaming smile. I'd like to think that the almost imperceptible shake of his head that came with it was a sign of admiration.

And even though they're not yet aware of one another, I also like to think that Sergeant Graves will one day marry my rotten sister Ophelia and carry her off to a vine-covered cottage just far enough from Buckshaw that I can drop in whenever I feel like it for a good old gab about murder.

But now there was Dieter to take into account. Life was becoming so complicated.

"Just begin at the beginning," Inspector Hewitt said, suddenly back from his reverie. "I want to make sure we haven't missed anything."

Was I detecting a note of sarcasm? I hoped not, since I really liked the man, although he could be somewhat slow.

"Mrs. Ingleby—Grace—was having an affair with Rupert Porson. Rupert had been coming to Culverhouse Farm for years because . . . Gordon supplied him with marijuana. It eased the pain of his polio, you see."

He must have sensed my hesitation.

"No need to worry about betraying him," he said, "Mr. Ingleby has been most frank with us. It's your version I want to hear."

"Rupert and Grace arranged to meet at the seaside, years ago," I said. "Robin saw them there together. He stumbled upon them again, later, in the dovecote. Rupert made a grab for him, or something like that, and Robin tumbled down the central shaft and broke his neck. It was an accident, but still, Robin was dead. Rupert cooked up the idea of having Grace take his body, after dark, to Gibbet Wood, and hang it from a tree. Robin had been seen by several people playing with a rope.

"It was Rupert, too, who invented the story that Robin had been playing out the scene between Punch and Jack Ketch—that he had seen it at the seaside puppet show. Punch and the hangman's tale is one that's known to every child in England. No one would question the story that Robin had accidentally hanged himself. It was just bizarre enough to be true. As a well-known puppeteer, Rupert couldn't afford to have his name linked in any way with the death of a child. He needed to erase himself from the scene of Robin's death. No one but Grace knew he had been at the farm that day.

"That's why he threatened her. He told her that if she didn't do as he wanted, he would spill the beans to Gordon—sorry, I mean that he would inform Gordon that he'd been carrying on an affair with his wife. Grace would lose both her son and her husband. She was already half mad with grief and fear, so it was probably quite easy to manipulate her.

"Because she's so small, she was able to put on Robin's rubber boots to carry his body up to Gibbet Wood. She's remarkably strong for her size. I found that out when she hauled me up into the dovecote chamber. After she'd hung Robin's body from the tree, she put the boots on his feet, and went home the long way round, barefoot."

Inspector Hewitt nodded and scribbled a note in his microscopic handwriting.

"Mad Meg came upon the body hanging there, and thought it was the Devil's work. I've already given you the page from my notebook, so you've seen the drawing she made. She's quite good, actually, don't you think?"

"Um," the Inspector said. It was a bad habit he was picking up by associating too much with Dr. Darby.

"That's why she was afraid to touch him, or even tell anyone. Robin's body hung there in Gibbet Wood until Dieter found it.

"Last Saturday at the church hall, when Meg saw

Robin's face on Jack, the puppet, she thought the Devil had brought the dead boy back to life, shrunk him, and put him to work on the stage. Meg has her times very badly mixed up. You can tell that from the drawing: The Robin hanging from the tree is a sight she saw five years ago. The vicar taking his clothes off in the wood is something she saw last Thursday."

The vicar went beet red, and ran a finger round the inside of his clerical collar. "Yes, well . . . you see—"

"Oh, I knew you had come a cropper, Vicar," I said. "I knew it the instant I saw you in the graveyard—the day you met Rupert and Nialla, remember? Your trouser leg was ripped, you were covered with chalky smudges from the road at Culverhouse Farm, and you'd lost your bicycle clip."

"So I had," the vicar said. "My trousers got caught up in the ruddy chain and I was catapulted into the ditch."

"Which explains why you went in among the trees of Gibbet Wood—to take off your clothes—to try to clean them up. You were afraid of what Cynthia would say— sorry, Mrs. Richardson, I mean. You said as much in the churchyard. Something about Cynthia having you on the carpet."

The vicar remained silent, and I don't think I ever admired him more than I did in that moment.

"Because you've been going to Culverhouse Farm at least once a week since Robin died five years ago, Cynthia—Mrs. Richardson, I mean—had somehow got the idea that there was more in your meetings with Grace Ingleby than met the eye. That's why you've recently been keeping your visits secret."

"I'm not really at liberty to discuss that," the vicar said. "The wearing of the dog collar puts paid to any tendency one has to be a chatterbox. But I must put in, in her defense, that Cynthia is very loyal. Her life is not always an easy one."

"Nor is Grace Ingleby's," I pointed out.

"No, nor is Grace's."

"At any rate," I went on, "Meg lives in an old shack, somewhere in the depths of Gibbet Wood. She doesn't miss much that goes on there."

Or anywhere else, I wanted to add. It had only just occurred to me that it was almost certainly Meg that Rupert and Nialla had heard prowling round near their tent in the churchyard.

"She saw you taking your trousers off beside the old gallows at the very spot where she had seen Robin hanging. That's why she drew you into her picture."

"I see," said the vicar. "At least, I *think* I see."

"Meg picked up your trouser clip in the road, meaning to use it for one of those dangling sculpture things of hers, but she recognized it as yours, and—"

"It has my initials on it," the vicar said. "Cynthia scratched them on."

"Meg can't read," I said, "but she's very observant. Look at the detail in her drawing. She even remembered the little Church of England pin in your lapel."

"Good heavens," the vicar said, coming round to peer over Inspector Hewitt's shoulder. "So she did."

"She came here on Saturday afternoon to return the trouser clip, and while she was looking for you, she happened to wander into the parish hall during Rupert's performance. When she saw the shrunken Robin on the stage, she went into a right old squiff. You and Nialla carried her off to the vicarage and tucked her in on your couch in the study. That's when the clip—and Nialla's compact—fell out of her pocket. I found the compact on the floor behind the couch the next day. I didn't find the bicycle clip because Grace Ingleby had already picked it up the day before."

"Hold on," the Inspector said. "No one's claiming to have seen Mrs. Ingleby anywhere near the vicarage—or the parish hall—on Saturday afternoon."

"Nor did they," I said. "What they *did* say was that the egg lady had been there."

Had Inspector Hewitt been the sort of man whose mouth was prone to falling open when astonished, he'd have been gaping like a gargoyle.

"Good Lord," he said flatly. "Who told you that?"

"Mrs. Roberts and Miss Roper," I said. "They were in the vicarage kitchen after church yesterday. I assumed you had questioned them."

"I believe we did," Inspector Hewitt said, cocking an eyebrow at Sergeant Graves, who flipped back through the pages of his notebook.

"Yes, sir," said Sergeant Graves. "They both gave in statements, but there was nothing said about egg ladies."

"The egg lady was Grace Ingleby, of course," I said helpfully. "She came down from Culverhouse Farm late on Saturday afternoon with eggs for the vicarage. There was no one else around. Something made her go into the vicar's study. Perhaps she heard Meg snoring, I don't know. But she found the bicycle clip on the floor, picked it up, and pocketed it."

"How can you be so sure?" asked Inspector Hewitt.

"I can't be sure," I said. "What I *can* be sure of, because he told me so, is that the vicar lost his bicycle clip last Thursday . . ."

The vicar nodded in agreement.

". . . on the road at Gibbet Hill . . . and that you and I, Inspector, found it on Sunday morning clamped to the rail of the puppet theater. The rest is mere guesswork."

The Inspector scratched at his nose, made another note, and looked up at me as if he had been shortchanged.

"Which brings us neatly back to Rupert Porson," he said.

"Yes," I replied. "Which brings us neatly back to Rupert Porson."

"About whom you are about to enlighten us."

I ignored his twitting and went on. "Grace had known Rupert for years. Perhaps since even before she met Gordon. For all I know, she might even have traveled with him at one time as his assistant."

I knew by the sudden closed look on Inspector Hewitt's face that I had hit the nail on the head. *Bravo, Flavia!* I thought. *Go to the head of the class!*

There were times when I surprised even myself.

"And even if she hadn't," I added, "she'd certainly attended some of the shows he put on round the countryside. She'd have paid particular attention to the electrical rigging. Since Rupert manufactured all of his own lighting equipment, I can hardly believe that he wouldn't have taken the opportunity to show off the details to a fellow electrician. He was rather vain about his skills, you know.

"I expect Grace took the keys from the vicarage and walked straightaway through the churchyard, to the parish hall. The afternoon performance was over by that time; the audience had gone, and so had Rupert. There was little chance of her being seen. Even if she had been spotted, no one would have paid her the slightest attention, would they? After all, she was just the egg lady. Besides, she and her husband are parishioners of St. Tancred's, so no one would have given her a second look.

"She went into the hall, and using the corridor to the left, and locking the door behind her, went up the two short flights of steps to the stage.

"She climbed up onto the bridge of the puppet stage, and scraped away the insulation from the wiring, using the bicycle clip as a kind of spoke-shave. Then she slipped the clip over the wooden framework of the stage, touching the bared electrical wire on the one side and the metal rod that released Galligantus on the other. Bob's your uncle! That's all there was to it. If you've had a close look at the clip, you've likely already found a small abrasion mark on the inside center—and perhaps slight traces of copper."

"S'truth!" Sergeant Woolmer let slip, and Inspector Hewitt shot him a look.

"Unlike most of the other suspects—except Dieter, of course, who built wireless sets as a boy in Germany— Grace Ingleby had the necessary electrical training. Before the war, before marrying Gordon, she worked in a factory installing radio sets in Spitfires. I've been told that her IQ is nearly equal in number to the Psalms."

"Dammit!" Inspector Hewitt shouted, leaping to his feet. "Sorry, Vicar. But why haven't we found these things out, Sergeant?"

He glared from one of his men to the other, including both in his exasperation.

"With respect, sir," Sergeant Woolmer ventured, "it could be because we're not Miss de Luce."

It was a bold thing to say, and a rash one. If what I'd seen in the pictures at the cinema were true, it was the sort of remark that could result in the sergeant becoming a road-mender before sunset.

After a nerve-racking silence, the Inspector said, "You're right, of course, Sergeant. We don't have the same entrée to the homes and hearths of Bishop's Lacey, do we? It's an area in which we could do better. Make a note of it."

No wonder his subordinates adored him!

"Yes, sir," said Sergeant Graves, scribbling something in his notebook.

"Then," I went on, "having set the trap, Grace went out by the hallway door at the right of the stage, and she locked that one, too—probably to keep anyone from going backstage and discovering what she had done. Not that anyone would, of course, but I expect she was under a great deal of stress. She's been planning to take her revenge on Rupert for a long time. It wasn't until she spotted the vicar's trouser clip on the floor that she saw exactly how it could be done. As I've said, she's a very intelligent woman."

"But," Inspector Hewitt said, "if both doors were locked, how did Porson get up onto the stage for the performance? He couldn't have locked himself in because he didn't have the key."

"He used that little staircase in front of the stage," I said. "It's not as steep as the two in the side halls, and it's only a single flight. Narrow stairs were difficult for Rupert because of his leg brace, and he took the shortest route. I noticed that about him last Thursday when he was checking the hall's acoustics."

"Quite an ingenious theory," Inspector Hewitt remarked. "But it doesn't explain everything. How, for instance, would the alleged murderer know that such a gimcrack bit of tin would result in Porson's death?"

"Because Rupert always leaned on a rail of iron piping as he operated the puppets. With all the lighting equipment that was hung backstage, the railing had to be grounded through the mains. The instant Rupert touched the live Galligantus lever, his lower body pressed tight against the rail as it was, with his right leg clamped in an iron brace, the current would have shot straight up his arm and through—"

"His heart," said the Inspector. "Yes, I see."

"Rather like Saint Lawrence," I said, "who, as you know, was done to death on a grill."

"Thank you, Flavia," Inspector Hewitt said. "I think you've made your point."

"Yes," I said, rather smugly, "so do I. Will that be all, then?"

Sergeant Graves was grinning away over his notebook like Scrooge over his ledgers.

Inspector Hewitt wrinkled his brow in a look that I had seen before: a look of exasperated curiosity held in firm check by years of training and a strong sense of duty.

"I think so, yes—except for one or two small points, perhaps."

I gave him that beaming, superior smile: all teeth and thin lips. I almost hated myself for doing it.

"Yes, Inspector?"

He walked to the window, his hands clasped behind his back, as I had seen him do before on several occasions. At last he turned: "Perhaps I'm a bit of a dim bulb," he said.

If he was waiting for me to contradict him, he'd be waiting until the cows came home in purple pajamas.

"Your observations on the death of Rupert Porson have been most illuminating. But try as I may, I have failed utterly to follow your reasoning in the death of Robin Ingleby.

"The boots, yes . . . perhaps. It's a possibility, I admit, but far from a certainty. Slender evidence when it comes to court. *If* the case is reopened, that is. But we shall require far more than a pair of child's boots if we are to prevail again upon their Lordships."

His tone was almost pleading. I had already decided that there were certain observations that would remain forever locked away in my brain: choice nuggets of deduction that I would keep for my own private delectation. After all, the Inspector had far more resources at his disposal than I did.

But then I thought of his beautiful wife, Antigone.

Whatever would she think of me if she found that I had thwarted him? One thing was certain: It would scotch any idea I might have had of sipping tea in the garden of their tastefully decorated maisonette.

"Very well," I said reluctantly. "There are a few more points. The first is this: When Dieter went running back to the farmyard, having just discovered Robin's dead body hanging in Gibbet Wood, the windows of the house were empty. No one was awaiting his arrival, as might have been expected. Surely the mother of a missing child would be frantic, waiting for the slightest scrap of news? But Grace Ingleby wasn't keeping watch at the windows. And why not? The reason is a simple one: She already knew that Robin was dead."

Somewhere behind me, the vicar gasped.

"I see." Inspector Hewitt nodded. "An ingenious theory . . . most ingenious. But still hardly enough to build a case upon."

"Granted," I agreed, "but there's more."

I looked from one of them to another: the vicar, Inspector Hewitt, and Sergeant Graves, their eager faces thrust forward, hanging upon my every word. Even the hulking Sergeant Woolmer slowed his polishing of the intricate lens.

"Robin Ingleby's hair was always a haystack," I told them. " 'Tousled' is perhaps the proper word. You can see it in his photos. And yet when he was found hanging from the timbers of the old gallows, his hair was as neatly combed as if he'd just climbed down from the barber's chair. Meg captured it perfectly in her drawing. See?"

There was an intake of breath as everyone huddled over the page from my notebook.

"It was something that only a mother would do," I said. "She couldn't resist. Grace Ingleby wanted her son to be presentable when he was found, hanging by the neck, dead in Gibbet Wood."

"Good Lord!" Inspector Hewitt said.

· T W E N T Y · N I N E ·

"Good Lord," Father exclaimed. "There's Broadcasting House. They've set up cameras in Portland Place."

He got up from his chair for the umpteenth time and hurried across the drawing room to twiddle with the knobs on the television receiving set.

"Please be quiet, Haviland," Aunt Felicity said. "If they were interested in your commentary, the BBC would have sent for you."

Aunt Felicity, who had barely got home to Hampstead, had hurried back again to Buckshaw as soon as the idea came into her head. She had hired the television for the occasion ("at ruinous expense," she hastened to point out), and because of it, was now enjoying vastly increased dictatorial powers.

Early in the morning of the previous day, the workmen

had begun erecting a receiving aerial on the ramparts of Buckshaw.

"It needs to be high enough to pick up the signal from the new transmitting tower at Sutton Coldfield," Aunt Felicity had said, in a voice that suggested television was her own invention. "I *had* wanted all of us to go up to London to attend the Porson obsequies," she went on, "but when Lady Burwash let slip that the Sitwells were having in the telly . . .

"No, no, don't protest, Haviland. It's educational. I'm only doing it for the good of the girls."

Several muscular workers, dressed in overalls, had lugged the set from the back of a pantechnicon and into the drawing room. There it now crouched, its single gray eye staring, like a flickering Cyclops, at those of us gathered in its baleful glow.

Daffy and Feely were huddled together on a chester-field, feigning boredom. Father had invited the vicar and told them to watch their language.

Mrs. Mullet was enthroned in a comfortable wing-backed chair, and Dogger, who preferred not to sit in Father's presence, stood silently behind her.

"I wonder if they have televisions in Portland Place," Feely said, idly, "or whether they might, rather, be looking out their windows?"

I recognized this at once as an attempt to twit Father, whose contempt for television was legendary.

"Television is a bauble," he would reply, whenever we pleaded with him to have a receiver installed. "If God meant for pictures to be sent through the air, He'd have never given us the cinema.

"Or the National Gallery," he'd add sourly.

But in this case, he had been overruled.

"But it's History, Haviland," Aunt Felicity had said in a loud voice. "Would you have denied your daughters the opportunity to watch Henry the Fifth address his men on Crispin's Day?"

She had taken up a stance in the middle of the drawing room.

"This story shall the good man teach his son;
And Crispin Crispian shall ne'er go by,
From this day to the ending of the world,
But we in it shall be remembered;
We few, we happy few, we band of brothers—"

"Nonsense!" Father said, but Aunt Felicity, like Henry the Fifth, pushed on, undaunted:

"For he today that sheds his blood with me
Shall be my brother; be he ne'er so vile,
This day shall gentle his condition:
And gentlemen in England now abed
Shall think themselves accursed they were not here,
And hold their manhoods cheap whiles any speaks
That fought with us upon St. Crispin's day."

"That's all very well and good, but they didn't have television in 1415," Father had said rather sullenly, missing her point entirely.

But then, yesterday, something remarkable had happened. One of the mechanics, who had been in the drawing room with his eye intently upon the receiver, had begun calling instructions out the window to a companion on the lawn, who relayed them, in a drill-sergeant voice, to the man on the roof.

"Hold it, Harry! Back . . . back . . . back. No . . . you've lost it. Back t'other way . . ."

At that very moment, Father had walked into the room, planning, I think, to heap scorn upon the entire operation, when his eye was taken by something on the snow-blown screen.

"Stop!" he shouted, and his word was passed along in ever-diminishing echoes by the mechanics, out the window and up onto the ramparts.

"By George," he said. "It's the 1856 British Guiana. Back a little!" he shouted, waving his hands to illustrate.

Again his instructions were carried aloft in a verbal bucket brigade, and the picture cleared a little.

"Just as I thought," he said. "I'd know it anywhere. It's coming to auction. Turn up the sound."

As Fate would have it, the BBC was at that moment transmitting a program on the topic of stamp collecting, and a moment later, Father had pulled up a chair, fastened his wire-framed spectacles on the end of his nose, and refused to be budged.

"Quiet, Felicity!" he barked, when she tried to intervene. "This is of the utmost importance."

And so it was that Father had allowed the One-Eyed Beast to sit in his drawing room.

At least for the time being.

And now, as the hour drew near for Rupert's inhumation (a word I had heard Daffy trot out for Mrs. Mullet's benefit), Dogger drifted off to the foyer to admit the vicar who, even though he was not conducting the funeral, nevertheless felt the professional necessity of wringing the hands of each of us as he came into the room.

"Dear, dear," he said. "And to think that the poor chap expired right here in Bishop's Lacey."

No sooner had he taken a seat on the sofa than the doorbell sounded again, and a few moments later Dogger returned with an unexpected guest.

"Mr. Dieter Schrantz," he announced at the door, slipping effortlessly back into his role as butler.

Feely sprang to her feet, and came floating across the drawing room to greet Dieter, hands outstretched, palms down, as if she were walking in her sleep.

She was radiant, the vixen!

I was praying she'd trip on the rug.

"Draw the drapes, please, Dogger," Father said, and as Dogger complied, the light vanished from the room and left all of us sitting together in the gloom.

Into view on the little tube, as I have said, floated the wet pavement of Portland Place in front of Broadcasting House, as the hushed and solemn voice of the BBC announcer took up the tale (it may have been Richard Dimbleby, or perhaps it was just someone who sounded like him):

"*And now, from every corner of the realm, come the children. They are brought here today by their mothers and fathers, their nurses, their governesses, and some few, I daresay, by their grandparents.*

"*They have been standing here in Portland Place for hours in the rain, young and old, each patiently waiting his or her* turn to bid a last, sad farewell to the man who captivated their hearts; to pay their respects to Rupert Porson, the genius who kidnapped them every afternoon at four from their everyday lives and, like the Pied Piper, led them away into his Magic Kingdom. . . ."

Genius? Well, that was stretching things a bit. Rupert was a brilliant showman; there was no doubt about it. But *genius*? The man was a scoundrel, a womanizer, a bully, a brute.

But did that disqualify him from being a genius? I don't suppose it did. Brains and morals have nothing to do with one another. Take myself, for instance: I am often thought of as being remarkably bright, and yet my brains, more often than not, are busily devising new and interesting ways of bringing my enemies to sudden, gagging, writhing, agonizing death.

I am quite firm in my belief that poisons were put upon the earth in the first place to be discovered—and put to good use—by those of us with the wits, but not necessarily the physical strength, to . . .

The poison! I had completely forgotten about those doctored chocolates!

Had Feely actually eaten them? It seemed unlikely; if she had, she wouldn't be sitting here with such maddening calm as Dieter, like a horse breeder admiring his filly over a paddock fence, gazed appreciatively upon her better points.

The hydrogen sulfide I had injected into the sweets was not sufficient to kill, at any rate. Once inside the body—assuming that anyone was stupid enough to swallow it—it would oxidize to hydrogen sulfate, in which form it would be eliminated eventually in the urine.

Was it such a crime, this thing that I had done? Dimethyl sulfide was dumped by the boatload into artificially flavored sweets, and no one, to the best of my knowledge, had yet been hanged for it.

As my eyes became accustomed to the dimness of the drawing room, I was able to have a quick look round at the faces illuminated by the television's glow. Mrs. Mullet? No, Feely wouldn't have wasted her chocolates on Mrs. Mullet. Father and Dogger were out of the question, too, as was the vicar.

There was a remote possibility that Aunt Felicity had scarfed them, but if she had, her outraged trumpetings would have made even Sabu's elephant bolt for the hills.

Therefore, the chocolates must still be in Feely's room. If only I could slip away, unnoticed in the semidarkness . . .

"Flavia," Father said, with a wave towards the little screen, "I know how difficult this must be for you, in particular. You may be excused, if you wish."

Salvation! Off to the poisoned chocolates!

But wait: If I slunk away now, what would Dieter think of me? As for the others, I didn't give a rap . . . well, perhaps a little for the vicar. But to be thought of as weak in the eyes of a man who had actually been shot down in flames . . .

"Thank you, Father," I said. "I think I shall manage to struggle through."

I knew it was the kind of stiff-upper-lippish response

he wanted, and I was right. Having made the required parental noises, he sank back into his chair with something like a sigh.

A froggish sound went up from the depths of the chair in the corner, and I knew instantly that it was Daffy.

The television cameras were cutting away to the interior of Broadcasting House, to a large studio piled to the rafters with flowers, and there among them lay Rupert—or at least his coffin: an ornate piece of furniture that mirrored the television lights and the nearby mourners in its highly polished surface, its silver-plated handles positively glistening in the gloom.

Now another camera was showing a little girl as she approached the bier ... hesitantly ... tentatively—pushed forward in a series of thrusts by a self-conscious mother. The child wiped away a tear before placing a wreath of wildflowers at the rail in front of the coffin.

The scene was cut to a close-up of a full-grown woman, weeping.

Next, a man in funereal black stepped forward. He plucked three roses from the wall of floral tributes, and presented each one delicately: one to the child, one to the mother, and the third to the weeping woman. Having done so, he pulled forth a large white handkerchief, turned away from the camera, and blew his nose with grief-stricken energy.

It was Mutt Wilmott! He was stage-managing the whole thing! Just as he'd said he would! Mutt Wilmott: to the eyes of the world, a broken man.

Even at a time of national mourning, Mutt was on the spot to provide the memorable moments—the unforgettable images required by death. I almost jumped to my feet and applauded. I knew that the people who witnessed these simple devotions, either in person or on the television screen, would go on talking about them until they sat toothless on a wooden bench, in a cottage dooryard, waiting for their hearts to stop beating.

"Mutt Wilmott," the Dimbleby voice went on, "*producer of Rupert Porson's* The Magic Kingdom. *We are told that he was devastated when news came of the puppeteer's death; that he was rushed to hospital for treatment of cardiac palpitations, but in spite of it—and against his doctor's orders—he insisted on being here today to pay tribute to his late colleague . . . although we are told on good authority that an ambulance is standing by at the ready, should it be needed. . . .*"

The view from a camera we had not seen before was now cut in. Shooting from a high angle, as if from a rotunda, the view came down and down into the studio, as it might be seen through the eyes of a descending angel, getting closer and closer to the coffin until, at its very foot, it came to rest upon a remarkable figure that could have been none other than Snoddy the Squirrel.

Mounted on a wooden post perhaps, the hand puppet, with its little leather ears, protruding teeth, and question mark of a bushy tail, had been carefully arranged to gaze sadly down upon the coffin of its master, its squirrel paws crossed reverently, its squirrel head bent in an attitude of humble prayer.

There were often times—and this was one of them—when, as if in the sudden, blinding flash of a news photographer's camera—I saw it all. Death was no more than a simple masquerade—and so, moreover, was Life!—and both of them were artfully arranged by something or other: some backstage celestial Mutt Wilmott.

We were puppets, all of us, set in action upon the stage by God—or Fate—or Chemistry, call it what you will, where we would be pulled on like gloves upon the hands, and manipulated by the Rupert Porsons and Mutt Wilmotts of the world. Or the Ophelia and Daphne de Luces.

I wanted to let out a whoop!

How I wished that Nialla were here, so that I could share my discovery with her. After all, no one deserved it more. But by now, for all I knew, she was already steering the decrepit Austin van up the slopes of some Welsh mountain to some Welsh village, where, with the assistance of some hastily rustled-up, real-life Mother Goose, she would unpack her wooden crates and, later tonight, raise the curtain for the gawking villagers in some far-flung St. David's Hall, on her own personal vision of *Jack and the Beanstalk*.

With Rupert gone, which of us now was the Galligantus? I wondered. Which of us was now the monster that would come tumbling unexpectedly out of the skies and into the lives of others?

"*Heartfelt tributes continue to pour in from Land's End to John O'Groats,*" the announcer was saying, "*and from abroad.*" He paused and gave out a little sigh, as if he had been overwhelmed by the moment.

"*Here in London, and in spite of the downpour, the queue continues to grow, stretching as far as All Souls Church, an beyond into Langham Place. From above the door of Broad-casting House, the statues of Prospero and Ariel look down upon the hordes of mourners, watching, as if they too share in the common grief.*

"Immediately following today's ceremonies at Broadcasting House," he went on bravely, "Rupert Porson's coffin will be taken to Waterloo Station, and from there to its place of interment at Brookwood Cemetery, in Surrey."

By now, even Feely could see that we had had enough.

"Enough of this maudlin trash!" she announced, striding across the room and flipping off the switch. The picture on the television tube retracted to a tiny point of light—and vanished.

"Throw open the curtains, Daffy," she ordered, and Daffy sprang to her command. "This is so tiresome—all of it. Let's have some light for a change."

What she really wanted, of course, was to have a better squint at Dieter. Too vain to wear her spectacles, Feely had probably seen no more of Rupert's funeral than a dishwater blur. And isn't it pointless being admired at close range by an anxious swain if one is unable to see said swain's rapture?

I couldn't help but notice that Father seemed to have overlooked the way in which our first television viewing had been so abruptly terminated, and that he was already slipping away into his own private world.

Dogger and Mrs. Mullet went discreetly about their duties, leaving only Aunt Felicity to protest weakly.

"Really, Ophelia," she huffed, "you are most ungrateful. I wanted to have a closer look at the coffin handles.

My charlady's son Arnold works as a set dresser at the BBC, and his services were especially requested. They gave him a guinea to ferret out some photogenic fittings."

"Sorry, Aunt Felicity," Feely said vaguely, "but funerals give me such awful gooseflesh—even on the television. I simply can't bear to watch them."

For a moment, a coolish silence hung in the air, indicating that Aunt Felicity was not so easily mollified.

"I know," Feely added brightly. "Let me offer everyone a chocolate."

And she went for an end-table drawer.

Visions of some Victorian hell flapped instantly into my mind: the caves, the flames, the burning pits, the lost souls queued up—much like those mourners outside Broadcasting House—all of them waiting to be flung by an avenging angel into the fire and molten brimstone.

Brimstone, after all, was sulfur (chemical symbol S), with whose dioxide I had stuffed the sweets. Bitten into, they would—well, that would hardly bear thinking about.

Feely was already walking towards the vicar, ripping the cellophane from the box of ancient chocolates Ned had left on the doorstep; the box with which I had so lovingly tampered.

"Vicar? Aunt Felicity?" she said, removing the lid and holding the box out at arm's length. "Have a chocolate. The almond nougats are particularly interesting."

I couldn't let this happen, but what was I to do? It was obvious that Feely had taken my earlier, blurted warning as no more than a stupid bluff.

Now the vicar was reaching for a sweet, his fingers, like

the planchette on a Ouija board, hovering above the chocolates, as if some unseen spirit might direct him to the tastiest confection.

"I have dibs on the almond nougats!" I shouted. "You promised, Feely!"

I lunged forward and snatched the chocolate from the vicar's fingers, and at the same instant, contrived to stumble on the edge of the carpet, my flailing hands dashing the box from Feely's hands.

"You beast!" Feely shouted. "You filthy little beast!"

It was just like old times!

Before she could recover her wits, I had trodden on the box, and in a clumsy, windmilling—but beautifully choreographed—attempt to regain my balance, had managed to grind the whole sticky mess into the Axminster carpet.

Dieter, I noticed, had a broad grin on his face, as if it were all jolly good fun. Feely saw it, too, and I could tell that she was torn between her duchess act and swatting my face.

Meanwhile, the hydrogen sulfide fumes, which my trampling of the chocolates had released, had begun their deadly work. The room was suddenly filled with the smell of rotten eggs—and what a stench! It smelled as if a sick brontosaurus had broken wind, and I remember wondering for an instant if the drawing room would ever be the same.

All of this happened in less time than it takes to tell, and my rapid-fire reflections were broken into by the sound of Father's voice.

"Flavia," he said, in that low, flat tone he uses to express fury, "go to your room. At once." His finger trembled as he pointed.

There was no point in arguing. With shoulders hunched, as if walking in deep snow, I trudged towards the door.

Other than Father, everyone in the room was pretending that nothing had happened. Dieter was fiddling with his collar, Feely was rearranging her skirt as she perched beside him on the sofa, and Daffy was already reaching for a dog-eared copy of *King Solomon's Mines*. Even Aunt Felicity was glaring fiercely at a loose thread on the sleeve of her tweed jacket, and the vicar, who had drifted across to the French doors, stood gazing out with pretended interest in the ornamental lake and the folly beyond.

Halfway across the room, I stopped and retraced my steps. I had almost forgotten something. Digging into my pocket, I pulled out the envelope of extra-perforated stamps Miss Cool had given me, and handed it to Father.

"These are for you. I hope you like them," I said. Without looking at it, Father took the envelope from my hand, his quivering finger still pointing. I slunk across the room.

I paused at the door . . . and turned.

"If anyone wants me," I said, "I shall be upstairs, weeping at the bottom of my closet."

ACKNOWLEDGMENTS

WHAT BETTER PLACE FOR a confession than at the end of a mystery novel? According to the great Eric Partridge, the words *knowledge* and *acknowledgment* come from the Middle English verb *knawlechen*, which means not only knowledge, but also *confession* or *admission*. So I'd better admit straightaway that I'm working with the assistance of a goodly number of partners in crime.

First and foremost among these conspirators are my editors: Bill Massey of Orion Books; Kate Miciak of the Random House Publishing Group; and Kristin Cochrane of Doubleday Canada. For their unwavering faith in Flavia from the very outset, I am forever in their debt. Bill, Kate, and Kristin have become family.

Again, my dear friends Dr. John and Janet Harland have contributed beyond measure. From brilliant ideas to animated discussions over happy meals, they have never failed to be the best of patient friends.

At Orion Books, in London, Natalie Braine, Helen Richardson, and Juliet Ewers are always marvels of friendly efficiency.

My literary agent, Denise Bukowski, has worked diligently to tell the world about Flavia. Also at the Bukowski Agency, Jericho Buendia, David Whiteside, and Susan Morris have freed me from worrying about the thousands of tiny details.

My deep indebtedness to Nicole, of Apple, whose

magic wand turned what might have been a tragedy into a perfect triumph of online support. Thanks again, Nicole!

At Random House, in New York City, Kate Miciak, Nita Taublib, Loyale Coles, Randall Klein, Gina Wachtel, Theresa Zoro, Gina Centrello, and Alison Masciovecchio provided a touching welcome that I will never forget. And having Susan Corcoran as one's publicist is every author's dream. And thanks to my copy editor, Connie Munro.

Thanks also to the American Booksellers Association for inviting me to their Indie Lunch at Book Expo America. Happily, I found myself seated at a table with Stanley Hadsell, of Market Block Books in Troy, New York, who epitomizes independent bookselling. We could have talked all night.

To Ann Kingman and Michael Kindness of "Books on the Nightstand," for their early and abiding faith. When I ran into Michael unexpectedly at BEA, I found out that in spite of living in the smallest town in the smallest county in the smallest state, he's one of Flavia's biggest fans.

In Houston, David Thompson and McKenna Jordan, Brenda Jordan, Michelle McNamara, and Kathryn Priest of Murder By the Book, made me understand instantly why so many people love Texas so much. Now I do, too.

Sarah Borders and Jennifer Schwartz of the Houston Public Library did double duty in arranging a question-and-answer session.

Special thanks to Jonathan Topper of Topper Stamps and Postal History in Houston, who took the time to spice up the evening with a fascinating display of Penny Blacks.

And to John Demers of Delicious Mischief, who managed to turn a steeplechase interview into a sheer delight.

Also in Houston, Random House representatives Liz Sullivan and Gianna LaMorte made me feel at home.

To that legend among booksellers, Barbara Peters of The Poisoned Pen in Scottsdale, Arizona, my profound thanks for being the perfect hostess. Although she's younger than I am, Barbara is nevertheless my long-lost twin.

Patrick Milliken, John Goodwin, and Will Hanisko, also of The Poisoned Pen, kindly allowed me a peek behind the scenes of a busy bookstore and plied me with refreshments.

Thanks, too, to Lesa Holstine and Cathy Johnson, for a very special evening during which we talked happily about everything under the sun.

Kim Garza at the Tempe Public Library put together a delightful afternoon of animated discussion. I still carry in my mind the image of all those happy faces. Thank you, Tempe!

In Westminster, Maryland, Lori Zook, Cheryl Kelly, Judy Pohlhaus, Camille Marchi, Ginny Mortorff, Wanda Rawlings, Pam Kaufman, Stacey Carlini, Sherry Drechsler plied me with soft drinks, cakes, and JuJubes (which, when we got around to recalling candy treats of long-gone movie matinees, they also taught me to pronounce correctly: It's "JOO-joo-bays," not "JOO-joobs").

Meanwhile, at Doubleday Canada, my publicist Sharon Klein has been a perfect dynamo. I must also admit that I'm in awe of Doubleday Canada's team, including Martha Leonard, as well as Heather Sanderson and Sharmila

Mohammed of the Digital Team, who have brought the Flavia Fan Club to life and provided a cosy haven for visitors.

And I'd be remiss indeed if I failed to extend special thanks to Brad Martin, President and CEO of Random House of Canada, who has championed Flavia from her very beginnings.

In spite of the worst blizzard of the year, Bryce Zorn and Curtis Weston of Chapters in Kelowna, British Columbia, managed a full house for the Canadian launch of the first book in this series, *The Sweetness at the Bottom of the Pie*. Thanks also to Paul Hasselback, who saw me safely home through black ice and all the windblown drifts.

Trish Kells of Random House Canada, who arranged a memorable book event in Vancouver, also acted as chauffeur and laughed at my jokes in spite of the rain.

Deb McVitie of 32 Books in North Vancouver was the charming sponsor of my first away-from-home reading and book signing. My co-readers, Hannah Holborn and Andrea Gunraj, helped to make it an unforgettable evening. If Hannah and Andrea are indicative of our up-and-coming young writers, we have no need whatsoever to worry about the future.

And finally, to my wife, Shirley, whose love, company, and patient support have allowed me the luxury of writing. Amadeus and Cleo have helped a lot, too.